Born Speaking Lies

Rob Lenihan

Fomite

Burlington, Vermont

ISBN-13: 978-1-942515-41-8
Library of Congress Control Number: 2015960525

Fomite
58 Peru Street
Burlington, VT 05401
www.fomitepress.com

Cover art - Zippo Lighter © RagnaRulz

For Mom and Dad…wish you were here.

I owe so much to so many. My everlasting thanks to
Sonia Pilcer and Louise Crawford for all the advice and
support; James Curran for putting up with all my questions, and to my family for all their love and guidance.

Part One: The Sea of Japan

1

Pennsylvania, sometime in the 1990s

BILLY THE KID is late for his own murder.

Afterwards when he looks back on this night, even Billy has to admit he was pretty much begging for it. With all the grief he had caused in those last few days, Christ, he probably should've been wearing a bulls-eye t-shirt and a toe tag just to speed things up.

And he had to give the bastards credit. They couldn't have picked a better time than right now, when Billy is so calm and serene, or a better place than right here, on this silent country road beneath a sky full of mutely exploding stars.

Beautiful, he thinks as he drains the excess beer into the dark; like talking to God on the telephone.

Sal and Vince, sitting back in the car, could never appreciate this, not if you grabbed them both by the hair and pointed their pig ugly faces straight up at the North Star. City rats like them aren't happy unless they're breathing in smoke, reading by neon, and stomping on concrete.

Billy zips up, closes his eyes and takes a long draw of sweet air to wash out the harsh fumes and loud music. Yes, he thinks on the exhale, God is good all the time.

He takes another blind breath and listens to the traffic noise drifting across the river from Jersey, eons away from Billy and his beautiful night. It was a good move coming up here, taking a look at his house-to-be and getting away from all the misery back home.

He loves this spot, the rest stop on 611, especially now, at this ungodly hour, when it's dark and devoid of life. It feels like nowhere.

Billy remembers something about young girl who was murdered and dumped here years ago. She went without a name for the longest time until the cops finally ID'd her body and got the animal who killed her. At least some people pay for their sins.

He opens his eyes and looks over the edge into the black empty. Damn, just imagine falling into that shit, bouncing off those carnivorous rocks. They'd haul your ass away in a sandwich bag.

Billy pictures his twisted body sprawled out dead in the woods below, sees his holy spirit rise slowly into the eastern sky like a B-movie angel.

Stars gather around him, satellites cruise around the earth and comets streak by on their way to infinity.

It's like the Christmas show at the planetarium, where they traced the origin of the Star of Bethlehem. Only now Billy's in the middle of the celestial ballet, instead of sitting in the audience with his mother.

From here Billy looks down at the river coursing toward the ocean, at the red-tailed Matchbox cars, rolling down the distant stripe of highway.

I will sail to the Sea of Japan…

It's all down there in the river, his life's work, shimmering just beneath the water's surface. His dearest memories, his most grievous faults, all preserved in an eternal photo album.

Jesus, Billy really was a pretty evil son-of-a-bitch, wasn't he? Thank God his sins are all the way down there; so far away, like they belong to someone else.

Do you still love me? Please, tell me. Do you still love me?

The voice is distant, scratchy, like it's coming from a sunken Victrola buried in the riverbed and it makes him wince. Leave me alone, for Christ's sake. Can't you see I'm trying to die now?

Charley would get a kick out of this. He'd love being up so high, looking down on this part of the world that meant so much to him. But Charley's gone, too, like so many others who get close to Billy.

You see that man there? He don't like you very much…

And just when Billy's ready to take that step off the embankment for real—you know, just for the hell of it—the voice of a mere mortal reaches up from the earth's surface and grabs him by the ankles.

"I'm sorry…"

Sorry? Sorry for what, you stupid bastard? You want to—ah fuck, Billy doesn't believe this, not now. He opens his eyes, reaches under the sweater Lucille gave him last Christmas, but Billy's going virgin tonight, his fingers grab nothing but wool, and by then it's much too late.

A red giant goes supernova in his face as he shrieks across the cosmos engulfed in flames. *Mayday! Mayday! We're going down!* And Billy crashes to the ground with the force of doom.

Oh, such pain, he wants to scream, he wants to die; he wants to burst into a thousand radioactive pieces. He gags as red-eyed demons scuttle up from below the rocks and gnaw on his throbbing brain tissue.

You gotta take the pain…

He's stretched out of the ground, like Frank Sinatra after the Nazis drilled him in the back, and his bleeding head hangs over the edge of oblivion. Voices float over him like mist from the river.

"Is he dead?"

"If that didn't kill him he'll live forever."

"Maybe you should go back there and check."

"Maybe you should suck my dick."

Billy lies motionless, crushed beneath the weight of time and space, and thinks, yes, of course, it would be these two ending his life. No one else could ever get so close.

"I'm just saying we ought to be sure."

"You wanna be sure? Take the fucking gun and go back there yourself."

"You want me to shoot him?"

"No, I want you to tongue kiss him, you fucking asshole."

Billy can't believe his dying ears. Finish the job, you brainless humps; finish what you started. Two in the back of the head, get rid of the body. Stupid pricks can't do nothing right.

The voices drift and Billy senses the car starting up and driving away. It's just him now, in this forsaken place, with his memory bank leaking into the abyss.

All right, he thinks, it's over. I'll just bleed to death here and that'll be the end. The lady on the white horse will come to him soon and Billy will be sailing to the Sea of Japan…

2

THEY TEAR DOWN 611 without saying a word and Sal's so spooked he can't even switch on the radio, certain that news of what he just did will screech through the speakers the second he touches the dial.

—murdered his best friend, shooting him through the head while the guy was taking a piss—can you believe that, ladies and gentlemen—?

He's angry, lost on this freak show of a road, and he doesn't give a fuck about nothing no more. He just wants to be gone, away from the trees, the meddling stars, and this goddamn river.

It's Vince who finally cracks the silence. Vince, his cousin, who never could keep his mouth shut.

"You said you were sorry."

"What?" Sal cranks his head toward Vince. "What was that?"

"Back there." Vince jerks his thumb. "Just before you did it. You said you were sorry."

Sal doesn't appreciated being quoted right now and he makes like he doesn't remember.

"I did?"

"Yeah. I didn't know what you were doing."

"All right…"

"I mean, you got nothing to be sorry for. He did this to himself—"

"All right." The words make Sal angry. "Who cares what I said? It don't matter now."

"But—"

"It don't matter."

He slows down when he sees town lights up ahead. All he needs is some yahoo cop to grab them for speeding.

But there's no one on the street, it's a ghost village, with the mandatory gas station, post office, and diner, and no signs of life, like they built it 10 minutes ago just to snag the tourists. Sal sees an on-ramp for the bridge to Jersey and makes the turn.

He drops his head as he hands the money over to the toll collector and takes off as soon as the barrier rises.

On the bridge, Sal looks straight ahead, because he knows if he turns to the side he'll see Billy climbing over the railing, soaking wet and stinking dead with the fresh bullet hole in the middle of his face.

Ditch the gun, Sal orders himself, ditch the gun now. Toss the thing into the water, you fucking idiot, you're right here. But his hands are glued to the steering wheel and the gun that killed his best friend stays in his pocket, getting heavier every second.

He threatens me, Sal. He walks into my club, my place, and threatens my life—right in front of you. And you just fucking sat there. So now what, Sal? What are you going to do about this?

It was an order, not a question and Sal thinks angrily, there, I did something, you crazy old crocodile. I did just what you wanted. You happy now?

Sal still can't believe what happened, what Billy did to bring this on, when that perfectly great evening suddenly nosedived straight into the shitter. Billy's party had broken up and Sal and Matty had gone to the bar to do a couple of shots, just the two of them. It was going to be a quiet little nightcap before they went home, that's all.

They talked about the trial coming up, how those scumbags in the FBI were indicting all the old timers for stuff that happened 40 years ago, for Christ's sake.

"Next they'll be digging guys up and putting their dead fucking bones on trial," Matty snarled.

Sal wondered what was up with Billy at the end of the night, he looked so angry and upset, snapping at his wife like that, and as Matty was shrugging like he had no idea, the door opened, the scent of gasoline filled the room, and Billy came walking toward them.

"Hey," Matty smiled broadly. "Speak of the devil."

And that's who it was, all right, coming through that door, Satan himself. That foul-smelling thing might have looked like Billy, sounded like Billy, but the eyes were blazing like a mongrel from the wrong side of Hell, glaring at Matty and speaking pure blasphemy.

"You fucking cocksucker…"

He was cursing, vicious, vile stuff, sticking his finger in Matty's face, and calling him every filthy thing you could think of and so much more. Sal and the old man were stunned, didn't know what the hell was happening.

"Yo, Billy, calm down," Sal shouted. "What the fuck is wrong with you?"

But Billy wasn't hearing it and the hatred was so poisonous that Sal was seriously wondering if people were going to reach for their guns here. And if they did, which way would Sal aim?

"Fuck you, Matty!" Billy screamed with tears running down his face. "Fuck you!"

Matty, who looked ready to climb out of his wheelchair, withered legs and all, and tear Billy's throat open, narrowed his eyes down to slits and glared at his top man.

"Billy," he said in a voice filled with murder, "this better be a joke…"

Only it wasn't. Billy stood there for a second, seething with immeasurable rage, reeking of gas like he took a bath in the stuff, and spewed this weird shit from the Bible or something, about the wicked going astray, and speaking lies, and Sal was like, what the fuck?

And then he left, did an abrupt about face, out the door he went, the gas odor still hanging in the air. Matty stared after Billy for a long stretch of time before he turned to Sal.

What are you going to do about this?

3

He jumps when Vince launches into one of his hacking fits and the car swerves in sympathy.

"What the fuck is wrong with you, coughing like that?"

"I'm sick."

"I can see that, shithead. But what the hell is it? You sound like you're going to hoist your lungs."

"I don't know what's wrong."

They come to the other side of the bridge and he looks for the highway home. Sal knows what's going on with his cousin but he won't let himself think it.

"So you know what a doctor is? Get your ass over to one and get some pills or something, dipshit. What—you die and it's gonna be my fault?"

"No—"

"You're goddamn right it's not. I'm not your mother, pal. In this fucking life, you take care of yourself."

They'd set this thing up just right, all by the book, at least at the start. Told Billy some story about taking a ride up to the Poconos, go to Matty's country place and then over to this house up in the mountains that Billy wanted to buy.

That's it, Billy said, pointing at the dark outline framed by stars. That's my new home.

Sure, big guy, whatever you want. Move up here, plant potatoes, and live like Daniel Boone. It's your fantasy.

They went to this bar in Delaware Water Gap, with an old deer head on the wall and a jazz band on the stage that got louder as the evening went longer. Filled him with booze and waited for the right time.

You think I'm going to Hell?

Billy, in the bar, leaning against the wall, his arms folded. Sal stared at him a few seconds before trying to make it a joke.

We're all going to Hell, big guy. Don't you know that?

No, you don't understand. Billy looked into his eyes. *I've done too much, too many bad things. I've committed too many sins.*

Well, it was really just one too many, Sal thought, and you did it to the wrong guy.

And he was burning up, dying to ask Billy, why, why in God's holy name did you pull that stunt on the bike path? Why did you take off on the Cigar like that?

Why are you making me kill you?

But the music kept getting louder, the crowd got thicker and Vince was monkey waving behind Billy's back to say it's time, let's go, do this fucking thing already.

So instead of asking his questions and trying to find out why it all went so bad, Sal slipped his arm around Billy's shoulder and eased him toward the door.

Big guy, let's get out of here.

4

"You sure he's dead?"

The question catches Sal flat-footed as he drives down I-80 on autopilot.

"What's that?"

"I'm just asking—"

"I shot him in the head, asshole." Sal hears his voice rise. "If you'd been with me, instead of hanging back like a little pussy, you would've seen it. His head snapped back and he went down. You think he faked that shit?"

"No, but—"

"But, nothing. What is he, Count Dracula, he's going to climb out of his grave? He's dead, all right? Can't you leave nothing alone?"

"It's not that—"

Sal twists the steering wheel hard to change lanes and shoots his middle finger up in response to an angry horn blast.

"I didn't see you taking the lead on this thing, Vince, you know what I'm saying? I'm the one who went out there, okay? You didn't do shit."

"I know, but Matty—"

"Fuck Matty, I did exactly what he wanted. Billy is dead, all right? I shot him, he's dead, have a nice day."

"Yeah," Vince says, "but we just left him there. Someone's going to find him."

"No one's gonna find nothing." Sal opens the window a crack to air out his doubts. "They got bears, coyotes, all kinds of animals up here. Believe me something will come along and make a meal out of him in no time at all."

He thinks of predators savagely tearing into Billy, of maggots taking whatever's left. Thinks what a sharp-looking guy Billy was and what he'll look like a couple of days from now. And he thinks how that picture is going to haunt him for the rest of his life.

Sal can't believe Billy was riding next him in the dead man's seat just a little while ago, his head rolling, talking some weird shit about a Japanese garden and a woman on a white horse, who the hell knows.

He drove down 611, no idea where he was going, Vince was sweating in the back seat so heavily you could smell him, and then Billy starts singing that goddamn song.

Glorious, glorious, one keg of beer for the four of us...

Vince looked at Sal in the rearview, Sal looked back, and they joined in, all three of them riding around that dark mountain singing glory be to God there ain't no more of us, 'cause one of us could drink it all alone.

"You'll get your Iron Cross now, Von Ryan!" Billy shouted when they finished and laughed, like something was funny.

Then he said pull over and Sal bounced a look off the mirror to Vince. Can you believe this guy? He's picking his own grave.

Sal watched Billy walk through the break in the wooden fence and disappear into the shadows. Vince prodded him, pushed him out of the car, do it, do it, follow Billy and Sal wanted to club the little bastard with the gun he was so pissed.

It was the worst of both worlds, that rest stop, with the stars glaring down on him like a billion eyewitnesses. They were on a deserted stretch of country road and yet the traffic noise from Jersey was deafening, a four-lane storm cloud of furious hornets.

Sal walked through the break in the fence and immediately felt colder, cut off from the rest of the world and his feet hardly touched the grass. This was a place for the dead.

He squinted through the darkness and saw Billy looking up at the stars, so close to the edge, as if he were going to jump, and Sal was going to shout, get away from there, you're gonna kill yourself.

But he remembered why he was here and he prayed, please, do it; you've wanted to die for so long now, just finish the job and let me go home to sleep.

Sal knew it could never be that easy, that Billy would never be so obliging. So he got closer and raised the gun just as Billy was turning back toward him.

I'm sorry…

He watched Billy fumble under his sweater, heard him cursing, and kept watching, long after he should have pulled the trigger.

When it happened, when he did it, when the flash nearly blinded him, and the recoil almost tore his arm off, and the echo began its marathon voyage around the world, Sal expected all those speeding Jersey cars to screech to a sideways halt, aim their headlights across the river and shine their virtuous beams upon him, gun in his hand, as he stood over his murdered friend.

I'm sorry…

5

VINCE STARTS TO laugh. They're coming into Newark, by the airport, and trucks roll by them like whales in a haunted ocean. Sal thought Vince was coughing again, but, no, he's laughing, in the same seat where Billy was sitting, laughing so hard his body trembles.

"What's so funny, Vince?"

"Nothing, it's just that—"

"Just what, Vince? Let's hear it."

"Fucking Billy." Vince snorts "He always wanted to get a place in the Poconos. Now he's got one forever."

Sal can feel his mind shutting down. Wires and cables that connect sanity and reality snap and break apart.

He squeezes the wheel with his left hand, makes the ugliest fist you ever saw with his right, and starts punching Vince in the head. He doesn't have to look; he knows he's going to land the blows right on target.

"Hey!" Vince wails and tries to cover up. "What the fuck—stop it!"

There's a jet dead ahead in the filthy sky coming in for a landing, all blinking lights and roaring engines, and Sal wants to rise up off the blacktop, kamikaze crash into its belly, and go up in a column of purifying fire.

Sal's knuckles are aching and bloody and that only makes him punch harder.

"I'm sorry," he shouts, tears running down his cheek. "I'm sorry, I'm sorry!"

Back by the river, a body lies in the shadows and waits for permission to die. Millennia pass, the sun goes out, the earth grows cold, dinosaurs rise to roam the earth again and then sink back into the mud. And Billy's still there.

I hear good things about you.

What? What do you hear about me, mother fucker? Tell me what you've heard; I'd really like to know.

I once told you, Ryan, if only one gets out, it's a great victory.

You should pray now, before it's too late, before you stand in front of God and attempt to justify what you did with your life.

Billy tries to remember his Act of Contrition that those horrible nuns had pounded into his head so long ago and it's coming in all fuzzy and crackling. Come on now; how the hell did that thing go?

The wicked are estranged from the womb: they go astray as soon as they be born, speaking lies.

His eyelids open slowly, creaking like one-hundred-year old hinges and a glacial smile grows on his bloodless face. Close enough.

Billy stands slowly, and braces for the sudden rush of pain rumbling through his skull, the agony that assures him that he's still alive. One more deep breath and he turns from the river and starts walking to the road. He won't be joining any lost spirits tonight.

He looks down the road and waits, he knows it's coming, any second now, and sure as shit, he sees the glow of headlights in the distance. That's it, big guy, just keep on coming.

The lights become brighter and the engine noise starts in. Billy waves a hand in the expanding beams and allows himself another smile.

Whoever you are, he thinks, you're dead. I don't care what your story is, I don't give a shit how many kids you got. If you stop, I'm going to kill you. I'm going to pull you out of the car, beat you down to the ground and kick your head until it cracks wide open. And the more you beg for mercy, the worse it'll be.

Come on, bitch, Billy thinks, don't keep me waiting.

He winces from the high beams and hangs out his thumb. Above the engine noise he hears a voice that might be his own singing so merrily.

"Dear, dear, what can the matter be…"

6

AND THEN HE'S *running*—

—as fast as he can, so fast flames streak from his shoulders and the ground shudders beneath his feet, so fast that nobody in this world will ever catch him.

"Billy! Billy!" His mother's shouts rip by his ears like tracer bullets. "Come back!"

He digs deeper, head down, arms pumping, so that he carves right through the wind. Billy's going to his sacred place and he won't let anyone, not even Jesus Christ himself, get in his way.

He thought it was going to be okay for a little while. Charley had just dropped them off at the Botanic Gardens, got them out of the house after the old man came home drunk and looking to start a fight. It didn't take him long.

"You're taking him to a goddamn garden? Oh, yeah, that'll make a real man out of him, won't it?"

"But he likes it—"

"—because you keep taking him there!"

Charley stepped in, as he always did, got between them and the old man, and took them to this calm, beautiful place. Once inside his mother bent down to look into his eyes and he could see the latest bruise on her face shimmering beneath frantically applied make-up.

She smiled and stroked his cheek, always so nervous and fearful and it wouldn't be until years later, long after she was gone that Billy would realize how beautiful she was with that long black hair and dark brown eyes.

"We're going to have a nice time today, aren't we, honey? We always have a good time when we come here, right?"

He nodded faintly, anxious to get away from her and begin his voyage.

"Don't worry about Daddy. He's going to be okay. He…he just gets upset sometimes."

Billy starts to squirm, no, he doesn't want any part of it.

"Is everything okay, honey? You're not mad at me, are you?"

He shakes his head no even though he really was mad at her and his father and everybody in the whole world. Everybody except Charley.

"I know you get scared when Mommy and Daddy fight…but everything is going to be all right."

Billy looks to the trees, people walking by, up toward the sky, anywhere but into those beautiful eyes, so needy and drenched with pain.

She's always saying that everything's going to be all right and it never is. It's never going to be all right in that house with that bastard and she knows that better than anyone. And yet she's still lying about it.

"Is everything okay, honey?"

Billy turns his eyes up to the sky, to the birds, and the expanding layer of gray clouds. He shrinks from his mother, pained by her critical demand for affection. She's ruining everything.

"Billy?"

He turns even more to avoid looking at her and the quick movement knocks the book of matches out of his pocket. He grabs for it in mid-air, but it crashes to the pavement cinder block heavy.

His mother's eyes widened with shock and disbelief when she sees the matchbook, and she looks so hurt, so wounded, like Billy drove a knife right through her.

"Billy…" She can hardly speak. "Billy, you promised you wouldn't do—"

"—I-I just found them that's all." He spits out the words rapidly. "I wasn't going to do anything with them."

"…but you said you'd stop. You promised."

He's about to burst into flames and he's got one second to do something, just one second to get away before she starts sobbing, before she drags him to the subway station for the roaring train ride back to that house.

There's only one second for him to twist free of his jacket, pull out of the sleeves like a magician on Ed Sullivan and leave his mother kneeling there with the empty windbreaker dangling from her fingers.

And then he's running—

"Billy!"

She yells, angry, then pleading, come back, please come back, begging him not to leave her and Billy runs even faster until her wretched cries are swallowed by the garden's lush stillness and there's nothing but the trees and the sweet air rushing into his face.

You promised!

He's knows it's wrong, that he's being so cruel to her, but he sees the wooden fence surrounding the Japanese Garden and he smiles.

Billy charges through the entrance, to the end of the viewing pavilion where he can look through his panting reflection into the lake as the catfish swirl in graceful circles and the snapping turtles patrol the waters like ironclad ships.

It's a weekday and there are so few people here he can pretend that this place was built just for him.

Billy doesn't have much time; she'll be here soon so he leans over the fence and peers deeply into the water, until the sounds of the world fade away and the ground disappears from beneath his feet. Let us pray.

I will sail to the Sea of Japan. I will ride a snapping turtle and roll through the waters with a school of catfish as my royal guard. Clouds will tumble through the sky at my command, all the rulers of the world will bow down before me. And I will reign forever.

Billy can ride beneath the waves with no fear of drowning, just a warm, powerful sensation as seawater passes through every cell of his body.

He sees sunken pirate ships with their tattered Jolly Rogers, schools of exotic fish bursting with every possible color, killer whales on their way to the Horn of Africa, deep sea creatures that no man has ever seen before rising from coal black waters just to pay homage to Billy.

This was Charley's idea. Charley, who saw how miserable Billy's real world was, helped him create this new one. Do it whenever you're lonely or scared, big guy, and you'll feel better in no time.

Billy smiles at all the living things around him. No one yells at him down here, and no one would ever dare raise a hand to the king. All the fear and tension that cloaks him every waking moment in his house now floats from of his body and drifts up toward the sunlight.

He is king down here and one day he'll enter this undersea world and never return—

"Billy!"

She's screaming, terrified, like she thinks Billy is going to jump into the water, and the harsh voice rumbles through his undersea world. A hand clamps on his shoulder and Billy closes his eyes so tightly, vows never to open them again. He feels his body being yanked up to the surface, away from his kingdom.

"No, no—"

"Billy, stop it!" His mother shakes him. "Stop it!"

He swings his arms, hits her shoulders, her face, screams at her to get away, to let go, he hates her, hopes she dies, and then he snarls, the way his father does when he's had way too many beers.

"Get your fucking hands off of me!"

She catches her breath, stunned by his ferocity and Billy is, too, horrified at what he said, and he stops struggling, waits for the slap across the face he knows is coming, knows he deserves.

Billy braces for the pain, but his mother doesn't hit him or shake him or do anything but stare at him for a few aching seconds.

And then she bursts into tears.

Part Two: The Poison of the Serpent

1

IT HAPPENS ONE evening, just before midnight, when Old Ethan decides that he's ready.

He's not frightened, no, not at all. He's been waiting for this moment for so long, looking for the sign, anything that would tell him the end was coming, that he was starting to doubt it would ever happen.

It got so bad that Ethan wondered if maybe people around here were right; that he really was out of his mind.

And then this morning, just eight hours ago, he saw the sign, by God, in huge, shrieking letters. Ethan saw the devil.

Right there on the main drag in Mount Pocono, driving a pick-up truck by the Galaxy, the Father of All Lies in human form.

It's been years, decades, since the last time they met. He was older now, but he couldn't fool Ethan, not for one second. It was him all right, the Son of Perdition, straight from Hell and loose upon the earth. And Ethan knew it was time.

He looks around the crumbling house where he was born, where he's lived for all of his 78 years. Stacks of newspapers and magazines piled around the living room, ancient furniture that hasn't been touched in decades, the old busted Motorola against the wall, layers of dust wherever you look.

Everyone in town says the place is a dump, not fit for pigs. His neighbors hate the sight of it, but it's still his property. Ethan balances the .357 in his right hand. It's still his.

This is his home and neither that judge nor that fat-ass cop who keeps coming around here is going to take it away from him.

"Liars," he mutters, "all liars…"

It's the town that went bad, not Ethan. There was a time when people around here helped each other, when you knew everybody and everybody knew you. We took care of our own up here on the mountain and everybody liked it just fine.

And then Ethan blinked and his small town became a city.

Those people, the ones from New York, the coloreds, the Puerto Ricans, they all started coming up here and brought all their garbage with them. You have to lock your door now, nobody knows their neighbors, and still they keep building, building, more and more homes.

And the things people say about you, accusing you of the most terrible acts.

Ethan lays his free hand on the Bible and the words travel up his arm and pass through his lips.

"The wicked are estranged from the womb. The wicked go astray as soon as they be born, speaking lies."

He knows they're all around him; whoremongers, murderers, idolaters, and they're going to get him—unless he does something.

Azariah, Ethan's old German shepherd, noses up to him, whimpering because he knows something is wrong, and begins licking Ethan's hand.

He's getting on, too, this old mutt. Can't run outside because of all the cars racing by. With the bad legs, he has to circle the floor half-a-dozen times before he sits down and it takes him forever to get back up.

Ethan looks down at his dog with a mournful smile. Poor old guy.

"You're the only one I could ever trust in this world," he says. "The only one."

Azariah looks up at his master's soothing voice and Ethan scratches that special spot right behind the old timer's ear.

"Yeah, you like that, don't you?" Ethan says. "Yeah, buddy, I know you like that."

Azariah is loving every minute of this, he's just so damn happy. It's time, Ethan thinks as he raises the .357, and shoots Azariah right through the head.

"Good boy." Ethan pats the dog's gory skull. "Good boy."

2

ONE HUNDRED MILES to the east, Vince sits dying on a barstool in Brooklyn, not a friend in the world, and thinks about the bears.

Five months, five months and there's no sign of him; no clothing, no bone fragments, no watch, ring or wallet, not one trace of the low-life son-of-a-bitch has turned up yet. He just floated up to heaven like the goddamn Virgin Mary.

Sal keeps saying the bears got him, dragged his carcass to a cave somewheres and had him for dinner, bones and all. Sal talks about the bears so much he should join the circus.

"Bears will eat anything," he says over and over, trying to convince himself. "They need a lot of food for the winter and shit. I'm telling you there's nothing left of him."

Yeah, sure, that sounds logical. It was the bears. Or the squirrels. Or the woodchucks. Or maybe the Loch Ness fucking Monster did the backstroke up the Delaware and dragged Billy's dead ass back to Scotland for a late night snack. Makes sense to me.

"Fuck!"

Vince pounds on the bar hard enough to get some of the regular rats to turn around and give him the look. Easy, big guy, he tells himself. Don't want to attract too much attention; not yet, anyway.

Fucking bitch, she leaves me a note—

This is a fine place to end it all, Gallagher's Bar & Grill, this sinkhole where his old man drank himself to death, where two of his brothers were well on their way to doing the same.

Vince swore he'd never come back here; wouldn't even look at these misbegotten fucks, let along drink with them. We all know how Billy felt about these mutts, don't we? He didn't hold his feelings back at all, one of the few times him and Vince saw eye-to-eye.

These are the kind of assholes you lean on, smack around for laughs. You certainly don't socialize with these shitheads, not if you're part of Matty's crew. You just wipe off your shoes and keep on walking.

And yet here he is.

Vince had no idea he'd end up at this dump when he came flying out of Delores' apartment and dove behind the wheel of his car. He only knew he wanted to run away, to vanish and reappear on the other side of the world.

Vince allows himself a smile at the memory of Billy getting the business at that rest stop. It was so sweet watching that prick go down. Ding-dong the witch is finally fucking dead.

Thought you had all the answers, didn't you? Never thought it could happen to you, did you, numb nuts? Never thought people would get so fed up with your bullshit that they— *that we*—would decide the world would be a better place without you?

It was always Billy this and Billy that, no matter what anybody else was doing. Matty just about shot a load every time Billy walked through the front door.

Vince was the only one that could see this bastard for what he really was. Up until Billy pulled that shit down by the bike path and topped it off by threatening Matty, fucking Matty, to his face. Then all of a sudden Billy wasn't so funny no more.

Of course Vince just about planted his foot up Sal's ass to make get him out of the car and pull the trigger, with all his cousin's weepy bullshit about Billy being his best friend and how this ain't right, and there's gotta be a better way, yeah, sure, fuck you, Sal.

Your best friend is going to get us all killed if you don't bury the crazy prick. Or we can drive back to the city and tell Matty that we fucked up royally and that Billy the Kid, the person the Cigar hates the most in this or any other world, is still alive and well.

That got the dopey bastard out of the car.

3

VVINCE TAKES THE joint out his wallet, reaches in his pocket for the lighter. Shouldn't be long now until they figure out where he is and come looking for him.

"Hey!"

Vince looks up and sees the bartender drawing a pitcher and glaring at him like he crapped on Old Glory.

"What?"

"Take that shit outside."

"What are you—?"

"—it's against the law, Einstein." The bartender releases the lever and it snaps back into place. "Where the hell you been?"

Vince glowers at this stupid hump. Where have I been? Does this douche bag know who he's talking to? Matty's boys smoke, fuck and scratch their nuts any place they want, any time they want, law or no fucking law. If we feel like honking a pound of blow out of Mother Teresa's sacred snatch, then that's what we'll do because we ain't a-scared of God. And anyone who gives us any shit about it gets hauled down the nearest alley for an emergency education.

Furious, Vince puts his hand on the bar, half-rises off the stool, all set to grab this cocksucker by his ratty head of hair and slam his empty skull against the bar a few dozen times until he curses his mother for giving—

But Vince makes the mistake of looking into the mirror and knocking eyeballs with the colorless fright mask that used to be his face.

Holy shit, he grips the edge of the bar to keep from falling to his knees and then the goddamn coughing starts all over again. Vince knew he looked bad, but even God ain't got the right to do this to people.

He sinks back to the stool, all his strength spent.

There's no crew, no back-up, no muscle, just a terribly sick man who meekly nods to the fuckhead bartender like a little fag while his twitching fingers struggle to put the joint back in his wallet.

"My mistake…"

—just like the rest of your goddamn life.

Vince sneaks another look at the picture, holds it close so none of these skanks here can breathe on her, Renee, his beautiful little girl. He strokes the smiling image gently with his index finger and fights the urge to cry.

Fucking bitch leaves him a note, a note, like something out a soap opera. She wouldn't talk to him, face to face like you'd do for anybody, even a bum on the street. Yeah, Vince was mad at her and kind of blew his stack, but who wouldn't? She wanted to take his kid away for Christ's sake.

"Renee," Vince whispers to his daughter. "Renee…"

He hadn't married her, like he kept promising, but he told her over and over that the miserable pig of a wife would never give him a divorce, which was bullshit, seeing as how Vince's wife had hit the bricks after she found out about Delores. But Vince wasn't looking for no new wife.

Delores didn't want to hear no excuses, threatened to take the baby—Vince's baby—back to Mexico and it just made him so crazy. After the diagnosis, after Vince found out what the hospital, that slaughterhouse, had done to him, Renee would be the only evidence that Vince had ever existed.

When her mother started running off with the mouth about Guadalupe, well, it set him off, and he started screaming about coming over there to the apartment he had gotten for her and burning the place to the ground. See? Billy's not the only pyro in town.

I set her and the kid up in the apartment, give her money to send to her old lady back home, and she thinks she's going to pull this shit on me?

He was streaking down 18th Avenue, a few blocks from her place, when he started to calm down. Maybe it was the other drivers cursing and honking their horns at him, or maybe it was the sound of the can full of gasoline bouncing on the passenger seat, but whatever it was, Vince had lost his seething fury by the time he pulled up to Delores' place.

And then he saw the note, crucified to the refrigerator door with a Little Mermaid magnet.

He got as far as "I'm so sorry—" before he tore her letter to pieces and began punching the refrigerator door, stupid wetback son-of-a-bitch, when I get my hands on her—

And then he jumped back horrified at the blood, foul, tainted blood spreading all over the refrigerator, so much that it looked like the cold white machine was bleeding, not him.

What if the kid came in here and touched that? What if you infect your daughter with this shit, you scumbag? Then you'll surely go to hell.

He tore open the kitchen cabinets, one after the other, jars and plates clattering around him, until he found a bottle of some kind of spray cleaner and scrubbed the refrigerator door with paper towels.

The smell of the cleaning fluid was making his head expand, the towels kept dissolving in his hands and every time he thought he was done he'd see another drop of blood, and then another, and another, and he knew no matter how hard he scrubbed his germs, his filth, would be somewhere on this rough surface and Renee would come in contact with it and she'd end up dying like her father—

"It wasn't my fault," he screamed. "It wasn't my fucking fault!"

His strength finally gave out and he slid to the floor sobbing. Blow out the pilot on the stove, a voice told him, pretend it's your birthday and make a wish. Let the place fill up with gas and clean this apartment the only way you can. Do what you promised.

Why the fuck not, he thought. Drop a match and let nature do the rest. He was a dead man either way, from his cousin or the sickness. Might as well let them know you were here.

He was pulling the grill off the stove when the phone started ringing.

4

VINCE ADJUSTS HIMSELF on the bar stool and takes another sip of his vodka. *Billy done this*, he thinks at the mirror, and his withered likeness nods in furious assent. Some how, some way, he's making it happen.

It don't matter we shot him in the woods and left him to rot, don't matter he's been dead for so many months, Billy somehow is behind all of this grief, pulling the strings, pushing the buttons as he tap dances around the Ninth Circle of Hell.

Vince tried to explain it to his cousin, Sal, he says, something is wrong here. It just ain't natural, all this bad shit happening at once. I'm telling you, that prick put some kind of curse on us and he's reaching for our throats from beyond the goddamn grave.

You'd think his cousin would listen to him, show him some respect, you know, after all the shit they been through together. But Sal just patted him on the shoulder and nodded like he was talking to some drooling mongoloid.

Vince, you gotta get a hold of yourself. Forget about Billy, for Christ's sake. Just forget him. We got a lot more important things going on around here.

Vince takes another hit on the Stoli's and tells his shriveled image, yeah, like I don't know that Sal thinks of Billy every other second, like I don't know about the nightmares he's been having, and that in spite of all the talk, he's just as scared as me. I know plenty, big guy.

He knew he shouldn't have answered that damn phone, that he should get on with the show and let that stupid ringing be the last thing he heard in this life.

But he couldn't help himself, even though he knew who was calling. He was still hoping Sal might listen to him.

And to give him credit, just for a second there, Vince actually believed Sal was on his side. Listen, big guy, Matty ain't mad at you. He's okay with everything. He wants you to come over so we can square things. Now just stay where you are and I'll come pick you up.

Stay where you are. Oh, sure, like Vince is going to fall for that one. He knows exactly how them bastards square things and he's not playing that game.

What am I retarded or something? I don't know what Sal and that rancid old mummy have planned for me?

I made plenty of them calls myself, damn it, talking the buddy-buddy shit the whole time you're planning how to get rid of the poor schmuck's corpse. I was standing right next to Sal when he made that call to Billy. I know what happens next.

You get two in the back of the head, an unmarked grave in a landfill somewhere and people you've known for years will suddenly make like they never heard of you.

Dying didn't make him stupid, but Vince played it that way, saying, sure, Sal, I'd like that. Come on over. I'll wait right here. Then he rang off, ripped the phone out of the wall, and ran down the stairs to his car.

Vince sees some of the regular cadavers dragging themselves through the front door, ready to foul the air with loser talk and low rent laughter.

Why, why couldn't any of these worthless scumbags get the bad blood instead of Vince? Nobody would miss these shitheels if the whole pack of them dropped dead on the count of three. Vince's got something to live for now.

He's thinking about what he'll do when Sal's people get here because you know Sal ain't got the balls to come down here himself. He'll probably send guys that Vince trusts, good buddies that he's hung out with, gambled with, guys he's had over to the house plenty of times.

And none of that shit will matter. When they walk through that door tonight, whoever they are, they'll be Sal's people. Down to the fucking bone.

Maybe Vince will smile and drop a smart-ass remark. Or give them a big hello, buy them a round, no hard feelings, boys, let's have one for the road.

Maybe he'll curse them, call them pussies and gouge at them with a broken beer bottle. Them faggots would trample the Baby Jesus to escape Vince's toxic blood.

Or perhaps he'll knock back his drink, throw that asshole bartender the biggest tip he's even had in his life, and walk out the door with his executioners fearless and silent. Vince will face death bravely, like Frank Sinatra in that dumb-ass movie that Billy never stopped talking about.

Whatever he does, Vince is not going to beg for his life, oh, no, he's done being scared. God knows he's not leaving much behind, so he wants to do this last part right.

Fucking bitch, she leaves me a note…

Vince drops his head low and stifles the urge to cry. He's never going to see his little girl again and his own cousin is going to have him killed. This is so fucking twisted.

He tries to stop it, does everything he can to hold it together, but his reflection starts crying and Vince can't help it, can't stop these stupid tears from rolling out of his eyes.

At least Billy didn't see it coming. He died happy, the arrogant fuck, looking up at the stars like a Cub Scout on a camping trip. He didn't have to spend his last hours knee-deep in blue-collar corpses waiting for his last ride. Fucking Billy gets all the breaks.

Vince inhales, wipes his face. He's okay now, got it under control. Thinking about Billy makes him mad and that's good, that's what he needs. No more whining, no more of this poor me bullshit. All his bags are packed; he's ready to go.

He feels a heavy shadow fall on his back. Shit, that was fast.

Fucking Sal, he's so scared of me he sent that iron-pumping roid-rager to make sure I don't cause no scene, no, we can't have that.

It must be that surfer boy psychopath who can't get through the day without maiming somebody. Matty's little mutant will have fun pulling Vince apart, putting the fear of God in the rest of the crew. And won't that make Daddy proud?

Enjoy it while you can, kid. Blood don't mean shit to Matty and one day that satanic old lizard will send someone for you, sure as Christ made little green maggots.

Vince gets a hard poke in the shoulder, turns to give the asshole the snake eye, and he's looking at some massive lowlife standing behind him on rocking heels.

It's under control…

He's big, this one, with a bloated moustache hanging over his mouth, beer gut cannonballing against his belt buckle, and a tattered flannel shirt with the sleeves rolled back to expose swollen forearms branded with scars and a tattoo.

It takes Vince a few seconds, wondering why this hump is eyeballing him so harshly, as if one of Matty's boys would ever have anything to do with a fuckwad like——

And then he knows.

That's his brother, the older one Rocco standing there, glaring at him with smoldering hatred. Jesus, you gotta be shitting me.

"Well, well, well look who's here." Rocco leans closer. "It's the big time hoodlum himself. So how's it going, tough guy?"

Vince looks beyond Rocco's hefty shoulder and there's Willy, the youngest, standing by the pool table and shrugging stupidly. No, no, this is not happening.

"I can't believe it's you." Rocco is close to bellowing. "Willy said it couldn't be you sitting here all by yourself at the bar, but I says, Willy, I says, I think that's him. I think that's our long-lost brother over there."

Vince looks down into his drink as if he'll find salvation there. Now? This fat drunken bastard, who's had a cancerous two-foot hard-on for me ever since I hooked up with Matty, he has to show up now?

"I got nothing to say to you, Rocco."

His brother stares at him for a long drunken moment like he's trying to decode a secret message.

"You got nothing to say to me?" Rocco steps into the face zone and breathes out a noxious cloud of bourbon. "Yeah, well, I got something to say to you."

"Listen, Rocco, I——"

"——you're a disgrace to our family. You hear me? You're a *disgrace*."

Is this schmuck serious—half the family in jail and the other half on parole? What's left for us to be ashamed of?

"You got that fag disease, don't you?" Rocco's eyes are suddenly clear and vicious. "That's what everybody is saying. They're all saying you got that shit that the queers get."

Rocco pokes his chest with two stubby fingers and Vince smacks his hand down.

"Get the hell away from me."

"Oh, look at this." Rocco spreads his hands out. "The little fag is going to scratch my eyes out."

Willy grabs Rocco by the shoulder and begins whining.

"Rock, please, don't start no shit here—"

"—I'm not starting *nothing*." Rocco says it loud enough to make the heads turn. "I just asked the little prick a question, that's all. I mean, he never comes in here no more, never talks to his own family, didn't see his own poor mother until she was in the goddamn box. Least he could do is be sociable, right?"

"Rocco—"

"How about it, Vince?" He jabs Vince again with the fingers. "You got that queer disease, don't you? You been sucking dick or taking it up the ass or whatever it is you homos do and now you got that sickness that only the fags get, right?"

—if I ignore him he'll get tired, he'll go away, he'll want another drink and then he'll be too drunk—

"Answer me!"

Rocco cuffs him on the side of the head and Vince being so sick, sails clean off the bar stool and crashes to the floor. His head rings as pure, un-diluted pain rolls through his body.

"Don't you ignore me, you little prick!" Rocco screams down at him and everybody in the place is laughing at him from their mile-high stools.

He's a kid again and his old man is shitfaced and wobbling, his fists up, challenging any man in the place, any one of you scumbags, to step outside, and all the frightened boy who used to be Vince wants to do is die and keep on dying until the end of time.

Rocco's kicking Vince in the guts with those Frankenstein work shoes, stomping on a dying man, and snarling through clenched teeth.

"Where's all your friends now, big guy? Huh, where are they? You gonna have me whacked, badass? Is that what you're gonna do?"

Willy's doing his best to pull Rocco back, almost crying as he shouts enough, Rocco, enough, fucking stop it, until finally two regulars step in and haul Rocco back up against the juke box.

"Get out of here, you fucking faggot!" Rocco yells with Tony Bennett backing him up. "Get out of here before I kill you!"

Vince crawls, on his hands and knees like an animal, for God's sake, toward the door, sobbing and choking as he staggers to his feet.

He's so weak he almost falls down again, but he summons up enough strength to whip around and look his brother in the eye.

"You're gonna burn for this, you mother fucker," he croaks. "I swear to God, *you're gonna burn!*"

The entire bar laughs and jeers at him while Vince staggers out onto Third Avenue, determined for once in his life, to keep his word.

5

Ethan steps quickly over Azariah and goes to work. His ears buzz from the sound of the gunshot and the smoke burns his eyes.

He has to move fast. People must have heard the noise, the strangers, the outsiders, will want to know what's going on. Ethan has to act quickly or they'll try to stop him.

He pours kerosene all over the newspapers, the furniture, the walls, drenches every inch of the room right up to the dog's body and hurls the empty can into the kitchen. No mistakes; no chance of a rescue.

They all want to judge him, all these people in this town. His neighbors, that fat cop who keeps coming around here—imagine him telling me there's a problem, the kid's family has lodged a complaint, Ethan should get a lawyer.

Ethan remembers that cop when he was just a snot-nosed brat who got picked on every day by the rest of them little bastards at school. Now that he's got the badge and the gun, he thinks can tell Ethan what to do.

They have venom like the venom of a serpent, like the deaf adder that stops its ear. So that it does not hear the voice of charmers, Or a skillful caster of spells.

Ethan strikes a match and holds it in his fingers, mesmerized for a few adoring seconds. Always loved fire, ever since he was a kid.

Didn't matter how much his mother yelled at him for playing with matches, how hard she beat him, Ethan never stopped. Fire is so pure, so powerful, it can cleanse any evil, purge any sin.

He looks down at Azariah, bleeding into the carpet, and it hurts him so much to see his only friend dead at his feet, brain tissue and bone spread around the floor. But they won't be apart for long.

The heat of the match reaches his fingers and Ethan raises the flickering light high over his head.

"*O God, break the teeth in their mouths*," he shouts, "*tear out the fangs of the young lions, O Lord!*"

He drops the match to the floor.

6

Sal sits at the kitchen table of his house on Staten Island, the lights off, and cracks one match after another.

It's the same each time; the match flares up in an angry burst, lights up a small circle around him, and dies seconds later, leaving him in the dark again.

It's insane to think this way, but each time, he's kind of hoping it will be different, that this match, or *this* match, one of these goddamn matches is going to stay on, burn like a highway flare all the way to morning. Sal's afraid to put on the lights with their harsh glare, but he can't stand the dark either.

He needs the primitive power of flame to protect him until dawn. But each time the match goes out and joins the pile on the white linoleum floor.

Drunk last night and drunk the night before, gonna get drunk tonight like we never got drunk before…

He listens to the refrigerator rumbling and clicking a few feet over his left shoulder. Goddamn thing is always busy making ice cubes, cleaning itself. Sal could drop dead right here on the spot, and that refrigerator would keep on doing its business. Somehow that doesn't seem right.

The stove is behind him over his left shoulder, so clean it looks like Sal and Iris moved in here yesterday, instead of 15 years ago.

Then there's the sink, which puts the stove to shame it's so spotless, and the microwave taunting him with a blue cobalt grin that spells out 3:33AM. *You're halfway there, son, halfway to the devil's number.*

But Sal can't go to bed, not after the latest nightmare. Trapped, he was trapped in a room that looked totally strange and terribly familiar;

surrounded by smoke and flames, he was still freezing cold, while someone stood on the other side of the door and kicking like a spastic jackass and singing, glorious, glorious, one keg of beer for the four of us.

The door flew off its hinges, heat and smoke flooded into the room, a dark figure came toward him, and, of course, this is where Sal wakes up, before he can see who is coming to get him. But, really, who the fuck else would be singing his way through a four-alarmer?

It was so real he woke up choking on phantom smoke and climbing half out the bedroom window before he realized it was just a dream.

"It's okay," Iris had told him. "Come back to bed now."

Sal lights another match, feels the heat spread around his fingers and silently begs, please, please, don't go, just this once, don't leave me alone here. But the son-of-a-bitch wavers, goes out, and another dead soldier hits the deck.

When he turned 40, the boys got him a cake with those trick candles, the kind that keep burning no matter how many times you blow them out.

Sal kept on blowing, and the boys laughed harder and harder, but he couldn't believe they'd actually pull such a stupid trick on him. But they did and he fell for it. Wish to hell I'd kept some of them candles.

But what's really fucked up about all this is that Sal should be the happiest man alive. A month ago, him, Vince, and Matty walked out of that courthouse, not guilty on all counts, to face a battery of TV cameras.

The Feds did everything but charge them with clipping Abraham Lincoln and they still sailed out of there free as the wind.

The reporters started calling him "Stainless Sal" on account that he couldn't be touched, nobody could take him down. It read good in the newspapers, but if those jerk-offs could just see him now they'd be calling him "The Spineless Wonder".

Jake was there, too, miserable Irish bastard, circling behind the ring of lights, cameras and questions with that baboon grin of his.

He should have been angry, furious that the three of them bounced; Sal half-expected him to pull out his weapon and gun them down in front all those video witnesses. Cops have been known to do demented shit like that when things don't go their way.

But Jake, that prick, he was all lit up like it was Christmas morning and he was smiling straight through Sal's body, wordlessly saying your ass is mine, fucknuts, no matter how many fires you light.

"That son-of-a-bitch," Sal snarls at the microwave, "he should die coughing up blood!"

Vince started going crazy a short time later, talking all this shit about Billy coming back from the grave to kill them all. It was like Jake knew what was coming and he thought it was the funniest goddamn thing ever.

So now Sal's got people out looking for his own cousin because that's what Matty wanted. Sal tried to tell the Cigar that Vince didn't have much time, at least let him die like a human being instead of being dumped in the woods somewhere. But Matty didn't want any part of that.

You need to relax, Sal, the old bastard tells him, go up to the country place for a few days and let the boys handle this thing. It'll be better that way.

If anyone else had suggested going up to that house of horrors Sal would have screamed "are you out of your fucking mind?" before chucking him down the nearest sewer.

But Sal didn't feel like being the next one to vanish in the dead of night so he made up some line about his wife wanting to stay in the city.

Seriously, though—go to the house that rightfully belongs to a dead man? That was the last place on heaven, hell, or earth that Sal wanted to be. He didn't even want to buy the goddamn dump in the first place, but the Cigar insisted, demanded, and Sal thought it would probably be a good idea if he did what he was told.

"You have to believe me, Sal," the old man said, trying to sound deep but only coming off as insane. "It'll finish things."

Finish things, my ass. Matty didn't want to this to end. He wanted to hate Billy right into the afterlife and making Sal buy that house was his little way of defecating all over Billy's memory, the sick old freak.

Sal had only been up there a few times since he got the place. Yeah, it was the country and the fresh air and the woods, but no matter what he did, Sal could never get a good night's sleep in that house.

Every time he closed his eyes he saw Billy standing at that rest stop looking up at the stars. And he'd jump out of bed at the slightest noise while Iris slept soundly next to him.

I don't belong there. I stood right next to the guy who wanted to buy it, listened to him talk about his dreams for the place, and I shot him, for fuck's sake. It's unnatural to be anywheres near that place.

Sal rises from his chair and sneaks over to the fridge, an intruder in his own home. He winces when the cold blast of automatic light hits his eyes, makes a blind grab for the milk carton, and hip checks the door shut.

"Salud," he whispers as he lifts the container to his lips.

He sits back down, low on milk and down to one match. Goddammit, Stainless Sal shouldn't have to live like this. The papers say he's one of the most feared men in New York and here he is hiding in his kitchen like the boogey man's banging on the back door.

It all comes back to that night at the rest stop. Sal sees every moment of that night, each frame of his own private Zapruder film with Billy jerking back, tumbling to the ground, not an ounce of life left in his body.

The whole business should have been over right there. The guy was dead. But the questions still plague him, even after all this time.

Did his hand shake? Did his wrist turn just a fraction when he realized he was shooting his best friend? Why didn't he lean over and give Billy the bon voyage?

And did he really think he could walk away from what he did that night?

Sal lights his last match…

7

THE FLAMES ARE all around him, consuming the house and everything inside it and Ethan smiles.

He wants the blaze to grow, to spread to the neighboring homes, down to Pocono Boulevard, then up the highway; he wants the fire to sear the top off of this foul mountain, burn all the new houses and the new people who don't belong here, the strip malls, the resorts, and the fast food joints.

Destroy everything new and shining and hurl it all into the lake of fire.

"Ethan!"

Someone is shouting at him, Ethan sees a form silhouetted by flames; the fat cop is coming toward him, trying to rescue Ethan when he knows he's already been saved. Ethan laughs. Let him try and be a hero. Let him die in my house…

Vince crushes his body against the cold bricks of Gallagher's and feels jukebox music thumping on the other side of the wall.

The beat is steady, miles away from Tony Bennett, and it sends him a tom-tom message to burn the bastards, burn the bastards, God wants you to burn the bastards. He nods fervently to the music. Thy will be done, big guy. Just watch me.

Vince sees the firehouse just a block away and laughs so hard he nearly drops the bottle from his hands. Oh, yeah, that's sweet. He's never really noticed the place before, never really saw it until tonight; never saw things so clearly until now. Better keep them big boots handy, boys.

Billy always talked about hell and fires and that son-of-a-bitch could've torched St. Peter's Basilica while the Pope was giving a sermon and all the guys in the crew would still think he was Christ on the fucking cross.

Fine; if you can't beat 'em, burn 'em.

Vince, the big time hoodlum, allows himself one sneaky peek through the bar's picture window and sees Rocco at the pool table, waving his arms and talking his bullshit to the whole room. Oh, yeah, that's it, pal, just hold that pose.

It was good thing he had that can of gasoline in the car, so now it was just a matter of taking the empty beer bottles from the floor of his car and filling the thing up with firewater.

He rips off a piece of his shirt, stuffs it down the bottleneck. It's like a school science project and Vince really wants to win that blue ribbon.

His hand shakes fiercely as his lighter hacks up a few useless sparks; c'mon, you bastard, don't do this to me. He didn't come this far, suffer so much pain, just to fuck up and Vince is so mad now, he's choking the bottle hard enough to snap it to pieces. Light, you scumbag, light!

He's about to start crying again when a flame springs up in his fist and he holds it under the dangling rag, giggling, here's a little fire for you, scarecrow.

It's burning for real, right there in his hand, bright red heat is racing toward the bottle, and his brain is screaming throw it, throw the fucking thing, you asshole, throw it, and Vince springs in front of the window, armed cranked back and ready to go long.

But when he looks into the bar, he doesn't see Rocco standing there anymore.

In this endless second, poised to launch his homemade fireball, he's looking right into Billy's eyes, Billy that miserable prick, who can't even die right, is looking right back at Vince, that lowlife sack of shit is laughing at him, mocking him, just like old times.

It's Billy that Vince sees holding the cue stick, Matty's little darling, alive and well and just begging to die all over again.

That's all it takes, that's the last thing to push Vince into action and make him hurl the burning bottle right through the big picture window.

"Die, mother fucker!" he shouts as he sets the bottle free.

It's strange, how it happens, the soundless gap that follows the shattering glass and a flash of burning wind hits him full in the face. There's nothing, no noise at all, and Vince feels wronged, cheated out of his chance for proper revenge. This is his show; he wants to enjoy the sound as well as the picture.

And then he hears it, oh, yeah, does he hear it, the roaring flames, horrified screams pouring out of the gaping hole in the wall that used to be the window. Only then is Vince satisfied.

The sluts are shrieking, and those bar rats, the same bastards that were laughing at Vince just a short time ago, now they're diving over tables, throwing themselves to the floor, terrified. Oh, God, this is beautiful…

And in the middle of it all, Vince sees a human flare rolling over the pool table screeching like a rabid chimpanzee.

"Burn, you bastard!" Vince jumps up and down on the sidewalk hard enough to rattle all the chinks in Shanghai. "Burn!"

Vince has never felt so strong, so powerful in his entire life, like Merlin zapping some fucktard with a lightning bolt. You see? I'm not dead yet, you scumbags; I can take you losers any day of the week.

And then his heart stalls in mid-beat. The screams coming from the bar grow louder and louder and there's a very bad smell pouring out of the window, an ugly burning odor, like hamburger that's been left too long on the grill. But that ain't chopped meat he's smelling.

Sirens and bells rip all around him, dark, hostile clouds rush over his head and Vince sees with sudden and shocking clarity that he's done something unspeakably evil. God is going to punish him for this and it's going to be very harsh indeed.

Vince looks around at the dark houses popping on their lights and then starts running, running as fast as he can.

8

THE GUN GOES off and Billy erupts from his grave, dirt and leeches clinging to his face, his fingers digging for the eyes of the lowlife motherfuckers who shot him so he can rip their——

Billy stops when he sees that he's clawing at empty air. His heart bronco bucks against his chest and his hand shakes as he searches his face for gore and gushing blood, but only finds sweat lacing his fingers.

He's alive, not decomposing in the woods or being chewed by animals. He's here, in this town, in this house. Billy looks to the other side of the bed. Next to this woman.

He tries to convince himself that it was just another nightmare. You get that close to death, even if you're Billy the Kid, it's going to leave a mark. But no one's trying to kill you, at least not tonight anyway. Go back to sleep.

He can't, though, not now. Billy squints through the late evening gloom. He knows he didn't dream that sound. Somebody nearby just fired a gun.

She was just inches away. The lady on the white horse was coming down to earth on a beam of light with a smile that washed over him like a wave of holy water. He felt so peaceful, so safe; he didn't want it to end. He was reaching up to the radiant white mane when the gun went off.

Billy turns to Lora sleeping next to him and he can't help but smile. He wants to caress her, wake her up gently, tenderly, so they can make love and drive away all this profane energy swirling around him.

His hand floats in the shadows just over her bare shoulder; all he has to do is to touch her, shake her slightly and everything will be all right.

C'mon, guy. It was never a problem before. When Billy wanted it, he didn't have to ask. But he pulls his hand back. That's not how he wants it tonight, not with her.

Wake up, he reaches out with his mind, please, wake up and make me stay here with you.

Billy looks to the window, drawn by the gunshot's echo and feels the stray dog desire to leave, to go out with no destination. Climb into Lora's truck and prowl around on back roads until the demented spirit that tortures him decides to let go for a few hours.

Last night he drove down 611 and turned off on to Gorge Road, the first time since he's been up here; first time in 35 years. He killed the lights and followed the road through a gauntlet of rhododendrons, and his hands were trembling because he knew it couldn't possibly be the same, everything around here had changed so much.

And then he saw a church where there used to be a beautiful vacation home. The little gray house on the hill, the one with the red shutters, wasn't there anymore, and the swimming pool, the beautiful pool that everybody used to gather around on summer nights, was filled in and covered with grass.

Billy was close to tears as he climbed out of the truck, almost crying like a little girl as he walked out to where the middle of the pool used to be, and as satellites circled overhead, he fell to his knees and hammered the cold ugly ground until his fists turned bloody.

"Bastards," he whispered so hatefully. "Dirty lowlife bastards..."

On the way back he tried to find the spot where Lora's brother got nailed, his head sliced off as he rode through a fog bank by a truck stretched out across the road. No skid marks, no sign at all that he knew what was about to happen to him. There are worse ways of checking out of this rodeo.

Billy turns back to the bed and feels the same warmth that coursed through him the first night he saw Lora. Almost half a year and he still roils in this purgatory, aching to get out, unable to leave her behind.

Stay, his normal mind says, stay here with her and live like a human being for once in your life.

He likes the sound of that, no craving to prowl around in the dark, no need to set fires, no one to beat, rob, or betray. No reason to lie.

Billy puts his head back on the pillow, closes his eyes, and takes a deep breath. Fuck it, if some hayseed shot his old lady for talking during Wrestlemania it ain't got shit to do with Billy. He belongs here, in this house, with this woman. He belongs with Lora.

And Billy almost buys into the fantasy, almost drifts back to sleep, seriously thinking that he'll get up tomorrow, take care of his chores and blend in with everyone else around here.

Then something tugs at him, a familiar odor he thought he'd left behind in another world, and his eyes creak open.

Do I smell smoke?

9

GLORIOUS, GLORIOUS, ONE *keg of beer for the four of us…*

Sal's stopped trying to banish that song from his head, figures it's his penance to hear this stupid tune until they lock him up or he puts a bullet through his brain.

He moves his arm blindly, knocks the milk carton to the floor and grimaces at that sound, so much like a gunshot he wants to take cover. Maybe God's dropping a hint.

He still hears the shot from that night, the noise rolls over his memory like country thunder. You'd think such a powerful blast, like artillery for Christ's sake, would erase any doubts about survivors. But it only makes things worse.

Sal sees the microwave's glowing teeth have reached 4 a.m., what his mother must have meant when she talked about an ungodly hour and that's the word, all right, ungodly. Far away from anything pure or holy, this is the devil's shift.

He hears a noise upstairs, Iris, getting out of bed and searching for him. Shit…

"Sal…?"

The hallway light snaps on and harsh light blazes down the carpeted stairs. Sal tenses his shoulders, shrinks into his seat. Maybe she'll turn around, go back to bed.

"Sal? Are you down there?"

Not a moment's fucking peace…

"Yeah," he barks. "I'm in the kitchen."

"What are you doing?"

Jerkin the gherkin, he thinks harshly, what else have I got to do? He can see her, even in the dark, the woman behind the long shadow at the top of the steps. Good shape for her age, the face a little worn, a little tougher. Lately she's been little more than a shadow to him, even in the middle of the day.

It's all fading away from him. His son, Ralph, is in college in Michigan and when Sal talks to him on the phone, it doesn't sound like his boy anymore. All the Brooklyn is draining out of Ralph's voice and he's sounding like all those other Midwest farm boys he hangs around with.

Pretty soon his son won't know what good Italian food tastes like, after eating enough of that overcooked shit spaghetti, blood red sauce and godawful Play-Doh bread they got out there. He'll marry some blond Nordic girl, have blue-eyed children and any trace of Sal will be wiped away in a generation or two.

But that's what Sal wanted—to get his son away from here, away from his life. Make sure he didn't wind up some dead end punk leaving rubber and busting heads. He didn't want Ralph to be like Billy's kid.

"What are you doing down there?"

"Nothing. Go back to bed."

"But—"

"—go back to bed!"

The shadow on the stairs mutters "asshole" and vanishes when the light clicks off. Her footsteps fade and Sal wishes he could tell her what he's feeling, what he's going through. He wishes they could sit down and talk to each other, even though he knows that talking really is the last thing people ever do in Matty's world.

He wishes for one more match.

Sal gets up when the microwave says 4:15 and walks to the doorway to turn on the kitchen light. It hurts, the brightness from above, and he flicks the switch down. It's time for him to say the closest thing to a prayer.

"Stay dead, Billy," he whispers. "Please, stay dead for everybody's sake."

He's just turning toward the steps when the phone screeches to life. He jumps, ready to run up the stairs and dive under the bed. Once, twice, three times it rings, but it won't stop. He picks up the receiver knowing goddamn good and well who it is.

"Hello?"

"*Sal!*" Matty screams into his ear. *"Do you know what your fucking cousin just did?"*

10

BILLY BLOODHOUNDS THE smoke trail around the curves on Fairview Avenue, window rolled down, one hand on the wheel. The son-of-a-bitch is big, Billy can tell. This isn't a trash fire in someone's backyard. A whole house is going up.

His head throbs with voices from all corners of his life, like a radio tower at the top of world. He curses himself for leaving Lora when his heart screamed at him to stay put; with all she's gone through in the last year she needs someone who's going to be there for her.

Drunk last and drunk the night before, gonna get drunk tonight like we never got drunk before...

He thinks of the woman on the white horse. Why her, why now? Is it a warning, a vision? Is somebody else going to try and blow his head off? Billy's got enough Italian in him to be wary of dreams, enough Irish to tag it all as guinea mumbo jumbo. He keeps driving.

Glory be to God there ain't no more of us...

The smoke covers the air like curtains in a funeral parlor, and Billy's almost there, driving by these small blank houses, ready to bear witness to this tremendous fire.

Maybe he'll call for help when he arrives. Or maybe he'll feed the bastard more kindling and sit back to enjoy the flames. Billy has no way of knowing until he gets there.

And then everything explodes in his face, as if someone hurled a battle ax from the dark side of the moon and hit him square in the forehead.

The pain is fierce and Billy goes to war with the steering wheel as the pick-up veers and bucks on the narrow strip of road. His eyes squeeze shut, but he still sees it, a huge blue Oldsmobile, big as a freighter, coming up the hill.

Everything slows down to a stop-motion scramble. The smoke sinks into his lungs like poisoned cotton, the vehicles move in a strobe light tattoo, and Billy hears singing, so happy and innocent, two voices chiming in, dear, dear, what can the matter be?

No, no, they don't exist. It's a mirage, a ghost ship trawling through the dark old mountains; it's in your mind, it's not real, unlike that tree that's coming at you now, big guy, getting bigger and uglier every second. Keep on going and you'll finish the job they started at the rest stop.

Billy yanks at the wheel, feels the truck weaving off the road, a few more seconds and he'll be taking out mailboxes, lawn statues, and crash clean into some poor fucker's living room.

Oh, Jesus God Almighty, he panic prays, get me the hell out of this.

He sees himself impaled in the wreckage, the volunteer firemen ripping away hunks of metal with the Jaws of Life, sawing and hacking until they free his shattered bones and MedEvac what's left of him down to Allentown. He'll be helpless, at the mercy of total strangers. And then everybody will know.

You some kind of fucking hero? Huh? You a fucking hero?

Somebody must be working the cosmic switchboard tonight. The pain subsides, his vision clears, and Billy is able to pull the truck's nose up and over just as he's about to crash through a row of hedges.

The world comes back into order. He's back on the road, his heart beat thumping down to normal, and there are no other cars, no one singing, no one else but Billy on this strip of blacktop.

He turns the corner.

11

THE OLD HOUSE is lit up with flames screaming out of every window. Billy sees an empty cop car out front flashing lonesome blue and knows what's happening as he jumps out of the truck and runs to the front door. It's got to be George on duty, coming to save the day.

Fully involved. That's what people are hearing on their scanners tonight, 10-55, fully involved. George must have gone in just before the blaze got serious and now he can't get his ass out.

The fire's had a good head start and it gnaws through the house methodically, relishing the rotted old wood and piles of trash before moving on to the next piece of the building.

Billy shouts for George, for anybody who might be in there, and hears nothing but the fire's demented cackle.

This thing is no an accident, this blaze that Billy's watching, no faulty appliance, no frayed wire or random bolt of lightning caused this disaster. Somebody really worked hard to make this happen and they did a goddamn good job of it. Billy has no doubt in his mind because Billy knows fire.

He has to admire the inferno for a just a bit little longer, appreciate the effort that went into destroying this place, that will leave nothing but the smoking foundation by the time the sun comes up.

And away we go…

Billy covers up peek-a-boo style and runs into the house. The heat is incredible, yeah, schmuck, big surprise, like walking through a furnace, predatory flames on either side of him, spreading wide, preparing to close in.

Mayday, mayday…

He looks up the stairway leading to the bedroom and feels a rolling wave of heat that rumbles and snarls and dares him to come on in. So powerful, so amazing, he'd just love to touch it, certain he will not get burned.

"Billy…"

He looks down at the croaking noise coming up from the floor and sees George on his knees, his nice blue uniform smudged and stained black; his face sweaty and ready to pop.

Georgie Porgie, local flatfoot. Always gave Billy dirty looks even when they're shaking hands. Billy knew George was gunning for him, looking for any excuse to screw him over.

He knows that George would do anything to be in his place, next to Lora in that warm, lovely bed. Good old Georgie, who could burn to screaming cinders for all Billy gave a fuck…

"Billy!"

You could just back the hell on out of here right now and let the fire take care of the stupid son-of-a-bitch. One less cop, one less thing Billy has to worry about. If George is dying to be a hero, Billy's not going to stand in his way.

We got any more goddamn heroes around here? Huh? Anybody else wanna save my life?

He turns and walks toward the door. Hell, he might even go to the funeral.

Billy stops when he hears George gagging on the vicious air. It's such an appalling sound, if you heard an animal make that noise, you'd do something. Billy turns back, walks toward the slumping figure; screw it, he can always kill this bastard later if he has to.

"C'mon, big guy, get up." He pulls George to his feet. "It's time to go."

They crash down the steps and George hits all fours coughing out soot. Billy, standing tall, hears sirens screeching through the stars and he's almost sad, knowing they're coming to kill this magnificent fire.

"I'll never forget this, Billy," George says between gasps, "not as long as I live."

"On the house, George; on the house."

Oh, this is rich, Billy saving a cop's ass. What would Jake say if he could see this now? Billy quickly looks away from George to keep from laughing his balls off.

They both turn when they hear someone yelling from the house and there's this old man, this crazy old man dancing naked on the front porch waving a blazing bathrobe over his head. He's screeching at Mach One, just as proud as he can be of all the destruction he's caused.

Billy looks at him, really looks at this maniac for the first time since he came to this town and feels something like recognition, but that's impossible, there's nobody left around here who would know him; but their eyes lock and the guy is nodding, yes, I'm reading your mind and Billy is reading his, looking at the world from Ethan's sockets, and picking the words that come out of his mouth.

"...Their poison is like the poison of the serpent."

The fire trucks rumble up Fairview and George struggles to his feet so he can wave them in. Billy's not moving, though; he's not even sure he's breathing.

Fuck you, kid.

Then the front of the building caves in, all the evil and hatred within the house ignites and the bloated fire rears up and belly flops right onto Old Ethan's head in a molten tidal wave.

"Jesus Christ," George shouts, staggering back from the spectacle. "Jesus Christ!"

Billy keeps his ground, the heat rolls over his body and he drinks in every beautiful second.

"Glorious," he whispers in reverent tones. "Fucking glorious."

Part Three: I Hear Good Things About You

1

He descends into the basement's moldy gloom slowly so that his eyes can adjust to the growing darkness.

The voices upstairs dissolve to a faint echo as he goes down the steps and that's just fine. This is Billy's refuge, below the earth's surface, crammed with piles of old furniture, boxes of yellowed papers and photographs, moldy clothes, and the oil burner's rumbling bulk. It's a mess, but at least nobody yells at him or kicks him like a dog.

Every now and then his old man threatens to clean out the basement, set up a nice rec room, with a pool table, TV and refrigerator just for him and his buddies—no wives allowed. A nice little hideaway, he calls it. But the great plan always dissipates in few days, like a fever, and Billy's sanctuary remains untouched.

Billy finds a spot near an old storage closet and his hands quickly fold a sheet of yellow paper until it becomes a B-29 Superfortress on a mission to destroy Berlin. He can see the crew, hear the captain's voice crackle through the radio as they fly into enemy anti-aircraft fire.

Billy strikes a match and watches the blue tip ignite, the flame expand and flex inches from his nose to illuminate the small circle of debris around him like a bursting flare.

He holds the burning match for few seconds just to admire its beauty and feel the heat crawling toward his fingers.

In this abandoned place Billy has the power of life and death and his hand trembles as he puts the flame to the airplane's tail and sends it through the air.

"We've been hit—!"

The plane holds the air for a few seconds while the flames work up its fuselage; it rises a few inches, buoyed by the heat. The fire grows, spreads to the wings, the cockpit fills with smoke as the aircraft begins a deadly spiral at 30,000 feet, trailing a desperate stream of exhaust.

"Mayday, mayday!"

Billy sees the plane tumble through the clouds, slam into the ground and tear a crater in the earth big enough to swallow a small town.

He looks down on the crumbling paper wreckage between his feet with God's view of the catastrophe. This is what He sees looking down from the place the nuns called paradise. A red speck burst followed by an updraft of newly minted souls whirling toward judgment.

The paper curls up black and turns to smoking ashes. His mother had always warned Billy that someday he'd burn the house down and right now that doesn't sound like such a bad thing.

Billy kicks aside the embers takes another piece of paper, another match, and begins to construct another tragedy.

"Mayday, mayday…"

He's so wrapped up in his handmade disaster, he doesn't hear the footsteps creaking down the old wooden steps, doesn't know a damn thing until the basement light snaps and he sees his father walking toward him, his eyes rolling, pulling off his belt.

"You little fuck…"

2

It's cold in the diner, cold as a bastard with the AC breathing all over the place, and for two cents Billy would turn around and go the hell home.

But Lora insisted on treating him to breakfast and after his vanishing act last night, Billy thought it was best not to argue.

"You deserve it," she said as she dragged Billy out of the house.

"I deserve to lay on my ass in bed all day, that's what I deserve."

No fucking way does Billy want to be here. Day after the big fire, that's all people around here are going to be talking about and you just know some douche bag will want to ask Billy about what all went on last night.

He followed Lora into the diner, his cap pulled low and his eyes even lower as he gently guides her through the frozen Muzak air to an empty booth at the far end of the building.

"Maybe we should just eat in the parking lot."

"C'mon, it's more intimate back here."

They slide into the booth, take their menus, and Lora slips off a sandal and rubs her bare sole up against Billy's ankle. You did say intimate, big guy.

He pretends to scan the breakfast column while doing a quick recon. There's a huddle of lifers at the counter slurping coffee beneath the TV; a waitress hangs over the cash register counting out singles and lip-syncing to the zombie version of "One More Night."

The dessert case slowly turns a selection of cakes and pies in a rotating morgue, and the juice machine, blazing with a photo of painfully bright fruit, screams *Enjoy Vitality!* in frantic white letters. Enjoy it or else…

Everything looks pretty much the same, just like it has ever since he's been coming here, but Billy senses that something's not right today.

He looks toward the door and starts wondering, you know, just for the hell of it, what would happen if some psycho walked into this place with a 9mm and started shooting.

No weapon, no place to run, and plus he's got Lora to worry about. He looks down at the butter knife at his elbow, blunt as a crayon and just as lethal. Nothing you could do, except die.

Trapped like a fucking rat…

You read about that kind of thing happening all the time. People sit down to eat, doing the place mat puzzles, talking about everyday shit, when they look up to see a gun barrel pointing at them. Their eyes bulge, mouths drop, seconds before their brains are splattered all over the table.

It's the worst nightmare or the craziest thrill, depending upon which side of the gun you're on.

"You okay?"

Lora's looking at him with those priceless green eyes and he gets the same chill he got the first time he saw her. Short brown hair, tender smile, it's all right. Even now, dressed like a goddamn field hand, with the worn jeans and one of Billy's old shirts, she can still drive him crazy.

"Yeah, yeah. Just stuff on my mind."

"Anything interesting?"

—maniac dancing naked on the burning porch, looking at me like he knows me, like we're family for fuck's sake—

"Nah," he squeezes her hand. "Nothing important."

She smiles and turns her head, supposedly looking for the waitress, but Billy knows better, knows she's giving him the profile just to rile him up. And she's succeeding.

The old timers are pointing up at the TV and Billy sees they're watching news video of Old Ethan's house burning away on the small screen. Billy had gotten his ass out of there just as a TV station van was rolling up in front of the place. Yeah, that's all he needs, getting his mug on the idiot box.

Lora reaches over to a nearby table, picks up a discarded copy of the morning paper, and looks down at the front page so she can read all the fuck about it.

"Oh, Jesus, you, too?"

"What?" She gives him the innocent look. "I want to see what they wrote."

"What do you want to know? The old mountain rat fried himself. End of story."

"It's big news."

Yeah, that's the problem; it's too big. Billy peers out the window to the sailor's knot of belly-crawling traffic where 611, 190, and 940 all come together, and just looking at those cars and trucks, he can sense the noise, the congestion, and the foul air as if it were all plowing straight through his head.

"I don't see your name."

"I keep telling you, I didn't do nothing."

Didn't take much to get George on board. As the firemen were rolling out their gear, training their hoses on those howling flames, Billy was helping George over to an ambulance and talking low and private.

C'mon, big guy, can't you leave me out of this? Poor old bastard's dead, the house is a total loss. No need to mention my name, is there?

Billy made it sound like he was so humble and shy, that he couldn't deal with all the attention, but the undertone was clear: do you really want everyone around here to know it was me, of all people, who saved your useless hide tonight?

Do you want all the folks in town, especially folks like Lora, to know how you stumbled through the house gagging yourself to death until I showed up?

George pulled away from him, roughly staggered the last few feet over to the ambulance, so deeply insulted by any suggestion of dishonesty, and Billy was like, get over yourself, lard ass, this is what makes the world go round.

He was still glaring at Billy when the EMT slipped the oxygen mask over his face and at his first long breath, George gave him the slightest nod to say that they had a deal. Billy turned away, smiling, fucking cops, they're all alike.

"Well, I don't think it's fair." Lora closed the paper and pushed it toward Billy. "You should get some credit."

"No, I just showed up when George was coming out of the building. He's the real hero here."

Another smile, another soft breeze through his heart.

"I think you're a hero, too."

3

SHE DIDN'T FEEL that way last night, that's for shit sure, when she seemed ready to carve Billy's head off his shoulders and mount it on the living room wall.

Billy had just left George at the ambulance when he sensed something, above the wicked smoke, frenzied lights, and deranged radio voices screeching out of dozen different speakers. She was here and Billy had to find her.

He scanned all the vacant faces flashing in the crowd before him, all these stupid bastards were closing in on him—

"Billy!"

She was running toward him, sidestepping one of George's cop buddies, her arms reaching out to him.

The whole reckless scene stopped the second their eyes met; the flames turned to stone, the firefighters stood fast, and the ferocious arcs of water stopped solid halfway out of their hoses.

They grabbed hold of each other while George sat a few yards away wheezing into the oxygen mask. Sorry, pal, I got this dance.

"What happened to you? Where did you go?"

She was shouting, with tears in her eyes, shouting at Billy the Kid, demanding to be heard over blaze that had abruptly returned to life.

"I-I couldn't sleep—"

"You could have been killed!"

Billy was stunned by her anger, shocked that someone actually gave a damn about him and he hated himself for putting her through this misery, for being just another loser who couldn't be there for her.

"I'm so sorry—"

Billy buried his face in her neck, desperate to be alone with her, to get away from this place.

The crowd was moving in on them and he wondered how many of these pricks were taking pictures of them right now, clicking away with their fucking cameras, no clue of what they were photographing, just pressing the button over and over.

He got into the truck and followed her old Honda like a bad dog. Lora was unlocking the front door when Billy caught up with her, pushed her into the house, and slammed the door shut behind them. Reeking of smoke, Billy half-dragged her up the stairs, pulling at her clothes as they went.

Lora was right along with him, biting his shoulder, clawing his back, fighting him one second and urging him on the next, stupid bastard, you stupid bastard. He kicked the bedroom door wide open, shoved her to the bed, and groped her with those soot-stained fingers.

Billy could feel the others trying to get at them, the dead, the ghosts from his earlier life, but he wouldn't let them in, wouldn't let all that evil come between him and Lora.

He finally rolled over next to her, his chest heaving, all the strength gone from his body, and Billy was thinking that they were alone now, no one else in this house, dead or alive, when he felt Lora's hand slip around his throat and squeezed just a little too hard.

"If you ever do that again," she whispered, "I'll kill you."

He smiled in the dark. God is good all the time.

4

IT'S GETTING COLDER in this cracker box and Billy cranes his neck to catch the waitress's attention, yo, bitch, get your ass over here before we starve.

He's fed up with this place with its atrocious elevator music and the Yukon air supply. He nudges Lora with his foot and feels her toes gently rubbing at his ankle.

"Let's get out of here," he says.

"We haven't ordered yet."

"Forget this crap. I got a nice sausage here all ready to go. Shame to waste it."

Lora smiles and eases back in her seat.

"I think I'll have the waffles."

Billy feels a sinister twinge in his head and this bullshit isn't helping any. She's not getting it. Billy makes like he's joking around, but this is serious; he has to get out of here, he has to make love to her, and it has to be right now.

They have to leave now before some head case with a 9mm walks in and starts shooting, or some prick on vacation from the old neighborhood walks in to get a coffee, ask directions, or take a leak, and sees Billy, realizes, shit, he ain't dead at all, and tear-asses to the nearest phone booth.

"Hey, Billy!"

Larry Nelson, a big grinning schmuck who lives on their street, comes toward them, yelling out every word like he's hanging off the side of a mountain.

"How's it going, bud?"

"Not bad for an old feller."

Standard greeting, standard response, now fuck off.

"That was some business last night, huh?"

"You got that right."

"That place burned right to the ground." Larry shakes his head like he's never heard of fire before. "I heard you ran into that house."

"Oh, no." Lora pinch hits for him. "Billy got there just when George was coming out."

That's it, kid. Billy gives her another nudge under the table. Stand by your man.

"Old Ethan, he sure was a piece of work, wasn't he?"

You don't know the half of it.

"This is really something. Everybody in town's talking about it."

"Yeah, that's for damn sure."

"Well, you guys take 'er easy."

Larry blunders away from them, thank Christ, and the waitress finally snaps out of her coma and starts walking toward them with her pad out and a mouthful of gum cracking with every step.

Billy's head is really starting to throb now, and, oh, look, here comes old Georgie Porgie himself waddling through the front door and heading their way. Jesus, can it get any better than this?

And then he looks down at the paper—

Pain, like he's never known in his life, like that bullet hitting his skull ramped up a few thousand times, I mean, fuck, this is killing him.

— bastards, they shot him, they got in here somehow, put a gun to his head and—

Everything goes blazing white as Billy grabs at the side of his head, tumbles out of the booth, and starts gouging at the dirty brown tiles like he's digging his way straight to hell.

Ah, look at him crying like a little girl…

"Billy!"

…somebody get him a skirt.

He tries to talk, tries to breathe, tries to stay alive, but it feels like his brain is going to blast into bloody chunks all over the walls. Billy's on all fours—

—collapsed on the side of the road, making like he needs help real bad, while the driver of the pick-up pulls over and parks. The blood rolls hot down his face, but he doesn't care because he's about to spill gallons of the shit all over this beautiful night. He sees a large rock inches away from his right hand and eases his fingertips up against the rough surface.

He hears footfalls getting closer, sees the ten-yard shadow stretched out by the head-lights. That's it, schmuck, come on over. Do your good deed for the day and get your skull caved in. Billy smiles cold and wicked. The only Good Samaritan is a dead Samaritan.

The driver stops right in front of him; he sees a pair of work boots as his hand grips the rock, ready for to attack, to claim the first victim in his holy war, and Billy cranks his head up and looks into a pair of priceless green eyes—

—he's fighting to get to his feet, he has to stand up because he doesn't want to die in this place, in this town, not when there's so many people he has to kill.

"What is it, baby? Please tell me, what's wrong?"

She's next to him, kneeling right beside him, stroking his neck, telling him that he's okay; it's going to be all right.

But her voice sounds so far away, so distant, like she's shouting down into a freshly dug grave. Other faces surround him, talking, jabbering, at the man dying on the floor.

"Get back, get back. Give him some air!"

"Call an ambulance—"

"No!" Billy forces his mouth to work. "No…ambulance!"

He puts everything he's got into getting off the floor and when he's up to one knee, Lora trying to steady him, Billy sees a holster, a gun butt, radio with the rubber antennae and pair of handcuffs, and a blue uniformed arm is reaching down to him.

"Get your fucking hands off of me!"

Lora gasps and everything snaps into focus. There's a circle of people around him; the regulars, the waitress with a coffee pot in her hand, even the freaking cook is here to stare. Oh, sweet Mother of Jesus, what Billy would do for a 9mm of his own right now…

Lora's kneeling beside him, her hand over her mouth and George is on the other side, all bewildered and hurt. Billy looks to Lora, begging her with his eyes, and says something he swore he'd never say to anyone on this earth.

"Help me," he croaks, "*please!*"

5

She struggles to get him out to the parking lot with his arm draped over her shoulder and his body pushing down on her so heavily Lora's afraid they'll crash to the ground.

"You're going to be okay," Lora whispers, not believing a word of it. "You're going to be fine."

Billy breathes hoarsely into her ear and his legs twitch with each step.

"Jesus…Christ…" He fights with every syllable. "Jesus…fucking… Christ…"

"You're going to be all right, Billy."

She winces as his fingers angrily claw around her arm.

"Bastards," he snarls down to the pavement. "Dirty fucking…bastards."

George trails after them with one hand on his radio and Lora can feel all those busybody sons-of-bitches staring at them through the smoked glass windows like they're watching a goddamn baseball game.

"Lora?"

She opens the truck's passenger side door and gets Billy into the dead man's seat as he calls it, only now it really seems to fit as he hunches over shivering like he's just been pulled out of an icy river.

"Lora, wait—!" George is right behind her. "What the hell's going on?"

"I don't know. He gets these headaches—"

"That's a lot more than just a headache," George says. "Let me call—"

"No!" Billy slams his palm against the dashboard hard enough to make them both jump. "Don't fucking call nobody!"

"But, I can't let you—"

"No, goddammit!"

George looks to Lora for some kind of explanation, but she stands there without a word to say while Billy's noxious rage burns up her back.

There's no time for this bullshit, she can't stand here arguing, so Lora reaches over and squeezes George's hand, silently implores him to be a friend now, please, and not a cop.

George nods reluctantly and steps back a few feet while Lora closes the door and runs around to the driver's side.

"Call me if you need me."

"Thanks…"

She closes the cab door and starts the engine. Billy curls into a ball, muttering "bastards, bastards," again and again, and Lora almost checks the rearview just to make sure there's no one else in the truck with them.

The radio squelches, hauls in stray signals from all over and hacks up jagged shards of static while she throws the truck into reverse, pops a U-turn and screeches across the parking lot, vowing to bull her way into traffic even if she's got to rip off a few fenders to do it.

"—bastards, bastards—"

Lora eyeballs a heavyset guy in a gray Nissan coming down 611 and he sees that it would be a really good idea to let her go ahead of him. Lora skips the thank you wave and charges toward the intersection. Stay green, you fucker, she threatens the dangling traffic light, stay green or I'll come here tonight and chop you down like a rotting tree.

The light shifts to yellow, close enough, and she sails down Pocono Boulevard with one eye on the road in front of her and the other eye on Billy as he shudders, coughs and curses.

"Those fucking bastards—!"

The radio snaps into sudden clarity, as if jolted by Billy's rage, and news about last night's fire erupts in the cab until Lora smacks the volume dial into silence.

"It's okay, hon," she grips the steering wheel. "I'm taking you to Pocono."

"No! No hospitals!"

"Billy, listen to me. We have to—"

"—no fucking hospitals!"

She turns to look at him, shocked by the ferocity in his voice. His eyes

blaze with pain and anger and right now Lora, who's always been so goddamn decisive, doesn't have the slightest idea what to do next.

"They're just going to look you over."

"I don't want no doctors touching me."

"But you could be having a stroke or something."

"No doctors." Another spasm jolts his body. "Just drive me home."

She sees the railroad bridge dead ahead and the spot just beyond where
Kenny got killed and here she is now with someone else who's going to die
on her.

Lora knows she should keep going right on down to the hospital in
E-burg, let him yell all he wants, but Billy is so furious that it takes her a few
seconds to realize that she's feeling a little afraid of him right now.

Billy leans back heavily in the seat, eyes closed, and takes in long, slow
breaths, each one of them sounds like his last.

So either she takes him home and hopes he lives or takes him to the
hospital and pray he doesn't kill her. The cab falls into an abrupt, unnatural
silence until Lora jumps at the sound of Billy's voice.

"Lamb of God," he whispers in deafening tones, "who takes away the
sins of the world…"

6

HER FATHER USED to say that any girl stupid enough to pick up a hitchhiker deserves whatever she got and if the old bastard could see his daughter right now, he'd laugh himself to death if the booze hadn't killed him already.

Lora had never done anything like that before. She'd helped the occasional stranded driver, sure, but nothing like that night down by the rest stop.

She had gone down to Mount Bethel to have dinner with her aunt. It was just a short time after Kenny's death and the divorce and she didn't feel like being alone.

It was the first the time in a long while she could relax and have a beer. And then another beer. And a few more after that.

Her aunt had wanted her to stay over but Lora insisted she was fine, perfectly fine, damn it, and she headed back home with the oldies station keeping her company.

She was coming up to the rest stop on 611 when she found herself thinking about a little girl who had been dumped here God knows how many years ago and wondering why in the hell she'd recall that awful business when she saw a man crouching on the side of the road like he had fallen to earth in a meter shower

Dead of night, stranger along the side of the road, she's all by herself and slightly buzzed; so naturally Lora had to stop. As she slowed down the truck, Lora heard her father's voice slurring from the great beyond.

— any girl stupid enough to pick up a hitchhiker deserves whatever—

Yeah, thanks, pop. You finally got what you deserved, didn't you? Drove Mom to her death and beat on your children until they ran off and left you to drink yourself into what people outside the family called an early grave, but what your kids knew was long overdue.

She put the truck into park, got out and slammed the door hard, knowing this was stupid, stopping here in the middle of nowhere, walking toward this figure on the ground without even taking the tire iron with her.

But the poor dummy was trembling like a whipped dog and Lora couldn't help but think of her brother because this was just the kind of mess Kenny would get himself into, all busted up with no one to help him and no way of getting home.

She came up slowly on the guy, ready to turn and run like hell for the truck and take off with a spray of gravel.

"Mister," she said, "are you okay?"

The guy lifted his head, blood streaming down his face from a horrible gash on his forehead and it looked like, in spite of all that blood, he was grinning, a really savage breed of smile, like he was planning to kill somebody and have a lot fun doing it.

Maybe he was just grimacing in pain, but whatever that look was, it vanished from his face when they looked at each other and the ferocity she thought she had seen in his eyes evaporated.

"Yeah, yeah, I'm fine," the guy said. "Just a little banged up."

Later, when she thought about it, Lora had this vague memory of the guy's fingers letting go of a healthy-sized rock and she'd wonder what in the hell he was planning to do with that thing, but at the time it rolled right by her and all she could think was that she couldn't leave this guy bleeding here like he's roadkill.

"What happened?"

The guy stood up with a bit more ease than he probably should have, like maybe he wasn't hurting as much as he let on.

"It's a long story."

They usually are.

"You need a doctor."

"No, that's okay. I'll be all right."

"But you're bleeding—"

"—I'm fine." He smiled at her, a genuine one this time. "Just need to get my bearings."

They stood there a few seconds, with the truck's motor running and the night getting darker all around them, until Lora finally shrugged.

"I'm going up to Mount Pocono—"

"That'll do just fine."

7

SHE GAVE HIM a towel that she had in the cab and, as he wiped the blood off his face, the guy told her about getting a lift from a bunch of college guys in Easton who started beating on him when he got out of the car to take a leak, she should pardon the expression.

Hit him with a flashlight, took his wallet and the last thing he saw was the taillights of their car vanishing up 611.

He was looking for a place to crash for the night before heading to New York to hook up with some very dear friends of his.

"They're not expecting me," he said.

"You're going to surprise them?"

"Oh, yes indeed…"

He said his name was Billy Vero and he repeated it a couple of times like he was trying it out for the first time. This guy was good, talked so effortlessly, but Lora knew just about everything she was hearing was a lie. She couldn't get angry with him, though, just like Kenny.

The radio voices picked up slightly as they rode into Delaware Water Gap, as if on cue, and here's Johnny Rivers singing "The Poor Side of Town," just as they passed the bar where Kenny used to hang out with that no-good lying sack of shit ex-husband of hers, where he had been drinking the night he got killed, and Lora felt the tears in her eyes. Goddammit, Kenny, why did you do this to me?

Billy didn't say anything, just gently rocked his head to the music.

They were just outside Mount Pocono, the railroad bridge right up the road, and she was wondering where this guy wanted her to drop him off, when Billy asked her to stop at the Yankee Inn.

"The what?"

He said there was this big hotel in the middle of town, drove by it when he was a kid vacationing up here. Their brochure said they had space for helicopter landings—helicopters, can you believe that?

"It's right across the street from the miniature golf course…"

Lora nodded as he spoke and got a faded memory of some old hotel, but that place burned to the ground so many years ago that the only people who remembered it probably died or retired down to Florida where they could die with a tan.

She didn't say anything until they reached the office complex where that hotel used to be and she could see the surprise on Billy's face, like he really expected that old place to be there. Maybe the beating did more damage than he realized.

"Jesus," he whispered. "It's like I dreamed it all up."

The seconds ticked by with Billy looking around until he finally pointed to the diner, closed, dark and deserted, and asked Lora to leave him there.

"Are you sure?"

"Yeah, that'll be fine."

She did as he asked; pulled into the empty lot, okay, whatever, buddy, have a nice life. He got out of the truck, closed the door and just stood there, like he was waiting for a beam of light to come down from the stars and take him away.

I'd better stick around for this, Lora thought, as she shifted into neutral.

When nothing happened, when he didn't ascend into Heaven or teleport back to his home planet, Billy turned to Lora with this confused look on his face. Oh, Christ…

"Look," she said, leaning out the window. "I've got a cot in my basement. You're welcome to stay there until morning."

Billy took a long time to answer, like he had a flood of offers coming in, and he was having trouble deciding which one to take.

"Sure…that sounds good."

"But just for tonight, okay?"

"Of course."

That was months ago and in that time Billy had moved from the basement to her room upstairs and Lora didn't know much more about him now than she did on that ride up 611.

8

Lora turns left on to Fairview, away from the goddamn bridge, gives in to Billy, and goes up the hill.

They go by Ethan's place and she has to crawl along because of all the gawkers and TV camera crews trying to get a look at the fire scene.

Billy sits up straight as soon as they clear the crowd and gives her a feeble smile.

"See? I told you I was all right."

"All right, shit, Billy. You almost died back there."

"You can't get rid of me that easily."

"This is serious, Billy." She's angry about his flip attitude, his latest lie. "This must have something to do with that beating those guys gave you."

His eyebrows squeeze together for a second as Billy remembers the fable he told her the night they first met and, give him credit, he bounces back quickly.

"Oh, now, I'm just a little worn out from last night." He gives her a dirty wink. "And that fire was pretty tiring, too."

Lora smacks his hand away from her thigh.

"That's enough of that. Just promise me you'll go to the doctor tomorrow and let him look at you."

Billy puts up three fingers of his right hand.

"Scout's honor."

"Yeah, like you were ever a Boy Scout."

"I ate a lot of Brownies."

She shakes her head while making the left to get back to Main. Billy's not going to the doctor, tomorrow or any other day.

"You were cursing up quite a storm back there in the diner."

"Really? Well, I was in a bit of pain."

Billy is folding his precious newspaper, slips it into his jacket, like it's no big thing; the way a magician gets you to look somewhere else. And another potential clue disappears.

"You lit into George pretty good."

"Did I? I don't remember that."

Yeah, right, you don't remember, like some fake-ass medium coming out of a trance.

You'd think she would have learned something about the bad boy types after that stretch with her ex-husband, who spent his free time drinking, stealing and swinging at Lora's head.

That bastard got his hooks into Kenny, with all those dirty deals, and the drugs, and the booze, and then one night George is knocking on her door to say Kenny's dead on the highway.

Static tears out of the radio as they get to the stop sign and Lora reaches down to adjust the dial, but Billy catches her wrist, not hard, but surprisingly fast and firm, the way those fingers wrapped around a healthy-sized rock.

She looks at him.

"I'm just fixing the channel."

His smiles and kisses her hand.

"Sounds just fine to me."

9

THIS SHIT'S BEEN going on every night and Jake still can't believe it. Anybody else you'd say this guy's a head case, a flake, a nut job. Put him behind a desk and give him a squirt gun. He can't do real police work no more.

This sort of thing could never happen to a rock solid, street smart, ball-busting gorilla like Jake, never in a million years. He's a tank, a machine; makes the Terminator look like a fudge-packer. Nothing gets to Jake.

Jake doesn't understand it. He takes his vitamins, says his prayers every night, and he hasn't touched a drop since Irene moved out last year. So why in God's holy name does this abomination come to him?

It's the guineas, he thinks with the covers pulled up to his chin, it's the goddamn guineas doing this to me, with their curses, and their omens, and their evil eyes; hear enough of that horseshit and you're bound to start seeing all kinds of spooks and hobgoblins.

Imagine what would happen if word of this nightly séance got around the job. Guys that he's known for years would sigh, shake their heads, poor old Jake, they'd say, he used to be a good cop, while the younger ones would stifle their laughter and make the crazy finger twirl whenever Jake walked by.

It starts the same way every night. He wakes up suddenly at some ungodly hour, lashed to this painfully empty bed by a net of graveyard air. His breath turns fast and shallow and Jake wants to yell so loud they'll hear him in Ohio, but he can't make a sound.

He knows he's not alone, but he won't open his eyes, not yet; Jake has to work his way up to actually looking at this thing.

Instead, he puts two trembling hands up to his face, feels the tears roll down his cheek, and begs the Blessed Mother, yet again, that if he must be visited by the dead, then let it be Connor, please, for just a few seconds. Let me hold him; let me tell him how much I love him, how much I miss him.

Are you telling me my son is dead?

Just this once, let me see my boy, and I swear I'll do anything you want. And then he prays.

Lamb of God, who takes away the sins of the world, have mercy on us.

Jake sees Connor's chubby face, with the glasses and that solemn, studious look that made Jake think of a cartoon owl. Such a beautiful kid, Jake thinks; you could never believe he'd been fathered by such an ugly bastard like Jake. And he closes his eyes even tighter until he squeezes the tear ducts dry.

Lamb of God, who takes away the sins of the world, please grant us some fucking peace.

But Jake's prayers are never answered and when he finally does open his eyes, it's not his darling little boy that he sees, but Billy, Billy the fucking Kid, sitting in the green folding chair by the window, looking right through Jake with the mournful eyes of a toppled saint.

There's no doubt in his mind. That's the Kid sitting in that chair, even though he's supposed to be dead, buried, and decomposing somewhere in the woods. No mistaking that face, even though it's drawn, devoid of color, with a scar over the right eye that was never there in life.

Billy just sits there, his head glowing faintly, his arms hanging by his sides as if he's holding an anchor in each hand.

They look at each other for the longest time, not speaking, because Jake knows that as bad as it is to see ghosts, it's much worse if you start talking to them.

The stare down continues, Jake hoping this specter will disappear and let him go back to sleep, but knowing full well that he'd never get off that easy. Finally, he breaks the silence.

"Big guy," Jake says. "You're a mess."

Billy nods and gives him a sad smile, as if to say, look who's talking, Jake. Even in death, Billy's a fucking smartass.

They met on a day when there were deaths in both families, and they headed toward each other like two lethal blips tearing across a radar screen, each one roaming the streets looking for an excuse to commit murder.

It was that unspeakable day when Jake, his first year on the job, had snapped at his son for running around the house, to stop making so much damn noise, to go outside and play.

Jake just walked up to the deli, two blocks away, that's all, to get cigarettes, a cup of coffee, and to shoot the shit with Emilio, the owner, and the old guys who hung around the place and talked about how this world was going to hell; about the Mets' chances this year, how it looks like we're not going to have a spring, but go right into summer, we never get a goddamn break.

Jake barely turned his head when he heard the ambulance fly by with the sirens going; you tune them out after a while; you have to if you live in this city.

He didn't think anything of it until he left the deli and started walking down the block; saw the ambulance stopped in front of his house, a delivery van cracked up on the sidewalk, and heard someone screaming, his wife, Irene screaming. He tossed the coffee away and began to run.

They sat in the waiting room, the place filling up with cops as word got around, and Irene sobbed and prayed. Jake had never raised a hand to his wife, but at that moment he wanted to slap her, tell her to shut up with the Hail Marys and the Our Fathers, it's all a crock of shit, that no merciful, loving God would ever let something like this happen to such a great kid.

But he couldn't shake free of the old habit himself and when he saw the doctor walking toward them his lips moved, Lamb of God, who takes away the sins of the—

Jake had his arm around Irene as the doctor started speaking. He was sorry, nothing they could do, wasn't any pain, and even though Jake was expecting this, Christ, he knew Connor was gone the moment he saw that derelict van, he didn't want any bullshit. He wanted an answer.

"Are you telling me my son is dead?"

The doctor paused briefly, a second or two of silence, before nodding slowly, such a simple movement, but just enough to extinguish any reason for Jake to live.

"Yes—"

Irene struggled for breath, buried her face in Jake's chest and screamed, such a terrible sound, that went clear through Jake's heart and carved into his soul.

He glared at the doctor like this was all his fault, like he was the one driving that van, and he thought how easy it would be to reach over and crush the guy's windpipe…

"It's not my fault," Jake blurts to the thing sitting in his bedroom. "You did this to yourself. It's not my fault, you son-of-a-bitch!"

Of course Jake doesn't believe that, not for a second. He's a good Catholic boy, certain he's to blame for everything evil in this world from original sin right on up to Armageddon and he thinks—he knows—in what's left of his rickety heart that Billy would still be alive today if Jake had just done…something.

"Don't you get it, Jake?" Stan asked him when they learned about Billy. "It's good that he's dead. The guy was a hard-on, not some mixed up little boy. We need more of these fucks to disappear on us."

Jake didn't want to hear that. He kept thinking that they should have pulled Billy in on that crazy business on the bike path, put him in protective custody so Matty and his animals couldn't get at him.

Billy would have been rotting in a cell, but at least he'd still be alive. And Jake would be able to get some sleep at night. Until he found another way to torture himself.

Hours after Connor died, Jake was walking brain dead through the neighborhood with little more than a pulse.

His home, the one where he wanted to raise his son, was full of mourners now, family, friends, neighbors, people he'd never seen before in his life.

They were all so sympathetic, so concerned, that Jake had to get out of there before he picked up a baseball bat and started bashing their heads in.

As he walked, he felt the unrelenting pull of home, the piercing guilt that told him he should turn around and go be with Irene, now, this very goddamn second if he were any kind of man at all. But he kept walking, a fugitive from everything he loved.

He told himself that there wasn't much he could do right now, that he'd only be in the way of all those kind-hearted bastards.

Let them help out, pitch in, pull together. Let them take care of Irene and feel like they're accomplishing something, Jake will be home soon, just one more block and he'll turn around, honest to God.

His eyes blindly registered stores, cars, people walking down the street, while Connor's terribly short life played through Jake's mind over and over.

He thinks of breakfast when Connor was eating his oatmeal at the kitchen table, and he rubbed the boy's head, such a thoughtless, mechanical act. Jake had no way of knowing that this would be the last time he would ever touch his son.

Jake stopped at a corner and saw the Fortway's marquee up ahead, where he and Connor had gone to see *A Goofy Movie*. Connor enjoyed it so much, laughed so hard at the tagline— *It's hard to be cool, when your dad's Goofy*—and Jake laughed, too. And then they went for ice cream afterward. How could anything bad ever happen after a day like that?

This is what life will be like from here on in, he thought. Everything you see, every sound, every face, whatever it is, you'll tie it to Connor.

The gears in his mind won't stop churning. It should have been me that died, for all the things I've done or failed to do. Connor was the only thing he'd ever done right and Jake hadn't been there to save him.

That's what Jake was thinking when he happened to turn his head a few degrees to his left and look through the window of the corner liquor store.

"What the fuck—?"

10

The insanity started right after the trial, that disaster, where the feds set out to nail Matty, Sal, and Vince on racketeering charges and came away holding nothing but their pathetically limp dicks.

Billy was supposed to be there on trial with the rest of them, but by then Matty had made sure the Kid was missing and presumed bear meat.

The verdict was no surprise to Jake; the trial had been a dumpster fire, a goat rope, a star spangled shit parade. He knew the case was going to go down the crapper before the first witness put his hand on the Bible.

Jake watched as one newly reformed scumbag after another got up on the witness stand and said whatever the feds told them to say. It didn't take the Cigar's mouthpiece long to recast the government's case as a shameless vendetta against three hard-working family men.

So they were cleared, not guilty on all counts, and the three of them faced a barrage of reporters in the courthouse lobby, sizzling under the TV lights like rats on a waffle iron.

That wormy little prick Vince, forever on the outside, looked like he was ready to croak right there on the spot—God willing. Jake could almost feel sorry for Vince after he got the bad blood at the hospital, the key word here being "almost".

Matty sat in his wheelchair like some arcade swami, his eyes blazing with hatred for everything they could see.

And there was Sal, twitching and looking over his shoulder as if he expected the jurors to change their minds, run down the steps and personally haul his ass off to jail.

Sal was always a coward, a pussy, so incredibly unsuited for his chosen profession that it was funny in a sick kind of way. The only reason he got away with scaring people was by hanging around Billy. It was kind of a halo effect, except that it came straight up from hell.

So for Sal to murder his best friend was sort of like a deep sea diver cutting his air hose. You might be free to move around the ocean floor for a little while, but what do you do when it's time to breathe?

Still the old man wanted Billy dead and that meant Sal had nothing like a choice in the matter. Billy had to go. Sal's only mistake was not shooting himself in the head right after he smoked Billy.

Jake was there in court that day, too, on the fringe of the crowd where he liked it, and watched that pathetic schmuck wilt as the reporters peppered him with questions. Sal was turning in every direction, twisted and sweaty, when he locked eyes with Jake, who tilted his head to one side and cracked his sweetest smile.

I know you killed, Billy, faggot, Jake said in his best ESP. *I'm going to nail you for it and there's nothing you can do to stop me.*

Jesus Christ, you'd have thought that Sal got caught reaming his own mother on the courthouse steps, judging by the horrified look on his face. He stood there, his mouth half-opened and you could almost hear his balls drop to the cold marble floor, one right after the other.

Stupid wops, Jake thought, I just love fucking with their heads.

And that night Billy came to him for the first time.

Jake couldn't believe his eyes. The guy behind the counter has his hands up in the air, while some asshole gestured at him with his hand in his coat pocket.

Jake took out his off-duty weapon and pressed it against his leg. This was so beautiful, so perfect, exactly what Jake needed right now, somebody he could honorably destroy. There would be no call for backup, not until this thing was over and there was nothing anyone could do to change it.

Jake was going to kill this hard-on who's got the nerve to pull a stunt like this in broad daylight; he was going to kill him because the guy deserved it, because the world would be better off without him, because Connor was dead and that was so wrong and Jake had to make someone pay.

The guy was backing out of the store, his hand still in his pocket; attaboy, don't look where you're going. Just keep inching out the door, just a little further, dipshit, so I can put you on a slab.

A Con Ed truck rumbled by and shook the earth beneath them. The bastard backed right into Jake and he pressed the gun against his neck, pressed harder like he was drilling for the guy's spine, and he was trembling he wanted to grease this loser so badly.

"Guess what, scumbag?" he whispered in the guy's ear. "You're gonna die."

It's still so hard to believe that Billy, the smartest one in Matty's crew, the old bastard's favorite son, had screwed up so badly, had done everything he possibly could to get busted, short of leaving a signed confession and directions to his house next to the body.

But that's what Billy wanted, all right, to get caught, be punished, and get nailed to the cross. If the cops wouldn't oblige, then Matty was happy to do the honors.

The Cigar must have had a stroke when he heard what Billy had done that night down on the bike path. The Kid had been pushing his luck with the old man for a while, but with the whole pack of them under indictment, a looming murder charge had turned Billy into walking poison.

And that crazy scene at the gas station by the bridge, the very same night, the victim's got both legs shot to pieces, but somehow he's still unable to give a description of the guy who put him on crutches. There are only a few people in this world who can terrify someone into that kind of silence. And now there's one less.

The word was that Sal and Vince took care of it, drove Billy up to the Poconos late one night and came back without him. That was the word; now all we need is the proof.

Matty and the other two mutts played stupid, of course, formed a retard's chorus of fake surprise and wonder at the news—what, Billy's missing? Jeez, that's terrible. Hope he's all right. Sure, you do, you lying scumbags.

Jake went to see Lucille at the house, partially out of genuine concern for her, but, also, well, he is a cop, after all, and a grieving widow might be moved to tell him something about the bastards who had murdered her husband.

But Lucille just sat there on the couch, looking near dead herself with her eyes all crying red and her face so pale, as she shook her head, I don't know, Jake, I just don't know what happened.

Oh, for Christ sake, you know goddamn good and well what happened. Those assholes murdered him and left him in an unmarked grave. What could you possibly owe those fucks after what they did to you?

That shitbag son of hers, Tommy, was standing behind her the whole time showing off his swollen tattooed arms in a sleeveless shirt and smirking in a way that made Jake want to get up and pistol whip the teeth out of his mouth.

Fucking punk, he enjoyed watching Jake waste his time. Whatever few good traits Billy had, he didn't pass them on to his son, that's for damn sure. This kid was just foul.

Jake finally left his card and a dead end request for Lucille to call him if she changed her mind. The last thing he saw was Tommy leering at him as Lucille closed the door.

Jake reached into the guy's pocket and found it empty, whipped him around, slammed his ass up against the door, because he wanted to look into this prick's eyes when he killed him, savor the moment when the guy realized his life was over.

Only when he looked into the bastard's face somebody had pulled a switch on him. This wasn't any career scumbag about to take one through the brain, this was just a kid, a teen-ager, whom Jake was all set to murder in Connor's name.

"What…what are you doing?"

The kid said nothing, just stared at him, like he'd been expecting Jake to come along any minute and blow his head off. Jake glared at him and got angrier as he thought about what had almost happened here, what he had nearly done.

"I could have killed you," he whispered, "I could have killed you just now."

He smashed the kid across the face, once, twice, fuck it, he stopped counting, just belted the kid again and again with his free hand, and the store owner came running out shouting kill him, kill that little cocksucker, until Jake told him to shut the fuck up, get back in the goddamn store, and people were staring at them, but this kid didn't cry or yell or nothing, just kept staring while Jake cracked his head from side to the other.

Jake was crying for the very first time that day. He hadn't cried when they told him about Connor or when his wife broke down, but now he couldn't stop.

"Stupid son-of-a-bitch," he wailed as he smashed the kid's face again and again.. "You stupid son-of-a-bitch..."

Jake had no way of knowing that Billy's father had croaked on him that same day, denying Billy's right to stomp the old man into his grave. And instead of beating some sense into his head, Jake had made Billy a martyr in the scumbag community and helped him get his very first audience with Matty Cigar. Nice going, big guy.

"Do you know who I am?" Jake asks Billy's ghost and gets another slow motion nod. He feels anger growing despite the fear and disbelief. At least Marley's ghost said what was on its mind, not like this hump playing Twenty Questions here.

Jake wants to grab this invading spirit by the throat and demand to know what in fuck's name does he want? Why won't he leave Jake alone?

Didn't I warn you about those pricks? Didn't I try and beat some sense into that concrete head of yours, the very first time I met you, so you wouldn't end up rotting in the woods like some slaughtered animal? I went above and beyond, mother fucker, above and beyond. It's not my fault you're dead, you miserable prick, so don't you dare look at me like that.

But Jake can't say anything. The dead haunt the living because they want something, justice, revenge, a wrong made right, and they can't leave this earth until it's been done.

Jake stares at those unblinking eyes until Billy's waves him over, c'mere, I want to educate you a little.

He does what he's told, leans in close and hopes he'll get answers, why all this is happening now and how he can make things right.

The bloodless lips move and Jake strains, strains like a bastard to hear something, but never picks up a sound on this or any other night, like he's been struck stone deaf.

The spirit starts to fade and Jake feels the wave of panic surge through him.

"Don't go," he croaks, "please, don't go!"

But Billy's ghost only nods and then he's gone, leaving Jake more alone than ever.

11

Sal stops outside the bar with his hand on the doorknob and looks down the deserted street.

Nobody's around this late at night, this early in the morning. This ungodly hour. The steel shuttered stores lining the block won't start opening up for a little while yet.

Sal remembers when the boys would come out of this place, the Good Friends Bar & Grill, at the break of dawn after a night of hard drinking, gambling, and whatever, and they'd laugh at these people, the baker, the deli owner, the candy store guy, as they arrived bleary-eyed to begin their day.

Fucking losers, working in their crappy little stores all day. They should die now and do us all a favor.

Sal isn't laughing now. He's wishing he was home in bed with Iris, even if it meant nothing more than staring at her back till sunrise; anything would be better than what he's going to do next.

Sal catches his ghostly reflection in the door's blackened glass, frightened, colorless, and so old, and he can't go one inch further.

It was like this the first night he came here, to Matty's bar, God knows how many years ago, back when he was breaking into cars, busting heads and making his parents miserable.

They did everything they could to set him straight but he only got worse. Looking back, he wonders why he was such a little shitheel.

They were good people, his mom and dad; worked hard, only wanted the best for their kids, but Sal couldn't stand that. It was like he had to punish them for having the nerve to love him.

Finally his Uncle Jack, an ex-con who could see that Sal would never change, never finish school or get anything like a decent job, pulled him aside for a talk.

Go down to that bar there, he said, and ask for Matty. He'll take care of you.

Sal froze at this very spot that first night, seconds away from running back home crying. Just like tonight. But he didn't run that time and he's not running now because, just like then, he's got nowhere to go.

He's reaching for the door handle when it flies open and Sal is facing Train, Matty's young maniac. Massive, dyed-blond hair, with a face that's just a little too familiar, he looks down at Sal with a deviant smile.

The night turns colder and Sal has this sickly feeling of being pulled from this street, away from this earth to a place where darkness never ends.

They look at each other, two generations squaring off, and it's deadly clear that Sal is the vanishing American in this little encounter.

"Hey, Sal, how's it going?"

"I'm good, Train. Real good."

"That's what we like to hear."

Train steps aside, holds the door back like he's helping an old lady at a bus stop, and waves his hand.

"Enjoy your evening."

Sal nods slightly and walks through the door.

They're all inside standing at the bar, just below the widescreen TV, always on ESPN, always on mute. Matty's top guys have been ordered out of bed in the middle of the night.

From the outside the place looks like any other neighborhood dive, but the locals know better than to walk through the front door. Only Matty's crew is allowed in here.

There's Teddy Farina, showing everybody his new goddamn cellphone; Paolo, bulky and wide from all the years at the gym; and Louie, gray, bloated and sucking on what's probably his twelfth cigarette in the last two hours.

The guys all turn his way, looking like the dearly beloved gathered together, and the faces all carry the same mixture of pity and relief. Sorry for your trouble, pal, but you're on your own tonight.

Sal walks into the room as they approach him one at a time to give the expected hug, and at least with Paolo it feels sincere, but maybe it's just because he's so strong. He even takes a second to pat Sal's cheek.

"You okay, big guy?"

"I'm good, Paolo. I'm good."

Sal steps back and looks into the eyes of each man standing around him.

Which one of you will do it? Which one of you will take me out the back door with a gun jammed in my back? Which one of my good friends here will murder me the second Matty so much as lifts his pinky?

Rex, the rat bastard who takes care of the place, is standing behind the bar leering at him like a short-eared jackass.

"Hey, Sal, good to see you."

"Good to see you, too, Rex."

"Some shit, huh?"

Fuck you, Rex. The guy thinks who he is because he's always kissing Matty's ass. Billy thoroughly hated this guy, saw him for what he was, and he always took time to rub Rex's face in shit. Rex doesn't seem to realize that things won't always be the same around here. Even Matty Cigar won't live forever.

Sal likes to think about what he'll do with Rex when the time is right, how hostile it's going to get, and how much he'll enjoy it.

"Yeah, Rex, some shit."

Rex stretches his grin a little wider and nods to the backroom.

"He's waiting for you."

A wave of cigar smoke reaches Sal, the way it came to him on his first night, when he crawled through a gauntlet of scowling old men and walked toward the streak of light at the bottom of the backroom door.

I hear good things about you.

The first words Matty Cigar ever said to him, after a long, cold-blooded stare. It was the first thing he said to any of the young guys who got this far into his world. And Sal couldn't believe it, couldn't believe that someone like Matty had ever heard of him, let alone talk to him.

It was the highest praise melded with the deadliest threat; a solemn oath, warning that if you didn't live up to everything that Matty expected of you, you'd curse your mother for giving birth to you.

Somehow Sal managed to keep from pissing his pants that night, somehow gave the right answers because the old man told him to go home and wait until he got a phone call.

The call came two weeks later, followed by many others, and Sal always answered. He did anything the old man wanted him to do, steal, stomp people, bust up stores, it didn't matter; the club was his home.

And when he was in good with the crew, after he had done so much, he couldn't possibly leave, he brought Billy in here, to the backroom, and told the Cigar good things about his friend, what a tough bastard his was, how he had taken a ferocious beating from that cop, Jake, and didn't so much as blink.

Sal was outside the liquor store that day and it was the sickest thing he'd ever seen; that cop wailing on his best friend, hitting Billy over and over, and Billy just standing like, thank you, sir, may I please have another?

One of them was surely going to die any second, Billy from the punches or Jake from the exertion.

If only Billy had cried, fallen down and begged for mercy. If only he'd shown some fear the day, Sal would never have told Matty about him, Billy wouldn't have joined the crew, and Sal wouldn't be standing here now.

But then Billy was always two-stepping with death. He wasn't trying to show everybody how tough he was that day; he wanted Jake to kill him. Only Jake ran out of rage.

So Billy came on board and quickly became Matty's boy, always running his mouth, making jokes, and Sal didn't really mind at all that his friend had eclipsed him in the old man's eyes. Guys at the top are such easy targets.

They'd play on that pool table, right over there in the corner, with the jukebox blasting, and Billy would strut around with a cue stick lining up shots no sane man would ever dream of trying, and you knew he was going to make even as you threw your money down saying no way, big guy, no fucking way.

All right, ladies, Billy would say, we're taking this one downtown.

Then he'd send the cue ball ripping down the length of the table like an ivory comet and Matty would lap it up, point and laugh with lines of smoke running out of his nose.

He's like a nigger, this fucking guy; crazy as a goddamn nigger.

Shit, Billy's crazy enough to be two niggers!

Matty liked to drop his little hints around Billy and the boys when he wanted them to do something. He'd sit back, puff on his cigar and calmly toss out the name of some poor stiff who was slow on his payments.

Boy, he'd say, it would be a real shame if that guy's store caught on fire some night and burned to the ground. A real shame.

Yeah, Matty. That would be terrible.

You hate to see shit like that, you know, but we live in a violent world, right?

You got that right, Matty.

The boys would smirk, look to Billy, who'd be racking up the balls like he wasn't even listening. No more had to be said and a day or two later somebody's place would be in flames.

Sal looks at the empty corner of the room, shakes his head and thinks *Jesus, it's hard to believe we were ever that fearless.*

"Sal!"

12

The voice comes through the office door and all the boys take a defensive step away from Sal, like he's radioactive for God's sake. What—you think Matty's going to strike all you assholes dead with a bolt from his cigar?

He straightens up, tucks in his shirt, and takes a quick look at himself in the mirror to see if his hair is all right.

Sal walks deliberately toward the office and tries so hard not to look scared, even though he's ready to puke all over the floor and crap his pants at the same time. It's a heroic effort because he really wants these steps, maybe his last on this earth, to look good.

Matty always says how you die counts for so much in this life. That's the one thing people will talk about, the one thing they'll remember about you. Did you die like a man?

Maybe Vince was thinking about that as he stood outside that rat bar, his brain twisted in knots, seconds away from torching his own brother. I'm gonna die like a man. Yeah, very good, Vince, you go out like some suicide bomber and get me killed while you're at it.

Sal steps into the office and closes the door behind him. Matty is behind the desk in his wheelchair, a cigar grafted to his right hand and a cloud of smoke hovering obediently over his head.

The face hasn't changed much in all these years. It's wrinkled, hard, carved out of a rotting tree, with dark brown eyes, flattened nose and the skullcap of white hair.

Matty is small, no bigger than a jockey, and ever since the shooting, he's been fused to that wheelchair.

There's a small TV on the desk broadcasting a flickering image and a line of talk about the late night firebombing in Brooklyn that-—

"Son-of-a-bitch!" Matty hammers his fist on the desk and almost sends the TV into the air. "He killed the wrong brother. Can you believe that?"

"Matty, I—"

"—I mean, what the fuck?" The Cigar's still looking at the TV. "He goes there trying to kill one of his asshole relatives and he fries the other one by mistake. Stupid fuck can't even get that right."

This is Matty's way when he's mad at someone. He takes his time getting into his victim, savors the singular pleasure of letting the poor bastard swing in the breeze by his nuts.

Finally he clicks off the TV, sits back in his wheelchair and turns his eyes on Sal.

"So tell me, Sal. What happened here?"

"Matty, I-I don't know—"

"I can see that, Sal!" Matty's voice erupts into a scream. "With my eyes closed and a bag over my head I can see you don't know what the fuck is going on here. What I want to know is why, why don't you know? I want to know why you let someone as sick, as crazy, as fucked up as your cousin walk around as free as you please."

"Matty, I had it all set up." Sal flinches at the child's voice squeaking out of his body. "I called him at that apartment and I told him to wait for me, that I'd come right over."

Matty's eyes pop out a little further.

"You told him to wait for you? So you call him up and tell him, hey, Vince, don't go nowheres because I'm coming over there to get you? And you don't think that would make him suspicious or nothing?"

Jesus, the story was bad enough the first time around, but it reeks like a mountain of week-old fish when the old man says it. Sal doesn't have the nerve to speak, so he nods like a dummy, yes, Matty, I know it sounds pitiful beyond belief,—

"What the hell is wrong with you, Sal?" The Cigar's voice pounds against the walls. "You could see he was fucking nuts; talking about Billy all the time, like the guy is still alive, he's coming after us. That sickness made him crazy—"

"—that wasn't his fault, Matty."

"It don't matter whose fault it is." Matty holds the silence for a few heavy seconds. "The point is, you knew he was out of his mind and you didn't do shit about it."

"Matty," Sal says, "he's got so much grief. He's sick, that greaseball or whatever she is ran off with the kid—"

"Fuck him, Sal. He don't have problems no more, he *is* the goddamn problem."

"But—"

"—where's this wetback at now?" Matty folds his arms. "How do we find her?"

"We think she might be in Queens with her family. We got people up there watching the house in case Vince shows up."

"That's just great. And the cops, they're not watching that place, too, are they Sal?"

"Well—"

"—they got no idea that she could be up there, so we got nothing to worry about, right?"

"N-no, it's just—"

"Of course they're watching the place, Sal." Matty waves his hand angrily. "What the fuck is going on with you?"

"Matty, I'm trying—"

"—the whole goddamn pack of you are hopeless. Junkies, psychos, guys who can't tie their goddamn own shoes. No balls, no brains. You're fucking hopeless."

Oh, God help me, here it comes…

"I took a bullet in my spine, for Christ's sake. I can't walk no more, Sal. You hear me pissing and moaning?"

"No, Matty, I—"

"You're goddamn right you don't!" Matty hammers the desk again. "Jake, that Irish prick, was one of the first ones there that night, and he comes right into the ambulance, leans over me and he says, 'who shot you, Matty? You're gonna die anyway, so just tell me his name.'"

And I'm in pain, fucking agony—

"And I'm in pain, fucking agony, but I put my head up and I says, 'your mother shot me, Jake. That's who.' See? I didn't cry, I didn't rat nobody out.

We took care of that business ourselves, remember?"

Sal has no trouble remembering that business, no, not at all. He'll never forget how they took care of things, even if you cleaved his brain in half with a chainsaw.

"Yeah, Matty…"

11

That's the night Billy came by his house, pounded on the door and told him Matty had been shot.

We don't know who, not yet, he said as Sal threw on some clothes, but we'll get the bastard. We'll get him tonight

On the drive down to Lutheran Medical Billy, whose wife was about to give birth at any minute, told Sal it was bad, real bad, and that the old man might not make it.

"I took the pain," Matty is saying. "I didn't turn on my own. I didn't rat nobody out. I took the fucking pain. That's what I been trying to learn you guys—sometimes you gotta take the pain."

The boys were all in the hospital hallway, with Vince cursing the loudest, swearing to get the no-good scumbags who done this.

But he fell into a glowering silence when the Cigar had the nurse call Billy and Sal, nobody else, just them two, into his room, and left Vince outside with the rest of the crew.

Once he saw Matty, Sal couldn't understand how he was still be alive, with the tubes running out of his nose, the machines beeping all around him.

His face was so drawn and colorless; it was like he was talking to them from beyond the grave.

"Jerry LaRocca." His voice was raw and reeking of death. "He's the one."

Billy and Sal knew Jerry, a legend among deadbeats, the kind of guy who seemed to owe Matty another pile of money every time he took off his hat.

It got so bad the Cigar was going to have Billy and Sal do Jerry some serious damage if the prick didn't come up with something, anything, right this very minute.

So Jerry came to Matty, whimpering like a little girl, took out a set of keys, trembled so badly the jingling sounded like the Good Humor Man coming down the block.

Here, he says, *here, Matty, take it. My house in the Poconos, it's all yours.*

Billy and Sal shot each other looks. Holy shit, the guy's giving up his house? Matty looked to them, his top men, like, should I do this? Of course, he was going to do it, but Matty pretended to be deliberate and thoughtful, looking at things from all sides. Billy nodded once, the Cigar snatched the keys from Jerry's hand, tossed them lightly in the air.

All right, Jerry, the Cigar said. *We'll put this business behind us, okay?*

Only they didn't. Jerry had a few days to think about it, a few days of hard drinking, no sleep, and late night screaming matches with his wife, to realize that he had lost his dream house forever. And a hell of a lot more.

He couldn't live with what he had done and he couldn't let Matty live either, so Jerry ambushed the Cigar as he was leaving the bar, shot him three times from such a short distance he could've beaten Matty to death with the gun.

The assassination attempt worked out about as well as all of Jerry's other plans and instead of killing Matty, he severed the old man's spine and made him the angriest cripple in creation.

Maybe Jerry hesitated, panicked at the idea of actually shooting someone like Matty, but whatever the story was, he made the unforgivable mistake of letting the Cigar live.

"Find him," Matty croaked, grabbing Billy's arm right at the Jesus tattoo. "You find him and make him curse his mother for giving birth to him. You burn that son-of-a-bitch! You burn him alive!"

This was the word of God. Billy and Sal left that hospital room, walked right by Vince and the others without saying a word, and went on a nightlong rampage, cracking on every mutt, every lowlife who so much as stood next to Jerry taking a piss in a public bathroom.

"It's our fault," Billy said as they drove. "We should've been there when Matty got shot."

They rousted guys out of bed, busted up backroom card games, hauled whining faggots into the nearest alley and kicked them bloody. It was onward Christian soldiers, trying to get to Jerry before Jake did, and they kept going until they found him holed up in a slop bucket hotel in Coney Island.

They encouraged the desk clerk to give them the key to Jerry's room, strongly suggested that maybe he should get lost for a little while and that he might want to keep his fucking mouth shut about what he seen here or he'd curse his mother for giving birth to him. Then they went upstairs.

Billy and Sal found Jerry in bed, twitching in the middle of a nightmare, his hand wrapped around a near empty bottle of Scotch.

The look on that loser's face when he opened his eyes, saw that he had company, the last company he'd ever have, was something that stays with you. At least it stayed with Sal for all these years.

They pummeled him, tossed him against the wall, stomped him, threw him on the bed, where they stretched out his arms and legs and tied him to the bedposts. The whole time Jerry was pleading his case.

"Billy, he took my house!" Jerry sobbed. "He took my fucking house!"

"I know, Jerry. But Matty says we gotta do this…"

"I was always straight with you Billy," Jerry said, ignoring Sal, like he was a shadow on the wall, "you and me, we never had no problems, right?"

"No, Jerry, we didn't. We always got along just fine, but this ain't got nothing to do with me."

"You don't know what that man done to me, what he done to my family!"

Billy waved the words aside.

"It don't matter, Jerry. All we care about is what you did to him."

"You'd do the same thing!" Jerry shrieked, "You'd do the same goddamn thing if you was in my place!"

Billy stepped back, stared hard at Jerry with the fury clouding his face.

"I'll never be in your place, Jerry." His voice was sharp, venomous. "I'm ain't no parasite, I don't pull on people's pricks, I don't keep on taking and taking and never giving nothing back. I'm not a fucking loser like you, Jerry."

Sal recognized those words from another time, but that all went out of his head when Billy picked up a can he had taken from the car and started pouring gasoline all over Jerry and that rancid mattress.

"Billy, please—!"

While Jerry was begging for his life Sal was thinking about how this was the first time the Cigar had ever asked them to kill anybody. Yeah, all the boys had sworn to do anything the old man said, but Matty wasn't fucking around now. When he said burn the son-of-a-bitch alive that's exactly what he meant.

Sal saw in that moment that he really wasn't the tough guy he thought he was, that he couldn't do this, could never set a man on fire, even a hump like Jerry LaRocca, and he ran out to the bathroom to yack up the little bit of food he had in his stomach. When he was done, he wiped his mouth and staggered back into the room, not even a shadow now, ashamed to look Billy in the face.

"I-I'm sorry—"

"It's all right, big guy. Look, why don't you go outside and make sure nobody's coming, all right?"

Sal knew Billy was offering him a way out.

"Okay…"

"Don't leave me here, Sal," Jerry's face was stained with tears and snot, the bastard finally acknowledging Sal's existence. "Please don't leave me here with him…"

But Sal wasn't about to stay in that room and he didn't even look at Jerry when he went out the door.

Once outside the bedroom, Sal listened to the sound of the gas rolling out of that can, the bass drum impact it made as Billy chucked it to the floor, Jerry wailing every inch of the way.

"Not like this, Billy, please not like this. This is wrong, this is evil—"

"I'd help you if I could, Jerry…"

"He'll do it to you, too, Billy. Mark my words, someday he'll stab you in the back, too, that sick old bastard's got no soul!"

"You don't gotta worry about me, Jerry. You don't gotta worry about nothing no more."

"Billy—!"

Sal braced for the crack of the match, the roar of the fire, the horrific screams. He waited and waited, Christ, just do it already so we can get the hell out of here. But instead of all the terrible sounds, it got quiet in there, strangely quiet and Sal had to peek through the half-opened door to see what the hell was going on.

He could just see Billy standing over the bed, like he was looking down on Jerry. He saw Billy's arm move a little bit and then he heard this gagging noise.

Sal couldn't go back into that room to see what was happening and he thought of how his parents talked about the old radio shows they listened to when they were kids, how good they were, when you didn't need no TV, you just used your imagination.

Sal used his imagination that morning and he could see Billy leaning over, putting his hand around Jerry's throat and squeezing, choking, so that Jerry's eyes bugged out, his arms and legs fought against the restraints, and Billy just squeezing, squeezing, the tattoo of Jesus swelling on his forearm, until the man in the bed fell silent and the body went slack.

And Sal was thinking, no, no, you're supposed to burn this loser to death, set him on fire so that his shrieks are heard all over Brooklyn and no low-life would ever dream of gunning for Matty Cigar for the next 1,000 years. You've got to make him curse his mother for giving birth to him because that's what Matty wants.

But Billy had disobeyed the old man's direct order and shown mercy when it was absolutely forbidden. Sal stared at Billy as he backed out of the room clutching a lit match between his thumb and forefinger, and thought, Christ, we both have secrets to hide..

"Get ready to run," Billy said, as he tossed the match.

And that's what they did.

Flames were climbing out of the hotel window by the time they reached the car and they took off in a streak of burning rubber.

Sal looked at the boardwalk, the parachute jump, thought of all the great times he had out here as a kid and how those memories would never be the same.

When they were a safe distance away, Billy pulled over and called his house from a payphone and learned that Lucille was going into labor and to get his ass down to Lutheran on the double.

"I'm gonna be a father," Billy shouted as he jumped behind the wheel and took off. "I'm gonna have a kid, big guy! Some shit, huh?"

We can stop by and visit Matty, Sal thought, tell him the good news about Jerry.

"Uh, look, Kid," Sal struggled for the words. "You know…back there…
I'm sorry, I just—"

Billy gave Sal a light rap on the arm with the back of his hand.

"On the house, big guy," he said. "On the house."

12

Sal knew that Billy had never told anyone about what happened that day, never told a living soul how Sal had run out of the room like a fag, like a pussy. Like a bitch. He had no proof of that and he didn't need it. He just knew that Billy had kept his mouth shut.

"So what are you going to do, Sal?" Matty's voice jars him away from the distant time, back to the office and the old man in the wheelchair. "What are you going to do about your cousin?"

Another challenge. Again he has to prove himself. And he has to do it before Jake finds Vince, because his cousin will crack in under two minutes and tell Jake everything he wants to know. Jesus, he'll probably make shit up he's so demented now.

"I'll find him, Matty, I swear to God. I'll find him."

The Cigar stares at Sal hard and unforgiving, relentlessly strips away the layers of armor Sal's built around his mind over the years until it's just like the first night they met.

"He's your cousin, Sal. You're telling me you got no idea where he is?"

"No, Matty, I don't."

"Sal…"

Matty leans forward and spreads his fingers on the desk.

"Sal, we all got family. Family is the most important thing we got in this life; it's what separates us from the fucking animals in the jungle."

"I know that, Matty."

"But sometimes family ain't enough." He flicks some ash to the floor.

"Sometimes the people we love become a danger to us. And we have to do something about it. You know what I'm saying, right?"

You're saying my life is hanging by a thread, that if you even think I'm lying to you, I won't leave this place alive.

"Yeah, Matty, I know what you're saying."

The Cigar gestures for Sal to come closer and Sal pauses just a second before he leans over the desk. The withered fingers wrap around his neck.

The old man's face is inches away. There's nothing to breathe except cigar smoke as he stares deep into Sal's eyes.

"I need to know the truth, Sal. And I know you'll tell me because we've been through so much together."

Sal tries not to breathe, sweat or think, nothing that might cause any doubts. He braces himself for the question.

"Do you know where your cousin is?"

Sal hears somebody outside coughing, bottles rattling as Rex moves a case of beer. He can hear the TV even though Matty switched it off. A jet crawls through the dark distant sky overhead, a baby cries in an upstairs apartment. Sal inhales the blue smoke.

"No, Matty, I don't know."

The Cigar studies Sal's face, the eyes boring into his brain, and Sal no longer cares about dying like a man because he wants to live, he wants to live so badly, and he wishes to God he had run home that first night outside the club, taken the abuse from his family and friends and became a working schmuck like everybody else in the neighborhood.

A few more seconds of this, of the old man staring at him, and Sal is going to burst into tears and leave this office in gory pieces.

Finally, after such a long time, the granite head nods, so unbelievably slowly, and Sal feels his heart beating again.

"All right, Sal. You know what you've got to do. Find your cousin and take care of this bullshit."

Take care of it. That means find your dying cousin and put him out of his misery; kill him like you killed your best friend. Take care of it or you'll curse your mother for giving birth to you.

"I'll take care of it, Matty."

The Cigar kisses Sal on both cheeks, gives him a powerful hug. His grip is strong, grown so powerful since his legs became useless. Sal returns the embrace and backs slowly away.

"You're all I got left, Sal. The only one I can depend on."

"I won't let you down, Matty."

He walks out of the office, away from the suffocating smoke, and steps into the bar. The boys are all pretending to watch the stifled TV, like they weren't cracking their eardrums to pieces just now trying to hear what was going on in the old man's office.

Sal wants to run out of this place so badly he's ready to crash through the window, but he says his goodbyes the way you're supposed to, the boys clap him on the back and tell him to take it easy. Rex's still got that grin on his mug as he holds up a bottle of Chivas.

"How about one for the road, Sal?"

Sal returns the smile as he thinks of a hotel in Coney Island, and how he and Rex will make a trip out there some day.

"Not tonight, Rex," he says, walking to the door. "But soon, real soon. I promise."

13

BILLY SITS BACK on the couch with his feet up on a cushion and watches Godzilla dropkick the Japanese army all over the tube.

That's it, big guy, he thinks, fuck them bastards up.

Billy's into his third hour of TV this morning, so incredibly grounded by Lora after his near-death spectacular in the diner.

He had told her he wasn't going to any goddamn doctor, not today, not tomorrow, not ever, and so she in turn told him that he wasn't leaving the goddamn house for the rest of the goddamn week, how does that grab you, buddy boy?

He knew better than to argue with her.

Billy made like he was all pissed off at being confined to base, but he enjoys being her patient and with the monster movie festival on cable, he doesn't mind plopping down in front of the tube and relaxing.

Get outta the way, stupid! You're blocking the TV!

And while Billy pretends that he's fine, never felt better and there's nothing wrong with him at all, he's actually a little concerned. First the headaches, now the seizure; whatever this shit is, it ain't getting better.

God, just the thought of being laid out on the floor, writhing helplessly before all those assholes gets his teeth grinding.

Billy's trying to keep a low profile here, but now every stiff in the Lower 48 will want to know what happened at the diner, what's wrong, did you go to the doctor? It also gives Officer Lard-Ass yet another excuse to spy on him. And I saved that fat hump's life because…?

"Fuck you, asshole!"

Lora's in the kitchen, late for work and ready to rip the kitchen phone out the wall by the sound of it as she screams at her ex-husband.

"I'm so sick of your bullshit!"

Billy shifts in his seat. No escaping the misery, is there? He recalls his last night with Lucille, the fiasco over that painting, where Billy was two seconds away from breaking her neck in 12 different places just as Sal and Vince showed up to take him for a ride.

I had to get him out of there...

He feels tension building around the scar and takes a long breath. Let's just watch TV, all right?

Godzilla approaches a set of power lines, the only thing standing between him and downtown Tokyo, and you can't help but root for the big green bastard.

He's getting closer, Billy, he's getting closer. Charley pokes his ribs, making him laugh one rainy Saturday when Billy's parents were out. *He's gonna get you, Billy, he's gonna get you!* And Godzilla hits the power lines with a torrent of shrieking sparks. Charley tickles him as he makes the shock noise—*zzzzt!*— and the young boy laughs even harder.

Billy winces as the monster turns a blazing white, pained by a sweet memory he doesn't deserve, and wonders if Hell is anything like this.

"Just get me the damn check or I'll have the judge on your ass!"

He looks toward the commotion in the kitchen. Billy's never met Scotty, Lora's ex, some former high school badass, who divides his time now between a trailer park and the county lock-up, but he's managed to form a severe dislike for the guy.

Lora blames Scotty for her brother's death since they were out drinking together the night the kid got his final haircut. It's probably not fair but if Lora hates this dipshit, that's good enough for Billy.

"Go to hell!"

He hears Lora slam down the phone and seconds later she walks into the living room and sits at the edge of the couch, red-eyed and trembling with rage.

"That fucker—!"

Billy snaps off the TV and sits up next to her with his arm coming down around her shoulders.

"Easy, easy." He gives her a squeeze. "Don't let this loser get you all upset."

"I'm so fed up." She's close to crying. "He's always trying to pull something."

Billy nods sympathetically and rubs her back. He's pretending to be calm and rational, but he's getting pretty angry seeing Lora so shaken like this.

"I know, I know," he says softly. "Some people are just lowlifes, but you know sooner or later they get what's coming to them."

Lora's back stiffens and she turns to give him a subzero look.

"Oh, no..."

"What? I just—"

"—you just nothing." She pokes her index finger under his nose. "I don't want any macho man bullshit out of you, buster. I'll take care of this, all right?"

Billy suppresses a wicked grin. Goddamn, she's good.

"I'm not going to do anything stupid."

"You're a man, you can't help yourself." She gives him such a nice smile. "Just stay here and rest, all right? If you can't go to the doctor, you can't go picking fights with people."

"But—"

"—forget it." She gives him a quick kiss on the lips. "I've got to go to work. There's some chicken in the refrigerator. Just put it in the microwave when you get hungry."

"You take such good care of me." He pulls her gently toward him. "What would I do without you?"

She eases away from his sly dog grip and pats him on the cheek.

"You'll have to manage for a little while."

She gets up and leaves through the kitchen. The house is suddenly empty, suddenly quiet and it reminds Billy that he doesn't belong here, that he should have left a long time ago before Lora started taking such good care of him.

He switches the movie back on to catch Godzilla in mid-roar and waits until he hears her car go down the driveway before he reaches beneath the sofa cushion and takes out the day-old newspaper.

"Where'd it go, big guy? Where'd it go?"

Billy at 5 years old, playing with Charley in the living room of the old house on Senator Street. Charley's just made a new JFK half-dollar vanish into thin air and now he's sitting on the couch with this mystified look on his face.

"What happened to it, big guy?"

Charley works with Billy's dad on painting jobs; deals with the customers because the old man is such a goddamn hothead they were losing too much business.

Unlike Billy's father, Charley knows how to talk to people, he's easy to get along with, likes to make everyone laugh, and even though he's a grown-up, he's Billy's best friend in the world.

The old man is there, of course, just a few feet away, stretched out in his sacred recliner, where he'd finally croak too many years later, scowling through a six-pack of Rheingold and a pack of Camels while the old Motorola spools out Ralph Kiner's play-by-play on the Mets' latest disaster.

It's early evening and the old man's already three sheets to the wind, as Billy's mom would say, and looking to hurt somebody.

"Where is it, big guy?"

Billy laughs as he pries open Charley's calloused hands, stained and scarred as if they'd been carved from wood.

"You're hiding it!"

"I ain't hiding nothing, big guy. It just disappeared."

Charley never raises his voice or starts any trouble; works hard every day, and even though the poor bastard's always struggling to pay his bills, he wouldn't dream of stealing so much as a stick of gum. Matty and his crew would laugh at him, call him a loser.

"Hey, look what I found!"

Charley reaches behind Billy's ear, holds up the coin in his fingers, and dangles it just beyond the kid's reach.

"Who's your, buddy, huh? Who's your buddy?"

Billy giggles and grabs at the half-dollar that keeps eluding him.

"C'mon, let's hear it. Who's your buddy?"

Decades away, Billy tries to focus on the movie and have fun watching that big-ass lizard destroy all those tiny buildings. But the question keeps nagging at him, even after all these years and it won't go away.

"You are, Charley," he says, as the tears begin. "You're my buddy."

"That's right!"

Charley laughs, rubs Billy's head, and hands over the coin.

Billy happily pockets the half-dollar, but he feels his old man watching them, smoldering over his beer as he tosses the can opener on the coffee table.

"Who's your buddy?" his father sneers.

Miserable bastard, he can't stand seeing Billy and Charley having fun together. Billy leans in close to Charley and drops his voice so his father won't hear.

"Tell me about the country," he says softly. "Tell me about Pennsylvania."

"Oh, it's beautiful up there," Charley says. "The trees go on forever and there's deer all over the place. And at night the sky is filled with stars; it's like you're flying through space. I got friends up there—"

On the TV screen, Ed Kranepool goes down swinging and the old man kicks the coffee table.

"Ah, shit, why don't you move up there, for Christ's sake?"

Charley looks hurt and confused, like he always does when he tangles with the old man. And, as always, he tries to reason with the bastard.

"I'm just thinking it might be good for Billy to get out of the city for a while."

"Yeah, well, I don't give a shit what you think, okay—buddy?"

Get mad, Charley, Billy thinks, pick up that ashtray and smash it of over the old man's head. C'mon, fight back, just this one time.

But Charley could never do that, not with the drunken driving convictions; he was afraid he wouldn't be able to get work anywhere else.

Charley has alimony, child support and there's talk that he owes a lot of money to some loan shark, a real nasty piece of work, is what Billy's mother says. Billy doesn't know much about this guy, except that he hangs around in a bar near the elevated tracks and always smokes a big cigar.

"Yeah, Tom, I know, but I think he'd have a good time there."

"I never went nowhere when I was a kid and it didn't do me no harm. Let him stay here with his mother and pick flowers."

Billy knows it's time to get out of here. He turns from Charley slowly to avoid any sudden movements, but the old man angrily shoves him aside with his foot.

"Get outta the way, stupid! You're blocking the TV!"

Billy stumbles forward, almost falls on his face. He turns and looks at his father, shocked at his brutality.

"Oh, look at him." The old man cracks open another can and gulps the foam. "He's going to start crying like a little girl. Somebody get him a skirt."

Billy can feel tears building up, but, no, he's not going to cry, he's not going to cry, even as the warm water rolls down his cheeks.

"Being a little tough on him, ain't you, Tom?"

"Tough nothing, he's got it too easy."

Hit him, Charley, please hit him—

"But he's just a kid."

"I know he's a kid, asshole; he's my kid, remember? If you paid more attention to your own kids, maybe they'd still be living with you."

The old man smirks, satisfied with the damage he's done. Charley gives Billy a quick nod to say you better go, big guy, and that's what Billy does, he leaves, roughly pushes away from his mother and heads out of the room just as the Mets get a base hit, and the old man leaps up from the recliner bellowing "go! go! go!"

His mother jumps at the outburst and nobody sees Billy's hand shoot out and snag a book of matches from the coffee table.

The old man is still cheering when Billy takes the pad from the kitchen table and goes down to the basement.

14

BILLY SITS BACK on the couch, still a little spooked about looking at the headline that almost killed him. But the fear makes him angry; it's just a piece of paper, you fag, he thinks in his father's voice, it ain't gonna bite you, and he cracks the paper open with a loud snap.

The front page is wrinkled all to hell, and he hopes the headline might have changed over the last few hours, but the words are still there, still spitting in his face: *Mobster At Home in Poconos.*

It might have run above the fold if that screaming freak of nature hadn't picked the same night to torch his hovel. But the story and the picture still had enough power to short circuit Billy's brain the first time he saw it and put him on the deck.

There he is, Billy thinks, there's Sal's fat stupid mug looking at the camera like he got caught jerking off in church.

Stainless Sal, that's what the New York papers said, the man prosecutors could not convict. Oh, please, if you think that guy's stainless shout "boo!" when he's not looking and he'll shit himself to death. That gutless bitch left plenty of stains in Jerry LaRocca's hotel room, that's for goddamn sure.

The paper wavers in Billy's hands as he reads about the reputed organized crime figure who owns a house near Saylorsburg a local resident, who wouldn't give his name, said he rarely sees Sal, but that he seems like a nice man, and that other alleged mobsters have homes in the Poconos—

"Bastard!"

Billy throws the paper on the floor while Godzilla is backhanding an office building into rubble, and he's raging, that son-of-a-bitch, that mother fucker, until his head starts to throb.

He wants to ignore the pain and ramp up the anger, but some logical bit of his mind says, easy, cowboy, we can't afford another brain blast or you might end up dead in front of the idiot box just like dear old dad.

But this shit is just so fucking wrong. That's Billy's house they're talking about, the one that he wanted to buy, the one he showed to Sal, told him how much it meant to him only an hour before that prick shot Billy in the head. Why don't you bang my wife while you're at it?

How could Sal possibly live there knowing what he did to get that house? Christ Almighty, it's so sick, it's unnatural—

Billy's thoughts stop cold and he nods slowly. Of course. It's Matty.

The old lizard hated Billy so much he must have forced Sal to buy that house just so he could give the finger to Billy's ghost.

You know Sal would never have the rocks to stand up to the Cigar; no, Stainless Sal did what he was told, bought a house that would forever remind him of the one thing he desperately wanted to forget. No wonder he stays away from the place.

Matty was the first one of the crew to have a house up here and it makes Billy so mad to think of all the work he put into the place to make it nice for the old guy.

Billy had just become a new father, but that didn't stop him from doing whatever he could to help out. Shit, he even went up there while Matty was still in the hospital and cleaned out all of Jerry's crap, clothing, furniture, pictures of his kids, any trace of that parasite that he could find within that house, Billy took it all, dragged it out to the backyard and set it on fire.

As the flames grew and Jerry's stuff burned, Billy sat down under a tree with a knife and slowly carved a sign that he wanted to hang over the front door.

There was a story going around that Jerry's wife got knocked up by somebody other than Jerry, somebody who ain't ascared of God, and some people wondered if maybe the Cigar had taken a lot more from Jerry than just his house.

You don't know what that man done to me, what he done to my family!

The smoke grew thicker as Billy's hand went to work, the same hand he used to crush Jerry's windpipe. Maybe he should have said a prayer while Jerry's worldly possessions burned to ashes; maybe he should have asked for the dead man's forgiveness.

But Billy was young and nasty back then, he wasn't ascared of God either, and he shoved the grisly memories aside, pushed them into the fire with the rest of the junk; you brought this upon yourself, big guy, and held out the sign to admire his handiwork.

The Hideaway. The name had jumped into his head the second he saw the place and he knew Matty would like it.

The work continued, with Billy clearing away the overgrown grass, getting a contractor to install a ramp so Matty could get into the place on his wheelchair, and then he painted the house gray and the shutters red. There wasn't any evidence of Jerry's place by the time Billy got through with it.

Matty almost cried when they wheeled him up to the front door, when he saw what Billy had done for him.

"Look at this guy," he said. "He's an artist, this guy, freaking Michelangelo, that's what he is."

Matty gave them keys to the place so his three top boys could use it whenever he wasn't around. The old man didn't want to know the details, as long as they didn't break anything or get in any trouble with the cops.

Matty had even talked about giving the place to Billy when he died. Billy was stunned that the old man thought so much of him, but he really wanted to start fresh. He wanted his own hideaway.

Naturally Vince, ass-kissing douche bag that he is, had to go get his own house in Marshalls Creek just so he could suck up to Matty, but it didn't matter because the Cigar just didn't like Vince worth a shit and never would.

God knows how Vince came up with the money—he could've been blowing sailors down by the docks for all Billy knew—but one look at that shithole was enough to tell you that whatever Vince paid, he had gotten screwed from pillar to post. And it couldn't have happened to a nicer guy.

But now that Sal had taken over Billy's place, all three of Billy's nearest and dearest friends had homes up here. Isn't that interesting?

Billy puts down the paper to look at the TV, sees Godzilla breathing atomic fire on a row of toy houses and setting them ablaze, and he smiles in a most evil way.

Big guy, Billy thinks, *you're reading my mind.*

15

On NIGHTS LIKE these, when she really wants to torture herself, Lucille takes the wedding album down from the shelf in the bedroom closet, pours herself a respectable shot of Johnny Walker and trawls through her glossy color memories in blurred disbelief.

The thing seems to get heavier every time she lugs it downstairs to the living room, over to the sofa that sits directly in front of that goddamn painting, and drops it on the coffee table like an ancient headstone.

Lucille knows this is bad, that looking through these pages will only make her feel worse than she already does and she'll end up like she has so many other nights: half in the bag, holding the photo album to her chest and quietly sobbing "Billy, Billy…"

The bedroom door slams upstairs and she jumps. It's dangerous, too, with that one upstairs stalking around the house. He hates it when she looks at the wedding album; he's doesn't want to know anything about the world before he was born.

Wait till he goes out, she tells herself. He'll leave in a little while, be gone all night, and you can look at this thing until sunrise.

But it makes her mad. This is still her house, damn it, no matter what the little gang banger upstairs thinks. No husband, no family, no friends, what the hell else does she have?

She raises her glass, to long life and happiness, and takes a drink. Now she's ready.

Once Lucille starts, she can't stop, as she lifts the cover, turns the first few pages and glides right to another world, where her parents are still alive, the future is still bright, and her closest friends are still around.

Lucille looks at the young bride in the photos, 20 years away, and she can't comprehend the joy in that woman's face. Yeah, you're happy now, sweetheart, great figure, beautiful smile. Just wait as the years burn away, wait and see what your life becomes. You've got no idea.

She looks at Billy, by her side in nearly every picture, so trim, so gorgeous, the son-of-a-bitch, wrapped up in that shining tuxedo; looks like a fucking work of art.

They warned me about you; everybody in creation told me you were trouble and that I should run like hell. But did I listen? Oh, no. I knew better. I always knew better.

It started in high school, when Billy was just a kid who sat in the last row of her sophomore history class and smiled whenever she looked his way.

They didn't have anything to do with each other until one morning outside Tech, when Jay McAvoy, this big stupid Irish bastard with the worst case of acne on the Eastern Seaboard, decided he was going to have some fun.

So he walked up to her, knocked the books out of Lucille's hand and yelled, watch where you're going, you fat ugly bitch!

She stood there looking stupidly at the books and papers piled up at her feet and McAvoy had about three seconds to laugh with his asshole friends before Billy stepped out from the crowd of kids and punched him right in the mouth.

Lucille will always smile at the memory of that punk going down on his ass, the shocked look on his pimpled face as he sat there touching his lips and studying the blood that laced his fingers.

Everything exploded then, boy; Jay snarling as he jumped up and charged into Billy, the street shuddering with the primal roar of 30 screaming teenagers. Lucille could hear her own voice shrieking above all the others, kill him; kill that fucking faggot!

Jay was beefy, easily 15 pounds heavier than Billy, and he threw hard, looping punches at Billy's head. Billy was fast and tricky, though, and unlike Jay, he wasn't interested in some schoolyard bloody nose. Billy wanted to commit murder.

He ducked under Jay's swinging fist, jumped forward and clamped his fingers around the kid's throat.

Jay's eyes bulged in shock; he hadn't planned to die that day. He tore at

Billy's hands, punched Billy's head as he desperately tried to break free. But Billy just grinned, took the shots, all the time squeezing, squeezing; the muscles in his forearms, expanding, twitching.

Tears filled Jay's eyes; his face turned a scary shade of red, his legs buckled and Billy was still holding on.

The kids around them slowly fell silent, not believing what they were seeing, and Lucille could taste blood-soaked energy churn through her body, knowing that Billy was about to kill for her.

Kill that fucking faggot!

Finally two of Billy's friends, Sal and Vince, stepped in, one on either side of Billy and gently tried to get their buddy to ease up. C'mon, big guy, Sal whispered, c'mon, let him go.

Billy didn't seem to be listening; his eyes were clear, no trace of psychotic rage. He was doing a chore, deliberately, efficiently, and he didn't want to be disturbed.

And then he just let go, released his victim, as if he had made his point and was ready for something else. Jay fell to the ground, his face bloated and scarlet, and coughed frantically for air.

Lucille's heartbeat slowed down to normal while Billy, his right eye swelling up purple, turned and smiled at her. That was all it took.

She flips the pages and sees those scumbags, Sal and Vince, crammed into so many pictures that some people might wonder who actually got married here.

She thought about cutting those bastards out of the photos all together, but she decided it would be better to keep the thing intact and hold onto to her hatred. Sometimes it's all Lucille has to get her through the day.

Sal was the best man, gave the toast with his glass raised high, wished the happy couple long life and endless happiness, and then hugged them both as the barrage of camera flashes opened up on them.

She glares at Sal's image. You fucking bastard. Billy was your best friend, for God's sake, he would've done anything for you. And this is how you pay him back?

Flip the page, get away from that lowlife, and now she's looking at that little rat Vince, whom she's hated ever since she laid eyes on him back in high school.

They say Vince is dying, very slowly, and it's made him so crazy that he burned his own brother to death and now the old bastard wants him dead in the worst possible way. A grin spread across Lucille's face. Now isn't that the saddest story you ever heard?

And, look, there's Lucifer himself, Matty Cigar, standing there next to his wife, poor woman, who had to die from the cancer just to escape that psychopath. Look at him; even when he's smiling he looks like he's going to reach right out of the picture and claw your eyes out.

He came to her a few days after Billy disappeared, rolled right in with Train, that monstrous young goon of his, and swore, swore on his grandchildren, the ghoulish bastard, that he had nothing to do with this, vowed he'd find the no-good sons-of-bitches responsible and make them pay, with their lives, you hear me, with their lives.

And the whole time she knew he was lying but she couldn't say it, only thanked him for being so kind and caring. She walked with him to the door and just as he was leaving Matty reached up quickly and pulled her down into a bear hug.

It was sick, being squeezed by the old invalid who had ordered Billy's death. Lucille wanted to flip over the wheelchair and bite off a chunk of his face. But she held back and tried not to gag when Matty kissed her on the cheek.

"We'll take care of you," he said.

Oh, yeah. He took great care of me all right, didn't he? Murdered my husband and left me to rot in this place, with that lunatic upstairs. Fuck Matty and all of his goddamn grandchildren.

Oh, and now here's Lucille's favorite, the buddy picture, with those three pricks crowding around Billy and raising their drinks with the dear friend they would murder a few decades later.

Jesus, Billy used to carry this photo around in his goddamn wallet. And that meant nothing to these animals.

They got married right after high school and moved into an apartment on Eighth Avenue two blocks from her mother's house. It was small, but just fine for the two of them, and Billy always made sure they had the nicest furniture and the newest electronics.

Sal and Vince were always there and most nights all three of them hung out at Matty's bar.

Everybody knew who Matty was, knew what he did, but Lucille never complained, not with the money Billy brought home.

He told people he was a painter, never mind the new cars in the driveway or the beautiful house he bought for her on Staten Island for their fifth wedding anniversary; never mind how Billy always said he'd roast in hell before he'd ever be a house painter like his scumbag loser of a father. Anyone asks, Billy's a painter.

Lucille knew where the money was coming from. But she didn't complain, no matter what her family or friends said; all the know-it-alls who told her she never should have hooked up with Billy.

What was she supposed to do—marry some dead-ender from the avenue who fixed cars all day?

So the fires continued. A store or warehouse, a small apartment building once, though the firefighters saved most of that one.

Lucille knew better than to ask, but she could always tell when Billy torched a place. He stunk of smoke and wildness, the savage pleasure he took from burning something to the ground.

When he came home from a job, and took her at night, he was completely out of control. She never complained about that either.

But it got for harder and harder for Billy to break off from his roughneck ways. When Lucille went into labor, Billy was nowhere to be found, middle of the night, their first baby, and she's got no husband. That was the day Matty got shot and everything was crazy, but, still, he just disappears and leaves her alone like this?

She was in the hospital bed at Lutheran, where they were treating Matty, more dead than alive, the baby wailing in her arms, her sister and cousin at her side, when Billy finally comes walking in with the fire smell all over him.

Lucille couldn't believe it, he's standing there just smiling like nothing was wrong, fresh from performing some terrible act, and she wanted to scream *get this animal away from me!*

But then he stroked her face, kissed her all over and whispered with tears in his eyes, you gave me a son, you gave me a son. Tommy, that's what I'm going to call him. My son, Tommy.

Later she read about a man who had been found in a burned out Coney

Island flophouse on Neptune Avenue, this guy Jerry, and she recognized his picture in the paper; he was one of Matty's crowd. So that's what Billy was doing the night she gave birth to their child. Committing murder.

Maybe that's why that one upstairs is such an abomination, she thinks. He was born with a curse on him.

It got worse after that. Billy didn't want to be a father, didn't want to be a husband, didn't want any responsibilities at all. He just wanted to run around with those assholes friends of his and bang anything in a skirt.

She cringes recalling the terrible fights they had, with Lucille holding the screaming baby in her arms while Billy shouted, kicked at the furniture and stormed out of the house. It was a nightly battle, slight variations of the same fight, over and over.

Most weekends in the summer he'd take off with Sal and Vince for Matty's house in the Poconos, The Hideaway. That's what they actually called the place, like Lucille couldn't guess what was going on up there, those three together with no wives around. Jesus Christ, how stupid did she look?

Tommy got older, crazier, and did everything he could to defy his father, cut class, start fights, terrorized the younger kids in school. Billy would beat Tommy something fierce, but it didn't change anything.

Lucille was trapped between a husband who ignored her and a son who walked all over her. She was drinking more, sleeping less, and all Lucille wanted was to get the hell out. Only Billy left first.

Five months ago, on Billy's birthday, that's when everything in Lucille's life turned to ashes.

They had all gone to Mexicali's on 69th Street, the same place he had taken her when he proposed to her all those years ago.

They were all there, Sal with his wife, Vince going stag after his old lady found out he had knocked up his little Mexican tramp.

Of course Matty had to tell everybody, yet again, about the first night Billy came into the club even though everybody in the room had heard it so many times before they could stand up and recite it in unison like the Mormon Tabernacle Choir.

"You never seen such a miserable little punk in your life." Matty shouted over the laughter. "He was trying to act like he was a tough guy, you know, and the whole time he's ready to piss himself."

Lucille looked around the table, at Billy, little gray here and there, but still so handsome. Sal was bulging out of his shirt and Vince was drained and withered, like he was getting ready to die before they served dessert.

"I love you like my brother," Sal said, the liquor making him warm and stupid. "I mean it."

"Ah, fuck you, big guy!" Billy shouted. "You ain't even got a brother!"

Everyone was laughing and joking and, and Lucille hadn't seen Billy so happy in a long time. Sitting there, she started to get this idiotic idea that they might actually work things out.

Billy had been talking more and more about moving out of the city, getting a place in PA. Maybe that's what they needed. Get Billy away from this town and all its grief. She squeezed his hand beneath the table and felt the warm strength in return. Get him away from Matty.

She should have known better. She should have known that some things, some people never change. The evening was winding down, they were all heading for their cars when Billy looked down the street and stopped dead with the keys in his hand.

Lucille turned to see what was going on and all she saw was this old gin rat stumbling down the block.

It was some hard case drunk, way beyond saving, the kind you ignore, thank God it isn't you and get on with your life. But not Billy. His face lost any trace of color when he saw that animated corpse and his eyes locked in on the guy as he staggered toward the pier.

Lucille gently nudged him to get Billy back from wherever the hell he was. Vince gave the "hel-lo" yodel and Sal just looked confused as his friend kept staring and staring until that shambling scarecrow disappeared.

Billy snapped out of it then, aware and angry that everyone was looking at him, and he snarled at Lucille to shut up and get in the fucking car.

They drove home without saying a word and Lucille thought, oh, yeah, things are going to change all right. They're going to move up to the country, raise chickens, plant vegetables, live the good life. Oh, please…

She knew enough not to talk to him when they got home. Whatever it was Billy wasn't going to tell her, which was just fine with her, fucking nut, Lucille left him in the living room and went upstairs to bed.

As soon as she put out the light, she heard the car roll down the driveway and she thought go ahead, asshole, go bang one of your sluts tonight. Don't ever come back for all I give a shit.

She fell asleep and then later, much later, at some ungodly hour, she woke up and sensed someone in the room. It had to be Billy, but something was wrong, terribly wrong.

He had a smell on him this night, but it wasn't fire; it was pure gasoline. Billy reeked of the stuff like it was coming out of his skin. And he was standing right over her.

She didn't move, didn't open her eyes, she sensed him standing on her side of the bed, and Lucille wanted to jump up, scramble into the bathroom and lock the door.

But she didn't move, knowing she'd never get beyond the night table. All she could do was lay curled up in bed, pretending to sleep, because she was sure if she made a move, made a sound, Billy would kill her.

He moved away from her. The bed sagged on his side and she felt his body taking up the space beside her, oh, please God, let me live through this night, please, just let me live.

She lay there for the longest time afraid to even draw a breath. After a while she felt the bed moving on Billy's side, gently at first, then harder. Jesus Christ, she thought, he's crying.

Lucille turns another page in the photo album and sees more good times. Her nostrils flare at an odor coming from upstairs and she knows the little puke is getting high up there. Atta boy, Tommy…

She was as shocked as anyone when she read about the old bum who had been found murdered on the bike path—strangled right below the bridge. It was the same night as Billy's dinner and not that far away.

She was in the kitchen making coffee the next morning and she thought how horrible it was; nobody should die like that, I don't care what you've done, but it had nothing to do with her. Or Billy.

She turned when he walked into the room, his head hanging low, and when he looked up, just at that moment, their eyes met, Lucille felt her blood turn to ice.

There was no way to talk to him about it, no way to approach him and say Billy, please, for the love of God, tell me you didn't do this terrible thing that even Jesus Christ Himself would never forgive? Please tell me you had nothing to do with it.

And even though she knew the answer, all she could do was watch her husband roil in unconditional agony. He stopped eating, wouldn't take any calls, and lit into her and Tommy at the slightest excuse.

A few more seconds, she thinks, just a few more seconds on either side of the clock and we would never had seen that boozehound, his tattered ass would have staggered by without us ever running into each other. He'd still be alive, more or less. And so would Billy.

Sal stopped by to visit, but Billy cursed him, chased him out of the house, told him to go back to Matty, you fucking pussy, go back and suck his cock with the rest of them scumbags.

There was no one she could turn to and she even thought about calling Jake of all people, tell him what was going on, and beg him to help them. But Jake would want one thing from Billy and one thing only and that was never going to happen. Billy would never do that to Matty no matter how much he hated him.

It got to a point when Lucille thought the tension, the suffering, couldn't possibly get any worse around this house. And then she brought the painting home.

She stops for a second to turn and look at the thing hanging on the wall behind her. Four clowns tumbling around inside a horse-drawn carriage, a fifth holding the reins as they rode through a forest of falling leaves.

Lucille saw it at the flea market on Victory Boulevard, and, shit, she just felt like buying the damn thing. She liked the colors and thought it would brighten up the room.

And she honestly didn't think Billy would care one way or another, the way he had been acting. Then he came home and saw the package on the kitchen table.

What the hell is this?

That look on his face when he saw the painting, swollen with rage, he looked at her with such fury, and screamed this is what you do with my fucking money?

Lucille screamed right back, tired of walking around the house on tiptoe, I'm just trying to make this place look nice. It got louder and louder, their words piling up into each other until Billy snarled you fucking bitch and grabbed her by the throat.

She couldn't breathe and the look on Billy's face told her he was going to do it, choke her to death right here in her own kitchen, over a fucking painting for God's sake.

She clawed at his arms, gouged for his eyes, and Billy kept squeezing.

This is what Jay McAvoy felt, back in sophomore year, while you were cheering kill him, kill that fucking faggot, now you know what it's like…

The room was spiraling around her head, you fucking bitch, you fucking bitch, they all warned her and now she was going to die—

Somewhere a car horn sounded and Billy let her go, just opened his hand, and she sagged to the floor while he walked toward the door.

Lucille sat on the floor inhaling, exhaling, inhaling, exhaling, terrified and furious, thankful to be alive and wanting to hurt this son-of-a-bitch before he got away.

She got up, wobbly at first, but steadier as she went upstairs to the bedroom closet, reached way into the back on the top shelf, grabbed the .38 that Billy thought she didn't know about and headed back downstairs to put an end to this bullshit once and for all.

Lucille came down the steps cursing, no good mother fucker, ramming bullets into the chamber and swearing to Jesus Christ and every saint in heaven that she was going to do it, she was going to kill that scumbag deader than shit.

Three shots for him, one for her so all they'll find here is two dead bodies and one clown painting.

But Billy was already out the door and climbing into Sal's car, and she should have asked herself why Sal was here, what the hell he could have possibly done to regain Billy's trust when she had failed so miserably.

But she was too furious to be asking such questions as she ran barefoot onto the damp cement, stopping only when she saw that red Cadillac turn the corner. Lucille stood sobbing with the gun pressed against her leg, you fucking bastard, you have no idea how close you got.

She had to say something terrible, she had to punish him in the worst way possible and the words tore from her body before she could stop them.

"Murderer!" She screamed, her voice ricocheting down the empty street. "Are you going to kill me, too?"

She started shivering violently as if it were the coldest winter night and she clamped her hand over her mouth, oh God, no, please, don't tell me I just said that, not here, in front of all these spying houses, I didn't betray him; please, God, strike me dead before I do something like that.

Jesus Christ, no matter how angry you are, no matter what he's done, you never give him up like that. What the fuck is wrong with you?

Lucille caught sight of that old sow across the street, Mrs. Nucci, peering at her through the spotless window, and she fought the outrageous desire to put a bullet right between those prying eyes.

She ran back into the house and slammed the door. She waited all night here on this sofa, lights off, gun in her hand, not sure what she was going to do when Billy got back, but certain she was going to do something.

Lucille sat in the dark and dredged up every foul memory she could find in her head, so she'd stay angry, really angry, this time. Lucille waited and winced at the occasional glow of passing headlights. Her anger slowly melted, slipped into worry, then fear, like it had so many times before.

He's up there with those shitheel friends of his, she told herself, they're up at Matty's cabin, banging some local girls and getting high. He'll be home any time, with a dozen roses and a line of bullshit. All he has to do is walk through the door.

Shortly before dawn, when he still hadn't come home, Lucille knew something was wrong, that something terrible had happened, and by the time Tommy came down for breakfast, she was rocking back and forth on the couch, whispering *Billy, Billy*…

16

JAKE CAME TO a few days later and told her, Lu, I gotta be honest here, this don't look good, Billy might not be coming home this time.

He seemed genuinely sorry, said they needed to talk; it was real important we get the people who did this, right? You want to punish these scumbags for taking Billy away from you, don't you? You don't have to be loyal to them bastards no more; look what they've done to you. Look what they've done to your family. You don't owe them shit.

Lucille refills her glass and wonders if Jake ought to have his picture in this album, too, seeing as how he's been a part of their lives for so long.

"What the fuck is going on here?"

She looks up and Tommy is right over her in the living room, no noise, no movement; like he melted down through the floor to appear before her.

"You looking at them stupid pictures again?"

Tommy shakes his shaved head and his ear lobe gives off sparks of reflected gold.

"I swear to God, you must be nuts."

"I'm just looking, that's all." Lucille gently pushes the glass of scotch away. "It's my business."

"Hey, it's my business if the neighbors all think you're a head case." He looks at the glass. "And a lush."

She bristles but says nothing. He's quite the little hoodlum now, her son, just 18 with swollen weightlifter's shoulders erasing his neck.

Commando pants, thin gold chain tight around his throat, black muscle shirt straining against his torso, Tommy is all set to go out and tear up the town. If only his father could see him now.

"Everyone on this block thinks you're crazy." Tommy taps his head with his trigger finger. "I hope you know that. The whole neighborhood thinks you're loopy."

"I don't give a damn what anybody thinks. It's my life."

"A life?" Tommy's smile is pure arsenic. "Look again, honey."

He seems bigger to her lately, larger beyond just working out. It's like his father's vanishing act allowed his body to grow wider, taller, more menacing. Without Billy around, Tommy doesn't have to sneak around the place to avoid a beating.

"The guy's dead, okay? Leave him in the fucking ground where he belongs."

Tommy never stood up to his father, the little faggot, didn't say boo when his old man gave him a look or cocked his head and said in a deadly soft tone, something on your mind, big guy? Oh, no, not Tommy; he'd get all quiet and sullen until his father left the house for the night and then turn on Lucille.

All the times I stood up for him, all the times I put my body between him and his father, to keep him from getting killed. She'd scream at Billy whenever he hit Tommy, you fucking coward, and Billy would end up beating her. Maybe that's why Tommy is so angry with her. She's the only witness.

"I'm going out."

He's got his arms folded across his chest, like she's supposed to jump up and do whatever he wants. Lucille doesn't move. Tommy leans over her.

"I said, 'I'm going out.'"

"Tommy, listen-"

His hand shoots out for her black leather purse resting on the end table, and he gets to it before she can stop him. She rises and pulls at the strap.

"No, Tommy, I need it—"

"So do I."

"No!" She holds the strap tight. "I've got to go shopping."

They glare at each other, the shoulder strap stretching under the pressure, his face inches from her, when Tommy smiles and clamps those big ugly fingers around her throat.

"What do you think you're doing?" Tommy whispers hoarsely into her ear. "You want me to break your neck? Huh? Is that what you want?"

She's trying to breathe, trying not to think that, it's happening again, Jesus Christ, it's happening——

"—drunken tramp, sit around here on your ass all day and look at your goddam wedding pictures—"

—pulling at the fingers, the hateful voice spilling over her…

"—where's your precious fucking Billy now, huh? Why don't you call him to come save you? C'mon, let's hear it, 'Billy, Billy'…"

She lets go of the purse and Tommy shoves her back into the TV, something falls to the floor, but she's just trying to breathe.

Her eyes focus on Tommy taking cash out of her purse while a car horn honks outside. He slips the money into his pocket and blows her a kiss.

"Don't wait up for me."

She doesn't start crying until she hears the car's squealing tires. Lucille sobs so hard, she can't think, her mind bouncing all over the place, traveling up the stairs to that place in the bedroom closet, way into the back on the top shelf—

The crying stops abruptly, like switching off a faucet. No, she's not doing that. She's not going to jail for that little shit.

Lucille wipes her face, picks up the wedding album and she's about to put it away, back in its sacred place when she stops and takes a long serious look at the thing.

She made it into something sacred, like the Bible, but it's more like an anvil now, a fossil from a time that's long gone and wasn't anywhere as near as good as she'd like to believe.

Lucille stands there in the living room for nearly minute before she tucks the album under her arm and storms out to the backyard.

She pauses a moment when she reaches the trash can, takes one last look at Billy and the fantasy version of herself with the champagne glass and that pathetic smile, and then dumps the damn thing straight into the garbage can.

She takes the lighter fluid from the cabinet under the sink and spreads it all over the beautiful binding, the smell mixes with the trash and she thinks, you like fire so much, here it is.

When the match makes contact, the sudden burst of flame almost knocks her down.

Lucille watches the wedding album burn, you bastard, burn, all those happy faces, all those forgotten friends, those false smiles and the rotted dreams of hope and happiness. Burn every goddamn bit of it.

The fire sags down to a whimpering glow and the biting stench of burning plastic reaches her nose. She gives it a few more seconds, just a few more seconds to make sure the thing is really gone, and then she crashes the lid down over the can as hard as she can.

Lucille stands there and listens to the abrupt stillness. She looks at the other houses around here, remembers when she and Billy moved into this place, all the plans they made about raising a family and being so goddamn happy.

We'll take care of you.

They owe her, those miserable fucks; they owe her for the silence she's kept, for all the pain she's suffered. Matty always talks about business, it's all business. Fine. Now Lucille's got some business.

She goes back inside, gets the phone and jabs out the number. It rings, once, twice, three times, until one of those bums finally gets up off his lazy ass and picks up the phone.

"Yeah?"

The voice is harsh, threatening, but Lucille is ready for it.

"I want to talk to Matty," she says. "I want to talk to him *now*."

17

SAL HITS THE speed dial as soon as he pulls into his driveway.

He can't wait, not if it means pissing down his leg or crapping his pants. Sal's going to make this call right now, right outside his house and then he'll scream himself raw and ram his head through the windshield.

Android beeps crank out the number at hyper speed, faster, you piece of shit, faster, and just as he makes the connection, just as the Cigar's number starts to ring up against Sal's brain, Jake and Stan, his fat ugly prick of a partner, fly up the drive in their unmarked shitmobile and come to a squealing stop inches from the bumper of Sal's car.

Sal should click off right this very second, call the old bastard tonight, tomorrow, any other time but now. But he won't let go.

He's got to deliver the message, can't keep Matty waiting, even while Jake and Stan, who grins and gives Sal the finger, get out of their car in door-slamming tandem.

Sal watches the two cops approach him. Stan, with his belly bulging through a stained yellow shirt, pathetic striped clown tie and that atrocious off-the-rack tan suit.

Jake is still going with the Sixties undertaker look, dark suit, darker thoughts, and Sal wonders if he gave these two stiffs money to buy new clothes would that be considered a bribe or a public service?

"Yeah?"

The Cigar picks up as Sal makes eye contact with Jake through the windshield. He's strung out between them, cops in front of him and the old man on the phone, and fucking Jake stares at him because he knows who Sal is talking to, and he knows exactly what Sal is going to say.

"Sal?"

He knows he should speak, but now he can't say anything, not in front of Jake, not when the bastard is eyeballing him so severely.

The old man is growling through the phone, and you'd better say something, fucko, or Matty's going to roar so loud these pair of losers will hear him from 10 feet away. He finally gets the words out.

"It's…done."

Sal lets out a long held breath and tries not to puke in front of the Bobbsey Twins here. He hears the Cigar exhale with throaty satisfaction as he savors news of the latest kill. Some days Sal swears death is the only thing keeping the old guy alive.

"All right then. Get some rest. We'll talk later."

"Okay." Sal watches Jake and Stan walk around the front of his car, getting closer.

"Sal…?"

"Yeah, Matty?"

The voice dangles in the air like it's coming in from Mount Fuji.

"I know it's been hard for you."

"Yeah…"

"But it's all over now. We can start fresh."

Stan raps his knuckles hard against the window and makes the roll down sign. Yeah, we can start fresh; with so many dead, we pretty much have to.

"I gotta go."

Sal clicks off the phone and powers the window open. He tries to look annoyed, indignant, like he's not scared of these two flunkies, but he can't do much but wrinkle his forehead.

"What do you guys want?"

Stan's blubbery face drapes into the car, accompanied by a sauerkraut cloud that comes off him like dime store cologne.

"Hey, Sal, how's it hanging?"

"I'm fine, Stan. How are you?"

"Oh, I'm just ducky." He gives Sal a wink. "So, big guy, have you heard the latest? Looks like your cousin caught the firebug from Billy."

Sal flinches at the sunlight sneaking over Stan's shoulder.

"I wouldn't know nothing about that."

"Now there's a fucking shock." He nods toward Sal's chest. "Who were you talking to you just now, dickhead? Don't you know it's rude to hang up on people?"

"I was done talking."

"Well, I hope you memorized everything Matty told you to say."

"I wasn't talking to him."

"Fuck you, Sal."

"Hey, I don't have—"

Stan's grin goes manic as he yanks the door open with sudden brutality and stares a hole into Sal's forehead.

"Your ass nailed to that seat, mother fucker?"

Jake walks up slowly behind Stan, his mug hanging down to the ground, as usual. Sal gives it a few seconds, just to stick it to Stan, gets out of the car real slow, and almost goes face down to the concrete he's so goddamn tired. He returns Jake's nod.

"Sal."

"Hey, Jake."

When was the last time he slept? Yesterday? The day before? He can't remember. Not since the old man called him at home, but he hadn't been sleeping much before that. And with all the driving he's been doing in the last few hours, he's close to slipping into a coma.

"How's Ralph doing?"

It's the warm-up, bouncing against the ropes before the fight starts. But you've got to give Jake credit; he does seem concerned, even while he's trying to put Sal away for life.

"He's doing good, Jake. Just fine."

"How's he like college?"

"He loves it. I'm real proud of him."

"And Iris? How is she?"

"She…good. She's good."

Jake looks up at the house, like he's thinking of buying it, as if that could ever happen on the miserable crumbs he gets from the City. He turns back to Sal.

"We've been looking for you, Sal," Jake says. "Couldn't find you any place."

"I went…for a drive." He can't come up with anything better. "I had to get away…you know, for a little while."

You're taking me up there? The voice cuts into his thoughts. *You're gonna kill me in the same spot you killed Billy? Please, Sal, not that; anything but that.*

"Okay, Sal, you know why we're here."

One sentence from Jake and Sal is suddenly naked out here in the harsh sun, his hands covering his shriveled dick, wind blowing up his crack, while these scumbags study him like he's an infected steer.

"I got a good idea, Jake."

"Then tells us where he is, asshole." Stan spits on the sidewalk. "We ain't got all fucking day."

"I ain't seen him."

"Don't pull that shit on us." Stan ups the volume. "You don't know where your own cousin is? You two faggots are joined at the crotch."

"I don't know where he is."

It's done.

Finding him was so easy, it was pathetic;. Sal drove over to Vince's house, his own house, the stupid bastard, and there he was, in the middle of the demolished living room with a kid's school bag over his shoulder, stuffed with clothes and toys.

I wanna see my kid, Sal. You gotta let me see her before I die.

Vince started crying, sobbed heavily into his hands. Sal wanted to shoot him right there, fuck the noise and the neighbors, put an end to this fiasco. Even if everybody in the building saw him leave, who would ever testify against Stainless Sal?

Get your jacket, Vince.

Sal—

Just shut up and get your jacket before the cops get here.

His cousin did like he was told; struggled to get into a navy blue windbreaker, the whole time looking dead in Sal's eyes. It's him or me, Sal told himself, it's him or me.

Are you gonna kill me?

Was he serious? Was his cousin actually asking him this? Torches that stinking dive in Bay Ridge, deep fries his own brother; has the whole crew looking at lethal jail time, and the brain-damaged little shit wants to know if he's going to get clipped for his sins?

Let's go, Vince.

Sal, we're family; we're blood, for God's sake. Don't that mean nothing to you?

Yeah, and his friendship with Billy meant something, too. His wife, his son, so many things mean a lot to Sal. But none of it means a thing to Matty Cigar.

"Look, guys, I'm telling you I don't know where Vince is." Sal leans against his car. "He's sick, all right? He's not right in the head."

Fuck, he's so tired. He's got to go inside, he's got to lie down for a few days.

"Hey, all he did was charbroil his own brother like a fucking hamburger," Stan says. "What's sick about that? Maybe he'll come after you next. I'd be worried if I were you, Sal."

"That's not going to happen."

Shit, he says it too forcefully, with a little too much certainty, and Jake turns his head to one side.

"What's that supposed to mean, Sal?"

Please, don't do this, Sal. Please, I'm your cousin, for Christ's sake. Tell Matty you couldn't find me, tell him I jumped into the Narrows, tell him anything, but please don't—

"It doesn't mean anything."

"Then why did you say it?" Jake, the all-seeing eye, takes a step toward him. "We want to talk to your cousin, Sal, so I'm warning you—"

"—Jake—"

"—if we found out you're holding out on us—"

"—you're gonna wish you had that AIDS shit." Stan steps in and finishes for his partner. "Just like your little homo cousin."

It comes over him gently, this strange desire to tell Jake the truth, to stop lying for once in his life, to stop holding things back, and drop this incredible weight from his back. He could finally get some sleep.

Sal feels the words forming in his mind, hey, Jake, you want to know about Vince? I'll tell you everything you want to know. He tries to shake it off.

"Hey, look, I'm tired."

"Yeah, you must be exhausted from sucking Matty's dick all night." Stan pumps his fist inches from his mouth. "Tell me something, Sal, do you hold the armrests on his wheelchair when you blow him or do put your hands behind your back like you're bobbing for apples?"

Sal looks to Jake for some kind of help, put a leash on this monkey, for Christ's sake, I deserve better; but he gets nothing.

"What's wrong with you guys? Huh? This is a terrible thing that happened here—"

"Oh, listen to this." Stan grabs his heart in the coronary pose. "Saint Stainless is worried about his fellow man. Hand me my fucking Stradivarius."

Sal feels anger building in him even as he knows that's just what this hard-on wants.

"Listen, I don't know where Vince is. He ain't called me and the last time I seen him he was three-quarters dead. He ain't got much time."

"Don't you wish, asshole?" Stan grins at him. "Maybe your cousin's got just enough time left to talk to us and put your ass in jail."

He wants to spit in the fat cop's face and roar my cousin ain't never gonna talk to nobody as loud as he can, but he knows that's the lack of sleep taking over, the godawful stress of the last several hours.

"I told you I don't know where my cousin is." He talks slowly, measures every word. "I got nothing more to say to you guys. You want anything else, talk to my lawyer."

It takes all the strength he has to get that out. Stan is still smirking, like he wants to haul Sal down to the station and toss him into the holding pen's freak stew of junkies, drag queens, and pedophiles, but Jake is calm. He's not giving up, Jake never does, but he knows when to pull back. He nods to Stan.

"All right, Sal. You know the drill, right?"

"Oh, yeah."

"Good. We'll see you around."

No doubts there; couldn't get rid of these two fucks with an elephant gun and a crateful of hand grenades. Stan shoulder checks him as he goes by.

"Give Matty a kiss for me."

They get in their car and reverse down the alley. Sal watches them back out on to the street and drive out of his sight. He tries to dismiss the confrontation and relax a little, but a caustic thought takes hold of his mind.

What if Matty told you to kill your son? Would you do that? Would you drive all the way out to Michigan and stand there on his doorstep with your hand inside your coat pocket wrapped around the butt of gun?

Sal can almost feel his fingers touching the cold metal nipple on the doorbell, hear the footsteps coming to the door. Ralph's eyes would widen in jubilant disbelief seeing his father appear out of nowhere and just as he embraces you, as he gives you that nice, loving bear hug, that's when you do it. Jam the gun into his ribs and pull the trigger.

He'd reel back, stunned by the pain and the betrayal. He'd stare at Sal not understanding as his life leaked out of the hole in his body. Maybe another bullet, in the heart, to end it, to wipe away that terrified look on his face.

Leave quickly, drive all the way back on nothing but coffee and anguish. And when you got home, pull out the cell phone and tell Matty it's done…

The ringing phone pulls him back to real time, stirs him to move, get out of the light and into the dark emptiness of his house. It keeps on ringing, but Sal won't answer it.

Part Four: Any Friend of Charley's

1

He wakes up instantly, no trace of sleep, and knows it's time to leave. The night has sunk to its deepest point and now, at this ungodly, hour, Billy can't stay in bed one second longer.

Sweat rolls from skin, his head throbs right at the scar point and it's bad, almost as painful as that time in the diner.

Lora is huddled next to him and it's so quiet that Billy wants to put his head back and howl just to make sure he hasn't died in his sleep.

I just wanted see how you were doing.

Billy shudders at a sudden stab of pain, yo, bitch, how do you think I'm doing? He wonders if the bullet from Sal's gun shattered more than just bone, that it might have cut deeper, destroyed some barrier in his mind and unleashed a storm of noxious memories into the present tense.

He looks at Lora and knows that she deserves better than this, her and God knows how many others in Billy's life that he's hurt, let down, betrayed or killed. But there's nothing he can do about it.

So Billy quietly slips away from her, gathers up some clothes and eases down to the kitchen where he dresses in under a minute.

And then he's gone.

"Hi, sweetie, are you okay?"

It's late, Billy is half-asleep, and his mother comes into his room unsteady and barely visible in the patchy darkness. He nods warily, not sure if she can see him or not, and watches as she sits down at the edge of his bed.

The old man probably hasn't come from Gallagher's and she's afraid to be alone. One of the neighbors is listening to the radio and the voice of Johnny Rivers singing "Poor Side of Town" drifts across the alley to Billy's room.

"I just wanted see how you were doing."

"I'm…okay," he says finally.

She's turns to the window, little more than a silhouette, and shakes her head.

"Billy, why do you keep doing this?" Her voice cracks a little. "Why won't you stop? Is it something at school? Is someone picking on you? You can tell me."

There's a strong smell coming off her and it seems like she's slurring her words. Billy doesn't say a thing.

"I'm so worried about you, honey. I-I don't want something bad to happen. Don't you see how dangerous this is?"

He wants to say he's sorry about the matches, about breaking his promise to her yet again, about being the cause of all the problems in the house. But nothing comes out.

"You know that Mommy still loves you very much…don't you?"

He nods again, so embarrassed by her needy demand. Why does she do this? Why can't she leave him alone?

"Just like I know that you still love me…right?"

She wasn't asking for much. Just another nod would have done it; she'd have gone to bed, gone to her grave satisfied that she had done one thing right. But Billy was still hurting and angry from his father's beating and he needed someone to hate.

So he just lay there, his mouth zipped tight, like a POW being interrogated by the Viet Cong.

She touched his face affectionately, rubbed his head, but Billy wouldn't give in. He was too tough for her and after a few moments, she rose, walked carefully out of the room and down the hallway.

A short time later Billy heard his mother crying in her room and so he closed his eyes and began his voyage.

"I will sail to the Sea of Japan…"

The yard is dead cold, hushed, the stars obscured by a sheet metal wall of clouds. A wave of night air brushes his shoulders and somewhere nearby a dog barks once and falls silent.

The can of gasoline he lifted from the garage sloshes a soft cadence against his leg and Billy sees the breath smoking out of his nose as he climbs into the pick-up and pops the brake.

He tries not to think about her as he free falls down the driveway, needs to concentrate on the mission, but those beautiful green eyes slide in between his brain cells and all he can think about is Lora alone in that bed.

He cranks the key in the ignition as soon as the pick-up touches down on the road, snaps on the headlights, and heads up to Pocono Boulevard, where the houses are dark, no people around, and Billy feels like he's piloting a submarine through a sunken city.

He rolls to a stop in the left lane at the intersection, hits the blinker and stares at the Mountain View Diner squatting dark and barren across the road.

Remember going there every Sunday morning after church? The place was always packed; the waitress called you "honey" and made sure to give you an extra piece of pie. Never thought you'd be back here decades later wandering around with a hole in your head or gnashing your teeth on the floor like a carnival geek, did you? Maybe you should eat at McDonalds.

The light changes Billy and steps hard on the gas.

Lora listens, just lies there and listens as the pick-up rolls over gravel in the driveway and coasts down the alley to the street. A few seconds later the engine comes to life and fades up the street, away from her.

Lora wonders where the hell Billy is going at 3:33 in the goddamn morning and what the hell is wrong with him. And she wonders why the hell she didn't say something before he left.

She woke up as he was leaving; half-asleep she saw a shadow moving around the room, flashbacked to her father on one of his rampages and almost screamed. But she managed to keep still.

If she had just challenged him, switched on the light and looked him in the eye, instead of pretending to sleep, and asked him what was going on she might have gotten Billy to open up and tell her why he's doing this.

But Billy would probably have some story to tell. He'd been doing it since they first met at the rest stop.

There's the obvious answer, of course; that he's got another woman some place. But she's not getting that. It's not like when her ex-husband was sleeping with every barmaid that bought him a round and coming home with that monumentally stupid grin on his face.

No, something else is pulling Billy away from her.

Strange how she thought of her old man. That bastard always picked on Kenny and Lora would try to defend him and the maniac would pick up the nearest blunt object and chase them out of the house.

They'd hide in the garage, Lora trying to keep Kenny from crying, and watching the long shadow enter the garage, the red tip of their father's cigarette getting closer. She'd done everything she could to protect her brother, but in the end it just wasn't enough.

A car slows down outside, almost to a full stop, and moves on. Probably George checking up on her before he resumes patrol. After that scene in the diner, she's glad Billy and George didn't run into each other tonight.

George was the one who told her about Kenny, pulled into the driveway the night, walked to the front door with his hat off. She knew what had happened just by the look on his face. And she fell apart.

George's a decent guy, do anything for Lora, but God forbid she'd actually take up with someone who was loyal, dependable, who'd bend over backwards to make her happy and actually stay in bed the whole night.

But George doesn't fit the profile. If they're not trouble, Lora's not interested and that just makes her angrier. Like some teenager on a bad boy kick. You'd think she would have gotten that crap out of her system after she married Scotty. When exactly is she going to wake the hell up?

She thinks of Aunt Ida, who never got married, who used to say that she was too young for Medicare, and too old for men to care.

Lora laughed when she first heard that line, liked how her aunt could joke about her life, but that was before Ida died so alone in her empty house and now she feels tears on her cheeks and she's getting mad all over again.

Shit, that settles it. Lora rolls over in bed and angrily pulls the blanket to her chin. She's going to lay down the law.

If Billy wants to go driving around in the fog all goddamn night long, he can find some other dope to put up with his bullshit. As of right now, Lora is through collecting mutts and nuts.

The stillness builds up in the room, makes her declaration seem so small and hollow, and Lora would be grateful to hear any kind of sound at this moment.

"Damn it, boy," she whispers. "Where the hell are you?"

2

WET CEMENT FOG rolls down the mountain, thick enough to keep any sane person at home and under the covers, but Billy switches the radio on to a band of gouging static and charges ahead like it's a bright summer day.

He spots the green glow of a traffic light floating above a swirling mass of fog, inviting him to come on in.

All right, bitch, Billy pushes down on the gas pedal, the light switches to amber in response and then he's sliding beneath a burning red eye.

"Just made it," he says.

The radio signal comes in clear for a few seconds, long enough for Johnny Rivers to sneak into the cab and bring Lora back into his heart before dissolving into an uproar of squelches and hisses.

He winces at a twinge in the side of his head. The truck is pulling away from him, easing into the opposing lane of traffic, but Billy doesn't seem to be able to do much about it.

You're dying, big guy, one of voices inside his head, *I hope you know that.*

Of course Billy knows that. He knows that the grief that took him down at the diner is going to happen again and again, and it's going to get worse each time, until his brain blows apart like an old fuse.

He doesn't need no doctor, he doesn't need no CAT scans, he knows what's going inside his body and he knows it's fatal.

It's kind of funny when you think of it. I mean, here you got Sal, who couldn't hit a bull in the ass with a tennis racket, who nearly puked himself to death when Billy did that job on Jerry LaRocca, fucking Sal finally did something right.

It's taking a little longer than Matty would like, but it's going to happen all right; Billy is going to die. Some shit, huh?

Do you think I'm going to hell?

Billy snaps back, sees where he's going. He tugs hard on the steering wheel and pulls the truck back over the double yellow lines.

"Not tonight," he says to whoever may be listening and plows on through the mist.

3

THE PICK-UP BLOWS right over the yellow lines like they don't exist and George sits up straight in his patrol car. All right, numb nuts, he smiles, your ass belongs to me.

It's been real quiet tonight, but George knows that won't last. Between this fog and idiots like that, there'll be plenty of wrecks before his shift is over.

Some of the younger guys love the crazy stuff, crashes, bar fights, domestic brawls, but George has been at this long enough to know that you don't have to look for trouble in this line of work because it's always going to come around.

He much prefers an evening when the radio has nothing to say except "10-22"—cancel your response.

The younger ones tend to think George is just counting the days until he puts in his papers. Some of his fellow offices have even muttered that they can't rely on him in a tight spot; that George is so desperate to retire in one piece that he'll hold back if the going gets tough.

It hurts to hear that kind of stuff, as if George would ever do something like that, but you can't do much about what people think.

He's all set to hit the lights on this nitwit when he sees that it's Lora's truck driving so recklessly, which is strange because he went by her house a little while ago, like he does every night he's on duty, and he assumed she was home. So we got a pretty good idea who's in the driver's seat, don't we?

He hasn't seen Billy since he went nutzoid in the diner and almost lunged for George's throat. He'd just as soon forget the fear that surged through his body when Billy roared at him. In spite of the gun, the mace, and the handcuffs, George was pretty goddamn scared for a few seconds.

Now what the hell is that bastard doing out at this time of night? Could be that he had a fight with Lora and she finally wised up and kicked his ass out the door. George might come home tonight to find a message from Lora on his answering machine, asking him to please come over as soon as he could.

He keeps his fingers on the switch for a few seconds and watches as the pick-up lurches like it's going to fly off the road. Be a real shame if something like that happens.

But the truck returns to the proper lane and George sees the taillights moving through the fog. He toys with the idea of pulling Billy over. The guy was clearly in the wrong lane and George would bet his next five paychecks that Billy doesn't have anything resembling a valid driver's license.

George knows there's a hell of lot more to Billy, if that's even his real name. Yes, George is hardly a disinterested party, but you don't have to be a gypsy fortune teller to know there's something very wrong about that guy.

The diner scene wasn't a fluke; that was the real Billy coming out to play. After all this time as a cop, George knows bad news when he sees it and this guy is strife in capital letters. Such a smooth bastard, with the smile and the jokes, and all that "big guy" crap; who the hell does he think he's kidding?

The glowing red eyes are fading away from him. It would just be the two of them alone in the fog and this time George would be ready for any wild man stuff. Billy would find out exactly what George is like in a tight spot.

No doubt, George could make life difficult for Billy. But Billy might do some talking and then Lora and everyone else on this goddamn mountain would ask if that's any way to treat the man who saved your life.

Everyone knows you've been mooning over Lora for most of your adult life and some people might think you're just a little bit of jealous of Billy.

Well, of course he is. George is so jealous, so ashamed of himself for being jealous, and so bug-eyed angry at the whole stupid situation he'd like to floor the pedal on this goddamn patrol car and carve screeching donuts in the middle of town until the tank goes dry.

It's just that he's known Lora for so long. They went through Pocono Mountain together and though they never actually dated it always seemed they would make a nice couple. But Lora didn't see it that way and George spent a good chunk of his emotional life on the sidelines.

First, Lora takes up with that lowlife ex-con sack of shit Scotty Fuller and George had to bite down on his tongue to keep from telling Lora to buy a house near the jail in Snydersville so she could save on gas when she went to see Scotty on visiting day.

But he didn't say anything because it wasn't his business and because just about everybody in town knew Scotty had beat the living shit out of George when they were in junior year.

He took to smacking Lora around, too, though she'd never admit it. George tried to help her, to get her to file a complaint. Just say the word, he told her, and George would have that fat slob in handcuffs so fast his head would spin clean off his shoulders. But Lora kept turning him down until she finally got mad at him, told him to back the hell off. And that's what George did.

He'd love to follow Scotty down to his favorite saloon in the Gap, sneak up on him in the parking lot, and pound the ugly bastard right into the ground with his baton. Then Lora could come visit George in Snydersville.

She finally pulled the plug on Scotty after her brother got killed on 611 near the railroad bridge, a 10-45 with entrapment.

George was the first one on the scene that night, when the fog was as bad as it is now, and the second he saw the remains of the car crushed beneath that tractor trailer like a beer can, he knew it was Kenny and he knew he was dead.

George didn't want to go any further; he didn't want to look inside that wreckage. He would've gladly stopped right there, but he kept walking, peered into the backseat and saw Kenny's severed head in the backseat looking right back at him.

To this day George doesn't know how he kept from puking all over the blacktop, but he came away looking greener than Kermit the Frog and turned around to face two smirking staties who had just gotten out of their cruisers and were watching the local boy fight to keep his dinner down.

George recovered, though; and he was the one who made the trip to Lora's house, not the Rambo brothers. He walked up to the front steps like an astronaut treading on the lunar surface, one slow, deliberate step after another.

The door flew open just as he lifted his hand to knock and Lora was standing and her face, that lovely face George has admired for so many years, was inches away, strained with fear and dread.

"Lora…"

That was as far as he got before she began screaming and crying, combining the rage and grief, and George eased her into the house.

And as he stood holding Lora in the kitchen, George tried not to think of the future, about what Lora would do now that her little brother had been so brutally taken away from her and that loser husband was clearly on the way out.

George did his damnedest to concentrate on his job because this was official police business and not date night for God's sake.

But he couldn't help thinking, just for a few seconds, that this might be his chance to finally be part of Lora's life, a real part, not a good friend, but to actually be the man in her life. George's marriage to Annie Mason had gone south a few months earlier after four long years of trying, really trying, to make it work, so it wasn't like he was cheating on anybody.

But he couldn't move in on Lora like some heartless ghoul after she dumped Scotty, not with the pain of losing her brother still so fresh in her mind. Let the girl grieve, put her life back together. Grandma always said slow and steady wins the race.

And then Billy shows up. Dead of night, in the middle of nowhere, bleeding all over the place, and Lora stops to give this guy, a total stranger, a ride.

George, back on the sidelines, was too stunned to be angry, I mean, Jesus, what is it with this girl and the goddamn rejects? Slow and steady, my, ass, it's a good thing Manson's still in the joint or Lora would've dragged him home, too.

Then just to put a nice red ribbon on the whole rancid mess, George had to blunder into Old Ethan's firetrap like a first class idiot and get rescued by Billy, the very last guy on earth that he wanted to see. And now that bastard is bulletproof as far as George is concerned. Nice going, chubber head.

There was one night at O'Hara's, before Billy showed up and after several beers had shut down his internal alarm system, that George, riding high on liquid courage, thought, what the hell, he'd just get things out in the open.

"You know," he said. "I always wondered what it would be like if you and I got together."

"Oh, c'mon, George," Lora said and swatted his arm. "You don't need a head case like me messing up your life. I saved you."

It was a good answer, had to give her that, and they both laughed it off, but when George saw Lora and Billy coming out of the Galaxy together, and got this singular ache in his heart, he wondered if this is what it feels like to be saved, can I please give damnation a try?

The taillights are little more than pinpricks now and George sure would like to know what that son-of-a-bitch is up to. Can't be anything legit; that's for sure.

Maybe George should sort of keep an eye on him, follow Billy at a discreet distance just to make sure he doesn't get into an accident or anything. These roads can be very dangerous if you're an outsider.

The radio squawks with a call, 10-45 with entrapment, and George eases up on the gas. The red eyes vanish into the fog and he prepares to make a U-turn and head back toward town. Some other time, big guy.

4

"WHAT DO YOU mean coming home at this ungodly hour?"

Billy wakes up to the sound of his mother's voice shouting at the old man who just came barreling into the house after a late shift at Gallagher's.

"I don't answer to you!" His father roars so the whole block can hear him. "I'll come home any goddamn time I want!"

"That's just great. And what about work—you have a job tomorrow morning, or are you going to stick Charley with that one, too?"

"Don't worry about my job. I pay the bills around here, not you."

"You pay the bills? If it wasn't for my father, we'd all starve."

"Shit on your father."

"Shit on yours!"

Her voice is coarse and angry, nothing like the woman who had come into his room earlier and begged for his love. This woman isn't Billy's mother at all.

"I see you've been bellying up to the bar, too." The old man snorts. "Jesus, some life I got. Come home every night to a firebug and a drunken tramp. How'd I get so fucking lucky?"

"Poor little man; the whole world is against you."

"Yeah, keep it up. You just keep it up with that mouth of yours and some night you'll go out of here in a box."

"Little man…"

The atmosphere out there is so charged that Billy can feel it in his bedroom. It's not like one of their usual arguments. Billy wants to warn his mother, tell her to be quiet before something bad happens.

But it's too late. The old man goes crazy, worse than ever, like an escaped mental patient, and Billy hears plates smashing, furniture being overturned, his mother screaming stop it, stop it, you goddamn animal. The noise stops then and the next thing Billy hears is his father's voice, rasping, deadly, barely human.

"You fucking bitch…"

He hears a blow being struck, something heavily hitting the floor and then the whole house falls silent.

Billy wants to believe it's over, that his parents had stopped fighting and he can go back to sleep, wake up the next morning and everything would be fine. But the silence is more frightening than anything he's heard tonight, so he gets out of bed and goes out to the living room.

Billy squints as the light hits his eyes and when he's finally able to see, he can't believe what he's looking at.

It's like the old man wanted to destroy any trace of the home he had created here. The dining room table is flipped over on its side, smashed plates and bits of broken glass are sprayed on the floor.

The living room lamp is in a corner, the shade torn and crumpled, the bulb somehow surviving the rampage and now throwing spookhouse shadows on the wall.

His father's in the living room, backlit by the TV's scorching test pattern, and straddling his mother, who is stretched out on the floor, his fingers wrapped around her throat. Her legs kick weakly into the air, while the old man chokes the life out of her.

"You fucking bitch," his father says in an ice block whisper. "You fucking bitch…"

Billy stands there for what seemed like an incredibly long time and watches his mother being murdered.

He can hear her gagging for breath, see the beads of sweat forming on the old man's face, and the tattoo of Jesus on his forearm pulsating and quivering as if the contorted image was going to rip to clear of the skin.

"You fucking…bitch…"

He's really going to do it; he's going to strangle his mother right here on the floor of their house while Billy watches.

He's terrified, but he can't let her die right before his eyes, and when his mother begins wheezing what could be her very last breaths, Billy pulls in a chest full of air and screams as loud as he can.

"Stop it!"

The old man looks up, startled, his fingers still clamped around his wife's throat, and glares at Billy.

The two stare at each other, while the catatonic TV squeals a burning monotone, and Billy watches as his father does the murderer's math, weighing the possibility of a double killing tonight, freeing himself of the wife and the little bastard in a few depraved moments.

His mother struggles feebly, scratches at the arms that hold her down, but Billy can't move, can't talk, can't do anything until his father decides if he'll let his son live or die.

The old man's fingers slowly loosen and Billy's mother eases to the floor, tries to breathe again. He stares furiously at his son, opening and closing those powerful hands.

Billy will never forget this night, the look in his father's eyes, a virulent combination of blazing hatred and paralyzing fear. All the brutal things he'll see and do over the years, he'll never see such harsh emotions in someone's face. Not until the night he watches Ethan die.

"Fuck you, kid," the old man mutters and walks down the stairs and out into the street.

He stood there for the longest time watching his mother cough and choke on the floor, rooted to that spot in the hallway, terrified that his father would come back and kill him the second he moved.

He finally walked over to her, the floorboards shrieking with every step, hovered over her as she lay face down on the floor, watched as her shoulders tremble violently, listened to her muffled sobs.

"Oh, God…oh, God…"

He touched her shoulder lightly, just tips of two fingers, and she jerked head up quickly, and Billy screamed, screamed like a girl, when he saw what the old man had done to her; one eye blackened shut, bruises covering her face, an ugly gash across her forehead, and angry red handprints still staining her throat.

He tried to back away but she clamped her hand around his wrist, pulled him forward until their faces were inches apart, he could smell the liquor, see her eye rolling in such complete terror.

"Help me," she croaked, shaking him down to his ankles. "Help me—!"

"Mom—!"

"Please!"

She released him and he ran to the wall phone in the kitchen, the receiver now dangling to the floor, found the number written on the wall in fading pencil and started dialing. He prayed while the phone rang at the other end, please pick up, please be there for us—

"Who the hell is this?" The words exploded in his ear after the eighth ring and Billy thought that he had the wrong number.

"Charley——?"

"Do you know what time it is, asshole?" The voice was harsh, the words garbled. "You call here again and you'll curse your—"

"—it's me; it's Billy."

There was a pause and it was like someone handed off the phone because the next man to speak was Charley, Billy's best friend in the whole world.

"Big guy? What is it? What's wrong?"

"You gotta come over, right now. It's Mom—"

"All right, all right, Billy. You just hold the fort and I'll be right there."

No questions, no more talk, the line went dead and Billy knew Charley was tearing down the stairs of his apartment building on Ovington Avenue, racing by the darkened stores on Fifth. You could run down the middle of the street at this time of night, so few cars and buses were around.

Hold the fort. This wasn't much left to hold, the fort had been attacked and overrun by a marauding savage.

Billy sat down next to his mother's huddled form and in a few minutes he heard Charley charging up the stairs, saw the horrified look on his face as he stepped into the apartment and looked around.

"Jesus Christ," he muttered, "Jesus Christ…"

Charley turned and saw them on the floor, a pair of refugees, knelt down and they fell on top of him, both of them sobbing uncontrollably while he held them tightly in his arms.

"It's gonna be all right," Charley whispered gently. "It's gonna be all right."

5

Tommy closes the door on his mother's whining, climbs into the dead man's seat of the stolen Mazda and plucks the joint out from between Eddie's fingers.

"What it is, bitch," Tommy says as he descends into crushed leather.

"What it is, son. You ready?"

"Fuck, yeah. Let's go."

Eddie U-bones into the path of an oncoming SUV and gives the driver the finger as he scars the street with a gash of howling rubber.

"Look out, mother fucker!"

Eddie giggles, so pathetically proud of himself. Tommy can only shake his head, bored by such juvenile stunts. This guy ever going to grow up?

Tommy looks around the interior of the Mazda, new, unspoiled, like it was built especially for him, bolted together minutes ago in a cascade of manic sparks and rolled off the assembly line just in time for the biggest night of Tommy's life, instead of being stolen from some douche bag who had walked out of the mall clutching a swollen shopping bag and a useless set of keys.

He wishes he could keep the car, dip it in bronze, mount it on a pedestal in front of his house, a monument commemorating what was about to happen tonight. But this thing is four-wheeled evidence and destined to be torched beneath some deserted overpass and left to burn.

"Nice ride, Eddie."

"Of course. Nothing's too good for my boy, especially on the night he pops his cherry."

Tommy shifts in his seat so he can feel the metal bulge against his waistband.

"Yeah, well, I'm way ahead of you, faggot, ain't I?"

"You have to be, son. You've got that name to live up to."

Eddie likes to do this shit. He enjoys digging at Tommy by bringing up the old man, without actually doing it, of course, the fucking smart-ass.

"So how's the old lady?"

"How you think, nigger?" Tommy swirls the joint's rocket red tip around his head. "Fucking loony tunes. I mean, she actually misses that cocksucker, the stupid twat. You believe that shit?"

"Shame on you, son. You should have more respect for your moms."

"Hey, I respect that drunken tramp." He passes back the joint. "I respect her so much I'd like to reunite her with that scumbag husband of hers. How's that for respect?"

Eddie tsk-tsks in time with the left hand blinker.

"I'm so disappointed in you, son. You have no idea."

"Go fuck yourself."

Eddie's a good man, no doubt, the only one Tommy would ever trust for this evening's excitement. But he doesn't know when to ease up on the ball-breaking and Tommy doesn't want to deal with his bullshit, especially tonight. And yet Eddie keeps pushing it.

Eddie's old man was in construction until the booze caught up with him and now he sits around the house all day draining his disability checks into his liver.

His mother, finally seeing what a first class fucktard the guy was, bounced right before Thanksgiving and hasn't been seen since. You've got to give the girl credit. Not all these bitches sit on their asses and do the woe is me shit.

Tommy and Eddie had hooked up in junior year after realizing that going to class was for gayrods and they quickly became the most feared names in school. They'd shake down any little piglet that got in their way, sold reefer, and boosted the occasional car. It wasn't bad at all.

For Tommy, there was always the misery at home, of course, with those matching assholes giving him grief.

The old lady would break Tommy's balls about his grades and the old man would beat the shit out of him if he didn't jump like some jigaboo houseboy.

"So, ninja, you ready for this?"

Tommy flashes up his t-shirt to show the butt of the .380.

"What's that look like, dick?"

"That looks like a gun. I want to know if you have the rocks to use it."

"How about I use it on you, cornhole?"

Eddie smirks as he glides the Mazda through a red light.

"Now, now, big guy, don't get excited. I'm just a little worried you might choke."

"Like how your sister choked on my cock last night?"

"Look, I'm trying to make a point here."

"You're trying to be an asshole."

Eddie cracks a monkey-boy grin.

"It's just that I really don't see you stepping up and doing the deed, son. You talk tough and that's fine as far as it goes. But it's just talk. This thing here, it ain't like bitch-slapping ninth graders at the bus stop. This is your moment of truth."

"I know what it is, fuckballs. I don't need you to tell me. Just drive the car like a good little fag and let a man take care of business."

"And what a man you are."

They slice between the empty tollbooths, get on the Verrazzano and the old memories stir. When he was young, maybe five years old, Tommy was terrified of riding on the bridge and he used to cry whenever the old man took him over to Brooklyn, convinced this monstrous piece of work was going to collapse.

Yeah, it was crazy, it was stupid, but Tommy was a kid, okay? He didn't know no better. Billy didn't want to hear that, though, oh no, he wasn't going to have his boy crying over this kind of crap. Billy the Kid was raising a fighter; he was raising a man. He wasn't having no queer for a son.

Jesus Christ, get him a skirt. He's crying like a little girl. Fucking asshole.

Tommy looks to his right, pictures the massive hulks slumbering in the Narrows.

The lights from Bay Ridge come up on his left, glow brighter, getting closer. That's his father's old neighborhood down there, where he and Uncle Sal took on the whole world for Matty Cigar.

Back then, they were all like family, those guys were always coming over to the house for dinner, drinks, maybe watch some football. They always joked around with Tommy, gave him twenty-dollar bills, and let him stay up late so he could listen to their rough talk.

Tommy loved those guys, and he always argued with his mother to let him stay up a little longer, c'mon, ma, just a little longer.

Naturally, those guys don't come by anymore, not after that shit with the old man, and Tommy's mother wanders around the house cursing them like a bag lady on the ferry.

Tommy knows he should hate Sal and Matty for smoking his old man, with the whole family honor, vendetta bullshit, but, fuck it; somebody would've capped that prick sooner or later. Maybe even Tommy himself.

"You know, son," Eddie says, "a lot of people are going to hear about this. The right people, you know what I'm saying?"

"Yeah, I know."

"This sort of thing could put you in real good with the powers that be. But if you drop the ball here, son—"

"—I'm not dropping no ball."

"I'm just saying if you do…" Eddie pokes the air for emphasis. "Your name is gonna be shit. If something goes wrong tonight—God forbid— you know what people are going to say about you?"

It's like hearing his father complain about how things have changed since he was young, that there's no real men around anymore, just these dicks who think they're tough guys.

The old man never mentioned no names or looked in his son's direction, but Tommy knew the message was meant for him: you're a pussy, kid, and you always will be.

"It'll be real bad, big guy."

The air becomes stale and tight and the road ahead of them seems to sway, the girders seem to tremble. Jesus Christ, get him a skirt…

"Hey, Eddie, enough now—"

"Everybody will think Tommy doesn't have the balls…"

"—shut your hole—"

"—lets some old hunyak push him around—"

"I mean it—"

— crying like a little girl.

"…never be like his old man—"

"You mother fucker!"

Tommy screams as he wraps his arm around Eddie's neck and jams the .380's barrel against the bastard's skull. The car swerves wildly as Eddie squeals and tries to keep inside his lane.

"Hey, what the—?"

"How do you like this, you cunt?" Tommy shrieks. "What do think about this, you little prick?"

"Tommy!" Eddie screeches, spitting out the joint, "what the fuck are you doing?"

"I'm testing your theory, bitch." He screws the barrel a notch deeper. "Let's see if I got the balls."

Eddie fights to break free, but Tommy's way too strong for this faggy little bitch.

The car screeches from side to side, horns blare all around them, and Tommy doesn't care, couldn't give a shit if they crash through the guardrails, sail into the Narrows and sink to the deepest part of the ocean. He wants an answer right now.

"You think I can't do it?"

"Let go of—"

"I ain't got the balls?" Tommy thumbs back the hammer. "Is that what you think, funny man?"

"You're gonna get us killed!"

"What it is, son!"

If only Tommy could have done with this with the old man, just to have that psycho bastard at his mercy for a few homicidal seconds; make him cry, make him beg for his life. He twists the gun a few malignant degrees against Eddie's head. Make him shit in his pants.

"Tommy, stop!"

"Answer me!"

"—we're gonna fucking crash—!"

"Answer me!"

"Yes! Yes!" Eddie screams, tears in his eyes. "You can do it! You got the fucking balls!"

Tommy cranks his bicep hard against Eddie's head.

"You sure, Eddie? Are you sure, you little lowlife scumbag?"

"Yeah, yeah, I mean it, I swear on my mother—"

"—fuck that slut, Eddie, you gotta do better than that."

"—on my grandmother, my fucking *grandmother*, for Christ's sake—"

Tommy shoves Eddie back into the seat like he's made of cardboard. He's sweating and there's this hammering inside his head, but he feels good. He's in control.

"Jesus Christ…" Eddie rubs his aching neck. "I mean…Jesus fucking Christ."

"You shouldn't have said that shit about my old man, Eddie. That was wrong."

Eddie clamps all ten fingers around the steering wheel and stares straight ahead.

"I was just trying to get you psyched, brother." He shrugs out a spineless chuckle. "Y-you did great, my man. I'm real proud of you."

Tommy folds his arms, sits back in his seat and smiles. They're coming off the bridge, getting onto the Belt. He looks around and sees nothing to fear.

"Thanks, son."

6

Billy's buried somewhere deep in the fog when the steering wheel starts tugging away from him.

He's crawling along with the hazard lights going, not sure if he's still on the road or on this earth, and it feels like the same unnatural force that pulled him away from Lora is now gently hijacking the pickup and guiding it through the low slung clouds.

He senses something familiar about his surroundings, despite the unrelenting mist, something so ingrained in his mind that it feels like he could just about let go of the steering wheel and read a paper with his feet on the dash while the truck takes him wherever it wants.

You are now entering—there it goeesss!

An exit springs up on the right and the truck rolls off the highway, travels a few miles beyond the fog's reach before pulling off to the shoulder and rolling to a stop beneath a willow tree.

He climbs out of the cab, looks around at the dark woods, picks a direction, and starts walking; gas can in one hand, tire iron in the other.

Billy moves quickly, his eyes looking straight ahead, and every animal, plant, and rock around here knows better than to get in his way. The crickets fall silent, the bushes step aside, and the stones roll out of his path. There's no sound except the leaves cracking softly beneath his feet that warn the whole countryside that Billy the Kid is heading this way.

He stops when he reaches a clearing and sees the place, The Hideaway standing before him, so heavily wrapped in shadows and gloom it looks like it'll vanish when the sun comes up.

It's not like those beautiful summer afternoons when Matty had his barbecues and the place was teeming with wives and kids, when the Cigar rolled around the backyard greeting everyone and patting children on the head like he was Old St. Nick in a wheelchair.

The boys hit a warehouse near JFK one night and came charging up here because they knew Matty wouldn't be around. They bounced into a local dive and reeled in some small town tramps with talk of life in the city and offers of free coke.

They got mockey-eyed, blasted the stereo loud enough to rattle the stars, and fucked like animals.

One of the skanks had to just about drag Sal upstairs and he looked so miserable, like he was going to face a firing squad instead of getting his dick wailed. Vince picked up a polar bear rug he had stolen during the break-in and ran around with the thing on his head, foam-spraying beer cans in both hands, singing glorious, glorious, one keg of beer for the four of us.

Billy was in a recliner, bare-chested, some giggling bitch on his lap, enjoying the show.

And Sal comes lurching out of the bedroom, wrapped up in a sheet like a Roman senator, his mouth hanging open and his eyes just a blur. He stood over right over Billy, rocking on his heels and ready to cry.

"I love…you, Kid." He said. "I fucking love you."

Billy smiled and nodded, deeply touched. He was still smiling as he reached over, ripped the sheet clean off Sal's body and left his best friend standing there ballsy-ass naked in the middle of the room while everybody screamed and laughed.

"I love you, too, big guy!"

Tommy and Eddie roll down Fort Hamilton Parkway and turn at the corner when they reach the Fortway movie house.

"He lives up there," Eddie says, nice and respectful now. "Middle of the block."

Tommy knows this place from driving around here with the old man when he was a kid, so he knows about the Fortway, even though he doesn't give a rat's ass.

Billy used to give his son the no-choice guided tour of his incredibly fucked-up life and this is where the stupid bastard tried to rob a liquor store the day Tommy's grandfather croaked and that cop Jake beat the flaming shit out of him.

His father was trying to show how tough he was but the only thing he did as far as Tommy was concerned was prove that he was a fucking asshole.

So he backs right up into a cop, gets his head busted, and you wonder why that nigger's not around no more. At least retards got an excuse for the stupid shit they do.

Yeah, Tommy heard all about the Fortway and the lights in the ceiling that looked like stars in the night sky. The place was falling apart by the time Billy and his friends starting going there, but you could still see—

Tommy clamps down on the memories. Let's keep that prick in his grave, okay?

Eddie turns at the corner, eases a short way up the block and double-parks under a tree. He shifts into neutral, switches off the headlights, gestures with his head.

"It's right up there," he says. "The house with the green light."

"Yeah…"

"He works a night shift, so he should be coming out in a few minutes."

Tommy nods. Routines are deadly, that was one of the old man's little gems. You do something enough times, people who don't like you are bound to notice.

He feels good, pleased that he's doing his business here, in his father's old neighborhood. Making his mark, the next generation, all that horseshit. He nods down the street.

"That fucking guy…he brought this upon himself."

"Oh, no doubt, son. You're definitely within your rights here."

"This shit was between me and that loser son of his. Didn't have nothing to do with him."

"Hell, no. Who asked his fucking opinion?"

"All I did was ask for my money, money that I had coming to me. And that little bitch stiffs me, the fuck, and then goes running to his daddy."

"You can't trust nobody no more."

Tommy was in the pool room on Clawson three nights ago, minding his own business, when all this shit started.

He knuckles were still sore from beating on the little scumbag for his money earlier that day, when this barrel-bellied polack with a head of thick white hair, like a glowing mound of cotton, walks right into the place and starts finger-jabbing Tommy in the chest.

"You stay the fuck away from my kid, you little cocksucker or you'll end as dead as your old man."

Tommy stood there, no idea who this shithead was or what kind of hairy bug he had crawling up his ass.

All he knew was that everybody in this dump was looking at Tommy and waiting for him to do something, instead of standing still like a fag and eating this guy's shit.

"Look, pal—"

"—my son don't owe you a fucking thing, you son-of-a-bitch. You go near him again and I'll come back here and break you in two."

And it was the goddamnest thing, facing this prick, with the mutant forearms, blubbery stomach, and the radioactive hair, Tommy was suddenly yanked back in time to Billy's last day on earth, when the old man nearly put him in the hospital.

"Stay away from my son, scumbag. I won't tell you twice."

One last poke to the chest and Tommy was back in the pool hall. He braced for a brutal shot to the gut, but the polack walked out and left Tommy with the cue stick in his hand and everybody in the room thinking he was a first rate pussy.

Somebody get him a skirt…

Tommy knew what he had to do.

7

Billy walks slowly up to the porch and stops when he sees his sign still hanging over the front door. *The Hideaway.*

He's amazed it's still here, assumed that Matty would have smashed that thing into splinters and dumped them into a vat of acid just to erase any trace of Billy. The old bastard must be getting soft.

He's an artist, this guy.

He walks up the ramp that he had installed for the Cigar and stands at the front door. It's a shame he lost his keys that night at the rest stop. Sure would have made things a little easier.

Billy puts down the gas can, grips the tire iron with both hands, spears the end into the doorframe as hard as he can, and pretends he's driving it straight into Matty's heart.

He buries the edge deep into the wood and pries, twists, against the door until the hinges squeal and the wood cracks with a splintered scream.

—freaking Michelangelo, that's what he is—

The door cracks open and Billy collapses to the floor, covered in sweat and breathing double time, and he's got 30 seconds, just 30 seconds, to get across the room, reach behind that stupid sailboat painting hanging over the mantelpiece and tap out the five-digit code to kill the alarm.

Billy staggers to his feet, trips over the goddamn polar bear rug that little suck-ass Vince gave to Matty, and stumbles toward the image of a sailboat gently floating in a beautiful blue sea, rips the thing off the wall, and jabs his index finger on the keypad, praying to Jesus, Mohammed, and the Great Akela that Matty hasn't changed the alarm code.

We'll just have to find a room for you, won't we?

Billy finishes, pulls his hand back and waits in the dark, while the broken door creaks on its hinges. He counts off the seconds; no call from the alarm company, no sirens howling in the dark.

Billy the Kid has come home.

"This guy needs to be taught a lesson."

"Definitely."

Tommy takes out the .380 and holds it on his lap, recalls the first time he saw his father with a gun.

He must've been around eight years old and Billy was sitting at the table in the basement, slowly cleaning a .38 with a cloth. His mother was out somewhere and it was just the two of them, father and son.

His father was telling him some story about running around the Botanical Garden, and this Japanese set-up they got, with snapping turtles, and grandma getting all frantic, but Tommy was barely listening.

His eyes were riveted on Billy's fingers, cleaning every bit of that gun, twirling the cylinder, snapping it close with a sharp click. He wanted to touch it so bad—

"Heads up, son."

Tommy's spine stiffens. He squints up the block and sees a figure coming down the front steps of the house. There's the potbelly, there's the white glowing hair, yeah, Daddy's going to work.

Fat load of shit, you probably took your kid to ball games and up to the mountains for camping trips, and you're so proud of him you can't help talking about him in front of all your friends, can you?

So what if he's a little junkie lowlife who won't pay his debts? You'll always be there to bail him out and show everybody what a badass you are.

Tommy buzzes down the window and takes a few deep breaths. He watches the patch of white hair float over to a Jeep parked a few doors down the block, sees the polack dig into his pocket for the keys.

Eddie starts up the engine, gooses the gas pedal a little, and pulls out of the parking spot gently, with the headlights off.

He's looking at Tommy, everybody's looking at Tommy, waiting for him to do something. Tommy raises his left hand, feels it vibrating with a thousand kilowatts of adrenalin.

It's all up to Tommy now, not Billy, his mother, Uncle Sal, or anybody else. This is Tommy's gig and all he has to do is drop his hand, his beautiful fucking left hand, and it'll begin.

—Billy's first was in a shitbag hotel when he and Uncle Sal torched some loser, big fucking deal, it took two guys to roast one deadbeat, and they did it on the very day that Tommy was—

The white head ducks and disappears inside the Jeep, Tommy hears the engine come on, sees the headlights shining on the back of a red SUV, and he's still got his hand up—

—you want Mommy to kiss it?

Tommy drops his hand and the Mazda roars up the block, a dark meteor tearing a hole in the atmosphere as they pull up alongside the Jeep.

For a second it's just the two of them, facing each other, like two fighter pilots hurtling miles above the earth at Mach 10. Tommy looks right into the polack's eyes, filling with shock and fear, yeah, Daddy, never thought you'd see me again, did you?

Daddy stomps on the gas pedal, but it's too late, Tommy's firing. The window explodes into mist, and the polack jerks as the bullet hits him in the neck. Tommy shoots again and again, and it feels like there's no gun, the bullets are coming right out of his hand, here you go, Daddy, how's that feel?

And one more, as he's leaning halfway out the window, right into that clump of white hair, that takes the top of Daddy's head right off and sends his body flopping into the dead man's seat and out of sight.

"Go! Go! Go!"

Tommy doesn't realize it's him screaming, and his cries meld with the squeal of the Mazda's tires, as Eddie rips down the block so fast they could set the trees on fire.

The interior of the car reeks of smoke and blood and Tommy feels so powerful, so fearless right now that he ain't ascared of God.

"Glorious!" he screams out the window in a voice he's never heard before. "Fucking glorious!"

8

Billy walks to main bedroom, goes straight to the mini-safe that Matty keeps in the closet.

The combination clicks easily in his hand, the door swings open, and Billy reaches inside where his fingers wrap around the butt of an old .45 Matty always kept there so he could go down fighting in case the Indians ever come back.

Billy lifts the weapon, checks the slide action, and savors the perfect balance. He points the gun around the room and takes out one kraut after another, bang, bang, bang, thoroughly in love with the killer weight in his hand.

He puts the barrel under his chin and presses, just to see what it feels like, after all these years of doing it to other people in Matty's name.

You know who I am, mother fucker? You know who I work for?

Yeah, Billy, learned them scumbags real good; made them see the light or made them curse their mothers for giving birth to them.

He pauses for a few seconds and puts his head down so the gun barrel slides right into his mouth, his approach for the real hard cases, the ones who thought Billy was bluffing, that he wouldn't dare pull the trigger.

Do I look like I'm kidding, asshole? Guys actually shit their pants when Billy did this little routine on them.

The metal taste fills his mouth, and Billy thinks how this would take care of the headaches lickety-split, watches his index finger inch worm its way around the trigger; feels the heavy tug and sees the hammer rise and crack back down.

Billy gags on the sudden snap in his throat, pulls the gun out of his mouth and tries to cough up a laugh. Hey, at least we know it's empty.

He reaches back into the safe, feels around until he finds the clip, slams it home, and slides a bullet into the chamber, his favorite sound in the world. He puts the gun in his belt and the bulge feels so good after all these months of walking around in the raw.

One more grab into the black hole and he finds it, the Bowie knife Billy got for the Cigar for Christmas a few years back, a foot-long piece of sculptured lightning that should be hanging in a museum it's so beautiful.

He looks around the room, at the furniture, the widescreen TV, CD player, and the bed, all made and waiting for Matty to come in and take a nap. He raises the knife up high.

"And here he is," Billy shouts at the empty house, "the man of the hour!"

Billy moves through that room like a storm system rolling across the Great Plains, tears into the bed, gouges out the guts of the mattress and spreads them over the floor. He stomps on the frame, kicks the night table over, and throws that TV against the wall.

He heads into the main room, grunting, snarling, wheezing as he destroys everything that gets in his way, windows, mirrors, glasses, junky little knickknacks.

He did so much work here, cleaning the place out, making it just right so Matty could get around in the wheelchair. It's a shame to trash it all, but Billy giveth and now he taketh away. Taketh like a fucking cyclone.

The knife cuts up carpeting, shades, furniture, that goddamn sailboat painting. He butchers the polar bear rug, kills the albino son-of-a-bitch all over again like he's a caveman fighting to the death. His shoulders ache, his hands and face are bleeding from the flying glass and he's struggling to get his lungs to work.

He might drop dead, keel over from a heart attack or a stroke, but he has to keep on going, move through every room to do as much harm as possible.

Finally, Billy stops, wobbling above all the debris, his head aching so badly it's about to break apart in chunks and fall to the floor.

He gets only a few seconds to savor his victory over Matty's house before he feels the rumble in his stomach. His throat pulls in, he gets a taste of the pork chops that Lora made a few hours ago in some distant fog-shrouded place, and, oh, Jesus, here it comes.

Something within his body yanks him down on all fours and Billy hauls up every scrap of food he's eaten since breakfast. He digs his fingers into the carpet, roars like a bear, and thinks, all right, that's it, there's nothing left, but he keeps on going, decorating Matty's house one last time.

He stops, finally, stops before he turns his guts inside out. Billy stays in the position for a long time and wonders if he'll ever be able to stand up.

Okay, big guy, a few deep breaths, you got this, just take it easy. He's up to his knees and then on his feet, staggering over to the porch to get the gas can. We're not done yet.

The night air clears some of the suffering from his head, the gasoline fumes revive him and Billy walks back into the place stronger, so he can anoint the house, in the name of the Father, the Son, and the Holy Spirit. He takes his time to make sure all this pristine rubble is doused and ready to burn.

Billy looks over his handiwork, the wreckage and ruin that used to be Matty's house and nods in satisfaction. It's like a whole boatload of evil spirits busted in on this place. Even the puke looks good.

He picks up an old copy of Parade from the floor, rips off the back page, bends and creases it, folds it over to make the wings, smooths down the nose, which ain't easy when your hands are rattling like you got the palsy, and in a few seconds he's got a perfectly respectable paper airplane.

The paper is a little thinner than Billy would like, but then it doesn't have too far to go.

He fishes around his pockets, searches for Lora's plastic lighter, hopes like hell he didn't leave the goddamn thing in the truck, and finds it in his back pocket, jammed up against his wallet.

Billy's moving super slow and cartoon crazy fast at the same time as he cracks up a flame, it sounds like a bone snapping in this obscene quiet, holds the trembling flame to the plane's tail until it catches fire.

And he sets it free.

9

THE PLANE GETS about halfway across the room before it begins a rapid descent, curling, spinning in tighter and tighter circles, mayday, mayday, while Billy backs up to the front door.

He's right there, right at the doorway when his aircraft touches down to the ground and the living room erupts into flames.

Thunderous orange light fills the room, newborn and starving, and it tears around the room feeding on the debris.

It gets brighter, hotter. Billy hears wood paneling crack, glass pop, and he's so proud, like watching your kid taking his first steps.

"Atta boy," he urges softly. "Fuck 'em up good."

Finally the heat is too much, even for Billy. He turns and he looks up to see *The Hideaway* sign hanging right overhead.

The fire grips the back of his neck, and Billy decides, no, he worked too hard on that thing, it belongs to him. He jumps, grabs the top of the sign, yanks it down and it feels like he's taking a scalp.

Billy jogs over to the tree line and watches the flames consume Matty's house. Look at all that smoke, twisting up in the air and joining the cloud cover. He closes his eyes and takes a long draw of hazy air. And they say this shit can kill you.

The fire punches holes through the roof and starts reaching to some nearby tree branches. 10-55, fully involved, that's what people will hear on their scanners tonight, fully involved.

In a few moments volunteers will drop whatever they're doing, leap out of bed, turn off the TV, run out to their cars, leaving wives, lovers, and children, all of them heading this way.

Billy grips a nearby sapling and squeezes while the fire tears off another piece of the roof; he's got to go, they'll be here soon, but right now, with his eyes shut, it feels like he's in the middle of the house, he feels the heat, hears the roar, but he's not burned at all.

The roof crashes in, like a bomb going off. Billy opens his eyes, hears sirens, getting louder, getting closer. Coming to kill his fire.

They'll be nothing left for them to save, Billy has seen to that. He walks back to the pick-up and it's too bad Ethan's not here tonight to see this because Billy knows exactly what he would say.

"Glorious, fucking glorious."

10

"C'MON, BIG GUY, we're going for a ride."

Charley was in Billy's room, the morning after the old man's rampage, gently shaking him.

Billy sat up as memories of the previous night came back to him. Charley pulling him from his mother's arms, while she cried and said no, no, don't take him away, and Charley softly shushing her, it's all right, it's all right, carrying Billy to his room and telling him to get some sleep before going back outside to take care of his mother.

"He's crazy! He tried to kill me!"

"Don't worry, it's gonna be okay…"

Billy heard Charley dialing the phone, talking to Frieda, his sister who lived on 72nd Street, and telling her that she had to come over right now because he needed some help here.

Charley took Billy's mother to the hospital as soon as Frieda got there and then she and her friends went to work cleaning up the house.

Billy fell asleep listening to these women, these strangers, talk as they vacuumed, scrubbed, and cleared away the debris. And now Charley was back.

"What about Mom? Where is she?"

"She's…okay." Charley paused just long enough to let Billy know that he wasn't telling the truth. "She's at the doctor's now, but she's going to be okay."

"And what about…Dad?"

"He's…he's gonna be all right. Now get some clothes together and let's get out here."

"Where are we going?"

"We're gonna see some friends of mine," Charley said on the way out the door.

Billy found out later that the old man had been arrested that night. After beating his mom and nearly demolishing the house he had gone to Gallagher's and started a brawl with some construction workers.

When the cops showed up, he began cursing and throwing punches at them, too, and they hauled him in. Billy wished he could've been there to see his father bashed with nightsticks, handcuffed, and thrown into the back of a police car.

He imagined the cops dragging his father down to the basement of the police station and beating him over and over until he cried like a little girl.

Billy dressed quickly, stuffed his school knapsack with a handful of shirts, a pair of pants, his G.I. Joe, while the women's voices come from the living room.

"That dirty bastard, he should have his legs broken."

"Look, the guy's been having trouble finding work and the drinking—"

"Oh, fuck him, Charley!" Frieda shouted. "That son-of-a-bitch needs someone to lean on him a little bit, you know what I'm saying? Someone should make a phone call—"

"—c'mon now—"

"—and then we'll see how tough he is, the piece of shit."

The voices stop when Billy creaks open his bedroom door and he walks out to the living room past a row of grim-faced, bulky Italian women who look down on him with hard-edged affection.

"Poor little guy," one of them whispers. "Gotta see his mother beaten like a *putana*."

"That bum, he don't care what happens to his own kid."

"He don't care about nothing. *Animale*."

Behind them Billy could see that the house is cleaner than it had ever been, like another family was living there. And that was fine with Billy. He never wanted to see this place again.

"Here, honey, sit down," Frieda said. "I'll make you some breakfast."

"We'll eat on the road," Charley said. "We want to beat the traffic."

"Charley—"

"—don't worry, we'll be all right."

Billy wanted to get away, too, afraid if he sat down at the table he'd never escape this awful house. Frieda put some oranges in a paper bag, handed them to Billy.

"Take this with you, sweetheart." She squeezed his fingers. "For when you get hungry in the car."

Billy took the bag from her, followed Charley down the stairs, climbed into his car, and the two of them drove away from that barren house.

He still remembers that trip, how they coasted over the Verrazano, nearly deserted on that hushed Sunday morning so it felt like they were the last people on earth.

"You're gonna love it up here, big guy," Charley said. "It's so beautiful, you'll swear you're in heaven."

The ride took a child's version of forever, with small towns coming up and quickly disappearing, and Charley called out like a tour guide, *"you are now entering—there it goeesss!"* and Billy couldn't stop laughing.

Charley did his best to keep Billy happy and make him forget about what had happened with his parents. He cracked jokes, told funny stories, and used his free hand to poke Billy in the ribs.

"Who's your buddy, huh? Who's your buddy?"

Billy laughed, tried to block Charley's tender assault as he said "you are, you are" between giggles.

The trip could have gone on until they reached California, just him and Charley driving until they reached the Pacific.

Somewhere along the way Billy fell asleep and when he woke up sometime around noon, he saw the highway had narrowed, the towns had all but disappeared, and Charley was turning on to a dirt road lined with rhododendrons, where the trees joined overhead to disperse the sunlight.

"Here we are, big guy."

Billy got a quick look at a sign reading "Miller's Breeze-Wood Lodge" and then dust was kicking up behind them, blocking out any sign of the outside world and all at once Billy was frightened; he wanted to go back home, as terrible as it was, he wanted to be back there rather than driving through this strange, wild land.

It was like a little village, this place. They came to a crossroads and a two-story white house stood in front of them. Up on the hill there was a small gray house with red shutters, barely visible behind the trees and bushes.

Charley turned down the hill toward this big old building that stood beside a beautiful swimming pool, and parked next to a blue Oldsmobile with a bumper sticker reading "God is Good All the Time."

"Wait here a second, Billy." Charley was talking as he got out of the car, closing the door and walking up to the house shouting "Junk man! Junk man!"

Billy heard voices, cries of greetings, and laughter coming out of the house and his fear began to dissolve. He got out of the car and looked over at the swimming pool that shone so brightly it seemed to be filled with sunlight.

He turned slowly, looked to the grounds behind the house, took in the ping-pong table, the badminton net, the swings set up between two trees, like they had grown there naturally.

"I had to get him out of there."

Charley's voice came from the house, reached Billy's ears amid the garbled chatter. Charley was in there with strangers talking about Billy.

He struggled to hear more, but the voices slipped back into noise. The screen door opened and Charley came walking toward Billy with an attractive older couple following him.

"And here he is," Charley made a theatrical sweep of his hand toward Billy, "the man of the hour!"

Mr. Miller was tall with perfectly trimmed white hair. He wore a white shirt and striped tie as if he worked in an office and he had a cigarette glowing between his fingers. Mrs. Miller was just so beautiful with a smile Billy could feel from 10 feet away and shiny red hair that he longs to touch even to this day.

"Hello, Billy." Mr. Miller spoke in a southern accent, like a character on a TV show. "How are you doing, young man?"

Billy just nodded and watched as Mr. Miller put out his hand, as if he were speaking to an adult.

"Charley speaks very highly of you," he said. "And I always say that any friend of Charley's is a friend of mine."

They were still shaking hands when Mrs. Miller came over to him.

"Well, hello, Billy. It's so nice to meet you. I'm sure we're going to get along just fine."

Charley had set this up, called the Millers at some point and begged them to take care of Billy until his father got out of jail and his mother got out of the hospital.

No one in Billy's immediate family wanted to get involved; they didn't want to face the old man, so Charley stepped in and called these people he had known for years.

They all had lunch and Mrs. Miller asked Billy about school, and the food he liked, and the games he played, and what it was like to live in New York, my, it's such a big city; and Billy looked like a fine young fellow and she was so happy that he had come to stay with them.

After lunch Charley said he had to get back to the city and even though the Millers and Billy tried to change his mind, he insisted, no, no, really, I got a whole bunch of things to do. He turned to Billy.

"All right, big guy, so you take care of things around here, okay?"

They all watched Charley's car disappear down the dirt road and as the cloud of dust faded, Billy wasn't feeling lost or abandoned. He felt welcome.

"Well, Billy," Mrs. Miller said, "we'll just have to find a room for you, won't we?"

11

The Breeze-wood Inn had three guests houses scattered around the property. The Laurel was the red brick house near the main building; The Vacationer was the large white building at the crossroads, but Billy's favorite was The Hideaway up on top of the hill that was barely visible behind all the trees and bushes.

Billy loved to go in there after guests checked out, before Selma, the cleaning lady, went to work, and pretend he owned the place, that he lived there all year round, greeting visitors as they walked up the hill and watching deer walk by his back window.

Mrs. Miller took him for long walks in the woods and she told him about growing up in North Carolina and meeting her husband. She told him about the daughter they lost to pneumonia who was just about Billy's age when the Lord called her home; and how they moved up here a few years later to take over the lodge.

She encouraged Billy to read instead of watching television. There was a shelf of children's books in the main house and though Billy wasn't interested at first, he wanted to please her, so he started with the history books like *The Great War* and *The War Between the States,* and the detective stories, like *The Mystery of the Haunted Skyscraper* with the Power Boys, and *The Case of the Stolen Dummy* with Brains Benton, a kid's version of Sherlock Holmes.

Every few days, Billy and Mrs. Miller would drive into Stroudsburg in that battleship of a car and ride down Main Street, where the cars parked on an angle instead of end to end.

First they'd go to J.J. Newberry's, so Mrs. Miller could buy Billy a huge ice cream sandwich and they'd walk down Main Street for some window-shopping.

Billy liked to run ahead and hide in a little alley on Main Street, plaster his body against the wall and wait for Mrs. Miller to go by.

She pretended to look for him, turning her head in all directions saying, "now where did that boy go?" That was Billy's cue to run up behind her and say "boo!" so Mrs. Miller could laugh and act surprised.

"You got me!" she'd say.

After dinner, the Millers would take Billy out for a ride around all the nearby back roads and look for deer. Billy sat in the back seat, peered into the woods for any sign of movement, any flash of brown amidst the green of the trees, and then he'd shout "deer!"

Mr. Miller played this trick where he'd point toward the woods and yell "deer!" and when Billy and Mrs. Miller looked, he'd start to sing, "dear, dear, what can the matter be?"

One night they came upon a field right after a rainstorm and there must have been a whole herd of deer, walking around, stopping to chew on grass; some of them were little more than shadows in the midst.

The deer didn't bolt into the woods like they usually did; they moved around slowly, unafraid. Billy and the Millers watched without saying a word, sensing they were in some kind of holy place, and it made Billy think of Limbo, where the souls of those who die in original sin must go until Judgment Day.

On some nights they drove through Mount Airy Lodge, the huge resort just a few miles from the Breeze-Wood, and look at the garishly lit buildings, the fountains that sprayed brightly colored water into the air. The people wore loud clothes and spoke in booming city voices.

"This place gets bigger every time we drive by," Mr. Miller said.

It was so different from the Millers' place Billy couldn't believe it, like someone had set up a circus right in the middle of the woods.

After the evening ride, they'd join the lodge's guests around the pool beneath a sky so brilliant with stars it was like the Millers had arranged it themselves.

The men would point up at the sky to track the satellites that passed overhead in the orbit around the earth. Billy could never see what they were pointing at, there were too many stars, but he pictured the satellites as huge, shining cylinders always watching everyone on earth.

The guests smoked, drank beer, and talked about politics, movies, traded stories about their lives back home. Billy usually sat in the grass listening to these people whom he viewed as characters in his own TV show.

There was Mr. Grogan, the salesman from Albany who seemed to be alone even when he was sitting with all the other guests. Mr. Williams wrote for television and lived in Manhattan. During the day, his wife used to sit around the pool in a leopard print bikini and Billy would sneak looks at her while pretending to read one of Mrs. Miller's books.

And there were the Langs, a heavyset couple whom Billy would have called fat if he didn't like them so much. The Langs lived in New Jersey and they always seemed to be laughing about something. One time Mr. Lang was telling everyone about how he and his wife were looking at a cigar store Indian in a local antique store.

"So this guy tells me that the thing costs $1,200," he said. "And I says, 'look, pal, I wouldn't give you that much for a *real* Indian.'"

Everybody was laughing and from his spot on the ground he could see that Mrs. Lang's cigarette lighter had slipped out of her pocketbook and fallen softly to the grass, just missing the cement walkway around the pool.

Nobody saw this except Billy and while the satellites sailed over his head, he leaned forward like he was trying to hear what the grownups were saying and slipped his hand over the lighter.

The thing was a beauty, he could tell by just by the touch, cool metal that radiated enough energy to start hundreds of fires. He closed his fingers around it and thought of the fun he could have with this baby.

She'd never notice that it was missing until tomorrow and by then she wouldn't know where she had dropped it. This is Billy's lighter now.

A freight train whistle rolled across the valley, the 10:10 was making its way through the night, the unofficial signal that it's time to go to bed, and a reminder of just how far away he was from his old life. Billy watched Mrs. Miller wishing the guests a good night and the stars shone even brighter as she smiled.

He stood up, took a step toward the main house, but he caught one more look of that lovely smile, and he turned to gently touch Mrs. Lang's hefty arm.

"Excuse me," he said, "You dropped this."

12

BILLY AND CHARLEY sat together in the Galaxy's benign darkness and watched Frank Sinatra tumble into eternal glory.

He still can't believe that Charley's really here with him. He just showed up unannounced this morning, walked right up to the front door with his "Junk man!" greeting and promised to stay the night.

"I wanted to check up on you guys," Charley gave Billy a quick tickle in the ribs. "See how things are going with my buddy here."

"Oh, everything's just fine," Mrs. Miller said. "Billy's been an absolute joy."

An absolute joy. That wasn't any trick memory talking there, that's what she actually said about him. No one had ever used those words about Billy.

And here they were, side by side in the little theater in Mount Pocono, watching Sinatra go down in a hail of German machine gunfire.

"Oh, man," Charley whispers.

Charley had driven Billy down to Stroudsburg that afternoon, the first time they were alone together and Billy had a pretty good idea what his friend was going to say.

"You know, big guy, your mom misses you very much. And your dad—he misses you, too."

Sure he does. Billy has no doubt that his father must walk the floor every night asking what happened to his son. He looked out the window and hoped Charley would talk about something else, anything else but his parents.

"She's getting better, your mother. And your dad…he's good, you know. They're both looking forward to seeing you again."

Yeah, but Billy didn't want to see them; he wanted to pretend his parents didn't exist, that they never happened. As far as he was concerned, his life had begun here.

"Yeah…"

When they got to town, Charley parked near Newberry's and got Billy an ice cream sandwich. They walked down Main Street and when Charley stopped to look in a store window, Billy ran ahead and ducked into the alley and hid. As Charley walked by, Billy snuck up behind him and poked his index finger in the small of Charley's back.

"Okay, big guy." Charley put his hands in the air. "You got me!"

When they came back for dinner and Mrs. Miller said there was an army movie, *Von Ryan's Express*, showing at the Galaxy in Mount Pocono. Billy looked at Charley, who smiled and gave him the thumbs up.

"Sure thing, big guy."

The movie house was so small, just a storefront, with no marquee; it was like a shoebox compared with the Fortway with the balcony and the lights in the ceiling that looked like stars. But Billy liked the Galaxy because it felt like it belonged to him.

In the movie Frank Sinatra leads a bunch of POWs who hijack a train and head to Switzerland. At the end, the POWs got into a firefight with German soldiers right at the Swiss border.

Frank fought off the German advance, tried to slow the krauts down so his men could get on the train and escape.

Frank's the last one, running down the train tracks while his comrades stood in the last car, urged him on as the bullets ripped through the air. Billy knew he wasn't going to die, Frank was the hero. He'll jump on that train and leave those stupid Nazis in the dust.

And just when you think he's going to make it, that Frank was on his way to Switzerland, a German officer yanked a machine gun away from one of his soldiers, took cruel, deliberate aim, and pulled the trigger.

Billy recoiled at the appalling blast of flame; Frank stumbled, sank slow and tragic to the gleaming tracks while the voice of the British major intones over Frank's fallen body like a priest giving last rites.

I once told you, Ryan, if only one gets out, it's a victory.

The POWs fell silent and watched Frank's body fade into infinity. Billy never thought death could be so noble.

"Wow," Charley said when the lights come on. "I didn't expect Frank Sinatra to get killed like that."

"Me neither." Billy nodded solemnly. "Me neither."

Frank laid down his life like so others could live. That's what the nuns said about Jesus dying for our sins. There is no greater love.

They walked back to Charley's car. It was cool out; cars were streaming on the street in both directions. The moon was high overhead; the satellites were doing their duty, faithfully circling the earth.

Billy felt like he was walking on top of the world when he abruptly sensed someone was staring with such intense hatred his skin seemed to burn. He looked over his shoulder expecting to see some demon, but found nothing but trees and darkness. A finger poked him in the ribs and Billy whipped around to see Charley smiling at him.

"Who's your buddy?"

In the morning, before Charley went back to Brooklyn, he took Billy for a ride on The Horn, a rough stretch of road somewhere around Tobyhanna.

The starting point was a sign that told drivers to sound their horns as the road suddenly shrank down to one lane.

There was a sharp right turn and then the road turned into long, crazy straightway with so many bumps and dips it could double as a carnival ride. Billy climbed into the back seat and happily handed himself over to the random will of speed and gravity.

"Here we go, big guy," Charley said as he stepped down on the gas pedal.

The car went faster and the first bump sent Billy straight up into the air, his head almost hitting the car's roof.

He'd come down laughing so hard, see Charley's smiling face in the rear-view mirror, and laugh even harder. The car would hit the next bump and Billy would be airborne again.

It was the kind of thing that would probably get you arrested today for endangering the welfare of a child or some such bullshit, but back then it was just fun.

Billy felt like he was defying gravity, defying everything and being happy, being a kid, in spite of all the heartache, all the misery back home. He sailed through the air like an astronaut in space, enjoying himself, and to hell with anyone who didn't like it.

Finally, when Billy couldn't laugh any more and the Horn ended, Charley headed back to the lodge.

Billy isn't sure where the Horn is now; the road was probably widened and paved over years ago so that it bore no resemblance to the wild place of his memory.

But even if by some act of God the Horn had remained untouched after all this time, Billy knows it would probably be nothing special, just a backwoods stretch of asphalt with a few bumps here and there.

He'd never fly out of his seat like he did when Charley was driving. He'd never laugh like that again.

They were all sitting around the pool one night, one warm, lovely night, when Mr. Lang said Hell didn't exist.

He and Billy had been talking about God and religion and Catholic school, and what happens to you after you die. The stars seemed close enough to touch, the satellites winked down at them as they passed overhead, and Billy felt like a real grown-up sitting on his beach chair talking to Mr. Lang.

Billy had said something about mortal sin and going to Hell and Mr. Lang shook his head.

"Oh, I don't believe there is such a place as Hell."

Billy thought Mr. Lang was teasing him. He was always making jokes, always had Billy laughing; he couldn't possibly be serious now.

"What do you mean?"

"I just don't believe it." Mr. Lang heaved his meaty shoulders. "I don't believe that God would create a place like that."

Billy started feeling a little nervous; dismissing Hell was inviting God to prove you wrong. In school, the nuns talked about Hell all the time, made you believe it was so real you could almost find it on the map. They made Hell as real as God.

"But God has to punish people," Billy said. "He has to make them pay for their sins."

"God is all-forgiving, right?" Mr. Lang said so gently. "If that's true, then

He'd never send anyone to Hell, no matter what they'd done. He'd forgive their sins."

Billy tried to find a way around the words. Of course God is all-forgiving; the sisters said that, too, even though they'd smash your face in for the least thing you did wrong. Even all-forgiving must have its limits.

It was strange talking about a place of endless torment in the midst of all this beauty and Billy didn't want to argue with Mr. Lang, but they were talking about their immortal souls. If there were no Hell, there'd be no reason to be good.

You little bastard…

Billy thought of his father's crushing hand around his mother's throat, the inflated face of Jesus twitching on the old man's arm. He thought of his mother curled up the floor, of all the abuse Charley taken over the years, he thought of all the evil in the world, all the bad people committing sins every second of the day, as many sins as stars in the sky.

The moon beamed overhead, satellites sailed through the darkness of space, and the 10:10 let out its lonely cry from the other side of the valley.

No, no, Mr. Lang is wrong. He must be. There has to be a Hell. There has to be a place for people like Billy's father.

13

Billy was out scraping leaves out of the pool one August morning when the phone rang in the main building.

It was another beautiful day in the Poconos, as Mr. Miller liked to say and Billy had been staying here long enough that this place was feeling more like home to him, while his life back in the city grew more distant.

When he heard the phone ringing, he jogged into the house and picked up the receiver.

"Breeze-Wood Lodge."

No one answered for the first few seconds and something told Billy to slam the phone down, cut the cord with Mrs. Miller's garden shears. But despite that warning he held on a little longer.

"Billy…?"

The voice was tense, fearful and instantly Billy knew he had made a mistake.

"It's Mommy."

His shoulders tense up and he looks around the room to see if anyone can help him, pull him away from this situation, but Billy is all by himself now. "Uh…hi…"

"How're you doing, sweetie?"

"I…I'm okay."

Billy doesn't want to do this. He doesn't want to talk to his mother, doesn't want to know anything about her or his father, and he'd give his right arm up to the shoulder if he could back up time two minutes, just two stinking minutes, so he can be back outside with the shining pool and the pure blue sky.

"Gee, honey, I haven't talked to you for so long. I miss you real bad."

She was so anxious, so frantic, like a drowning victim clawing through the surface of the water, and Billy was frightened, afraid she'd pull him down with her.

"I know it's been rough on you, baby, with me…being gone and all. It was bad and it never should've happened. I'm feeling much better now."

"Yeah…"

There was a long throbbing pause and Billy couldn't say anything, didn't want to speak at all, he was a kid for Christ's sake, why was she putting him through this? His mother finally spoke up.

"So, ah, are you having a good time up there, honey?"

Billy really wanted to tell his mother all about the Millers and all the great things he was doing up here. He wanted to share it all with her, tell her about the Langs, and the satellites, and the fountains at Mount Airy.

He wanted to tell her about going to the rodeo in Newfoundland, where real cowboys raced around poles planted in the ground.

He wanted to tell his mother about the young woman on the huge white horse that came riding right up to them just as they were leaving. Billy couldn't believe what he was seeing as this massive animal stood over him, the great head turning down and the big soft eyes looking right into his.

The horse looked so powerful, like it could leap right up into the sky and keep on going. Billy watched as the cowgirl leaned over and handed a pink prize ribbon to Mrs. Miller.

"This is for the little fella," she said.

She looked at Billy then, smiled, made the *tick-tick* noise out of the side of her mouth and cantered away.

"Well, Billy, look at you." Mrs. Miller said. "You're a real cowboy now."

She handed him the ribbon, which had the image of a horse in the center, and Billy knew he shouldn't have anything pink because it's a girl's color, but this was different. This was like a soldier getting a medal.

"You take good care of this now, Billy."

Billy nodded vigorously, swore to keep his prize ribbon for the rest of his life. And now, with the phone pressed against his ear, Billy wanted to tell his mother all about that fabulous day, how great it felt when the cow-girl handed over the ribbon and how much Billy wished his mother could have been there to see it all; he wanted to tell her so badly his chest was about to burst open, but the words wouldn't come, and so Billy's mother never heard the story about the beautiful white horse.

"It's all right," he finally said.

"That's…nice." Her voice was strained, reaching. "I had some trouble after I…y'know…got hurt, but I'm okay now."

"Uh-huh."

She paused, a warning sign that his mother was about to tell him something Billy didn't want to hear.

"I—I've been talking to Daddy."

Billy's heartbeat began to accelerate and he felt his father's presence in the room with him, here in this lovely place, like the old man was standing over him, sleeves rolled up, the Jesus tattoo stretched out over the pulsing forearm muscles.

"He's real sorry, Billy. He feels real bad about…what happened."

Fuck you, kid.

"He w-wants us to be together. He wants us to be a…a family again."

No, no, Billy shakes his head from side to side, strains the telephone cord, because she's lying, the old man doesn't want a family, he wants victims he can abuse, punching bags so he can let out all of his frustrations. He doesn't want anything like a family.

"Ah, all right, honey. I better go now. Y-you take care of yourself and maybe we could drive up there sometime soon and see you. We could meet those nice people you're staying with. Would you like that, Billy?"

No, Billy wouldn't like that at all, he wouldn't want his father coming anywhere near the Millers.

"All right, honey, you take care now…"

There was another pause and Billy knows what she's going to say now even as he thinks don't say it, please don't say it.

"I love you."

Billy flinched. Mrs. Miller was in the kitchen washing the dishes and he turned away from her, afraid the old life from Brooklyn would contaminate his new home.

The receiver felt as heavy as a stone in his hand and Billy just wanted to get away from this damn phone and go back into the glistening sunshine that beckons him to come out, come out right now.

C'mon, couldn't you say it just this one time? Couldn't you tell this poor woman that you loved her? Couldn't you do that for your own mother, you little shit?

He could hear her on the other end of the line, waiting for Billy to say it, just this one time. But he could only think of his father coming back into his life.

"All right," he said, "goodbye."

Billy could sense the pain vibrating through the phone line, he knew that she was a second away from bursting into tears, and he hung up quickly so he could run outside to the sun's healing light.

14

THAT NIGHT MRS. Miller took Billy to the carnival in Tannersville.

Mr. Miller was supposed to come along, too, but he said he felt tired and joked about not wanting to slow the young folks down.

So Billy and Mrs. Miller got into her big white car and followed the searchlight beam that cut through the night sky right down 611 to the carnival's parking lot.

Billy saw the Ferris wheel turning over the tents, the swarms of people, and he half-dragged Mrs. Miller toward the lights, the music, the food and the sound of people laughing like they'd never stop.

They ate hot dogs, popcorn, all that awful crap that Billy loved so much, went into the tents for the games of chance, where a mouse called Little Richie acted like a living roulette ball, scurrying across a giant spinning wheel, while the barker squawked "place your bets, place your bets," into a portable speaker.

They went on just about every ride, even the Ferris wheel which loomed so high over them.

Billy's back stiffened when the carny brought the safety bar in front of them, shut his eyes, terrified by the great height and the sick pull in his stomach when the wheel came down, like it was going to break free and roll right over them.

"You're not afraid are you, Billy?" Mrs. Miller whispered into his ear. "Not a brave boy like you."

She didn't make fun of him, call him a girl and say he needed a skirt. Her voice was warm, comforting, so that Billy could open his eyes when they reached the top, loosen his grip, and look down on the carnival below, like he was riding a satellite through the Milky Way.

Billy and Mrs. Miller were among the last to leave and they walked slowly back to the big Oldsmobile sitting by itself at the far end of the field.

He was so happy at this moment he felt like he could jump straight up to the moon. But as they walked across the empty lot, Billy's sense of joy and contentment faded, and he felt like they were isolated, trapped on this dark patch of ground. And Mrs. Miller, sensing his anxiety, took hold of his hand.

"Dear, dear," she sang softly, "what can the matter be?"

Billy could see the bumper sticker on her car, *God is Good All the Time* and he had just allowed himself to believe that they were safe, that he was imagining things, and that they'd get home okay, when he saw a man come out from behind a parked station wagon, as if he were lying in wait for them.

"...Johnny's so long at the fair..."

And then he was on top of them, a specter come to life. His clothes were torn, filthy, his hair was wild, and his eyes blazed with searing fury. He glared at Billy with a look of tortured rage.

Billy couldn't move; he never thought he'd ever be in any kind of danger up here, not here in this beautiful place with this woman he loved so dearly, and now the ragged man was staring down at Billy as if he were his worst enemy.

"The wicked are estranged from the womb," he croaked in a rusted voice. "The wicked go astray as soon as they be born, speaking lies."

The carnival and all its pleasures were instantly wiped away and it was just the three of them in the parking lot. This deranged man could do anything he wanted and there was no one to help them.

Mrs. Miller took a step forward and stared into the man's eyes.

"Leave us alone." She spoke in a level, forceful tone. "You just go home right now and there'll be no trouble."

But the stranger ignored her, came even closer, and reached over to Billy with his filthy hand spread wide, jagged fingernails streaking toward the boy's eyes.

"Their poison is like the poison of the serpent."

There was a loud crack as Mrs. Miller smacked that outstretched hand with all her strength and the ragged man yelped as if he'd been burned, pulled back, his face twisted with fear and anger.

He's going to hit her, he's going to tear into her with those awful hands—

"I'm warning you." She had a finger up in the man's face. "You go home right now or so help me God I'll have you locked up."

Her voice was tight and cold in a way Billy hadn't thought possible. The three of them stood motionless in the parking lot. Billy could hear the carnival noises, the distant music, the faint laughter, and he felt like it was all a mirage that would disappear the second he looked over his shoulder.

The ragged man stared at him and Billy knew that look, had seen it before when he stood before his father in the living room. He's doing the murderer's math.

Billy prayed, please God, swing that big searchlight over this way, shine it on this terrible creature and drive him back to Hell.

The ragged man took a step back, then another. He muttered something about the blood of the wicked and disappeared back into the dark. Billy and Mrs. Miller stood watching the shadows for nearly a minute before they dared to move.

"That poor man," Mrs. Miller said finally. "He needs help."

"Who is he?" Billy asked.

"He lives in his family's place up on Fairview." She said. "His name is Ethan."

15

EXHAUSTION OVERWHELMED BILLY as soon as he got into the car. With the excitement of the carnival and the confrontation with Ethan, Billy could barely keep his eyes open as Mrs. Miller drove down 611.

He was aware of the car rolling over gravel and coming to a stop, of Mrs. Miller gently shaking him, guiding him out of the car and into the house. Billy heard the train whistle, saw the beam of light slicing over the trees like God's index finger.

"Such a big day," she whispered as she tucked him into bed and stroked his chin, "you'll sleep well tonight, won't you?"

Billy closed his eyes and slid away from her and sank into a world of stifling darkness where monsters exploded from the grounds and clawed at his eyes. Billy couldn't breathe, couldn't see, and all he could hear was a woman shouting, oh, God, oh God

He opened his eyes, realized the voice was real, it was Mrs. Miller, and he got up and ran into the kitchen.

Wincing in the harsh florescent light, Billy saw Mr. Miller sitting in a chair, his shirt collar unbuttoned, his face drained off all color.

Mrs. Miller turned when she heard Billy enter the room.

"Billy," she whispered hoarsely, "help us!"

Mr. Miller wouldn't let her call an ambulance, so they walked him out to the car, his legs shaking, and headed to the hospital in East Stroudsburg.

The dirt road leading to the highway was black, nothing like the bright sunny day when he first came here with Charley; the trees were tall and menacing, and Billy sitting in the back seat thought he spotted dozens of red glowing eyes reflected in the headlight's glare.

Mrs. Miller floored the pedal once they reached the highway, so fast Billy was worried they might crash. She whispered to her husband, *we're almost there, we're almost there* as they flew by slumbering towns.

Billy looked up at the sky for any sign of the star and satellites, but the clouds had moved in between him and God.

They finally reached the hospital, helped Mr. Miller into the emergency room, and he seemed to be getting older with each step as the life leaked out of him.

The orderlies took him away in a wheelchair and Billy sat with Mrs. Miller in the waiting room. For the first time he saw how tired and weary she looked, how old she was. She squeezed his hand tightly.

"Billy, we've got to pray." Mrs. Miller whispered as if they were in church. "We've got to ask God to help us."

He tried to pray, he really did. Billy blessed himself, closed his eyes, pressed his hands together to ask God to help these people who had been so kind to him, who had taken him into their home when he had nowhere else to go.

Billy wanted to say the Hail Mary and the Our Father, but the prayers had been wiped from his memory and all could hear in his mind was the voice of that ragged man from the carnival.

"The wicked are estranged from the womb…"

They sat in that ugly, harsh room for so long, Billy's head drooping, his eyes closing, and shaking himself to stay awake, to stay with her.

"Mrs. Miller…?"

And the doctor said he was sorry, but there was nothing they could do, and Mrs. Miller stared at him for the longest time.

"No…"

That's all she said, just the one word, but with such intensity, that it carried through the entire room and other people around them stopped whatever they were doing and looked at the old woman in the corner.

Billy could feel her trembling, like her whole body was coming apart, and she squeezed his hand harder and harder, and he wanted to do something, anything to help her, but he couldn't because he hadn't prayed right, it was his fault that Mr. Miller died, and that ragged man was right about Billy after all—

Her grip went slack and she slipped away from him, collapsed to the floor while Billy started screaming and orderlies and nurses surrounded them.

He yelled and kicked at them, cursed just like his father, get your fucking hands off me, but they kept pulling him away from her. They carried him away from her, down the hall, and he strained to see her but she was lost in all the swirling bodies.

Mr. and Mrs. Lang drove down to the hospital and took Billy back to the lodge. They told him Charley was coming up from the city in the afternoon and Billy couldn't wait to see him.

He wanted to tell him his plan of living here with Mrs. Miller, helping her run the place and making sure she wouldn't be alone. She needed him now that Mr. Miller was gone. He could go to school here, live up in The Hideaway, and never go back to the city. Billy knew Charley would understand.

He was in his room when he heard Charley's car pull up, the engine's sound was unmistakable, and he ran outside to meet him. The tears started as he burst through the screen door and there was Charley, dropping to one knee, and he ran right into his arms, put his face in his buddy's chest and began crying.

"Hey, big guy, take it easy…"

"Charley—"

"—it's all right, it's all right—"

"—I tried to help—"

"It's okay, it's okay." Charley whispered into his ear. "Now you gotta go inside and pack your stuff, okay? We're gonna go back home."

Billy pulled away and looked into Charley's eyes.

"No, I can't leave. I have to stay here with her. She needs me—"

"Billy, listen, you can't stay here. You gotta come back with us."

He was wondering what Charley meant by "us" when the car door slammed again and he looked up to see his father, his fucking father, in this beautiful place, sneering down at Billy. His mother came up behind him, a timid smile on her face.

"Hi, honey…"

Billy glared at Charley, his best friend, now a traitor, who cast his eyes to the ground.

"Let's go, kid," his father growled. "I'm not waiting around this place all goddamn day."

16

Billy watched himself pack, clear out his room like he was looking at some character on a movie screen. It was strange, but as terrible as this was, it also seemed right to Billy.

It was right that he was being taken away here; it was right that he was going back to live with his father. This was what he deserved.

So he said nothing when his father took the pink ribbon that the lady on the white horse had given him, shook his head in disgust, and slowly closed his fingers around it, so Billy could hear it cracking one atom at a time.

"Get your ass in the car," the old man said as he dropped the ruined medal to the gravel.

They rode up to the church in Mount Pocono for the funeral, the last time Billy ever saw Mrs. Miller. She looked down at him, her eyes filled with such sadness, and touched his cheek.

"You take care of yourself, Billy."

They drove down 611, Charley at the wheel, his father in the dead man's seat, polishing off another can of beer and mumbling to his reflection in the mirror.

"Fucking kid," he breathed, just as they cleared the railroad bridge. "Been a curse from the day he was born."

His mother gasped and the car swerved as Charley turned to look at his father.

"Jesus, Tom," he whispered, "what the hell—?"

"What?" The old man raised his voice. "Why shouldn't I say it? It's true."

His mother put her face in a tissue and started to cry, soft, choking noises that she tried to disguise as coughing. Billy stared at the back of his father's head and wished for a knife he could drive straight through the bastard's skull.

He looked down and saw something on the floor of Charley's car, waited for his mother to turn away so he could snake his hand down, grab the prize and squeeze it tightly in his fingers.

A book of matches…

Part Five: The Wicked Are Estranged From the Womb

1

THE PUNCH COMES from somewhere out by the Milky Way, lands flush on Scotty's chin, and sends his sorry ass down to the gravel in a rolling crash.

Oh, mother, put out the cat, he thinks as his body tumbles over the pebbles and dirt.

Scotty knows he's been hit hard, extremely hard, actually, so fucking hard that he doesn't feel anything for a few sweet seconds.

But the pain is waiting on him, giving him a chance to catch up, and when he comes to his knees, oh, sweet Jesus, a solid brick curtain slams down on his brain and he flops back down to earth.

Scotty looks through the raging clouds of hurt and sees his favorite baseball cap on the ground, just inches from his bleeding mouth, his life story spelled out across the front: *Instant Asshole—Just Add Alcohol.*

Christ, he thinks, truer words were never writ.

A kick strikes his ribs and Scotty curls up in reflexive agony. Goddammit, now that was just plain uncalled for.

"Who's your buddy, mother fucker? Who's your fucking buddy now?"

The voice is low and so choked with fury, like this bastard's talking to somebody else; somebody he really wants to kill. Shit, pal, at least let me die for my own goddamn sins.

Neon hisses through the Bud sign in the bar window; traffic crawls through the Gap down below in the toll plaza, all them New York fuckhards heading to their weekend cabins while he's down on the ground getting the ever-loving shit beat out of him.

Nobody knows what's going on here and probably wouldn't give a twenty-pound rat's ass even if they did. What the hell kind of world we living in?

A pair of legs straddles his quivering body and Scotty cringes up for the coup de jour. Oh, man, five minutes ago I was a happy little cunnerman and now I'm going to die outside this dump and that is so un-motherfuck-ing-fair it's not funny.

As the five-ton shadow falls on his neck Scotty asks himself one simple little question, as he has so many times before in this three-ring disaster he calls his life.

How the hell did I get into this mess?

Well, let's see. He'd been drinking too much, of course, and, as usually is the case when he gets wasted, Scotty turns heavyweight stupid.

He liked coming down to this little joint to get shit-faced. It was so close to the highway that if the ever-increasing burden of all his busted fantasies, stupid tricks, and ugly incidents, finally got to be too much, he could imag-ine himself paying his tab, walking down the hill, and sticking out his thumb.

It was that simple: leave the car, leave the trailer, really leave that fucked up ex-wife of his, drop this whole goddamn minstrel show and hit the bricks. Yeah, you just see if I don't, you tinhorn white trash losers.

I'm not like you fuckers, he wants to shout to the rafters. I'm better than this.

Scotty is somewhere in the vicinity of his eighth beer, watching the TV flicker Australian rules football or some such horseshit when he asks him-self why, why in fuck's name did that useless dick of an ex-brother-in-law of his have to get himself killed like that?

I mean, me and Kenny were both right here that night. I drank as much as he did, and I watched him walk to his car, straight as an arrow, give or take. Simple run up the mountain and you're home—how could anyone fuck that up?

They had made plans, the two of them, they were going to do great things together, and Scotty was feeling like, damn, my luck is really changing this time.

The whole thing had been put together beautifully, all laid out to happen the next night, just 24 fucking hours away, where Scotty and Kenny were going to take down the Van Why place in Stroudsburg.

The old bastard was supposed to have a coin collection worth an estimated shitload of money, no alarms, no Dobermans, no bars on the window, none of that crap these city pricks like to install in their homes before they even unpack.

Scotty was going to be the front man, take all the risks, and all that stupid tweaker asshole had to do was stand by the door and keep an eye out for the cops.

Hell, a monkey could do that much, for God's sake, and that's probably where Scotty went wrong.

The two of them had done plenty of gigs around the county, kicked open the doors of weekend places and took everything they could fit into the truck. Middle of the day, didn't matter in these developments, with so few cops or security guards. The places were practically begging you to bust in. Just like the Van Why place.

Kenny swore up and down he was ready for this, ready for the big time. He was going to use his share of the take to get his life together, get off the shit, and make a man out of himself. They shook hands in the parking lot and off Kenny went, no more than 20 minutes from his house.

Yes, Scotty was thinking, we're really going to turn the corner on this one.

So what does that card-carrying shithead do? He dies, that's what he does, the dumb bastard, punches his ticket less than a mile from home.

Kenny was flying up 611, straight into the fog like he's A.J. Foyt streaking toward the checkered flag at Pocono Raceway and just before the railroad bridge, he managed to shear off the whole top his car beneath a tractor-trailer that had pulled out across his lane.

It was one pisscutter of a wreck, no doubt, with Kenny's empty head bouncing around the car like a runaway watermelon, and Scotty sorely wishes he had been there so he could have drop-kicked that useless blob clean into Ohio.

And so Kenny gets a closed-casket send-off and Scotty is left waxing his carrot in the hinterlands. Goddamn Kenny, he could never stand a good deal, couldn't face the fact that he might actually get a winning hand for once in his no class, bargain basement sale of a life. Probably got himself killed on purpose.

Yeah, just a few more beers and Scotty figures he'll go over to the cemetery in E-burg and gleefully piss all over Kenny's grave.

"Stupid bastard," Scotty slurs as a herd of Australians maim each other. "You deserved to die."

Naturally, Lora blamed him for killing her precious baby brother; about the only talent that malicious bitch had was pointing the finger at Scotty.

Oh, Lord, how she cursed him, words he didn't think she knew. It was a big ugly scene right in front of the house and if the neighbors hadn't been watching from behind their curtains, Scotty would have cleaned her clock right down to the gears.

The marriage was three-quarters down the crapper anyway and Kenny's demise made it official, so Scotty just packed his shit and rolled.

Her lawyer sent him some papers a short time later, which he signed without reading and put an end to that little horror show.

Scotty heard Lora was shacking up with some shitheel from New York and just thinking about that makes the beer go bitter in his mouth.

Yeah, more of them fucking bums up here, that's just what we need. This county is already the goddamn sixth borough of jungle bunny land, so what's a couple more greaseballs here and there?

I mean, shit, what the hell do people around here need to wake the hell up—a goddamn race riot?

"This seat taken?"

Great. Now he's got an asshole drinking buddy to keep him company. How lucky can a guy get? Scotty skips eye contact and gives a suit-yourself shrug. He knows a New Yorker when he hears one and this scumwad pulling up the stool next to him is hot shit on a bamboo stick.

Give it a few seconds, that's all. They'll tell you about how you can't get good bagels or decent pizza around here, and the roads are too narrow, and there's always traffic on the weekend, and there's nothing to do, and Jesus God Almighty, you want to grab the nearest bottle and christen the misbegotten bastards into a coma.

Like the rabbi said, if you don't like it here, numb nuts, take 80 East.

"Buy you a beer?"

Scotty's never been one to turn down a free bottle of the Jesus juice, but even he can draw the line someplace and he will be goddamned if he'll get stewed on some goddamn New York shitbag's tab.

"I can buy my own, skip. It's check day."

"Fair enough." The guy signals for beer and nods up at the TV. "So who's winning?"

"Fuck should I know? Bunch of faggots from New Zealand climbing all over each other don't mean shit to me."

Scott feels pretty good about that one, figures that should end this little chat real quick. But the stumby's still got that shit-gargling smile on his face.

"Yeah, right? It's like soccer. What's the story with that? Bunch of grown men running around in shorts kicking at a ball—that's a sport? Give me a break."

He's a weird-looking fucker, whoever he is, with those strange eyes and the scar on the side of his head, just odd enough to make Scotty take an instant dislike to him.

"Hey, pal, do I know you?"

"Well, not exactly, but—"

"—so then you got no reason to talk to me, do you?"

"I think there is—"

"—I don't give a Dixie fried fuck what you think, Tony, or Vinnie, or whatever the hell your name is. Just get your ass away from me and there won't be no bloodshed."

And now the bastard laughs, puts his head back and laughs out loud like Scotty just told him the funniest joke he's ever heard.

"Listen, buddy-"

"I'm not your buddy, shithead."

"Lighten up, all right? Your name's Scotty, right?"

Scotty eyeballs the guy real hard.

"What of it?"

"Oh, nothing. I hear good things about you."

"Do you now?"

"Yeah," the guy says. "You see, my name's Billy and we have a mutual acquaintance here—this lady in Mount Pocono—"

"Wait a minute." Scotty backhands a belch. "Don't tell me you're the one shacking up with that tramp? You? You're banging my ex-wife?"

This Billy character makes a guilty little grin and nods, and Scotty just about laughs himself silly.

"Oh, Jesus…"

"We got a little thing going. I hope that's not a problem…?"

"Hell, no, son. That stupid bitch is out of my life. You can hump her till shit don't stink, it's no skin off my hairy ass."

Scotty gets ready, expecting that something was about to start, an excuse for him to bust somebody up, but goddammit, he's wrong again. This dopey prick is still grinning at him. Leave it to Lora to reel in a fucking head banger.

"I'm glad there's no hard feelings. I'm not that kind of guy, you know?"

He's so polite, so good-natured; it's really pissing Scotty off. He wants to take this smart-ass out to the parking lot and kick him till he bleeds from his eye sockets.

"What do you want, buddy? That bitch blame me for starting the Chicago fire now?"

"No, no—"

"—it wasn't my fault that stupid ass brother of hers got his head lopped off. He couldn't hold his liquor, simple as that."

Billy shrugs and smiles some more.

"You know, in their grief, people will say all kinds of things they don't mean. It's human nature."

"It's bullshit."

"Okay. But the past is the past and right now there's more important things facing us."

Scotty's fingers tighten around his beer bottle.

"There's ain't no 'us,' dickhead. There's just *me* getting sick of *you*."

"Take it easy, big guy. I'm just talking about financial obligations. People have debts that they have to pay in order for things to run smoothly and avoid…bad feelings."

Scotty sits there on the stool and plays the words over again in his head at 33 and 1/3. The asshole is nodding at him, people are talking on either side of his head, and he can feel his beer going flat right there in his hand. Then he starts to laugh.

"You son-of-a-bitch, you're putting the squeeze on me, aren't you?"

"Now, hold on a second—"

"—that pig's got you working as a bill collector, huh?" He turns up the volume. "You come in here and expect me to just hand you a stack of cash because the tramp says so? Man, you got more balls than a bowling alley."

"No, no," the greaseball's waving his hands. "It's nothing like that."

"The hell it isn't, you lowlife New York scumbag." Scotty jabs the guy in the chest with the bottleneck. "Get the fuck out of here, faggot, and I mean right now. And tell that brainless slut I said to go fuck herself."

"Ah, now," Billy says, "why do you want to act like that?"

All right, that's it, that's the signal Scotty's been waiting for all night. He's going to get up and beat this cut rate pimp right through the floor, the nerve of that twat sending this monkey down here—

And then he stops breathing.

It's not by choice, of course, because Scotty would really love to be taking in oxygen right now, but his air supply's been cut off instantly like someone threw a switch.

This Billy character is sitting across from him, still working the hyena grin. Only now he's got his hand clamped around Scotty's throat and a bear trap couldn't be any tighter.

Scotty wants to scream, call out to the bartender, who's just 20 lousy feet away. But the air is squeezing out of his head and when he tries to speak, nothing, not even a decent gag, comes out of his mouth.

He feels pressure building around his neck, thinks of Kenny's head bouncing like a basketball, sees them Australian bastards playing that stupid game and he gets this urge to cry like a bitch.

"Let's go outside for some fresh air, huh?"

Oh, yes, air, that's exactly what we need, for the love of Christ, give some me air. The psycho eases Scotty off the stool and out the front door, and not one of these crack-smoking mountain freaks so much as looks up from his drink. Goddammit, I'm being murdered over here, you assholes. Don't any of you fuckers get it?

Scotty's been cut off from the space module, he's tumbling ass over tin cup through the cosmos while mission control is jerking off in the men's room.

He can barely feel the night air touching his face and then the vise is released and Scotty stands there, legs wobbling, breathing again, oh Allah, be praised, I'm breathing again. He looks up and sees how beautiful the world really is, except, of course, for this huge fist that's coming straight at him...

"Get up."

The words come as a surprise to Scotty, who's got his eyes welded shut and his body fetal crunched, expecting to be dead any second. So he doesn't move.

"I didn't hit you that hard, lard-ass," the voice says again. "Now get up!"

Scotty opens his eyes, rises real slow, so as not to look the least bit hostile. He's shaking pretty bad and he knows he'll hurt like hell and then some tomorrow, but at least he's on his feet. And looking into those weird blue eyes.

"You got a debt, Scotty. Don't you?"

"Oh, yes. I know, and don't you worry—"

"Shut up, asshole." The guy's voice is as final as death. "You're here to listen, not talk. Normally, you'd be in the river by now for half the shit you said to me. But I'm in a good mood tonight."

"I'm really glad to hear that because—"

"—thought I told you to shut up?"

Scotty slams his gums and prays this animal won't hit him again.

"You got a bill to pay, lard-ass. You got responsibilities to your ex-wife, and you just blew them off. So I'm thinking five yards ought to take—"

"Five thousand? Are you—?"

A direct hit from those eerie eyeballs is enough to shut Scotty's mouth again. No way in hell he's got that kind of money, but there's no way in hell he's going to admit that to this screaming loony.

"So we've got an understanding here?"

"We sure do."

"And you'll have the money…?"

"—in two weeks."

"How's that?"

"I mean one week…five days, tops. No problem at all."

"Good to hear, Scotty. You get the money together and I'll drop by your place on Monday."

"Oh, yeah, sure thing."

The bastard turns toward the pick-up, the one that used to be Scotty's prize fucking ride, but looks back like he forgot something.

"Oh, and Scotty?"

"Yeah?"

Too late. He gets a fist square in the gut that knocks his internal organs up into the trees. Back down to the gravel we go with Scotty choking for his life. Oh, Lord, this just ain't my night.

"Don't call her a slut no more, okay?"

"No…problemo."

This time around Scotty doesn't move a goddamn muscle until he hears the truck pulling out of the lot and vanish down Main Street.

When it feels safe, he rises, slips his hand out to the hood of the nearest car to keep from hitting the deck again and shakes his aching head.

Some piece of work Lora's found for herself. And now he's found me.

Scotty listens to the traffic noise below, all those cars, all those people, going to all those places. He could always join them, like he's been threatening to for all these goddamn years. Now would be a perfect time to fade from this little piece of scenery.

But to be honest, Scotty knows that no matter where he ends up, it'll only take him a month or so before he's neck deep in shit all over again. Some people just have the knack.

And this fucker here, you just know he's the type that will follow you right up to the Bering Strait and feed your nuts to the nearest polar bear.

Use your brain, cunnerman. Somebody who's that socially maladjusted must have all kinds of enemies in this world; the sort who'll pay good money to know where he is.

Scotty turns and walks back into the bar, uncertain if he's hit the daily double or just signed his own death warrant. Either way he needs another beer.

Billy, young and ferocious, walked up the stairs of his house after an all-nighter with Sal and Vince determined to murder his father.

As he climbed the steps, he could hear the Rheingold jingle howling full blast out of the TV, knew the old man would be in his recliner, barricaded behind a line of empties and an ashtray full of crushed Marlboros, his stubbled face stupidly aimed at the afternoon game.

….it's not bitter, not sweet, it's the extra dry treat…

Yeah, I got a treat for you, asshole. Right between the fucking eyes. His mother was visiting her cousin in Staten Island so there was no danger that they'd be interrupted, which was good because Billy was going to settle things today.

This had been building for so long, ever since Billy had dropped out of the womb, actually, but things shifted to critical this morning when he had crashed on Sal's couch at some ungodly hour and dreamed he was strangling a man in a hooded sweatshirt, squeezing and squeezing the loser's throat until Billy's skin turned to fire.

He woke up shaken, covered in sweat, and barely able to breathe. And he knew his father had to die.

Billy saw it all in his head, a private 3-D screening of the entire battle, as he stood before his father, kicked over the coffee table and roared, c'mon, big guy, let's go!

And then they'd tear into each other, oh, fuck, yeah, full on *Five Fingers of Death*, busting up furniture, crashing through walls, gleefully demolishing this cursed house until one of them was stretched out on the dining room floor beaten, butchered, and deader than Kelsey's nuts.

This is going to be great, Billy thought, as he reached the landing. This is going to be fucking glorious.

Sure, he might get killed, or maimed for life or go to jail for the next 20 years, but Billy didn't give a shit about any of that as long as he got the chance to inflict some phenomenal damage on his father before the cops showed up.

He walked into the living room and there was the old man, useless fuck, wearing his boxers and sleeveless t-shirt, eyes locked on the game. Billy approached him slowly, his muscles coiled and ready to snap.

His brain clattered like an abacus, taking inventory of every brutal act his father had ever committed, every beating, every harsh word and deed, all of his unforgivable offenses lined up in Billy's memory

Okay, scumbag, now it's your turn.

Billy knocked the coffee table aside, taking down the skid row of empty beer cans, sending the brimming ashtray to the floor, and squared off in his most wicked Little Dragon stance. Let the game of death begin….

But something was wrong, seriously wrong with this picture. His father wasn't moving, wasn't reacting at all.

Shit, Billy had done enough to get this psycho son-of-a-bitch flying out of the recliner with both fists up and his eyeballs rolling like dice in a wind tunnel. But the old man just sat motionless in his chair, his face paralyzed in a Halloween mask of rage.

Billy took a step forward, looked closely and saw that his father wasn't breathing.

He could faintly hear Ralph Kiner talking about what a bad day it had been for the Amazins, how they had blown a three-run lead in the bottom of the ninth inning, and you didn't have to be Columbo to figure out that Billy's father couldn't handle the torment of seeing his favorite team suffer yet another senseless defeat.

The Mets beat you to it, big guy. They killed the old man deader than shit.

And now Billy was standing there with all this anger, all this fury tearing through his heart, and there wasn't a goddamn thing he could do with it. This bastard had caused more pain, more misery than all the plagues of Egypt combined, but he got to ease out of this life like an old German shepherd taking a nap.

"No, no!" Billy screamed, glaring into his father's lifeless eyes, "No, you mother fucker!"

He fell to his knees and smashed on the floor with his fists, no, no, the prick can't get away this easy. We got business him and me. Fuck the eternal fires of Hell, even if they do exist, Billy needs his vengeance in this world, not the next.

He wanted to pound his father's chest, restart that vile heart, just so he can beat the bastard to death fair and proper. Billy has to humiliate his old man, stomp him so brutally that he starts crying, crying like a little girl. He'd waited so long for this day to come, Billy can't believe it's been stolen from him.

He rose, grabbed the old man's t-shirt and pulled, felt the dead weight resistance as his father's head lolled to one side. There's nothing here, big guy, not one shred of life. He's gotten away from you.

Billy stepped back, reared up to roundhouse kick this shitbag square in that mirror-cracking face of his, but he stopped himself when he realized how useless it would be. He looked at the corpse that used to be his father

"Lucky you," he whispered and walked out of the room.

He had to leave, get away from this goddamn place, and so he stormed out of the house, tears streaming down his face, down Senator Street, across Sixth Avenue, walking against the light and in front of honking cars, through the park, crashing into anyone who got in his way and over the highway.

Billy didn't know where the hell he was going or what he wanted to do when he got there, but he was going to do it in a big way.

He finally stopped when he reached the Fortway, distantly recalled the good times he'd had there when he was a kid, and looked around for a target, someone or something he could attack.

His eyes hit on the liquor store across the street, to the asshole sitting alone behind the counter and Billy hated the prick the second he saw him, a hopeless fat slob sitting on his ass all day. He paused for a minute, dug his hand deep into his jacket pocket just like the old movie gangsters, and walked toward the door.

This is going to be fucking glorious…

2

THE SMELL HITS them as soon as they turn on to the driveway, a paralyzing stink of burnt wood, seared fabric and melted plastic that crashes down on the property line like an invisible wall.

Sal grimaces, even with the windows closed the odor is killing him, and he struggles to keep the muscle bound Buick in line.

Matty sits silently in the dead man's seat as Sal guides the massive vehicle down the narrow dirt road. The stench grows stronger, Sal's almost in tears it's so bad, but the old man refuses to pay any respect to the crippling air that's filling up the car.

Sal hasn't been to The Hideaway in over a year and he remembers when the house was a refuge for him, a place where he could hang with his buddies without having to worry about anything.

That's all changed now. The woods seem thicker now, wilder. Dangerous. The trees hang lower, branches scratch at the side of the car, and pebbles kick up against the windshield as if nature itself is trying to run them off.

He hears voices coming from the undergrowth, taunting him like a whore on a dead end street. Come on, big guy; come here and see what I got for you.

And the car, this goddamn rhinoceros, is fighting him every inch of the way, like it knows what's waiting for them down there and doesn't want to go.

He yanks the steering wheel, stomps on the gas pedal, sweating heavily and cursing under his breath, worthless pile of shit, for two cents I'd drive you into the nearest lake.

When they pull around that last bend and see what's actually happened, Sal's grip on the steering wheel goes slack and his voice sinks to a whisper.

"Oh, my fucking God…"

Matty doesn't speak, doesn't make a sound, like he croaked right here on the spot and Sal, still in shock, has to hit the brake to keep from crashing into a tree.

The two of them sit in the idling car and stare at The Hideaway's mortal remains.

"Help me out of the car," Matty says hoarsely.

"But—"

"Help me out of the goddamn car, Sal."

Sal kills the engine, climbs out of the Buick and the smell hits him full on, Jesus, like talons tearing at his lungs.

He tries to avert his eyes from the debris as he walks to the trunk to get the wheelchair, but he can't; he's got to look at the devastation.

The house, the place that Matty took from Jerry LaRocca a generation ago, is gone. What's left, this gutted carcass, is surrounded by yellow tape like a corpse at a murder scene.

Only the front steps and the ramp are intact, untouched by the fire and leading to empty air.

The outer walls are nothing more than jagged stumps and a pile of mangled furniture, seared by flame and blasted by relentless jets of waters, squats in the middle of what used to be the living room like the entrails of a slaughtered animal.

Sal can see straight through to the back of the house where a surviving piece of the rear wall holds a solitary window in place and he catches himself stupidly looking through the shattered glass to the trees in the back.

It's like something from the Bible, he thinks, like God destroyed the place with a lightning bolt.

You can feel the hatred coming off of the rubble, long after the fire's been extinguished; evidence that somebody really wanted to destroy this place, to wipe it off the face of the earth.

The local fire chief, a big hayseed with a red Viking beard, said the place burned so furiously that the volunteers had to come back just before dawn, and beat the flames down a second time. A re-kindle, he called it.

Sal's heart lurches when he spots a pair of eyes staring at right at him from the center of the pile, but he sees that it's the old polar bear rug, charred and tattered, the head glowering at anything that crosses its lifeless line of sight.

Sal had picked up the local paper on the way over, and there it is in the back seat with the front-page photo of the house in flames; the word "Inferno" jumps out from the sub-head.

The photographer should probably get some kind of prize for that picture, it's that good, but Sal knows Matty will want to have the guy's arms broken.

"Sal…?"

He jumps at the old man's voice, pulls open the back door and unfolds the wheelchair. Matty turns in his seat, and Sal comes around quickly to help the Cigar into the wheelchair and rolls him up to the yellow tape.

Matty is quiet for a few seconds, looks over the debris like he's trying to identify a beloved child. He sits back heavily in the wheelchair and shakes his head.

"Twenty years, Sal," he whispers. "Twenty years we had this place…"

"I know, Matty, I know."

"All the work we put into this house. All the great times we had here, all the memories…and it's all just…fucking gone."

The old man's head goes down, the shoulders start shaking, and, oh my God, is Matty, Matty fucking Cigar crying?

Sal's never seen the old man even come close to shedding tears, not once in all this time, and he'd sooner dive head first into the smoldering ruins than watch Matty go to pieces like this.

"What happened here, Sal?" Matty makes no attempt to wipe his face. "What happened to our house?"

"Well, Matty, the cops said—"

"Don't tell me about the cops." Matty whips his head around and glares at him. "I don't want to hear about no fucking cops. Tell me what you know."

Sal hangs limply in the scorched air.

"Matty…this kind of shit, it happens up here all the time. These people up here, they're inbreds; they're all fucking crazy. They got nothing to do, but get high and burn down houses."

"What about the alarm?" Matty backs up to get even with Sal. "How come the alarm didn't go off? These people you're talking about, they know the goddamn code?"

"I-I don't know—"

"What the fuck else is new?"

3

SHE WAS CRYING, that's what Sal remembers most from this morning, sitting on the couch after another night without sleep, and watching Iris wipe her eyes, telling him that she couldn't take it anymore, that she had to get out.

"You're like a dead man!"

The TV was on, no sound, just the video of a plane crash somewhere in the world with flaming wreckage and stacked body bags. Sal knew he should do something, anything, instead of sitting on his ass while his wife walked out on him, but he was so tired.

The phone rang, it could only be Matty, like the old man was calling to claim credit for the disaster. See that, Sal? I did that. I can strike anywhere in the world.

His wife left as he picked up the receiver, slammed the front door behind her as she went, and then Sal was behind the wheel of the car, driving Matty up I-80.

Every 20 miles or so the old man would mutter "I don't fucking believe it" and then fall silent.

Sal was dimly aware that he was driving, but it was all instinct. He was barely awake, barely alive, behind the wheel, and his pulse only started to quicken when he saw the Delaware coming up on his left.

They must be across the river from the rest area on 611, the spot where he shot Billy.

I'm sorry—

He kept his head down, his eyes on the back of a fruit truck creaking ahead of him. Sal wouldn't look over at the Pennsylvania side; he didn't want to see Billy's ghost smiling at him across the dark water.

"Hey, Sal," Matty said, "will you go around this asshole already? Drive any slower and we'll be going backwards for Christ sake."

Sal did like he was told; he always did what Matty told him to do, so without looking at his mirrors, he drove into the path of the biggest 18-wheeler known to man.

It was like the thing dropped from the clouds, beamed onto the highway doing 70 mph. The screaming horn almost lifted him out of his seat and he threw the car back into his lane.

"What the fuck are you doing?" Matty shrieked into his ear. "You trying to get us killed?"

"I-I'm sorry, Matty. I didn't see the bastard."

"How the hell could you miss him?"

Sal didn't answer, didn't say anything about Billy's angry spirit blinding him to the rest of the world. He kept his mouth shut, fixed his eyes on the fruit truck's rear end, and didn't look anywhere else until they drove through the toll plaza.

The cops were useless, of course. Sal and Matty tried to tell the fire marshal, a pumped-up state cracker with a buzz cut and full-time smirk, that they really had no idea who would do something like this, that they were the victims here; but they could see the prick didn't believe anything these two greaseballs from Brooklyn had to say.

That cop knew who they were; the son-of-a-bitch was obviously glad Matty's house burned down and standing here now looking at the ruins, Sal realizes that he feels the same way.

No, seriously, Sal's happy that the house is gone, that the Cigar's precious fucking castle has been cooked. He's glad somebody torched this dump that means so much to this old bastard. He only wishes he'd had the balls to do it himself.

Look at the stupid old man, Sal thinks, staring at this pile of ashes like he can order the charred house back to life. Good luck with that, grandpa. The house ain't ascared of you at all.

Sal feels so powerful, so strong, he could pick Matty up, wheelchair and all, and toss him into the ashes. Here, tough guy, let's see you fix this—

Matty turns his way at that very moment, like he was mindreading him, and Sal almost craps his pants.

"You know, Sal," the Cigar says in slow motion, "if I didn't know any better…"

Oh, Christ, here we go.

"…I'd swear Billy had done this."

"Matty, c'mon—"

"I know it sounds crazy, but I swear, if I didn't know that scumbag was dead, I'd say he burned our house down."

"Yeah, but that's impossible." Sal swallowed quickly. "Billy's dead."

"Yeah, yeah. But it would be just like him to do something like this. It's… it's almost like he's still with us."

Maybe you should go down there. Maybe you should suck—

"Billy's dead." Sal's voice rises. "He's fucking dead."

Matty gives him a look that says you ought to know, pal.

"Yeah, I know that, Sal. It's just this shit with the code. I can't figure that."

The perspiration squeezes out of Sal's skin, like the temperature has suddenly jumped 50 degrees.

Who cares about the goddamn code? The place is gone; it doesn't matter anymore. These freaks with the computers can crack into Fort Knox if they feel like it.

"Yeah, Matty, who knows? Maybe Vince did this."

"Sal…"

"No, really." His voice gets louder. "Maybe my cousin came back from the dead and set the house on fire"

Are you gonna kill me?

"C'mon, Sal. Stop talking like this."

Sal feels heat on his face and neck, there's a dozen pairs of eyes staring at him from behind the trees. Where are you, you fuck? Show yourself, for Christ's sake. Get this goddamn thing over with.

"Maybe I did it, Matty. Huh? Maybe I got up in the middle of the night, drove all the way up up here and torched the fucking place."

Sal tries to look defiant, righteously angry, but the resentment fades as Matty stares into him.

"Cut it out Sal. We don't got time for this bullshit."

But Sal doesn't want to stop; he's not a dead man, he's alive and well, and he furiously points at what's left of the Hideaway.

"I'm gonna find the fuck who did this," he says, near screaming. "I don't care what I gotta do. I gonna find this scumbag and when I done with him he's gonna curse his mother for giving birth to him!"

Sal steps back, reeling from expending energy he doesn't have. But he feels good now, like he's shown the old man what he's made of.

And then the cell phone in his coat pocket starts drilling a hole straight through his chest.

4

Lora drinks her coffee at the kitchen table while reading about the big fire last night.

Four companies responded, nobody injured; the house a total loss. Look at those flames coming out of every window, like the blaze that destroyed Old Ethan's place. Sure been a lot of fires around here lately.

The paper said the house belonged to some alleged mobster from New York who was recently acquitted of criminal conspiracy charges in federal court. Lora tries to read some more, but she's thinking about Billy coming home this morning just before dawn.

He moved so quietly like someone used to sneaking around, but she heard him come up the stairs, go into the bathroom, and seconds later the shower came on.

Billy tried to run it low, but at that time of night it sounded like a downpour. He was cleansing himself, but of what?

And then he came into the room wearing nothing but a towel, fresh and powerful, and slid into bed next to her. As soon as she moved, they were going at it, wild and rough, like he'd just got out of prison after a 10-year stretch.

Lora was going to have it out with him this morning over breakfast, demand to know what the hell's going on around here, why he pulls this disappearing act every night.

But she didn't say any of that, just put out the food on the table, made some useless chit-chat, and watched him go out the door humming that "Glorious" tune with a plastic bag under his arm.

Lora knew what was in that bag, without even looking inside the damn thing; it was Billy's clothes from last night and she knew that he was going to throw them away some place far from the house. He was going to destroy the evidence.

And now here she is reading about the big fire, looking at Billy's windbreaker that's hanging on the cellar doorknob, the one piece of clothing he forgot to take with him this morning, and she's asking herself one simple question.

Do I smell smoke?

Matty glares at Sal, irritated at the sound of the cell phone. He hates cell phones and beepers; hates them like a witch doctor hates penicillin, and he hates them even more when they go off while he's performing major surgery on somebody's asshole.

You could never explain to him that cell phones are a necessity nowadays; pretty soon everybody and his brother's going to have one. Matty had decided that they were a menace and he didn't want nothing to do with them.

The screeching bites into Sal's chest again and the old man's scowl deepens.

"You gonna take care of that?"

"No, Matty. Whoever it is, they can wait."

But the goddamn thing goes off again and now the old man's staring at Sal and gripping the handles of his wheelchair. Sal pulls out the phone, prays it's Iris calling to give him another chance, but he already knows who's calling. He smiles weakly, takes out the phone and wonders why in hell he ever bought this goddamn thing.

"Yeah?"

"Sal…"

"Hey, how's it going?" Sal puts a sham lilt to his voice as his stomach pulls in. "How you been?"

"Please, I'm crawling the fucking walls here."

"Oh, really? Well, listen, we'll have to talk about this later—"

"I seen him, Sal, I fucking seen him with my own two eyes, right outside the house."

"No, I don't really think that's possible"

"Please, you gotta get me out of here."

The phone burns around Sal's head like it's going to melt down the side of his face. He's got to hang up.

"Okay, so I'll talk to you later—"

"Please, Sal, for Christ's sake, you gotta help—"

He switches the phone off on the sobbing squawks. A thin shell of sweat lines his forehead and his legs tremble beneath him. He coughs a few times before turning back to Matty.

"That your wife?"

"Uh, yeah."

"Everything all right between you two?"

"We're having some problems." Sal forces himself to shrug. "You know how it is."

Matty nods and looks back to the house. It seems like he's decaying before Sal's eyes; a fast-forward nature film of a rotting corpse. The fire has hurt the Cigar like nothing Sal has ever seen.

"Let's get the hell out of here."

5

MATTY'S OFFICE IS hot enough to double as a sauna and all the eyeballs burning in his direction jacks the Fahrenheit up another 50 degrees, but Billy is all smiles tonight.

He proudly bares the hideous bruises that Jake inflicted upon him outside the liquor store, the swollen jaw, the right eye three-quarters shut, and yet somehow these appalling injuries manage to look good on him. Fucking Billy, how does he do it?

The legend of Billy and Jake is only a few days old, but people around here know the story the way school kids know about George Washington and the cherry tree.

Matty Cigar sits before him, looks Billy up and down like he's a prize racehorse he's thinking of buying. Sal stands behind his friend sweating so fiercely he's liable to slip through the floorboards.

He'd bent back far enough to yodel up his asshole to get Billy this audience with the Cigar and it's got to go perfectly for Christ's sake or they're both heading for the landfill.

And now Matty blows out a column of smoke to pave the way for his sacred words.

"I hear good things about you."

That's it, that's the phrase that'll take you out of the sewer and right to the Promised Land, no humping around the desert for 40 fucking years, no eating other people's shit until you die.

The room is silent, nobody dares to speak, breathe or think. It's up to Billy to show the old man the respect he's due. He's got nowhere to go and he can't possibly afford to fuck this up. But Billy holds onto that smile of his and adds a shrug.

"Yeah, well, I've heard some good stuff about you, too."

He can hear Sal fighting to hold down his dinner. What the fuck, Billy? You're supposed to grovel before the Cigar, give thanks to Almighty God that he even looks in your direction, let alone considers taking you on.

What kind of psychopath cops an attitude with the most terrible person who ever lived?

But Billy doesn't want to be no houseboy, not after growing up under the same roof as his fucking father. No, you've got to take Billy just as he is or you can kiss his ass.

Any other loser would've been facedown on the floor already and bleeding from a score of fatal wounds. But Matty does the unthinkable and smiles back at the young upstart.

"Oh, really? And what is it that you've heard about me, Billy?"

Billy pauses to take a look at all the guys in the crew who are trying to stare him into submission.

"I hear you don't take no shit from nobody."

"Yeah, Billy, I guess you could say that. From what I hear, you don't either."

"Oh, you shoulda seen it, Matty," Sal jumps in on a rescue mission. "I thought that fucking cop was going to drop dead, he was wailing on Billy so hard--"

His voice goes dim when Matty and his best friend give him a solemn look.

Billy doesn't need Sal's help, not Sal's or anybody else's. He's already connected with the old man in a way that no one in this bunch ever has.

"I do what I gotta do," Billy says.

"That's good, Billy." Matty takes a long draw on his Cuban. "That's the kind of guy I'm looking for. Somebody who ain't afraid of no cops, who'll keep his mouth shut, and do what he's told. How's that sound to you?"

Billy, this punk, this nobody, he actually pauses, the son-of-a-bitch, like he and The Cigar are forming a partnership.

"Yeah," he finally says, "that sounds pretty good."

Pretty good? Why you worthless little hard-on, everyone in that room is thinking, where the fuck do you get that kind of nerve? Everyone except Matty, of course.

"Okay, then, Billy," Matty stands up, extends his hand. "Thanks for coming by."

"My pleasure." Billy takes the Cigar's hand. "Anytime."

"And since you know so much about me, then I don't gotta tell you what happens to people who fuck me over."

"No, I got that already."

The two men embrace, and it's real, a boundless love charges through Billy's heart, conjoined with a searing hatred; and he's ready to shed tears of joy and sink his teeth Matty's jugular hard enough turn the walls of this hovel a deep shade of crimson.

And it'll be like that for as long as they both shall live.

"Billy," the Cigar says, smiling. "Billy the Kid."

"That's me."

Billy turns around, tosses Sal a wink as his walks out the door. Sal pauses, nods to Matty and follows his friend out into the dark.

Lora is taking the trash out to the back when she sees that the shed door is ajar.

She was trying not to think about the smell coming off Billy's jacket or last night's four-alarmer. Is she going to blame him every time a house burns down somewhere in the county? Jesus, give the guy a break. But still...

She shakes the thoughts away, turns to go back inside, but there's that door, open just an inch or two. There's nothing of any real value in there, but you don't want to invite trouble.

Lora walks over to the shed, pulls back the door to give it a good slam, and stops when something on the ground catches her eye.

She bends down, picks up a piece of carved wood, and she's really wishing she had stayed the hell out of here.

It's a sign, painted dark green with white letters and when Lora reads the words she almost forgets to breathe.

The Hideaway.

They reach the toll plaza as the sun is going down. Sal had prepared the lie about having his place painted so they couldn't stay tonight, but he didn't need it. Matty wanted to get back to the city.

The old man stares out the window while Sal's brain involuntarily replays the phone call, that desperate, terrified voice.

"Fucking people…they're all the same," Matty says. "They think they can fuck me over and I'm just gonna put up with it?"

"Matty, I told you, we're gonna get the bastards who did—"

"I'm not talking about that."

What is it then?

"That…*tramp.*" Matty snarls over the word. "She's putting the arm on me. I don't got enough to worry about, I got to deal with her bullshit, too."

"Who?"

"Billy's wife, that's who!" Matty shouts. "That skank is trying to shake me down."

"Lucille? What'd she do?"

"She wants to meet with me, the bitch. She calls up the club and demands, she fucking demands, that I drop whatever I'm doing and go see her, for Christ's sake."

Sal can't believe Lucille did something like that. And he doesn't understand why he's just hearing about it now.

"But what does she want?"

"She wants money, Sal." The old man shakes his head in disgust. "She's a broad. That's what they all want. You're old enough to know that."

He hasn't seen Lucille in months, not since the service for Billy when she glowered at him with such unrestrained hatred that Sal wanted to run out of the church.

"Who does this bitch think she is, pulling this crap on me?" Matty says. "I don't take that shit from nobody."

"Matty, please, let's not—"

"—that…that whore is trying to order me around like I'm some fucking nigger. And after all I done for her."

Sal almost wrenches his neck to keep from doing a double-take. What he's done for her—like murdering her husband, destroying her family, and driving her to drink?

"She's still hurting over Billy."

"So what?" Matty shrugs. "I gotta worry about that slut because that lowlife bum she married finally got what he deserved? Give me a fucking break."

This is how it always starts, with somebody hitting the Cigar up for money. And it ends with somebody dead.

"Matty, you're not gonna…do nothing, are you?"

"What do you mean, Sal?"

Sal squeezes the steering wheel.

"I mean you're not going to…hurt nobody, right?"

They're coming up on the death spot, the point across the river where they left Billy. Matty shakes his head sadly.

"Sal, what's wrong with you? The woman's got a kid. I mean, Jesus Christ, what do you think I am?"

I know exactly what you are. I know better than anyone.

"It's just that I don't like her coming on so strong like that, that's all." He looks into the river. "But there's no way I'm going to hurt a woman."

You lie like a rug. They used to say that to each other when they were kids. You lie like a rug. It's sounds so stupid now, but it was a big deal in the playground. Sal has to bite down on his lip to keep the words from breaking free.

"I'm gonna meet with her tomorrow, hear what she has to say."

"So what time you want me to pick you up?"

"No, don't worry about it. I'm going to have Train take me."

"Train?"

"Yeah, I wanna start giving him more to do." Matty looks at him. "That's okay with you, Sal?"

"Sure, Matty, that's fine."

Sal guides the Buick down the highway and recalls the first time they all made this run, so many years ago, to take care of that loser who was hiding out in Stroudsburg.

He thinks how strange, how sick it is that after all these years, that trip has come back to torment them all.

A re-kindle, they call it.

6

BILLY SLIDES THROUGH the woods like a grizzly stalking its supper, nails a spot behind a tree and looks down at the house that is rightfully his.

That's it. That's my new home.

He is so angry right now, so furious he could uproot this tree he's using for camouflage with one hand and spearchuck it right through the front window.

Billy should be inside that house right now. He should be enjoying his life, smoking a cigar, drinking some brandy, and watching Frank Sinatra on the widescreen; not humping around the tree line waiting for his head to explode.

The house looks terminally empty, like even ghosts wouldn't want to haunt the place. No cars in the driveway, no lights on inside, no signs of life at all.

Billy came here to do business, packing the tire iron, lighter fluid, and a soul full of malice. He feels good after deep-frying Matty's place; so good he can't wait to do it again.

He smiles, certain the old man must've gotten the news by now; he must know that his hallowed Hideaway's been burned to shit. You gotta take the pain, big guy.

The Cigar must be heading up this way now, with Sal doing the spook work behind the wheel. Hell, they might be here already.

Billy would give both lungs and a kidney to see the look on Matty's face when he gets there. He'll get so mad, smoke will pour out of his ears, and he'll scream, oh, Christ Almighty, how that old bastard will scream. Shame to miss it.

Billy had considered an ambush. Pick a spot nearby, bum rush them two faggots and blast them bloody with Matty's own gun. It would be over in seconds. But there might be cops, volunteers, and other assorted losers hanging around the fire scene.

So he came here instead to give Sal the treatment, so the backstabbing prick can see how it feels. And if those two just happen to swing by here this afternoon while Billy is on the premises, then we'll have a nice little reunion.

Billy figures to crack the rear door and go in through the kitchen. It'll be good to tear through Sal's worldly possessions, deface every thing that fat scumbag owns and then set the whole mess on fire. It'll be like the Fourth of July.

Only he hasn't moved from his spot behind the tree. All these evil thoughts, all this rage, and here he is still looking at the place, still thinking how it was all supposed to be different.

This is necessary, big guy, you can't afford to be sentimental here.

But he wonders how different his life would be if he had lived in this house, if he would suddenly stop fighting with Lucille, stop cheating on her, stop hitting her. He wonders if he would've gotten along with Tommy if they had all moved up here as a family. And he wonders what he would have done if Matty called him from the city and said some stupid son-of-a-bitch needs a little fire drill.

When I grow up, Charley, I'm gonna have my own house up here and you can come stay with me any time you want.

Billy kicks this big goddamn tree as hard as he can, over and over, chips off bark in all directions and probably breaks half the bones in his foot.

He's stumbling back a few feet to get some more distance when he sees something moving in the bedroom window.

Billy stares hard at the house, scans the place for any sign of life. Maybe it was just sunlight bouncing off the glass or maybe somebody's spying on him. Matty's gun hangs heavy on his belt and Billy eases his fingers around the grip.

Something snaps behind him and Billy whips around, the gun in his hand, to see bushes moving just so slightly, as if brushed by the wind or a fleeing animal.

Billy stands motionless, holds on to the silence, and pulls it apart in search of any sound that doesn't belong.

His head starts to throb, connecting with the pain climbing up his leg; and Billy suddenly feels pretty stupid standing here aiming a gun at nothing. He thinks maybe he should pay a visit to Vince's house and torch that shithole instead. Let Vince be next on the hit parade.

He puts the gun away, turns back to the house for a last look.

"See you soon," Billy says and walks back to the car.

7

Lucille hides by the reptile house with her car keys in her hand and spies on the old man at the picnic table.

Look at him sitting in his wheelchair reading the paper. If you didn't know any better, you'd think he was some nice old grandpa out enjoying the warm weather.

People walking by don't pay attention to him, probably don't even see him; but if they knew who he was, they'd grab their kids and run to the nearest exit.

She keeps watching Matty, as he thumbs through *The Daily News*, sips a cup of concession stand coffee, and waits, waits at the table because that's what Lucille told him to do.

She still can't believe the way she screamed at Matty; shrieked herself hoarse at one of his mutts until she finally shamed the old bastard into coming to the phone.

Now you listen to me, goddammit—

She went crazy, blamed him for just about everything that ever went wrong in her life, called him a coward, a scumbag, a murderer, yes, she actually called him that, and she didn't give a damn if J. Edgar Hoover was listening in from beyond the grave.

He took it; every curse, every accusation, every vicious word. Matty let Lucille swear at him, threaten him, and demand that he meet her someplace and not his godforsaken rat's nest, hell, no, but out in the open so they could sort out all this bullshit.

Jesus, nobody screams at Matty Cigar, at least not more than once. Look what happened to your husband.

But that was Billy, not Lucille. He was the one with the death wish, not her. Lucille isn't trying to get herself killed out of some sick desire to pay for her sins. She wants to live, damn it.

Her eyes scope around the picnic area looking for the back-up; she scans faces and body types, mothers with baby carriages, fathers holding screaming kids by the hand, until she spots that steroid-sucking no-neck with the dyed blond hair standing by the trash can in a blue warm-up suit. No more calls please, we have a winner.

Train is just far enough away from the old man to look like they're strangers, but close enough to get to Matty's side if he's needed. Christ, that guy looked so much like the old man you'd think it was a father and son outing. And poor old Jerry went to his grave knowing that.

Matty cranks his head like an old monitor lizard and Lucille would love to see the zookeepers throw a net over him and drag him to the nearest cage. He's the most dangerous animal in this place.

The old man turns her way and Lucille ducks back out of sight. She's heard how snakes hypnotize their prey before the kill and she's not taking any chances.

She wishes she hadn't picked this place. A mall, a diner, even the ferry would've been better. But the zoo was the first thing that came to her mind when Matty asked her where she wanted to do this thing.

Lucille hasn't been to the Staten Island Zoo in years, not since Tommy was a little kid, and three of them had come here as an attempted family.

She always hated snakes, fucking things gave her nightmares, but the boys had insisted on going to the reptile house and she didn't want to be the killjoy.

So Lucille followed Billy and Tommy into that dank, man-made cavern, where the sign warned visitors not to wave anything at the snakes because "some of them have a nervous disposition and might injure or kill themselves against the glass."

They have a nervous disposition?

Each snake had a sign indicating their names and eating habits. The deadly ones all had a single word of warning spelled out in bright red block letters: venomous.

They had timed it perfectly that day, of course, arriving just as the snakes were being fed their ration of dead rodents, so she had to stand there with her husband and child and watch a block-long python slowly, so unbelievably slowly, suck down a white rat carcass.

She saw other women lifting their kids up so they could get a better view of this obscenity, but all Lucille could do was stand there paralyzed and pray for it to end. It was worse than any horror movie she'd ever seen and naturally Billy and Tommy couldn't get enough.

They laughed as each rodent's corpse disappeared, right down to the tail, and laughed harder when they saw Lucille's face work through five shades of green.

"Hey, Lou," Billy shouted so everyone in the place could hear, "where do you want to go for lunch?"

She'll never forget how her stomach pitched and tumbled that day; she's never felt that sick before or since. Until today. She drops the keys into her purse and takes a deep breath.

It's feeding time.

8

MATTY LOOKS UP when Lucille approaches the table and for a second she sees a flash of raw animal rage cut across the old man's eyes. But it disappears as the Cigar pulls his yellowed teeth back into a bloodless smile.

"Lucille!" Matty spreads his arms wide. "It's so good to see you."

She walks toward him like she's just learning how, one foot in front of the other, left foot, right foot.

"Yeah, Matty, you, too."

She forces herself to lean over, kiss those dusty wax cheeks, while his arms come up around her and squeeze, just hard enough to let her know he could hurt her if he felt like it.

"I swear to God," he says as Lucille sits down across from him, "you get more beautiful every time I see you."

"Oh, stop." She stifles the urge to spit in his face. "I'm just so glad you could meet me like this. I know how busy you are."

"C'mon, Lou, you know I always got time to see you." His grin widens. "And how often do I get to go to the zoo?"

They laugh together, just like they're supposed to. It's the ritual, the dance that they're required to do before they get down to the real subject.

It doesn't matter that he really wants to throw his coffee into Lucille's face or that she wants to leap across the table and claw his eyes out. They've got to do this right.

"So, tell me, Lucille, how are you doing?"

She coughs lightly to swallow the curses bubbling in her throat. How am I doing? Is that what the son-of-a-bitch asked me?

"Well, it's been tough, Matty." She looks down at the table. "Ah, listen, I'm sorry about the way I acted over the phone—"

"—please, Lucille." Matty holds up a benevolent hand. "Don't even think about that. I know it's been rough on you, losing your husband, raising a son on your own. If you're not entitled to blow your stack every now and then, who is?"

"Yeah, it's just that…with Billy, you know—I miss him so much."

"Of course, you do, sweetheart. We all do, crazy guy that he was. I tell you, he was like one of my own. And that's the God's honest truth."

"Oh, I know that, Matty." She shifts slightly on the bench. "And he felt so close to you. He told me that all the time."

I'd like to get close to you, you prick.

"Yeah, God rest his soul. And how's the boy—?"

"Tommy ."

"Yes," Matty nods like he actually recalls the name. "He's a good kid. Little wild, maybe, but all boys are like that at his age, right?"

She nods agreeably. Okay, here's where it starts.

"Yeah, but I've been thinking that maybe the city isn't the best place for him—or me. You know he's in that house, being reminded of his father all the time. I think it's bad for him. And he's getting in with a rough crowd."

Matty Cigar looks at her and the confusion on his face is the first sincere reaction he's had since she sat down at the table.

"What—you're saying you want to move?"

"Yes, Matty, I do. I'm on my own and it's been so difficult. I really think moving away from here would be the best thing."

Matty wrinkles his eyebrow and Lucille figures the old bastard's trying to decide if it's better to have her close or out of his life for good.

"All right, I guess, but where were you thinking of going?"

As far away from you and your pack of animals as I possibly can.

"I'm not sure yet. But I was thinking of going out to California, or the Pacific Northwest. You know, Oregon, Seattle, whatever."

The old man frowns, as if she's talking about mythical kingdoms.

"Jesus, Lou, so far?"

"Like I said, Matty, I think it would be best. We want to forget the past."

"How does Tommy feel about this?"

"He was a little upset at first, but he's coming around."

Tommy's got no idea what Lucille is planning. She's going solo on this one; she's going to leave that psychotic little punk behind and he can starve to death in that goddamn house for all she cares.

"Well," Matty says, "I can understand why you'd want to get away from all these…bad memories. How much do you think you'll need?"

"Well…Matty, I was thinking something like…fifty."

Matty doesn't react. It's one of the reasons he's survived so long because you never know what he's thinking.

Lucille watches, guessing what kind of fury must be going on inside his brain, how much energy he's expending right now to keep from leaping out of that chair and strangling her.

"That's…that's a nice piece of change, Lou."

"I'm gonna have a lot of bills to deal with, Matty."

"Yeah, the bills." The Cigar scratches his throat. "They sure can pile up, can't they?"

Matty looks away from her and the sounds of the zoo swell around them, kids shouting and crying, parents yelling after them. Lucille feels a twinge in her heart looking at these happy young families. People with normal fucking lives—is that so much to ask?

The silence between them deepens and she wants someone to say something, damn it, but Billy always said you should keep your mouth shut at times like these, make the other guy cave.

Matty knows this routine and he only opens his mouth to take a slow, dignified sip of coffee; shit, he's probably the one who taught that trick to Billy.

He wants you to quit. He wants you to give up and go back home to your miserable little life and leave him alone.

Matty moves his shoulders around, coughs into his hand, and slowly pours the remains of his coffee on to the ground where it puddles around his wheelchair.

"All right." His voice sounds clogged, like he hasn't spoken in weeks. "God knows how much you've suffered."

"Matty, I'm not—"

"No, no." He gently cuts in. "I promised you that I'd take care of you and that's exactly what I'm going to do."

The old man studies the empty coffee cup in his hand, like he's discovered a dinosaur egg. And she waits a little longer.

"Go and start your new life, Lucille. Take the money, go wherever you want with your son and you live, all right? Life is too short to waste even one minute being worried or upset."

"Thank you, Matty, thank you so much. I know Billy would be very proud of you right now."

Matty smiles and she thinks of the sign in the reptile house with a poisonous snake's head all nicely diagrammed with gripping teeth, venom duct, and fangs.

"I'll send some around to your house in the next day or two, okay?"

"That's just great, Matty. As soon as we get settled I'll send you our new address."

"You do that, Lou."

She's lying and they both know it. They'll never see each other again and that's exactly how they want it. She forces herself to lean over and let him kiss her on the cheek, squeeze her hand.

"Take care of yourself, Lucille."

"You, too, Matty."

Train is suddenly there, wrapping his hands around the grips on Matty's wheelchair. She turns and starts walking, forcing herself to go slowly as she tries to corral the thoughts ricocheting around her mind.

It can't be this easy, he's not going to let you leave this place alive, the snakes are going to break free from their cages, drop from the trees, and swallow you whole before he'd ever let you get away with this stunt.

Some of them have a nervous disposition.

The goon in the tracksuit is the decoy, the one she's supposed to see. Matty's got somebody in the trees aiming a rifle at her right now. One of his thugs is masquerading as a parent, ready to slash her throat the second she walks by.

Maybe the old bastard himself will pull out a .45 and empty the clip into her back. Who cares about witnesses? No one would ever dream of testifying against Matty Cigar, not if he shot the pope on live TV.

Lucille feels herself slipping into panic as she looks around for a way out of here. Keep walking, just keep walking; get away from Matty now before something happens.

A familiar sound reaches her, a bus pulling into the stop outside the zoo, and she walks faster, they're not going to kill me, faster, heels clicking on the pavement, I'm getting my money, and I'm getting out here.

She walks onto Broadway, turns and follows the bus fumes across the street to Colonial Court, where she parked the El Dorado Billy got her after she heard he was banging that waitress at the Green—

"Shit—"

Her hands shake so badly the car keys cowbell jangle until she's ready to throw them down a sewer and call car service when she steps back, breathes, and slides the key easily into the lock.

She's still alive as she opens the car door, still alive when she slips into the driver's seat, locks the door and starts the engine.

Lucille doesn't start crying until she reaches Clove Road and she's angry because she promised herself she wouldn't do this, but she's so happy to be getting out of this cage she's lived in for so long, she can't help it.

She skates beneath a yellow light as a dark blip appears on the rearview and she goes cold.

There's nothing behind you; no one's following you.

She holds onto the steering wheel with both hands and leans forward. No more ghosts, no more fear, no more wasting her days mired in the past. When she looks in the mirror again, the world behind her is all clear.

9

HE KNOWS IT'S wrong the second he touches the doorknob. And there's nothing he can do about it.

Billy wasn't going to leave the house tonight. Honest to God, he wasn't going to climb into the truck and haul ass out to Vince's dump. His plan was to stay the hell home, eat potato chips, and stare at the tube all night.

Billy was on his own this evening. Lora's visiting her cousin in Easton for her niece's fifth birthday party, won't be back until late and now Billy's kicking himself square in the ass for not going with her.

She tried to get him to come along, told him it would be fun, better than sitting around here by yourself. But Billy said no, he was tired and he didn't feel like going anywhere.

"All of those kids," he said, "you don't want some cranky old bastard getting in the way."

"You're not that cranky."

He smiled to say nice one and gently shook his head.

"No, seriously, I just want to rest."

Lora gave him a look that pretty much said she knew he was lying even if he didn't know it yet himself, but she kept it all in her eyes.

"Suit yourself. There's a ton of food in the refrigerator. I'll call you tonight."

Billy sits by himself in the living room watching Australian football, wishes he had gone with her because now his mind is amped up over how he choked outside Sal's house. Everybody knows Billy the Kid never bails on a job.

Maybe he was too attached to the place, unlike Vince's house, which he could cheerfully destroy, rebuild, and burn down all over again, seeing as how he always hated that spineless little queer.

But that place has been empty for months and Vince is either dead or so close to it that he's beyond knowing or caring what happens to his Pocono dream house.

Fuck it, there's nothing to prove by roasting that dump and all you'll do is pull Lora one step closer to your insanity. You don't want that, big guy.

Pressure builds in the back of his neck and Billy tries to ignore it, adjusts his seat, leans back, props his head up with a cushion, but it still feels like all them Aussies are piling on top of him, pushing him through the floor.

The pain spreads north; sweat leaks out of his forehead. The scar throbs in double time and the beer bottle he's holding jiggles in the same tempo. Lora's supposed to call him, she said she was going to call, so where the hell is she?

The guy next door starts plunking at his electric guitar, at this time of night, the son-of-a-bitch, cranking out some blues number and Billy starts thinking about Vince, what a whiny bitch he was, pissing and moaning about on thing or another; fucking hard-on, always talked a lot of shit but never delivered.

Billy's amazed he never got around to killing that asshole, Sal's cousin or not. Vince had been gunning for Billy for years, why the hell didn't the Kid strike first?

Matty would've pretended to be angry and Sal would've acted all grief stricken, but in their hearts they'd be grateful to Billy for clipping the little fruit and things would've gotten back to normal in no time. Even Jake wouldn't have cared. But instead Billy waited, just fucking waited, until that rat bastard made the first move.

Is he dead?

Billy went to Vince's place one time, a few years ago when that loser invited Matty and the rest of crew up for a cookout.

Billy doesn't remember much of that day, except that he got mockey-eyed in record time, ragged loudly on Vince's shitass K-mart house and pissed a gallon of beer all over the stupid fawn statue that Vince had put out on the front lawn.

Yeah, that was classic. Vince was shrieking *what the fuck*—? while Billy drained the lizard all over that defenseless deer. Christ, you'd think it was *La Pieta* the way that asshole acted. Lucille glared at him in disgust and Matty sat up on the porch laughing and saying "fucking Billy, fucking Billy" over and over.

And now that scumbag's house is sitting up there just a few miles away, safe and quiet as you please.

It's like the place is mocking him, calling him out for being a pussy because he's sitting here with his thumb jammed up his ass instead of doing what God put him on earth to do.

Billy's getting really wound up over this bullshit, when the phone screams out like a fire bell and he pounces on the goddamn thing before the first ring dies.

"Hello?"

"Hey, big guy. How's it going?"

He hears Lora's voice and the pain backpedals a little.

"Hey, yourself."

"You okay?"

She senses the desperation in your voice.

"Yeah, sure; I'm doing fine."

Billy hears kids laughing in the background; there's a TV on and he can just make out a song from one of the Disney movies. A woman, Lora's cousin, is telling everyone to settle down and behave and it all sounds so normal, so simple and so right.

"So what are you up to?"

"Ah, nothing much," Billy shrugs into the receiver. "I picked up a couple of strippers hitch-hiking on 611 and we're all going to get into the shower together."

"Good for you."

"Yeah, too bad you're not here."

"I'm sure you've got everything under control."

Billy's got nothing, absolutely nothing under control, the freaking walls are sliding in on him, and he's thinking it might be a good idea to jump into the truck right now and haul ass down to Easton.

"I think I can handle it. What's happening down there?"

"Well, we got pizza, ice cream, a stack of movies and a bunch of wild kids bouncing off the ceiling. Not all that exciting, I'm afraid."

Tell her you're coming down. Tell her you'll be down there in a little while. Tell her—

"Did you get to your cousin's place all right?"

"Oh, yeah. Little traffic here and there, but nothing major."

"How's your cousin doing? She all right?"

He can't break the connection, not yet; he needs to hold her on the phone a little while longer.

"Yeah…she's fine…"

"—because you know, I—"

A kid shrieks in the background and something crashes to the floor.

"—oh, boy. Listen, Billy, I'd better go. The natives are getting restless."

"Okay, sure, sure. Ah, listen, I was thinking—"

"—see you later."

The phone dies in his hand, the sound of all those happy people terminates abruptly and Billy stands there in the middle of this empty fucking house with the TV hanging over his shoulder and those Australians slamming into his neck.

Call her back. Call her back right now and tell her you're coming down to be with her. Don't hang around this place by yourself because you'll—

"Bastard!"

Billy hurls the phone across the room as the pain boomerangs around his head. He can't go to fucking Easton; he doesn't belong there, he doesn't deserve to be there. Just imagine an animal like Billy being around all those kids.

He struggles to put on his windbreaker, he's got to get out of here, let the Australians kill each other, go out in the yard, he thinks, as he yanks back the kitchen door, get some fresh air; take a few deep breaths and you'll be fine.

And when that doesn't work, when he's standing in the dark, like he has for so much for his life, and his fingers tap uncontrollably against his palms, and his head expands like a cheap balloon, and the guy next door keeps on twanging and twanging on the guitar until Billy's ready to vault the fence and crack the stupid bastard's head open with a shovel, he finally jumps into the truck and rolls down to the street.

He just wants to take a short ride around town and then get back to the house, watch some more tube, maybe read a little, and go to bed. Billy just needs a little bit of night air to help him sleep.

The road keeps twisting and turning on him, though, and he can't find a decent place to make a turn. The miles slip by, he's getting get farther and farther away. And closer and closer.

Somewhere during the ride, for just a few seconds, Billy thought he was being followed, like when he was outside Sal's house.

Years of being tailed by cops, angry husbands, and scumbags who had a hard-on for him over one thing or another taught Billy to sense enemy aircraft tracking him and this one pair of headlights behind him was driving a little too close for a little too long.

The beams turned off just as Billy was thinking about jamming on the brakes and greeting the mutt with the tire iron, and he drops the thought from his mind. He's got to keep driving.

Billy comes down to Gallagher's one night a week after his first meeting with Matty to get a few beers and escape from that goddamn house.

The old lady's on another bender and Billy doesn't want to hear her bullshit, so he comes down to his father's old hangout to relax and mock all the losers.

It's the next best thing to desecrating the old man's grave. He's playing darts with one of the living dead regulars when Sal walks in.

"Hey, there he is," Billy says, doing the power handshake with his friend, "the man of the hour. Fuck you doing here, nigger?"

"I need to talk to you, big guy." Sal nods to a place in the corner just below the TV set. "You got a minute?"

"Yeah, sure, but I'm telling you right now, you can't suck my dick, no matter how much you beg."

Billy should've known something was wrong right there, when Sal didn't laugh, give him the finger, and return fire. He should've picked up on the ugly vibe coming off his friend, but he's feeling too good to let anything bother him. He's going to be a big man soon.

They take a table below the Met's game and Sal lights up a Marlboro.

"I want you to know that Matty is very impressed with you."

"That's nice. I was pretty impressed with him."

"C'mon, Billy, quit fucking around now."

"All right, all right." He signals the bartender for another beer. "I'll be good."

"Okay." Sal pulls his chair closer. "Matty wants to start throwing work your way; he really does. But he needs your help with something."

"My help? For what?"

Sal pauses, looks around the way people do when they know they're going to ask way too much of you.

"Matty's trying to find this loser; a real deadbeat, owes the old man big time for God knows how long and the prick went and skipped town."

"Yeah, well, that's tough, but what's it got to do with me?"

Sal leans in and drops his voice a few notches.

"We think…we think it's somebody you might know."

Billy nods, understands instantly what this is all about and who Matty's looking for. It plays back in Sal's eyes, when Billy told his best friend about one of the sympathy cards they had received after the old man croaked, with a familiar name and a Pennsylvania address. Billy told Sal, who went and told Matty and now the Cigar needs Billy's help.

His eyes stalk the length of the bar, taking in the alkies, the burnouts, hardcore boozers from his father's day and the next generation right beside them, all destined to die in this cesspool.

He came here to lord it over these rejects, but the truth is that Billy's desperately afraid of becoming one of them, of making the downhill run from this dump to the graveyard, working for monkey wages and dreaming of the good life right up until they hammer down the lid.

Billy takes in the whole place, all the worthless talk and pointless bickering, pictures being one of these saps, nowhere else to go for refuge, and he gets an abrupt bestial urge to burn this place clear down to the ground.

He turns back to Sal.

"What does Matty want me to do?"

10

Billy sees the house coming up on his right, dark and lifeless, no use to anyone, but he keeps driving like he's heading someplace else, goes to a spot where he could easily cut the U-turn and head for Easton, even as he parks, switches off the engine, and picks up a can of lighter fluid.

He walks through the woods, his head full of Disney cartoons and children's laughter, and his fingers grip the metal can hard enough to leave a dent.

Billy could go on like this all night, for the rest of his life, walking beneath a starless sky, but Vince's house comes into view and he realizes that Lora was right about him going out after all.

Lucille gags for breath, tries to break free of the hand crushing her throat, but the grip is too strong.

Someone's on top of her, choking her to death. The face is obscured by shadows but it's someone she knows. Beneath the panic tearing through her mind, Lucille hears her own scolding voice.

Did you really think Matty would let you shake him down like that? Did you really think he'd let you live?

She hears something that sounds like a scream and if she doesn't do something now, she's going to die.

Lucille bolts upright and looks around. She needs a few seconds to realize she's at home, alone in bed, no one strangling her. The phone on the night table screeches at her and sends the clock clicking over to 3:33 am.

Her head hurts, a reminder of the drinks she'd been pouring herself since noon. The last thing she remembers is coming up here for a short nap at around five. That dream, it felt so real that Lucille touches her throat, expecting it to be tender and aching.

The phone rings again, startling her. Someone calling now; at this ungodly hour? It's a wrong number or one of Tommy's asshole buddies looking for their leader. Or maybe it's Matty trying to find out if she's home, so he can send Train over to pay her a visit.

Whoever it is, they're shit out of luck. Lucille's not going to answer. Just leave a message at the tone and I'll get back to you when hell freezes over. No goddamn way she's picking up a phone at this time of night.

The phone rings again and Lucille recalls the happy housewife voice she used when she recorded the voice mail greeting. *Hi, we can't answer the phone right now…*

Lucille almost smiles when she thinks of that recording. We can't answer the phone. A stranger calling this house and hearing that voice would think there's a joyful family living here, civilized people who sit down to dinner together, cheer at Little League games, and take yearly trips to Disney World.

Yeah, like there was ever a home here, like the miserable people in this goddamn house were ever a *we*.

The call is one ring away from tumbling into voice mail when Lucille reaches out, picks up the receiver and presses it to her ear.

"Hello…?"

There's someone on the other end. She tries to hear something, but only a gnawing silence comes out of the receiver. A few seconds slip by before Lucille hears someone sigh wearily, as if they're lost with no way of getting home.

"Billy?" she whispers as the line goes dead.

11

Tommy and Eddie have been driving all over the island for hours looking for bitches and trouble. They're mockey-eyed now, but Tommy still isn't feeling right.

Something's working on him from the inside and it's immune to beer, bourbon, reefer and all the other shit he's put into his body.

He had felt a little better after schooling that asshole at the mall. The loser had actually tried to snake a parking spot ahead of them and Tommy didn't yell or curse, didn't say shit. He just pulled the guy out of the car and pounded him into the pavement.

They drove away with the guy stretched out on the ground trying to put his jaw back together while dozens of other dickheads just stood by shitting their pants.

"Tommy is the man." Eddie giggles behind the wheel. "Tommy is one bad motherfucker."

And you're one flaming asshole. Tommy closes his eyes, eases back in the dead man's seat, and replays his most beautiful moment again. The old guy's eyes widening, the glass exploding, the white head of hair snapping back, no video game could ever give you this kind of rush.

I killed a guy, he thinks, I fucking killed a guy. Some loser is dead solely because of me and that feels so good I can't believe it.

"You're all over the news, son," Eddie says. "That's all these mutts are talking about. It's like, the mystery shooter, where will he strike next?"

"I'm gonna strike you next if you don't shut your hole, dickbreath."

"C'mon, big guy, lighten up."

"Lighten up, shit." Tommy's back stiffens. "You keep running your mouth like that it could to get back to the wrong people. And if that happens, God help you."

"Hey, Tommy, you know I'm solid. The cops could sweat me all night, all day, I wouldn't tell them my phone number."

"That's only because you're too fucking stupid to remember it."

Stupid or not, Eddie's right about Tommy being all over the news. It's crazy watching the TV schmucks talking about something that he did; talking about him. He should be signing autographs.

But being the top story has its problems. That Polack was a big name in the unions who went down in a big way and the cops want to nail somebody for it so bad they're jizzing in their little blue suits. It's not like Tommy slammed some crack-dealing spic; this is serious shit.

Tommy looks at Eddie struggling to change lanes. Eddie can brag all he wants about keeping his mouth shut, but Tommy knows he'd shit through his ears if a cop asked him for the time of day.

And that makes Eddie a problem.

You know what the old man would do, big guy, without pausing a second to think about it. Look at how his own people treated him. The minute they thought he could damage the outfit they took him for a ride in the country. Problem solved.

Eddie catches Tommy looking at him.

"What's going on, son?"

"Nothing."

"You sure? You look like you're doing some heavy thinking."

Tommy turns to the window so he doesn't have to look into Eddie's eyes.

"Nah, just enjoying life."

"What it is. So you wanna hook up with those bitches we met the other night?"

Tommy shakes his head. He doesn't want to be around Eddie right now.

"Think I'll call it a night."

"Ah, shit, you can't mean that."

"Yeah, afraid so. Just want to relax tonight. Drop me off at my house. I want to see if the old lady's drunk herself stupid yet."

Eddie grumbles but he does like he's told. Tommy watches him work the steering wheel and it comes to him, he finally realizes what's been nagging at him all night and how there's only one thing he can do to get rid of it.

He needs to kill again.

12

SHE JUMPS WHEN she hears the front door fly open, heavy footsteps trudging into the house followed by the sound of something crashing to the floor and Tommy roaring "mother fucker!"

Lucille shakes her head. God forbid he should fall down and break his neck. That would be a tragedy.

She looks at the receiver dial-toning in her hand, almost forgetting why she's holding and then remembering, yeah, the phone call, Lucille calling out to Billy, of all people. As if the guy is still alive.

She hears Tommy thudding against the living room wall and more slurred curses rumble up the stairs. Yeah, that's it, kid. Bust up the house all you want. Doesn't mean shit to me anymore.

Another lurching stumble and something fragile hits the floor and smashes to pieces, probably the vase on the bookshelf, though it could be the glass-framed photo of her parents on top of the bureau.

She almost wants to join him, help him tear this house down. Maybe we could set the place on fire just like your old man.

But she's angry, too. Little prick thinks he can do anything he wants, break stuff, make noise all night long, and nobody is going to do anything. Well, no one here really has, not since Billy disappeared.

She tells herself it's not worth getting angry, not when she's so close to leaving this place forever. He's not worth it.

But Lucille has taken so much crap from this punk for so long and so she gets up, yanks the bedroom door open, and steps out onto the landing.

"Hey, keep it quiet down there. People are trying to sleep."

There's a long pause before a roughneck voice comes up from the darkness.

"Fuck you…*bitch.*"

She bristles when she hears him laughing at her. God, if she could only have Billy here for a few minutes, just long enough to go downstairs, throw on the light and scare the shit out of that little bastard.

Lucille turns to go back to bed when a bottle shatters against the wall inches away from her head. She jumps back, nearly falls to the floor, and when she turns she sees the stain dripping down all over the carpet.

"Fucking bastard…"

Lucille pulls on her robe as she goes down the stairs, switches on the light in the living room and sees broken glass, the coffee table on its side, and Tommy leaning against the wall, drunk, stoned, and very dangerous.

He's miles away, this one, with his eyes half-closed, arms dangling at his side.

"What the hell is going on here?" Lucille steps over the broken bits of glass. "Are you out of your mind?"

"Hey, there she is," Tommy mutters into his chest, "the mother of the year."

"Look at this mess." Lucille waves her arms at the debris. "Just look at it."

Tommy grins stupidly and mocks her gestures.

"Look, look." He snorts. "Hey, honey, why don't you look at a fucking mirror? That face of yours could make a buzzard puke."

Lucille bites down on her lip.

"I'm not cleaning this up, okay? I'm not your goddamn maid."

"If you were my maid I woulda fired your ass a long time ago."

Lucille shakes her head. This would be a great time to turn around, go back upstairs and forget all about this asshole. But her mouth, her goddamn mouth, can't stay closed.

"Boy, your father would be very proud of you."

Tommy's quiet for a few beats as the words make the voyage through his clotted brain, time enough for a car to drive down the block, fill the room with its faulty muffler rumble and fade away.

"What was that?" Tommy's eyes flame over. "What did you say?"

Go back to bed. You don't have to prove anything to this scumbag.

But after this business with Matty, the nightmare, and that phone call, Lucille is done being afraid.

"You heard me, big guy."

He's right on top of her, moving so quickly despite his condition, and his eyes roar out of his head. She sees some of Billy there, but this is much worse. Billy was never this crazy.

"You're so fucking smart, aren't you?" The words slur out of his mouth. "Aren't you?"

His body expands before her. The veins in his biceps, the cords in his neck, are pumping wildly.

"You're better than everybody, right?"

"Look——"

"——fucking bitch!"

The back of his hand catches her high on the cheek, knocks her back into the bookcase, and she slides to the floor.

She tries to stand up, her brain reeling, but she can't get to her feet. Lucille looks around for something to use as a weapon and he falls down on top of her, two hundred pounds of brute rage, pinning her to the carpet, tearing her robe open and ripping at the nightgown.

"Get off me, you goddamn animal!"

At first it doesn't register what he's doing. How could it? There's no way her mind could grasp something so hideous.

But even when it does, even when she realizes the unspeakable thing that's being done to her, she refuses to believe it, as if denying it will make it go away, no, it's not possible, not his own—

"Tommy!" she shrieks. "Stop it!"

He punches her in the face and snaps her head back against the floor. Tommy is forcing her legs apart with his knee while she screams *stop it, stop it, you fucking—!*

Lucille claws at his face, goes for the eyes and scratches up his cheek. Her teeth sinks deep enough into his arm to draw blood and he's so whacked he's just laughs at her, as he keeps grunting, moving on top of her.

This is not real, she thinks, *this is not happening.*

She screams again, even though nobody is going to help her, no one hears anything coming out of this place, and this freak, this monster drives into her, drooling, cursing and slamming her body against the floor, fucking bitch, fucking bitch. A hand clamps around her throat and she can't breathe.

"I used to hear you and lover boy going at it all the time." His voice comes from all directions. "I'd be in my room and I'd hear you squealing and old Billy snorting away like a fucking pig. That's what you two sounded like, dirty stinking pigs rolling in the mud."

She sobs, bites into her lip, and tries to say a prayer that will deliver her from this outrage. Billy, Billy, she remembers that sigh on the telephone, and she wants Billy to save her from the nightmare that's coiling around her. Billy, please, help me.

Is this how Billy did it? Is it nice and hard, like Billy? Tell me, sweetheart, is this how Billy used to do you?

Tommy growls, his body arcs and strains in an obscene release and then it's over. She shoves him off her and rolls away. Tommy staggers to his feet, zips up, and stares down at her as if even he doesn't believe what he's done.

"Fucking pigs," he mutters.

He stumbles toward the front door, opens up the house to the outside world, the sounds, the streetlights, and she winces, please, please, don't let anyone see me like this. The door closes and she hears footsteps drifting down the street.

Lucille curls up into a trembling ball and tells herself with the one strand of sanity left in her mind that she has to get up, go to a hospital, call a doctor, do something for Christ's fucking sake.

But before she does anything, Lucille sits up, inhales every molecule of air in the house, and shrieks loud enough to split the sky in two.

13

BILLY STANDS OUTSIDE the house holding a can of lighter fluid while all kinds of bad omens are cracking through his guts.

It's like he's lived this night over and over. And here he is, back on the same spot, memory wiped clean, like some dumb ass cartoon character ready to get flattened by a 500-pound anvil.

Billy jiggles the doorknob again and the alarm in his brain rattles through his skull. Run now before it's too late.

He squints across the lawn and locks on the painted gaze of that god-damn fawn statue paralyzed outside the house, head tilted, foreleg raised forever pointing at nothing. Too late for what, Bambi?

A rogue wind blows through him and Billy shivers from the ankles on up. Another sign to back out of this thing.

Look at the little faggot crying his eyes out, just like a girl.

He puts his head back and breathes deeply until the voices fade and every-thing is still. No, he's not quitting; he's not giving into some stupid black magic horseshit. He's Billy the motherfucking Kid and he ain't ascared of God.

Putting down the lighter fluid, Billy drops to one knee and starts on the lock. It's a welfare number if ever he's seen one, typical Vince, and even though Billy should be able to go through it easily, right now the thing's giving more trouble than a death row prison cell.

Maybe this is the curse, he thinks, genuflecting before the dark house, I croak trying to bust this fucking thing.

A car engine's growl rolls down the road and Billy holds steady, his hand flat against the door.

He waits, stiff as the fawn statue, one-one-thousand, two-one thousand; a state trooper maybe, making the rounds; three-one thousand, or a week-ender who can't find his ass with his two hands once the sun goes down, four-one-thousand, five-one-thousand.

High beams slice through the black cross-roads and pause, six-one-thou-sand, seven-one thousand, just long enough to make Billy nervous and then and veer off to the left, the motor's rumble trailing a few seconds behind.

Billy allows himself to exhale and smiles as the door gently swings open for him as if he were an honored guest. Child's play, he thinks, as he steps into the blackness and closes the door behind him.

14

TOMMY DOESN'T LOOK right or left, as soon as he hears the scream, he's running down the block, blind with terror, into the street, through a firefight of headlights, squealing tires, horns and curses. And he keeps going.

Fucking bitch, he thinks, fucking psycho bitch—

She'll go to the cops, that cunt, tell them all kinds of lies and they'll believe her. Everybody will believe her, even though she's a stupid old drunk, they'll believe what she says about him.

The cops will cripple Tommy if they get hold of him, take him into a cell and kick the living shit out of him until he tells them whatever they want to hear.

Fucking savage, how could you do something like that to your mother—your own mother? Even that scumbag father of yours wouldn't sink that low. Oh, and by the way, stud, we got this little homicide over in Brooklyn and we're hoping you could help us out...

He falls to the ground someplace behind a row of houses, crying, like a bitch, like a little girl, at the thought of going to prison for the rest of his life. Wiping his eyes, Tommy pulls out his cell, calls Eddie to come get him, no fucking questions, just get the hell down there right now and pick him up.

It takes forever for the little hard-on to show up and when the car slows down Tommy sees Eddie behind the wheel with a shit-eating grin on his face and two young girls in the back seat.

"What the hell...?"

"You sounded a little tense on the phone, big guy," Eddie said. "I figured you needed to unwind."

15

Madame Medusa is dressing down her underling and Becky, the youngest, has fallen asleep on Lora's lap, but she doesn't want to wake her yet. Let the birthday girl rest a little longer.

It's just down to her cousin's three kids, the last of the partygoers having gone home after *The Little Mermaid*.

They watched *Snow White* after that and now it's *The Rescuers*, the Disney cartoon where the mice go save the little girl. God, did she actually see that at the Galaxy when it first came out? No, never mind. I don't think I want to know.

She'd been looking forward to this visit all week, but now she feels like she shouldn't be here. There's something wrong back home and she should be back there. With Billy.

Lora was a little surprised when he answered, certain that he had gone out and she'd get the machine. Of course he could've had been putting on his jacket and fishing out the truck keys the whole time he was talking to her, but she didn't think that was it.

Lora knew something was wrong by the way he picked up so quickly. She heard it in his voice, too, even though he was doing his damnedest to hide it; she could tell something was boiling inside him.

He was asking her for help, maybe not how he did when they were at the diner and Billy looked ready to die, but it was a distress signal all the same.

Damn it, she invited him to come down three times and he turned her down. What else could she have done short of roping him like a steer and tossing his ass in the trunk of her car?

"Everything okay?" Mary, her cousin, whispers. "You look a little preoccupied."

"Yeah, yeah. I'm fine."

So much for the poker face. Lora's pretty sure she could reach the phone on the nightstand without waking up Becky. She could call Billy, keep her voice down, just to see how he's doing. Lora tries not to let the next thought pass through her mind, but it's already too late —and hope like hell he's still there.

16

It's so dark in here, Billy groping his way around, severed from the world of the living.

Wicked vibrations course through him and shake the fillings in his teeth. Shit, he's as jumpy as a high schooler hoisting a ten-speed.

Look how his hand trembles as he opens up the lighter fluid and pours a long crackling stream of firewater all around the floor. See how unsteady he is as he digs in his pocket for the cigarette lighter.

The fuel spreads across the linoleum and Billy waits for the luscious smell to carry him off to the Sea of Japan.

"C'mon, baby, do your stuff," he mutters.

But tonight it's all wrong, seriously fucked up, and out of control. The fumes that usually smell better than Chanel No. 5 betray Billy now, rip down his throat and crush his lungs.

His eyes melt into tears and he sags against the refrigerator, coughing brutally, dimly aware that his legs are buckling and not particularly giving a fuck.

Somebody give him a skirt…

His fingers go numb, the can sails to the floor and spills its guts all over his shoes. Pull up, pull up, stand on your goddamn two feet, you pathetic sack of shit.

Mayday, mayday…

He grips the lighter, once twice, he cracks the flint, c'mon, bitch, don't crap out on me now. He gives it one last try before turning to leave and the whole place erupts around him with a searing light that gouges at his pupils.

Nice going, asshole, you finally cooked yourself. No one to save from the horrible death you so richly deserve like that night at the gas station, no, now you're going to get fried in an empty house. Serves you right.

The people from his life pass by his sightless eyes, Lucille, Sal, Charley, while old Ethan laughs and shouts for Billy to come on in, son, we've been waiting for you.

Somewhere deep in his heart Billy is actually relieved that it's over, finally over, all the bloodshed, all the dreadful things he's done, annihilated in a burning black mass. And he smiles when at last the only face he wants to see finally appears before him.

Lora, dear Lora, please pray for me.

Billy tucks his chin into his chest and waits for the heat to join the murderous light, take him away from this mortal world, and carry him to the place where the fires burn for all eternity. C'mon, baby, do your stuff…

When nothing happens, he lifts his eyelids a crack to see the quivering lighter flame in his hand and realizes that the shocking brightness washing over him isn't a budding four-alarmer, but the kitchen light shining over his head.

The old guy in the bathrobe glaring at Billy with a .38 in his shaking hands and the elderly woman cowering behind him aren't spirits sent here from beyond to usher him into the afterlife, but real people, real goddamn people who live in this house.

Oh, fuck me…

17

Scotty hides in the woods just down the road from where that scumwad Billy stashed the pick-up truck, my pick-up truck, goddammit. He tracked that prick for about 50 yards, watched him bust into that crappy-ass house, and disappear.

What in the fuck he's doing in there, Scotty has no idea, but one look into Billy's roving eyeballs will tell you logic ain't part of that guy's anatomy.

He's been tailing this bastard all day. First to that house where Billy hid behind a tree so long it looked like he was having an affair with the fucking thing and now to this dump. Either this bastard's working on his real estate license or he's got serious business with the homeowners.

Scotty wishes he had put an end to this bullshit earlier today. All he had to do was pick up a nice flat rock, hide in the bushes and smash the fucker's brains to guacamole when he went walking by. Stomp my ass, take my truck, and bone my ex-wife? Prepare to die, shitball.

Naturally Scotty didn't do jiminy jackshit, being extremely reluctant to tangle with this son-of-a-bitch in light of their first go-round. And when Billy turned his way and waved that big-ass cannon, Scotty just about pissed his pants as he beat a hasty retreat to his rusty old Honda.

You're probably in there sniffing panties and crawling on all fours like a Doberman, aren't you, you sick bastard? Enjoy it while you can, you miserable prick, because Scotty intends to grand slam your shriveled cajones right out of the park. And the crowd goes wild…

Scotty feels good about his old fat self right now and he's thinks about celebrating with a healthy bucket of suds. He wonders when that spooky crackhead in there is going to call it a night so Scotty can stop scratching his privates and start some hardcore drinking.

And then he hears the gunshot.

"Oh, fuck me…"

"What are you doing here?"

They're standing in the kitchen, this elderly couple in their robes and pajamas, with fear and anger churning in their eyes and aimed straight at Billy. The old man gestures with the gun and shouts again.

"What are you doing here?"

Billy's eyes rip a savage rotation around the room and take in the modest furniture, the shelves holding a lifetime's worth of knick-knacks, the bureau crowded with photos of this nice couple, their children, grandchildren, and friends.

He sees images weddings, graduations, trips, Rotary Club picnics, volunteer fire department and the ladies auxiliary, all those happy moments from the last half-century of these fine, church-going people, a whole volume of lives that had absolutely nothing to do with Billy until this moment.

Jesus, just imagine an animal like you being around people like this.

He sold the house, Vince, that lowlife son-of-a-bitch; he sold the goddamn house.

Yes, of course, he did, Vince was always up to his ass in debt, so naturally he got rid of the place and left Billy here to face this lovely old couple who want to blow his fucking head off.

"Don't move!"

The old man's voice is hoarse, panicked and his hands twitch the pistol into a gunmetal blur. Billy looks at them, the lighter fluid's stink crawling up his nostrils, the flame flickering in his hand, and he has exactly no idea what to do next.

"Don't you move or I'll shoot!"

Christ, you could laugh your ass off it's so ridiculous, this fossil talking to Billy the Kid like that. Sure you will, gramps, and your dentures will fly out of your mouth from the recoil. Fuck, Billy could leap over there right now and stuff the gun down his throat.

There's a photo on a shelf just over the old man's shoulder of a guy in a navy uniform and it takes Billy a second to realize that it's the younger version of the man standing before him, so proud of serving his country.

"Take it easy," he says, his hands raised. "Just take it easy."

The husband and wife speak in terrified tones but Billy's having trouble understanding them, the pain in his head is so bad that it sounds like monkeys jabbering at him.

The woman, that poor woman, looks at him with such fear it could break your heart. Billy wants to put his arms around her and let her know there's nothing to be afraid of, that he's not the bad guy they think he is.

"There's been a mistake," he says. "Just let me leave and you'll never see me again, I swear to God."

It's sounds so stupid, the words coming out of his mouth. Yeah, sure, big guy, you can go. Just close the door on you way out and watch out for the fawn statue.

The couple stares at this evil spirit standing in the home and Billy wonders if they understand what he's saying. The old guy looks at the puddle on the floor and flinches at the smell.

"—what is that?"

"—just put down the gun and let me go."

"—what are you doing?"

"No, no, it's a mistake, I'm telling you, it's a goddamn mistake!"

Billy is screaming by the time he's done, his eyes shut, his head thrown back, wailing up to the Moon's deepest crater. The noise, these old people, the knowledge that he's fucked up so badly has got him nearly blind with pain.

He opens his eyes, hoping he'll be somewhere else, back in time, on the couch watching TV and waiting for Lora to call. But nothing's changed; he's still with these people, in this house, only now they're even more frightened.

"—the police—"

No, no police; if they call the cops he'll go to jail and he'll die in some prison hospital and those bastards that did this to him will go free.

The wife reaches for the phone and Billy glares her to a halt.

"Don't…"

The husband says call the police, call the police, and Billy shakes his head no, don't do that, but the woman's hand is lifting the receiver.

The gun looks like a howitzer aimed straight at his head and Billy feels

the animal instincts kicking up, the rage building on itself, creating such virtuous anger that he can justify anything he does.

"Don't point that fucking gun at me!"

Billy launches himself across the room, crashes into the old man and
grabs at the gun. The wife screams, the husband yells, and it feels like the
whole house is tumbling down a mountainside.

The floor and ceiling roll over and over; Billy curses, pulls, twists, to
get this old bastard to let go. Plates fly off the shelves and all these framed
memories rain down on them and smash to pieces around their feet.

The old man wheezes and gasps for breath, but Billy's got so little left in
the tank he's not sure if he can hold on much longer.

The wife is yelling to stop it, please stop it, and Billy feels the gun slipping out of his hand, and you know this old timer, this Navy man, will kill
him if he gets this weapon back.

Billy tugs his finger and the gates of hell fly open.

18

Scotty hangs on to the gunshot's echo for a few beats as it crackles through the air and fades into the dark. He's motionless for a second, but when the screaming starts, he knows it's time to hit the bricks.

He fires up the Honda, rips a U-turn with the lights off and tears down the road like a pipe bomb's been slammed up his keester.

He peels off a hefty chunk of road before he throws on the high beams and the whole world is whittled down to nothing more that two yellow lines on the black top. Move, nigger, move; you don't want to be caught anywhere near this shit.

Well, we wanted dirt on this fucker and from the sound of things back there, it looks like Scotty hit the mother lode.

"Fucking Billy," he says with a seasick smile. "Fucking Billy."

The thunderclap cuts through the two bodies and Billy's not sure who should be falling to the floor. The sound wraps around them, imprisons the two men in a deafening echo.

He smells gunpowder, feels inky warmth rolling on his arm, and hears someone coughing out for breath.

The old man lets go of the gun, steps back with a monstrous hole in his chest and slides down to the ground like he's falling backwards out of an airplane.

"No!" The woman says in a terrified whisper. "No!"

It's just a heartbeat, one-one thousand, until the old lady starts screaming and clutching at her husband's out-stretched arm.

Billy stares at the gun in his hand and he doesn't understand, he just wanted to take the thing away, that's all. He didn't want to hurt anybody.

"Oh, God, please…"

She's screaming so loud, her husband's blood stains her hands, and there's no doubt he's dead, no doubt Billy killed him. He wants to run away from this place as fast as he can, but he feels something nagging at him, a vile thought that he refuses to believe.

She knows what you look like, big guy; she can identify you.

He lifts his arm slowly and levels the gun at the old woman as she kneels over husband's body.

She can put you on death row.

Billy puts the gun up against the head of white hair and his hand shakes so hard.

"Please," he says softly, "please stop it."

Just a little pressure and it's all over. C'mon big guy, don't leave her a widow. These two belong together. Do the murderer's math, count to three and pull the trigger. One-one thousand, two-one thousand—

He wraps both hands around the gun and shudders until he's about to break apart. The gun falls to his side; he pulls himself away from the old woman, and stumbles out of the kitchen door and into the dark.

And then he's running, charging across the yard, he has to get away from this place, but he crashes into something and tumbles to the ground.

He looks up at a pair of glassy eyes, the deer statue looks right into him and Billy smashes the head to pieces with the gun barrel, kicks the ceramic corpse aside, and runs with the woman's faded screams still in his ears.

Lora, dear Lora, please pray for me.

Part Six: You See That Man Over There?

1

BILLY AT 18, getting the call…

They're waiting for him outside Matty's bar. The cold beam of the block's only working streetlight shines down on Sal, Vince, and the Cigar, all huddled around the old man's big blue bastard of a Buick.

Billy makes like this is nothing special, just hanging out with some friends, even though Sal had just phoned his house to say the words he'd give his right arm to hear.

Matty wants to see you.

"Here he is." Sal gives Billy the power handshake. "The man of the hour."

Vince shrugs and turns away, the little prick; Matty gives him a slow nod.

"How's it going, Billy?"

"All right. You?"

"Thank God," Matty says. "Look, we're going for a little ride tonight. We're gonna be gone most of the night and it's gonna get a little unfriendly. You up for it, big guy?"

Up for it? Billy's so up for this he's dodging jets taking off from JFK. Matty, Matty fucking Cigar, is taking him out on a job. But Billy has to pause before answering, just for a second, so he don't look like no loser.

"Yeah, sure…why not?"

"All right!" Sal slaps his hands together. "Let's kick some ass."

Billy smiles while he tries to purge the memory of his mother sitting mockey-eyed in the old man's battered recliner squinting at Walter Cronkite.

He tries to forget how she grabbed him, dug her fingers into the face of Jesus freshly tattooed onto his arm, and begged him to stay because she knew that something bad was going to happen tonight.

And then she looked at him with those sunken bloodshot eyes and dropped the bomb.

"Do you still love me?"

He doesn't want to think about how he brutally yanked free of her, shouted "just watch the fucking TV already!" as he stomped out of the house, her cries slurring down the stairs after him, *Billy, Billy*. The Cigar wants to see him and that's all that matters.

"Okay, then." Matty opens up the Buick. "Let's go."

The big car rolls down the avenue, Billy and Sal in the back, Vince in the dead man's seat, so desperate to be near the Cigar that he'll crawl straight up Matty's ass if he gets half a chance.

Matty switches on a Tony Bennett tape when they reach the Verrazano. Billy bites into his lip to keep from asking where they're going and what they'll be doing because he knows that the Cigar doesn't like questions.

You're gonna love it up here, big guy. It's so beautiful, you'll swear you're in heaven.

"Now tonight," Matty says, "we're gonna send a message—and not just to one asshole, but to the whole pack of them. We're going to let them know that if you don't pay your debts, then you gotta take the pain."

Billy looks down at his fingers, closing into fists, aching to hurt someone. So much anger, stuck with that hopeless drunk in that house, a future so constricted he'll die painting houses and drinking himself stupid every night just like that dead loser of a father if he doesn't do something right now.

"People like to pull on my prick." Matty tugs at the air with a free hand. "They think they can just skip out on what they owe me and I'm not going to do nothing about it."

Matty's voice gets louder as the car picks up speed.

"Parasites, that's what they are," he says. "Fucking parasites; the more you give, the more they fucking *take*!"

He's roaring by the time he's done and the boys know the Cigar's not even talking to them; he's out there on his own, screaming at the world and they've got nothing to say.

The miles go by; Tony Bennett gives way to Frank Sinatra, then Vic Damone, and then silence. Vince's head droops, Sal's eyes are closed like he's meditating and Billy looks out the window to see towns fading away, woods growing deeper. He knows this route, even at night, even in his sleep.

You are now entering—there it goeesss!

Billy can feel Matty watching him. The Cigar makes like he's looking straight ahead or checking the other cars, but every so often his eyes flick up to the rearview mirror to look at Billy.

This is part of the test. Matty wants to see if he'll crack tonight. He wants to know if Billy can be trusted.

They drive through Jersey, come around the Gap. Billy looks over to the other side of the river, where it seems so dark and empty, and he wishes he could be there now, alone, just him and the stars. How great would that be?

They slow down at the toll plaza, cross into Pennsylvania. The Stroudsburg exits come up and Vince sounds off an artificial laugh.

"Hey, look at that," he says. "Park Avenue. You believe that? Park Avenue? These hayseeds kill me."

"That's on the south side," Billy says into his window. "There's some nice houses over there."

"Oh, yeah, I'll bet they're fucking mansions."

Vince chuckles too loudly at his own joke. Matty acts as if the passenger seat is empty.

"Billy, this prick we're looking for, he likes to hang out at a bar at Fifth and Main. You know it?"

"Yeah." Billy points over the front seat. "Get off here and turn right, get on to Main Street."

Billy takes a pearl diver's breath as they turn off the highway and drive into Stroudsburg. He guides Matty past the waterfall, by Ann Street, and on to Main.

The town seems so much smaller now, like a toy village below a Christmas tree. They turn left on McConnell and the huge car is so alien to this place, the men inside clearly up to no good, Billy wonders why the fire alarm doesn't blare out a warning.

Another left onto North Fifth, down to the corner, and then right on Main, lined with its rustic streetlights.

"What kind of fucked up town is this?" Vince is still bitching. "It looks like they made it out of Lego blocks."

"Hey, Vince." Matty puts a finger to his lips. "I'm trying to think here."

Vince shuts up and you know the little shitheel's face must be flushing up as red as a fire engine. Sal looks at Billy, nods toward his cousin, mouths "asshole" and Billy smiles in agreement.

Matty turns on to Main, passes the bar, and parks in front of a Chinese restaurant. He turns off the lights, kills the engine, and adjusts the mirror so he can scope the corner behind him.

"You guys wait here."

Matty gets out, walks by the bar, and casually looks through the window. Apparently satisfied, he turns around and walks back to the car.

"He's in there, the bastard." Matty slams the car door. "Getting shit-faced on my money."

"You want us to go in there and get him?"

"Nah, let's wait until he comes out." Matty checks his watch. "Shouldn't be too long."

2

Matty sends Vince into the Chinese joint on a food run, lights up a Cuban, and adjusts his seat so he can look at his boys and keep an eye on the bar at the same time.

Vince slides back into the car with a steaming bag and pungent smells fill the car the second he rips back the staples.

"Stupid chink bastards; took them forever to fill the order. I swear I hate them fucks."

"You get the duck sauce?"

"Yeah, Sal, I got the fucking duck sauce." Vince waves a small plastic envelope between two fingers. "What's this look like?"

"All right, slick, take the rag out, huh?"

Matty blows a smoky barrier between the two cousins.

"Hey, boys, it's time to eat."

Sal tosses Billy an egg roll, pops open a container of wonton soup and drinks half of it down in one draw. Vince chomps down on his spareribs and wipes his mouth with the back of his hand.

"What a cesspool," Vince says between bites. "Shit, Billy, I don't know how the hell you could stay in a place like this."

"What are you talking about, jerk-off?" Sal polishes off his soup. "You're out here in the country, you got the lakes and the woods; it's beautiful up here."

"Oh, yeah," Matty says. "I'm thinking about getting a place up here for myself. It'd be nice to get away from the city on weekends, enjoy the fresh air. Just like our buddy in there."

The Cigar smiles coldly and the boys laugh just like they're supposed to, Billy, too, even though he's being pulled so hard in opposing directions he's about to snap in half.

He wants this night to be over; accelerate until it's years behind him and it's a hazy speck somewhere deep in his memory, but the seconds won't oblige as they inch by so goddamn slow.

"Son-of-a-bitch…"

Billy looks up at Matty's coarse whisper, sees him glare angrily out the back window, and knows it's time. A numbing silence fills the car and Matty raises his hand, the cigar burning red between his fingers, ready to unleash his dogs.

"Matty, wait…"

"What is it, Billy?"

Yes, Billy, what is it? What do you have to say right now? That you changed your mind; that you want to go home? Maybe this life isn't for you after all; maybe you can't take the pain. Maybe somebody should get you a skirt.

"Let him walk a little bit," he says. "There's an alley about halfway up the block."

"You sure?"

Now where did that boy go?

"Yeah, I'm sure. We can take him in there so nobody will see us."

They all turn their heads as a figure lurches by the passenger side of the car and walks up Main Street.

"All right, Billy. What do you got in mind?"

How about that, big guy? Matty is asking for his advice, you lucky bastard. Now let's see how you handle it.

"Sal crosses the street, goes up a ways, and comes back down on this side of the block. I follow the guy and Vince stays behind me as the lookout."

"Hey, fuck you, Billy!" Vince throws his hands in the air. "I'm no lookout—!"

"I like it." Matty's words come down like boulders. "We'll do it your way, Billy."

Sal raps Billy's leg and smiles wide, so pleased with his boy. He hops out of the car, crosses the street and heads up the block at just the right pace and attitude.

Matty nods and Vince, still sulking over his bit part in this deal, gets out, and begins walking. The lights in the Chinese restaurant go out, closing time, the street is darker, and now it's just Billy and Matty Cigar.

"All right, Billy, let's get you a little closer."

Matty turns the key in the ignition and Billy's pulse surges with the car's engine. He inhales the Cuban's stale aroma deeply and uses it to blot everything else but here and now.

They see their man, head down, hands tucked into the pockets of a torn sweatshirt and Billy hates this guy from the ground up, hates him for being a loser, a drunk, a scumbag. A parasite. He has to hate him or he'll never be able to get out of the car.

"Here you go, kid." Matty slows down. "Now make me proud."

Billy opens the car door and he's a commando dropping behind enemy lines. He hits the street in a trot and falls in step behind his man, left, right, left, right. He senses Vince, behind him, sees Sal crossing over to this side of Main and walking straight toward him.

Now make me proud.

It's a perfect autumn night, winter just over the horizon, ready to roll in and cover the world. There's no one else on the street at this ungodly hour and Billy sees it all from a satellite high in space, a military assault carried out with flawless timing so that all forces will collide at the mouth of the alley.

It was so beautiful here on summer afternoons, walking down Main Street with Mrs. Miller, looking in all the store windows— Billy walks faster, swings his arms briskly to shake off stifling memories. He's got work to do.

He looks at the back of the tattered sweatshirt and listens to his own breath coming in fierce animal bursts.

Billy takes long liquid steps, as if he's running through clouds and he wants to get hold of this guy before the screeching alarm in his head drowns out his rage, before his mouth betrays him and shouts out a warning to the enemy.

This is life and death, him or me, a harsh lesson in survival of the fittest right here on Main Street USA. He grabs the guy's shoulder, roughly spins him around.

And looks right into Charley's eyes.

One hundred miles to the east, Billy's mother wakes up in the recliner fighting for breath. It's like that night her husband almost choked her to death and she trying to call for help.

But no one's around, she's all alone, and so she forces herself to stand, get away from the recliner, and falls heavily to the floor.

And while the TV station signs off for the night, the last thing she hears is the Star Spangled Banner, the last thing she sees is Old Glory waving grandly in a slow motion breeze, as she chokes out the last words she'll ever say in this life.

"Billy, Billy…"

3

THEY STAND BEFORE the alley staring at each other, neither one believing what they were seeing, neither one knowing what to do next.

You got me!

Charley's face, unshaven, worn by time, and bloated by alcohol, brightens slowly with dazed relief. You got no idea why Billy's standing here in front of you, do you, big guy?

Look at him, he's shit-faced; mockey-eyed, you could smell the booze coming off him. He's a goddamn drunk, just like the old lady.

"Billy…?"

Hearing his name sends the cold dark street rushing back to meet them, and Billy feels such hatred that this scumbag would say his name, act as if they're still friends with Matty just a few yards away in the car.

"What are—?"

Billy slams his shoulder into Charley's chest as hard as he can and Charley grunts, his eyes wide in shock, and staggers into the black hole of the alley, Billy right on top of him. Sal charges forward and crashes into Charley from behind.

"Heads up, asshole!"

All three of them vanish into the alley. Charley chokes, tries to speak, tries to say something to the boy he once knew, but Billy is all machine now and his right hand is wailing, bang, bang, right into Charley's face.

"Wait…" Charley says through bloodied lips. "Please…"

"We're done waiting, shitheel." Sal punches Charley in the stomach and bends him over. "Now we gonna fuck you up."

Charley puts his hands up to show he means no harm and tries to speak, but Billy won't let him say a word.

"Shut up!" Billy punches Charley again. "Shut your fucking mouth!"

He looks down to avoid Charley's eyes and puts his fists to work, in the head, the stomach, the ribs, I don't owe you nothing; you brought this on yourself, big guy, and now you gotta take the pain.

Billy forces himself to remember how angry, how hurt he was on that last day at Breezewood when Charley brought his father up from the city.

He reminds himself how furious he was when he came home to find the old man's body, how he had been cheated out of an exquisite chance to release his hatred. And now he's got a second chance. Keep calling up those memories, big guy, keep ripping open those wounds and you'll get through this yet.

Billy and Sal take their man to the ground, punching and kicking at the curled up body. Vince abandons his post at the head of the alley, hops around the outskirts of the assault, tries to get his piece of this loser; but this is Sal and Billy's show all the way.

Billy grabs a handful of Charley's hair, cranks his head back and points to the Buick that's pulling up outside on the street. Matty's watching, big guy, he's watching everything you do.

"You see that man over there? You see him, fuckhead?" Billy shakes the battered face. "He don't like you very much."

"And if he don't like you," Sal says, "*we* don't like you."

"Please…let me talk to him-"

"He's done talking to you, bitch. Now you deal with us."

Billy pulls Charley to his feet and slams his body from one side of the alley to the other, spreading blood on the walls like graffiti. Charley is sobbing, a little faggot crying just like a girl. Somebody get him a skirt.

"Billy…"

"Don't talk to me, mother fucker!" Billy snarls. "You don't know me! You don't say shit to me!"

Charley tries to say something, but Billy elbows him across the face. Matty is watching and if Billy fucks this up he'll never get another chance to prove himself, the Cigar will never trust him again, and Billy will end up a loser, a nobody, like this hapless prick here. He grabs Charley by the throat and squeezes.

"Who's your buddy?" he whispers so only the two of them can hear. "Who's your fucking buddy now?"

Charley gags, claws at Billy's fingers. Billy feels a hand pull on his shoulder and he angrily shoves it away. A car horn is going off and somebody is shouting, *Billy, you're killing him,* and he nods, yes, that's exactly what I'm doing. And it's long overdue.

"Hey!"

A scalding beam of light ignites the alley and petrifies the entire scene. *"What the fuck is going on here?"*

The voice is gruff, full of authority and coming closer.

Maybe it's God intervening to put an end to this thing, but it's only a local cop walking toward them with a flashlight in his hand.

"Nobody fucking move!"

Billy steps back, his face streaked with his sweat and Charley's blood, releases his grip so his best buddy in the whole world can slide to the cold pavement bleeding and coughing.

The cop holds the flashlight like a spear and for a second there Billy can't help but think of the search beam waving through sky telling everyone it's carnival time.

"Jesus fucking Christ…" The cop aims the beam to Charley.

"What the hell happened to him?"

"Nothing." Billy slips his bloody knuckles behind his back, squints when the light hits him. "Nothing at all."

"Nothing my ass. You were choking the living shit out of this guy."

"I wasn't choking nobody—"

"The hell you weren't, greaseball; I saw you."

The cop bounces the light from Billy to Sal to Vince and down to the body on the ground. In the dim light, Billy could see that the cop is an older guy, gray hair around his cap, a little heavy, one hand resting on the butt of his gun.

"Hey…" The cop prods Charley with the beam. "What happened to you?"

"He tripped," Billy says.

"I'm not talking to you, asshole; I'm talking to him."

"But it's true, officer." Sal chimes in with an altar boy's innocence. "We're walking down the street, we look in here, and we seen this guy keeling over."

"Yeah." Vince joins the lie. "I think maybe he's drunk or something."

"Really? And what happened to his face?"

"Yo, don't blame us," Billy says, "he was born with that!"

The boys' laughter recoils off the bricks and the little tin cop burns angry behind his flashlight.

"You some kind of fucking smart-ass?"

"Hey, I'm just telling you what happened, big guy."

The cop steps up to Billy.

"It's 'officer', okay, scumbag? Now tell me what you're doing here."

"We come up from the city to relax a little."

"Yeah," Sal says. "We like the fresh air."

Billy can just see some movement to his left, Charley struggling to his feet. He keeps looking at the cop.

"You staying in town?"

"Nah, we're just here for the day."

The cop points to Charley.

"And you were just walking by and you see this guy flopping around on the ground, all busted up?"

"You got it…officer."

The cop smiles harshly and shakes his head.

"You're a goddamn liar."

It goes quiet in the alley and the only sound is Charley coughing and wheezing as he tries to remain standing. Billy stares straight into the flash-light's eye.

"I'm a liar?"

"That's what I said, asshole. You deaf?"

"Oh, no…" Billy stretches his bloodied fingers. "My mother always said I got ears like an eagle."

"Is that right?"

Billy ticks his head to one side, looks to Sal, who steps alongside him and nods to say, yeah, why the fuck not? Vince falls in next to his cousin and all three of them face the cop.

"Oh, yeah." Billy's face is ghostly white in the cold beam. "And if my mother said it, you know it's true."

The boys are all set to go. The coughing grows louder, Vince's hand slaps a rapid rhythm against his thigh, while Billy and Sal get ready for the rush.

They're going to tear into this tiny blue man, drag him right through the heart of his pathetic toy town, and hang him upside down from the nearest streetlight. It's just a few seconds away…

"Is there a problem here, officer?"

The cop swings around and shines the light down to Matty, who is walking slowly down the alley. It's like steam coming out of a bursting radiator, the boys step down, their bloodlust chilled.

Billy can barely make out the words, amazed at how soft Matty can be when he wants to. Years of dealing with cops, lawyers, and prison guards come into play. Yeah, they work for me; they're really good boys, get a little wild sometimes, sure, but didn't we all at their age? They was just trying to help the poor guy that's all, and hey, you sure you're not Italian?

Charley staggers forward, one hand on the wall, his eyes pounded into slits. Matty and the cop are still talking when Charley's jagged voice cuts through the alley.

"I'm all right…"

The cop turns to Charley.

"All right? Christ, you can hardly walk."

"I said…I'm all right." Charley wheezes out the words. "I was feeling a little sick, I got dizzy, and I fell down. These guys…were helping me out. That…that's all there is to it…"

The cop looks at the outsiders who have invaded his town. He knows Charley's lying and everybody in this alley, rats included, knows he can't do shit about it. He sighs and shakes his head.

"You sure about this?" He asks Charley. "You don't have to be afraid of anybody. We'll protect you."

"No, no, I'm fine." Charley looks straight at Billy. "They're good boys."

"You want me to call you an ambulance?"

"No, no, I just want to go home now."

The cop nods grimly. He wants to lock up this pack of New York hoodlums so badly he could scream, but he's got no victim.

"All right," he says finally. "Go ahead."

Charley brushes by Billy as he limps down the alley. Billy tries not to watch the beaten man stumble toward the street, but it just takes so fucking long, as if somebody had stretched out this narrow passageway out for miles.

Please, for Christ's sake, Charley, just go already.

And the poor bastard finally answers Billy's desperate prayers, vanishes like he never happened.

They're driving down Main Street a short time later with Billy rubbing his swollen knuckles and looking out the window for any sign of life.

That cop could barely rein in his fury, but he had nothing on them and after checking IDs, asking some useless questions, he told them to get into their goddamn car and don't ever fucking come back here if they know what's good for them. Billy made the smooch noise with his lips, the boys suppressed their laughter, and the cop could only glare at him.

The street is dark, so much darker than it was a few minutes ago, and he's telling himself that what happened tonight, it's just arithmetic, Charley on one side of the equation, Billy on the other. If Billy hadn't dragged him into that alley tonight, it would've been somebody else.

He's a curse, always has been since the day he was born.

And Billy decides at this moment that there is no God up in the sky watching over us, protecting us, answering our prayers. There can't be, not after what happened tonight.

The only thing up there are the satellites, soulless machines spinning in a freezing orbit, never helping, never intervening, just recording everything that happens good, bad, or neutral and moving on. Down here on earth, you've got to deal with guys like Matty Cigar.

"You guys did good," Matty says. "I'm real proud of you."

Sal turns to Billy.

"Shit, big guy," Sal says, "I thought you were going to kill that loser."

"Too bad you didn't," Matty says. "Fucking prick."

Billy joins in with the laughter, but he's not feeling much of anything inside now. He's learning how things work. He sees now that just giving up an address would never have been enough for Matty Cigar. No, any lowlife could do that.

If you want to get anywhere in this crew you've got to get the blood on your hands; you've got to do such terrible things that you hate yourself so much, you won't have anyone else to turn to except Matty.

"You know, Billy," Vince says in a fake casual tone. "That guy seemed like he knew you."

"He used to work for my old man…until my father canned him. But I ain't seen him in years."

Vince doesn't want to let it go.

"It looked like more than that to me. It looked like you guys were really tight."

Billy sees that he's made an enemy for life this evening and he knows just how to handle it. He stretches his arms out wide, pretends to yawn.

"Hey, Vince, weren't you supposed to be the lookout tonight—you know, warning us in case somebody was coming?"

"That's right." Sal eyeballs his cousin. "Why the fuck didn't you say nothing about that cop?"

"I did—"

"No, asshole, you didn't. You come down that alley, even though Matty told you not to, and we didn't know shit until Matty blew the horn and that cop was right on top of us."

"I-I was helping you guys out. I was backing you up."

Vince is nervous; he turns to Matty for salvation, but all he gets is a granite profile.

"We're supposed to work together," the Cigar says very slowly, eyes forward. "We're supposed to be a team. You stick to the plan so things don't get all fucked up."

Vince shrinks into the dead man's seat and stokes his hatred for Billy. He won't say a word for the rest of the evening.

Billy eases back in his seat and folds his arms across his chest. They did good tonight and he was the best of them all. And if Billy can do something like this, something so heartless, so cruel then nobody in this world will ever be able to hurt him.

He looks out the window, sees a battered figure near the corner by Newberry's, bent over, like he's puking his guts out. Or crying.

You let a bum like my father walk all over you. You stiffed Matty until he had to hurt you. You're a parasite.

Matty turns left on Seventh Street, heads over the bridge to get back on 80, and, as Billy loses sight of the guy, Cronkite's sign-off comes to him.

He looks out on the headlights moving west. They should be home by the time his mother sleeps it off. Billy thinks he should do something nice for his old lady, get her some flowers, take her out breakfast.

He can do anything he wants now. He's Billy the Kid.

Part Seven: This Ungodly Hour

1

IT'S HARD TO believe that this is the day, the special day, that Lucille is supposed to make her great escape.

Get the money from that rat fuck bastard Sal, take off on out of here,
and leave Tommy and the rest of this hideous world far behind.

But that's all over. It all ended last night, at some ungodly hour, right
there on the floor with Tommy grunting on top of her. No point in going
now; this stain will be with her for the rest of her life, wherever she goes.
There is no new life waiting for her.

Lucille would really like to believe that the best thing to do would be to just
go, start over, and let God take care of Tommy in His own good time.

But she's not waiting for God to get around to punishing this animal.
Lucille brought him into this world, so she has to take him out of it. The
kid's a curse to everyone around him.

This is more than just revenge, though. Lucille finally sees that Tommy
is evil, an abomination that should never have been born.

She's going to do this right, just like the boys in the crew. They're good
at handling people close to them.

Switch off the lights, draw the curtains, crank up the TV nice and loud
to distract him, and sit here below the clown painting with her head down,
the gun on her lap and out of sight.

Lucille hasn't touched the gun since that night with Billy. After she had
cooled off, she shoved the thing to the back of the bedroom closet shelf
and tried to forget about it. But now she needs it.

There'll be no wavering, no hesitation. She sees it so clearly in her mind that she has no doubt she'll be able to do it. And there's nothing Tommy could say that would stop her.

Put three in his chest, then stand right on top of him and put the last two into his head.

Once it's over, well, Lucille knows she can never live as a fugitive; the endless running, constant lying, she doesn't have the strength for that.

The best thing to do is to wait till the cops get here. God knows she's got enough evidence of abuse and she can use Matty's cash to get a good lawyer. A lot of people will call her a hero for this, though a jury might think different. And Lucille wonders if she could ever survive in jail.

That meeting with Matty, it seems so far away, like it happened in another century. She remembers how strong she felt afterwards, so proud that she had stood up for herself, showed the old bastard that she wasn't going to take his crap. And Tommy took all of that away from her in just a few minutes.

Boy, your life turned out really well, didn't it? Your husband murdered by his friends and you're about to gun down your only child and spend the rest of your days behind bars. Could you ever have imagined any of this misery on that day you posed for your wedding pictures?

Lucille walks to the front window and looks out at the street, the gun in her hand hanging just below the sill. She's so lost, so far away from the world on the other side of the glass.

There's Mrs. Nucci in her usual place across the street spying on everybody like she's been doing for so many years, but she doesn't hate the nosy old bitch, not anymore. She's not hurting anybody. Let her look, that's about all she's got in her life. And she'll be getting quite a show today.

Maybe she'll use the gun on Sal when he gets here. Step out onto the front stoop and blow a hole right through him as he walks up to the front door; stand over and taunt him through his dying breaths. Is this how you did it to Billy, you fuck? Is this how you murdered my husband?

The phone rings and Lucille turns around, the gun raised. It's a repeat of last night, when the nightmare started with the telephone ringing. That phone can be silent for days at a time, but lately it's sounding off every other minute.

She walks over to the phone and stares until the thing falls still. Angry, she reaches down, yanks the plug out of the wall and throws the phone across the room. Now let's see anyone try calling me.

Lucille looks down at the rug, at the exact spot where it happened. And she can't stop from seeing it again.

"Dirty fucking bastard…"

There's a noise in the kitchen, the slightest sound of the door easing open. Gutless faggot's trying to sneak back in here. Lucille picks up the remote, clicks the TV on to an infomercial and sends the green volume bars up as high as they'll go.

She presses the gun against her leg and starts walking. Remember, don't say a word, just raise the gun and start firing. Whatever happens after that isn't important. First you've got to kill this fuck.

Lucille stops just before the kitchen. The scene is all wrong; this isn't Tommy standing there by the back door, it's Matty she sees for a moment before she realizes it's Train standing in her house, grinning viciously and aiming a gun straight at her while the TV howls about flat abs and a money back guarantee.

And even though she has a gun, too, right there in her hand, and she's yelling at herself to shoot, shoot, shoot, the thing is cemented to her leg, and all she can do is scream along with the television while the bastard son opens fire.

He wakes up in daylight with no memory of the last few hours. And he likes it just fine.

A delicate ray of sunlight shines down straight from heaven and it glows in him, with him, and through him. Birds are singing in the trees, the aroma of bacon and eggs floats up from the kitchen and wraps around him.

The only thing Billy knows right now is that he's warm, rested, and safe.

He wonders if he's still back at the rest stop, his life ebbing out of the side of his head and everything that's happened since then has been nothing more than a dying man's dream.

Charley, it's me, Billy. Do you know me?

Perhaps he's been reincarnated, so that when he looks into the mirror he'll see an eight-year-old boy eager to go out into the sun and counting the days until the carnival comes to town.

"Another beautiful day in the Poconos," he says in a whispering smile.

A radio crackles to life directly below him, a sharp electric voice that pierces the floorboards and fills the room.

- searching for the suspect who shot an elderly man to death—

Billy explodes out of bed and nearly crashes to the floor with last night's memories mainlining into his brain. He recalls everything that happened, everything he did, in slow sadistic detail.

Caucasian male in his forties with graying hair and a small scar over his right eye, the radio voice gets louder, angrier—

She saw your face, gave the cops a description. Aren't you sorry now that you didn't take care of business when you had the chance?

"Billy?" Lora calls up to him from the bottom of the stairs. "Are you okay?"

"Yeah, I'm fine." He fakes a cough and gets to his feet. "I tripped getting out of bed."

The silence from downstairs goes on for a little too long

"Okay," she says. "Breakfast will be ready in a minute."

He had gotten home last night at some ungodly hour, after a suicide sprint through a blur of dark roads, flak bursts of oncoming traffic, and a brake-burning near miss with a pack of terrified deer. Somewhere along the way he vaguely recalls stopping to throw the old man's gun into a black lake, but he might have dreamed that and the murder weapon could be sitting in Lora's truck right this very moment.

And the whole time he drove Billy cursed that old man, that stupid old man for causing all this grief.

You brought this on yourself, big guy.

He climbed into bed shortly before Lora got home, lay there with his eyes closed, while Lora hovered about the room so quietly, pretending to believe that he was actually sleeping.

He showers in a blast of steaming hot water that nearly takes the skin off his bones and stifles a howl of pain. Never should have come back here, big guy; you should have stayed on that tormented road and gotten far away from this place.

Billy shuts off the water, steps out into a cloud of choking steam, and switches to outlaw mode.

Climb out the window, take Lora's truck, drive as far you can, steal a car and drive some more. Repeat until you're miles away from the one person in this world who actually gives a damn about you.

Billy towels off, wipes the mist from the mirror and sees the battered face of a frightened old man. He looks at himself and wonders who'll be the next one to help him, the next one he'll destroy.

Fucking kid. Been a curse from the day he was born.

Billy steps away from the mirror. It won't be long before the cops crash through this place like a pack of wild dogs and the whole town will know that Lora was shacking up with a murderer.

Those pricks will nail her for harboring a fugitive, resisting arrest, drinking on the Sabbath, any kind of insane bullshit charge they can yank of out their asses, the lying scumbags, and then won't those old bastards at the diner have plenty to talk about over their morning coffee? Fucking cops, he hates them more than ever right now.

Billy dresses, slips on his jacket, and finds Matty's gun waiting for him in the right hand pocket. He pulls the weapon out slowly, so slowly it seems to take hours and the barrel feels like it's three feet long. He raises the gun up to his face to look it over. Nice piece of work, that's for sure.

Billy brings the gun barrel up to his mouth and clicks back the hammer. There's no doubt now, big guy, no games; this thing is loaded. You pull that trigger this time and the back of your head will be all over the windows.

Finish it. Finish the job that Sal started. Make up for all the misery you've caused for so long.

Oh, shit, now look at him; he's crying like a little girl. It starts off softly and he thought he could stop it, but the tears gather momentum until he sobs and the gun shakes so violently in his hand the thing is ready to go off.

That's it, big guy, just shake a little more and end this business.

"Billy, breakfast is ready."

The tears subside and the trembling fades away. Just hearing her voice is enough to make him put the gun away, wipe his face clean, and go downstairs to be with her for one last time.

2

BILLY FOLLOWS THE sound of a local car dealer's dumb fuck jingle to the bright burning kitchen. Lora's at the stove, her back to him, and he comes up behind her, slips his arms around her waist, and buries his face in her hair.

She smells so good and he wishes, oh God, how he wishes he had stayed the hell home last night so he could enjoy these beautiful seconds without seeing that old man die and hearing the woman scream again and again.

"Good morning."

"Same to you." She reaches up to touch his cheek. "Hope you're hungry."

"Starving."

He sits down at the table and watches as Lora stands over him and loads eggs on to his plate.

This used to be his favorite time of the day, these mornings with her, when he felt so calm, so far away from his old life it was almost liked it never happened.

The radio sounds off with the traffic report and Billy spots the morning paper neatly folded on the kitchen table exposing the letters "MUR-"

Billy would rather put his head in the oven and crank it up to broil before he'd touch that thing and read about the horrible crime he committed, but the paper is part of his morning ritual.

Billy picks up the paper, slides off the rubber band, and unfurls the page one photo of Vince's old house, sealed off from the rest of the world by a streak of yellow crime scene tape. A fifty-foot headline roars "ELDERLY MAN MURDERED" loud enough to knock Billy off his chair.

There's a blurred photograph of the man that Billy killed on the right side of the page, taken perhaps at a party. He's smiling, one hand up, and someone's arm is around his shoulder.

Billy stares at that picture, at that face, a good, decent man who didn't deserve this brutal death. He wants to look away but his eyes are nailed to that photo. Look at him, you prick, look at the man you killed.

"How'd you sleep?"

She's standing right over him, filling his coffee cup.

"Oh, just fine."

Billy senses Lora lingering there as he reads about the murder of this father and grandfather, a U.S. Navy veteran who worked for 35 years at a machine parts plant in Allentown.

"You know, Billy…" Lora says slowly. "I called here last night and there was no answer."

"Really? You must've called when I went out to get some beer."

"I called three times, Billy." Her voice is flat, unemotional, like an elevator announcing each floor. "You weren't home."

Billy puts the paper down, relieved to finally take his eyes away from the front page.

She's looking right at him with those beautiful brown eyes and he wants so badly to throw his arms around her, confess to every bad thing he's ever done, so that she'll forgive him and everything will be all right.

But he's not pulling her any deeper into this business and he shifts to the innocent act.

"What is this, Lora?"

"You tell me, Billy. Tell me what's going on here."

"Nothing's going on. I went out to get some beer and then I drove around a little."

"Drove where?"

"Where?" Billy fakes a shrug. "Here and there, back and forth, what the hell difference does it make? You know I'm having trouble sleeping."

"You were sleeping fine last night…or at least it looked that way."

"That was after I got back."

"And what about that, Billy?" Lora asks. "Why can't you sleep at night?"

"I don't know." The blood pulses softly on the side of his head. "I get these…headaches."

"But you won't go to the doctor."

"Oh, Christ—"

"We still don't know what happened to you, Billy. We don't know why you collapsed in the diner. You could be really sick."

Billy closes his eyes and rubs his temples.

"Look…I don't need any help with this."

"No," she snaps. "You've made that clear enough."

Lora gets up, goes to the sink and angrily yanks the faucet on. He looks at her, a cloud of steam rising up around her face and imagines Lucille talking to him like this, how he'd whip her around and backhand her across the mouth.

Remember how she used to shrink from you, trying to cover up? Remember how she cried and screamed as you hit her? Remember the night you nearly choked her to death?

"C'mon," he says. "You think I picked up some skank from the truck stop?"

"No, Billy, I don't think that at all."

Sweat beads up around his forehead, his tongue grows thick in his mouth.

"Look, there's some things in my life. It…it's got nothing to do with you."

"No kidding."

"It goes back a while—before I even met you."

Lora turns off the water and stares at him.

"Really? And does it have anything to do with that fire from the other night?"

He looks at her, honestly confused.

"What fire?"

"Jesus Christ, Billy, that house fire from the other night—the same night you drove off in my truck."

"So I went out for a drive, that's all. It doesn't mean I set somebody's house on—"

Lora reaches to the cabinet under the sink, pulls out a piece of wood, and slides it front of him.

"I found this in the woodshed."

He stares at that *The Hideaway* sign he carved outside Matty's house so many years ago.

"I wanted to throw it out." Lora's voice floats over his head. "I wanted to forget I ever saw it, but I put up with one guy's bullshit right up to the day the cops kicked in the door and took him out of here in handcuffs. I'm not going through that again, Billy. Not for anybody."

Billy's got nothing to say. That…thing, it doesn't belong here, shouldn't be anywhere near this house. Lora kneels down beside him and speaks softly into his ear.

"A man got killed last night, Billy. The police are saying that someone was trying to set his house on fire. Another fire, Billy. Another fire. Now is there something you want to tell me? If you know anything about this, please tell me."

Sweat drips out of him and his right hand twitches on the table. Billy's taken some pretty serious beatings in his life, from the old man, Jay McAvoy, Jake and half the cops in Brooklyn, and he never said a word. But this is torture, cruel and unusual punishment—

—tell her. Tell someone close to you the truth for once in your miserable life.

"I have to know what's going on. Please, don't lie to me anymore. Don't keep me in the dark."

They always want something, these bitches; never fucking satisfied. They want you to be stay home at night, stay away from other women, buy them every goddamn piece of jewelry they see. They want to know if you still love them.

"Whatever happened," she whispers, "I'm sure it was an accident. I know you're a good man. I know you never meant to hurt anyone."

But she's so wrong. Billy's not a good man and he's been hurting people ever since he drew his first breath. They closer they get to him, the more they suffer.

His right hand shakes so badly he wants to drive his fork through it, pin the bastard to the table.

Lora puts her hand on his wrist and softly squeezes, still looking at him with those pleading eyes, and Billy is ready now, he's ready to tell everything and do anything she wants because he can't stand hurting her like this any longer.

But the second he opens his mouth, the very goddamn second, the telephone screams off the wall and his right hand lashes out, knocks his breakfast plate clean off the table and sends it exploding to the floor.

Lora jumps back, stares at him in shock, and down to the mess at her feet, while Billy stupidly holds up his treacherous hand, now calm and steady as a marble statue, and tries to say, no, that wasn't me doing that, not the real me.

"Billy…?"

Her voice is shaky, so full of hurt, it's killing him. The phone rings again and Lora turns and walks out of the room, leaves him there alone in the kitchen.

Billy gets up to follow her, to apologize, to explain, but the phone sounds off a third time and he halts in mid-step. He takes hold of the receiver and brings it to his ear.

"Yeah?"

"Hey, Billy boy." Scotty's voice rolls into his head. "How's it hanging?"

3

Billy says nothing for a few seconds. Of course it would be this cock-sucker calling right now at the worst possible time imaginable.

Lora goes upstairs, probably to pack his bags while Billy's got her scumbag ex-husband breathing industrial strength venom over the phone lines.

"Look, I can't talk now."

"Oh, I'm sorry." Scotty's voice is heavy sarcastic. "Am I calling at a bad time? Well, tough shit, mother fucker."

"What do you want?"

"Me? Hey, I don't want anything. I was just calling to congratulate you for making page one this morning."

"I don't know what you're—"

"—don't even try lying to me, dipshit." Scotty's voice scrapes over the line like sandpaper. "I saw you with my own two eyes going into that poor old man's house last night, so cut the crap."

"Is that a fact?"

"It sure is. And I'm betting the cops would love to know what I know."

He hears Lora moving around upstairs and he wants so badly to go upstairs to be with her, try and fix the mess he made before she walks out.

"You still there, Billy boy?"

"I'm here."

Stupid, so fucking stupid, Billy's supposed to be the smart guy from the city who knows all the angles, and somehow he let this backwoods barrel of shit stick to him like a cheap bumper sticker.

He can just picture Scotty squatting in his rust bucket trailer in his boxers, scratching his balls, sucking down a Rolling Rock and wet dreaming himself into a new pick-up.

"Look, I don't have much time."

"Then you better make time, scumbag, because I'm sure them staties would be happy to give me all the time in the world. So take your face out of my ex-wife's crotch and listen real good."

Yes, listen, by all means; listen to this born loser. The fat fuck hasn't held a winning hand since he dropped out from between his momma's legs and all those dead ends have fried his brain cells. A guy like this will do anything to get on top once in his life and you have to handle him like toxic waste.

"Okay, you got my attention. Now what?"

"What do you think, shit-for-brains? You want me to keep my mouth shut, numb nuts, it's going to cost you."

"You think I have money? You serious?"

"Don't give me that shit, you asshole," Scotty screams. "I swear to fuck I'll go straight to the cops and hand your ass right over to them and if you think I'm kidding, just fucking try me!"

He hears Lora coming down the steps and then she'll be out the door and away from him.

"All right,take it easy. We'll work this thing out."

"It's already been worked out, shitheel. You come up with a serious pile of money or I'll see to it that you and that slut are up to your eyeballs in misery."

Billy smiles now because Scotty has brought Lora into it. And that's going to make things so much easier. It's going to be slow and awful, and this time Billy won't listen to any pleas for mercy.

"Billy?"

Lora is standing in the kitchen looking straight at him. Billy raises his index finger and mouths *one second.*

"Billy, put the phone down and talk to me."

"Don't you do that, Billy boy." Scotty drills into his skull. "Don't let that bitch put you on death row, buddy."

Billy cups his hand over the mouthpiece.

"Wait," he whispers.

"No, Billy, I won't wait. Hang up the phone and talk to me now."

"Please."

"Hey, Billy." Scotty cranks his voice up. "I'm getting a little impatient here."

Billy takes his hand away to speak and in that instant he loses her; Lora walks out and slams the kitchen door behind her. He stares at the broken plate, the splattered eggs and they're looking so much like brain tissue and skull fragments.

"Okay, big guy, I hear you loud and clear."

"Shut the fuck up with that 'big guy' stuff. I'm calling the shots here."

He hears Lora's car start up and sees her backing up so she can go down the driveway.

"Okay, okay. But we've got to do this right. I don't want Lora to know what's going on here. It would be bad for both of us."

"Yeah, so?"

"I did some work for a guy in Portland and he owes me a shitload of money. I'll go down there today and collect from him, clean out whatever I got in the bank, and hand it all over to you."

There's a long silence at the other end of the line and while Scotty's rodent mind chews on the scenario, Lora goes down the driveway and disappears.

"All right. And where are we going to do this?"

Billy smiles into the phone, his hand clamped around the gun.

"I know just the place," he says.

4

SAL IS HALFWAY over the Verrazano when the bridge disappears right from underneath him.

It's impossible, of course. Shit like this doesn't happen in real life; huge monstrosities like this bridge don't just vanish before your eyes like some David Copperfield stunt. This ain't Vegas.

So where is the goddamn thing?

Sal tries to remain calm, even though his heart is ready to pump clear through his chest, and he tries to recall what the hell happened just before he got marooned in the ozone layer.

He was driving to Matty's house, taking his time just to piss the old bastard off. The radio was playing "One More Night" and he switched from the easy listening crap to get some news.

Sal was expecting to hear the usual grief from other parts of the world with people getting killed in earthquakes, floods, and bombings. But instead there's a breaking story about a missing mobster's wife gunned down in her home by an unknown assailant.

"He promised me," Sal's voice cracks. "He promised me he wouldn't hurt her."

Sal's known Lucille since high school; best man at her wedding, stood with her at Tommy's christening, all those weekends in the Poconos. How many times has Sal gone to her house for dinners, parties, the holidays, or just to escape his own family?

That old bastard did this on purpose. He wanted her dead, but he didn't want to Sal to know about it until it was over. Sal's supposed to be Matty's right hand man, like a son to the old guy, yet he had to hear about it on the radio like all the other losers.

Matty don't trust you no more. You been cut out of the inner circle. You seen this happen to other guys and it always ends with them getting into a car one day and never coming back.

That's when he looks up from the radio, and sees that the Verrazano's huge towers, miles of cable, the road before him, the other cars and trucks, they all evaporated so it was just him tearing through the air 200 feet over the churning black water.

"No," he sputters. "No, no…"

This can't be real. He's just in shock. This is going to pass any second now.

But it doesn't. His car keeps going straight for a few Looney Tune seconds before Sal feels the awful tug of gravity, the hood dips forward, and then the car starts to whistle through the sky like a 20-ton bomb and all Sal could do is jam on the brake pedal as the car heads toward the ocean.

Mayday! Mayday!

He tries to think rationally, that he has to be ready when the car hits the water so he can swim to safety, even though he can barely get around a backyard swimming pool without going into convulsions. There's no way he can survive this, Sal's going to die with all these sins clinging to his soul.

You could have done something to save her; you could have stood up to that sick, crazy old man, warned him not to do nothing to Lucille. That's what you would've done if you had some balls.

Sal screams, loud, long, and high, his eyes clamped shut, face planted against the steering wheel, because he knows it's going to be awful and he knows he's going to hell, straight through the freezing water and right to the everlasting fire.

His voice cracks and he starts coughing and choking, and yet he still hears screaming, loud, inhuman wailing; so he opens his eyes a crack, the faggy tears roll away from his eyes, and he sees everything is back to normal.

The bridge, the cars, and buses are all back in place and an oil truck is behind him, crawling right up Sal's rear end.

The driver pounds on the horn again, and Sal sees that his car is coming to a stop. So he's not going to drown, he's not going to meet his maker. He's alive.

And now he really wants to see Matty.

5

MATTY'S HOUSE SQUATS at the end of the street there like a giant brick spider, biggest home on the block, with a huge picture window shamelessly displaying a massive spiral staircase that Matty will never use.

Every Christmas the old man shells out a ton of money to decorate the place like it's Rockefeller Center, with the lights, reindeer, and a sound system blasting Christmas carols right up to midnight. Nobody ever complains about the noise.

On Memorial Day he hosts a backyard barbecue and invites everybody in the neighborhood to eat his food and kiss his ass. Everything in the surrounding area is drawn to this place, ensnared by its gravitational pull.

Sal stops at the corner. The block is quiet, especially at this time of the day. Matty is probably in the living room now, huge TV switched to one of those stupid talk shows, sipping his third cup of coffee and thumbing through the *Daily News*.

Sal, we gotta stick together. This thing we got, it's more important than just one person. I know it's rough, but you can't just fall apart over something like this. You gotta take the pain.

The radio shifts into static; bits of some strange language pierce the noise, like the car is speaking in tongues and Sal decides that he hates Matty's house like he's never hated anything in his life. He presses down on the gas pedal.

The car picks up speed. The other homes on the block streak by on either side of him, the static grows louder, and it's almost like Billy is in the back seat, urging him on, that's it, big guy, show him who you are.

"Lamb of God who takes away the sins of the world," he whispers, "have mercy on us."

His phone starts to ring, probably Matty wondering where he is. Sal won't touch it; his eyes are aimed out the window and it feels like he's sitting still while the house rushes toward him, breaking free of its foundation to charge out and crush him.

The phone rings again and Sal wonders if it's his son calling from college, just to say, hello. Yeah, the kid only calls him when it's Father's Day or if he needs money, but Sal wants to believe it's his boy; he wants to believe his son is reaching out to him in the last few moments.

You have a chance here to atone for your sins. Wandering around your house, never sleeping, the fear gnawing at you every minute of the day. No one on this earth will miss you. Show everybody you're fearless and crazy, just like Billy. Show everybody you ain't ascared of God.

Sal figures if he hits the curb just right, the car could crash right through that picture window and take out that spiral staircase. With any luck Matty will be wheeling by at that same moment and the low flying car will grind the old man into pulp before it explodes and burns the place to the ground.

He is so close to that house, so incredibly close to actually doing this thing, when his survival instincts explode into action, when the frightened little man overrides the kamikaze brain waves, and Sal stomps on the brake, brake, you son-of-a-bitch, brake—

The car twists wildly to the right, sending up clouds of burning rubber, Billy's ghost isn't in the car anymore; it's just Sal frantically pushing his foot through the floor to make the goddamn car stop.

But he's just along for the ride now and through the windshield he sees Train charging out the house with his hand under his jacket, ready to kill whoever's behind the wheel of the runaway car.

Everything stops a second later, the car just inches from the curb, the engine panting like a dying husky.

"What the fuck are you doing?"

Sal lifts his head, as heavy as a bowling ball, and sees Matty at the end of the driveway. Train stands alongside the old man, in Sal's old spot, his hand still under his jacket.

Sal glares at Train in this near death moment, the murdering son-of-a-bitch who killed Lucille, who's got this look on his face that says, so what are go going to do about it, asshole? You know who my daddy is…

Sal climbs out of the car and staggers up the driveway. He's covered in sweat and breathing like he ran all the way here from Staten Island. People are racing out of their houses to see what all the noise is about and the old man glares a hole right through him.

"What the hell is going on here, Sal?"

It takes a few seconds for Sal to get the words out.

"Why…?" he takes a deep breath. "Why did…you do it?"

"Do? Do what, Sal?"

Sal leans over and gets close to Matty.

"You know what I'm talking about. I just heard it on the news—"

"Sal…"

"—on the radio, Matty, the fucking radio. That's how I find out?"

"Listen to me—"

"How could you do that, Matty? How could you do that to her?"

The old man looks at Sal for a few seconds, as if he's about to say something, offer an excuse for the vile thing he's done, beg for forgiveness and then have a 20-megaton coronary and make the world a better place.

But instead Matty leans forward and slaps Sal across the face.

The hand is hard, like a piece of petrified wood, and Sal is so weak, he almost tumbles to the ground. He stands there, touches his burning cheek and stares at Matty. Did he just fucking hit me?

"Get out of here, Sal." The old man's eyes are glowing. "Get the fuck out of my sight. Don't you call me, don't you come by, don't do nothing until I tell you to."

"But—"

"Don't say a fucking word to me, Sal. Just go."

Sal stands there, a ghost in human form. This stunt is going to cost him his life. Train smiles, eyeballs Sal in a malicious way that says they'll be meeting again very soon.

The old man jerks his head and Train wheels him back to the house. The door slams and Sal is alone. The house looks down as Sal staggers into his car and starts up. The neighbors retreat into their homes and Sal's car lurches down the block, heading back to the vanishing bridge.

6

Tommy finds out while he and Eddie walk down Richmond Avenue, mockey-eyed and fearless, laughing at every stupid thing they see.

People look at them and that's just what they want. Everyone has to be watching them.

The assholes who stare from their cars, the faggots walking on the sidewalk, who cut a wide arc around them because they know what will happen to them if they don't, anybody else who might be around, they all have to stop and look at Tommy and his boy having so much fun.

When Eddie's phone goes off, they laugh even harder.

"Excuse me, bitch," Tommy says, pointing low, "but your snatch is buzzing."

They go crazy over that one, roar and point at each other in amazement because it's just too fucking funny.

Eddie pulls the phone of out his pocket, struggles to hold on to it like it's a wet bar of soap and Tommy gives him the jerk-off sign.

"Fucking retard—"

"—hey, blow me—"

"—can't even work that thing; I mean, what a dick."

Eddie gets the phone out of his pocket, pauses to give Tommy the finger, and snaps the thing open.

"Yeah," he slurs. "Who the fuck is this?"

Tommy feels good, strong, a hell of a lot better than last night. He looks around at all these losers scurrying to the mall or their stupid jobs like cockroaches running for cover. They're just waiting to be stepped on.

"What?" Eddie shouts into the phone. "Speak up, asshole, I can't hear you."

Tommy smiles at his boy. Eddie sure came through, didn't he? They went back to his house with the two bitches and headed down to the basement while Eddie's old man was stretched out on the living room couch sleeping off his latest bender.

Tommy didn't say nothing, just grabbed the dirty blond, shoved her to a threadbare sofa, and started pulling off her clothes.

Eddie and his slut vanished into another room leaving Tommy to climb all over this tramp and make her yelp, cry, claw at his back and bite into his shoulder. He didn't care if he killed her, just as long as he broke free of the fear that was gripping him.

Get off me, you fucking animal!

Later, after she fell asleep with her head on his chest, Tommy looked through the darkness at the tiles on the ceiling and thought about his next move.

He wasn't going back to the house, that's for goddamn sure. And maybe it was the lack of sleep or all the shit he had gone through in the last few hours, but Tommy was thinking about maybe stopping by Uncle Matty's place, asking if he could be part of the crew.

That got him laughing, laughing so hard he could barely hold it in. Christ, how fucked up would that be, working for the guys who buried the old man?

The girl murmured and moved against him and he got the urge to wake her up, tell her who he is and what he's done. Let her know just whose dick she's been sucking.

You seen that shit on TV, that old guy getting killed? Well, that was me, bitch, how you liking that?

But then he started to think that she was just an ugly little pig, barely worthy of his time or his cock and his hand just kind of slid up to her throat, and it was such a perfect fit; the flesh was so soft, so fragile.

Her body stiffened and he saw that she was awake and staring at him. Tommy squeezed a little harder and her eyes opened a little wider.

She didn't move, didn't blink, she just watched him because there wasn't much else she could do. Tommy listened to her anxious breathing for a few seconds more before relaxing his grip.

"Get the fuck out."

7

"*WHAT?*"

Tommy turns when he hears the shock in Eddie's voice. He sees Eddie's mouth hanging open and his eyes bugging in Tommy's direction.

"What the hell are you talking about? That's impossible." He tilts the phone away from his ear. "It's Sergio over on Lincoln. He just seen something on TV..."

"So what?"

Eddie stares at Tommy for a few seconds.

"It's about...your mom."

Tommy grabs Eddie's shirt and yanks him up close.

"What about her?"

"She's—"

"She's what, you little prick?"

He pulls Eddie up on his toes, shakes him hard, and fed up with the asshole's babbling, Tommy takes the phone and shoves the little homo aside.

"What the fuck is going on?"

"*—it's all over the news, there was a shooting at your house, cops are there right now, they're saying your mother is dead—*"

"You're lying." Tommy says it calm and soft. "You're a lying mother fucker and when I get my hands on you—"

"*—no, it's true! I'm looking at the TV right now—*"

Tommy holds the phone right to his ear while the voice tells him that his mother's body was found in the kitchen of their house, that there are TV new vans parked up and down the block.

They're all in there, he thinks, cops walking through his house, going into every room, opening the closets, the drawers, looking over and touching everything, and taking picture after picture.

You've been threatening to kill her for so long and now somebody's saved you the trouble, got rid of the only other person in this world who really knows what happened last night. Somebody did you a big favor, son.

The old lady used to call him her little man when he was a kid and she'd hug him so tight, but Tommy doesn't want those memories, he wants them gone, cranking his arm back, he wants to cut them clean out of his brain—

"Bitch!"

Tommy hurls the cell phone out to the street, into the path of an oncoming bus that crushes it to nothing.

"My phone!" Eddie squeals. "My fucking phone!"

Tommy's not listening, not caring. He turns and starts pounding on the nearest parked car as hard as he can, over and over, smashing the windows, scuffing the body as the alarm screams *get off me your fucking animal!*

"Stop it! Stop it!" Eddie shrieks, trying to pull him back. "We gotta get out of here!"

Tommy shoves Eddie aside and works his way down the length of the car's body, leaving a trail of dents, scratches, and footprints.

Sick, demented old man, he's going to pay, he's going to pay so bad.

"Listen, Tommy, we gotta go." Eddie is frantic. "The cops are going to be looking for you…"

The alarm gets louder, memories from last night become sharper, and Tommy is going to keep on kicking this goddamn car until it's a pile of a scrap. People stare at him and that's just what he wants. Everyone has to be watching him.

"Tommy, c'mon—"

Eddie hauls him back and Tommy is ready to start pounding him, when he catches sight of some asshole staring at him, looking at Tommy like he's some freak in the circus. He tears the gun out from under his shirt.

"What are you looking at, mother fucker?"

Tommy goes right up to the bastard, the gun aimed at the guy's face. God damn, he wants to cap this fuck so bad. People are running away, jumping behind parked cars, while this schmuck stands there unable to make a sound.

"You like me, faggot? You wanna suck me off? Is that it?"

"Tommy, please," Eddie says, "we gotta get out of here!"

He knows Eddie is right, but Tommy can't let this thing go. The urge to kill is back, stronger than ever, and here he's got a perfect target for all this hatred. Be so nice to pull this trigger.

"Listen," Eddie whispers, "my uncle's got an empty house in Flatbush he's trying to sell, we can go there until we figure this shit out…"

Tommy nods, has to admit the little bastard is right. He'll never get to Matty if he gets nailed for blowing away this piece of shit.

He holds the gun in the asshole's face for a few seconds longer, lowers it very slowly, glaring at the prick the whole time like he could change his mind any second and shoot him right between his eyes. When the gun reaches his side, Tommy smiles.

"Some other time, little man."

They run the street, Tommy limping badly, like maybe he busted something kicking that car.

"You're crazy," Eddie snaps, "you're out of fucking mind, I swear to God!"

Tommy nods. No argument there, son. And people around here are going to find that out soon enough.

8

"Eternal rest grant to her, O Lord," Jake whispers over Lucille's covered body as he taps out a stealthy Sign of the Cross, "and let perpetual light shine upon her."

It's madness all around him, a small scale invasion in the middle of this poor woman's kitchen.

Local precinct detectives, guys from organized crime, uniforms, and CSU taking photographs, putting everything they see into evidence bags, stomping around upstairs as they march into the home's most intimate places. Paging Dr. Clusterfuck….

In the midst of all this activity, Jake feels like a wax dummy in a wrinkled suit. Jesus, he thinks, you better move a little before somebody throws a sheet over you.

So unbelievably cruel. Lucille had suffered so much as Billy's wife and even more as his widow. And now look at her, for fuck's sake, lifeless and bleeding in her own home.

Jake should have known something bad was going to happen after Billy's ghost failed to visit him last night. He had stared at the empty chair until the sun came up and the sanitation trucks did their T-Rex rumble down the street, but that son-of-a-bitch never showed.

He was thinking that it's pretty sick to be blown off by your own hallucination when the phone rang and Stan was telling him to get over to Billy's house.

There was such a crowd around the place—a herd of neighbors, TV news crews, photographers—cramming around the place as if they were crashing a movie premier.

He wanted to turn around when he saw them, go back home and wait for Billy to stop by, but he forced himself to walk through a squadron of gawkers and bloodsucking cameras.

Jake can't stop looking at Lucille's body. He wants to tell everybody in the room to stop, stop whatever the hell they're doing right now, and show some respect for this woman.

I knew her, goddammit. I sat right there in the kitchen with her after her husband disappeared. She's not just a victim or a statistic; she's a person.

It's stupid, of course and Jake's embarrassed for even thinking this way. This is a crime scene, dick, not a soap opera; if you can't help, go stand outside and take pictures with the rest of the freaks. And don't let the door hit you in the ass on the way out.

"Excuse me, Father, do you have time to hear my confession?"

Stan materializes next to him and Jake tilts a thumb down south of his belt buckle.

"Kneel down, my son."

"I'll meet you behind the church." Stan nods toward Lucille's body. "Looks like the shooter entered and exited through the kitchen door and, of course, none of the neighbors saw or heard a goddamn thing."

"That son-of-a-bitch." Jake says. "Couldn't leave her alone."

"We're talking about Matty, of course?"

"Who else?"

"You think she was putting the squeeze on the old bastard?" Stan asks. "Maybe she was giving the Cigar a hard time over Billy."

Jake lets the questions float by. It doesn't take much with Matty. It doesn't even have to be true.

"Tommy might have done this. People heard them fighting all the time. Maybe the kid finally finished her off."

"No, he didn't." Jake is certain. "It's the old man. And we've got to find Tommy before he does something stupid and gets himself killed."

"Yeah, what a fucking tragedy that would be."

"It's like Matty's trying to wipe out the whole family," Jake says. "He wants to erase Billy's bloodline."

"Who is this prick—King Herod?"

There was no way Sal would have signed off on this thing. He'd never stand for killing Lucille, which means Matty had it done without telling his second in command.

Sal's not man enough to stand up to the Cigar, so he must be roiling in guilt and terror right about now, shut out by the crew with nowhere to turn. How long before tortured spirits start invading his bedroom at some ungodly hour?

Jake walks into the living room, pretending to be investigating, when all he really wants to do is turn away from the body.

His eyes stop at a painting on the wall over the couch and he wonders absently if it had been there when he came to visit Lucille.

A bunch of clowns riding through the woods in a horse-drawn wagon—a seriously bad piece of work, the kind of thing that makes the dogs playing poker thing look like *The Last Supper*.

Jake could just imagine what his wife would say about a monstrosity like that. She would've come up with a pointed, biting assessment because she had an eye for such things and it's really too bad that's she's not his wife anymore, that she's been gone for more than a year now, moved to Florida with her new husband.

"Jake…?"

No doubt she's much happier now, free of Jake and his misery. She's far away, living in a houseboat under the bright sunshine with someone who really cares about her and doesn't hide in the past—

"Jake!"

Stan says his name sharply enough to turn a few nearby heads. He steps in closer and sinks his voice to a graveside whisper.

"What the hell is wrong with you?"

"What?" Jake plays the innocent card so well. "I'm fine."

"Fine, my ass. You were having a three-way conversation with yourself for Christ's sake."

"I was just…thinking, that's all."

Stan says nothing, but holds out a tissue, and Jake wonders what that's about until he feels the moisture leaking down his cheek.

"Oh, shit…"

"It's all right. Just take care of it."

Jake dabs his eyes and slips the tissue into his pocket.

"I'm sorry…I haven't been sleeping well."

A camera flashes somewhere behind them and Jake feels penned in, trapped between the crowd of cops in here and the nosy mutts outside. And he notices that his partner, his buddy, is eyeballing him, giving Jake the hard, pitiless stare usually reserved for punks, lowlifes and other enemies of the state.

It's really uncalled for. But Jake knows how to return fire, how to look as holy as an altar boy even if you've got a pound of coke stuffed under each arm and the Lindberg baby hanging off your hip. All of these years of grilling Grade A hard-ons like Billy and Matty Cigar have taught him a thing or two.

"Jake," Stan says after an eternity, "you got some vacation time coming, don't you?"

He thinks of landing in some strange city, with no one to meet him, standing alone by the luggage carousel, while his fellow passengers are greeted warmly by their friends and family and scatter in all directions.

"Yes, Stan, I believe I do. Why do you ask?"

Stan's face turns to concrete.

"C'mon, Jake," he says. "Do I have to talk to somebody about you?"

Somebody. That's the code word for a shrink who will disembowel Jake's every word, dissect his every gesture, put him on modified duty, take away his weapon, so all the young cops will do the crazy sign every time he walks by.

"No, Stan, I'm okay. Seriously."

"A lot of guys say that Jake—just before they eat their guns."

"C'mon, Stan, it's nothing like that and you know it."

"Do I?" Stan raises an eyebrow. "I've been to too many funerals, Jake; I don't want to go to yours."

"You're not invited, Stan."

Jake's going for the joke, but Stan is not smiling.

"There's some real nice travel deals in the paper today, Jake."

"But—"

"But, nothing. Get your ass home and start looking. And the next time I see that God-ugly face of yours, it'd better be sunburned."

Arguing would only make things much worse, so Jake takes one last look at Lucille, hopes that there really is a perpetual light shining upon her, and goes out to face the clicking mob.

9

BILLY SLIDES INTO the first seat at the counter, two chairs down from a road-blasted trucker slurping a bowl of tomato soup loud enough to drown out the Muzak.

It's freezing in here, as usual, and when Billy turns in his seat the squeaking gears set his teeth on edge. Shit, people, how about a little oil over here, huh?

He looks at the TV, volume down, flickering high over the end of the counter, does a smooth scan of the faces around him and sees only strangers. He eases back in his seat. All clear.

Billy checks his watch and sees Scotty has less than two hours to live. Plenty of time to get a cup of coffee, black, two sugars, before heading to the Gap to grease that pig.

Some guys will tell you that it's bad luck to come back to the place where you almost croaked, like camping on an Indian burial ground or dropping slugs in the poor box. But Billy sees poetry.

He was reborn on that morning, returned to the land of the living while that guy he was pretending to be, that imposter with the easy-going manner and the nice girlfriend, stayed behind. stretched out lifeless on the cold tiled floor.

This is where Billy the Kid hauled his way up from the darkest pit of Hell, shook off the burning embers, and proudly declared that he wasn't ascared of God. He is risen…

"Hey, Billy, how you doing?"

That waitress, Marie, Marianne, some fucking thing, comes toward him with a two-watt grin on her face and drags a sponge over Billy's slice of the counter.

"Not bad for an old feller."

"You sure look better than the last time you were in here."

"Been taking my vitamins."

She lets out a shrill laugh that makes him cringe. As she walks off to get the coffee pot Billy drums two fingers on the counter and reviews the plan.

Get down there early and find cover. Stay out of sight until that backwoods baboon shows up, beat him until he's three-quarters dead, soak him down, and light him up. That fat fuck ought to cook all night long.

You really shouldn't have threatened Lora like that, big guy. Ordinarily, Billy would've let you off with two behind the ear and called it a day. But you've earned yourself some very special treatment and before this day is over you'll be cursing your mother for giving birth to you.

You burn that son-of-a-bitch!

Billy flattens his palms on the damp surface, feels the tombstone coldness seep into his fingers. You're going to take the pain.

"Here you go, big guy."

His head snaps up and there's the waitress standing right over him pouring his coffee. Where the hell did she come from? He feels exposed, as if all his homicidal thoughts are being blared out on the TV.

Billy suppresses a shudder. He's plotting a brutal murder here and the waitress catches him with his hand down his pants? Last time that happened you wound up with a hole in your brain.

"Thanks."

"Get you anything else?"

"Yeah, how about a fur coat to wear in this ice box?"

"Oh, now, Billy, don't tell me you're cold."

"Oh, no." He rends two sugar packets with one tear. "It's just that I always thought 'when hell freezes over' was a figure of speech."

The waitress lets go with another screech owl laugh and slaps Billy's hand.

"Oh, Billy, you kill me. I swear, you honestly kill me."

Don't give me no ideas. Billy raises the steaming cup to his lips while the waitress goes over to give the soup-sucking trucker a refill. Now, now, best save the anger for our chubby little friend.

He puts the mug back in the saucer and looks around at the people in the booths, walking outside in the parking lot, coming and going in the bright sunshine.

As soon as he pays for his coffee, Billy's life here is over. Whatever happens, wherever he ends up, he knows he'll never come this way again.

He looks down at the spot on the floor where he collapsed that day, when he peered up through the agony to see Lora, tears in her eyes, doing everything she could to keep him from slipping away.

She's the reason he survived that day. It's nothing a doctor would accept, but Billy knows it's true. He's not rotting in his grave right now only because Lora wouldn't let it happen.

The cash register clangs out loudly, like Quasimodo swinging in the bell tower. The temperature keeps dropping and Billy's alarm system goes off, like it did when he was standing outside Vince's house, telling him to throw some money on the counter and vacate the premises *muy pronto* before some seriously terrible shit happens.

But his body refuses to move. He came here to prove he wasn't afraid of omens or hexes or little green men and he'll be goddamned if he'll turn tail and run. He's Billy the Kid and he'll leave this place when he's good and fucking ready and not one minute before. Hell, he just might treat himself to a piece of pie.

He turns toward the door and almost tumbles out of his seat when a woman walks into the diner looking so much like Lora that he's certain it's her, coming here to forgive him.

And Billy was ready to slide Matty's gun down the length of the counter, take Lora into his arms, and walk out of this frostbitten hellhole with her and move to Wisconsin or Wyoming, or anywhere else she wants to go.

He's all set to speak to her when the woman changes before his eyes, the molecules of her face rearrange and there's someone else, a total stranger, who bears no resemblance whatsoever to Lora, standing there looking at him nervously.

Billy—

He whips around, looks beyond the trucker crushing crackers into his soup bowl, down the counter, and up to the TV screen and sees Lucille looking down upon him.

It's impossible; she can't be on TV, even though he knows he's seeing her with his own two eyes; Lucille can't be on that screen.

He blinks, realizes it's a photograph, grainy and dated by her short haircut and her smile, so joyful, he hardly recognizes her.

Billy tries to place the situation, when and where that picture was taken. Why she had been so happy when the shutter clicked and why he wasn't next to her. Billy can't retrieve the memory, but he knows Lucille is dead. And he knows that Matty killed her.

The counter starts to lift toward the ceiling, like a ship riding through a typhoon and Billy holds on tight. The whole building threatens to tumble over, break apart all around him, and he pushes down hard to keep the place together.

A fragment of the news report reaches his ears.

—gunned down in her home—

Her home, Billy's home, the one he bought for her, the one that he abandoned.

The photograph disappears and there's some blow-dried asshole with a microphone standing in front of Billy's house, his home choked off by yellow tape and encircled by a mob of gaping monkeys who wave and point at the camera like it's a tailgate party.

Tommy, what about Tommy? What happened to his son?

Billy stares at his house and it's like he's been gone for 20 years. Something catches his eye, someone in the background walking behind the reporter, his head down, heading for the front door.

"Jake…?"

The figure disappears into the house and Billy fights to hear what the reporter is saying, but these goddamn hayseeds all around him are talking, slurping soup, ringing bells, and humming along with the Muzak for Christ's sake.

He wants to scream at all of them to shut the fuck up—

—wife of missing mobster—

Blood pounds into Billy's head. Missing, who's missing, you scumbag? I'm right here, right in front of the TV, can't you see me, you stupid son-of-a-bitch? Everyone knows me, I'm Billy the Kid, and I ain't ascared—

And now he looks at his own face, dialed back several years to the time when he had the moustache Lucille had hated so much. It was from one of the barbecues at Matty's house and he's just waiting for one of these douchebags around him to do the double take, look at the face on the TV, then to Billy and back again, holy shit, is that guy…?

His first instinct is ease out the door without making a sound, but Billy holds his position. A quick exit, no matter how smooth, could give him away. He forces himself to pretend he's casually interested in the story about some gangster's wife.

Gee, what a handsome young man. He takes a sip of his coffee. I wonder how the pie is today?

—who is presumed dead—

No, goddammit, Billy's not dead. Down here, shithead; I'm hiding out in this jerkwater town pretending to be a human being. Billy the Kid is alive; it's just everybody else around him who ends up dead.

You see? That's why he had to let go of Lora because he knows that if he stuck around she would be the next one shot down in her home, the next one on the TV screen, and he looks at that cold counter top, churning with that knowledge, that truth, until he rears back and knocks the coffee mug to the floor.

Everything goes spooky quiet. The only sound is "One More Night" on the speakers and the voice on TV, loud and clear now, done with Lucille's murder and talking about a traffic accident that's causing all kinds of head-aches for area motorists.

Billy doesn't move. His hand is nailed to that stained surface and he doesn't dare look up because every pair of eyes in the place is aimed at him.

The waitress, Marie, Marianne, some fucking thing, approaches him slowly, her eyes wide, holding a big red menu in front of her like a shield.

"Billy… you okay?"

"Yeah, yeah." His voice crumbles like tin as he struggles for an excuse. "I…just forgot something back home."

What home, big guy? You left the one you shared with Lora and the one back in the city is a crime scene. You ain't got no home.

"You feeling sick?"

She's worried he's going to hit the deck again, scare away the customers.

"No, no, I'm fine."

His hand trembles as he reaches for his wallet, to pay his bill and get out of this place, and his back stiffens when his fingers brush the gun bulge in his belt. And at that second Billy wants so badly to use this weapon on every living thing he sees.

Start with the waitress, end that screeching laugh forever, and go down the line, nail the trucker, mix his blood with the tomato soup, and then the salesman, the nurse, the butcher, the baker, the candlestick maker. If Lucille can die, why can't all these losers join her?

It would be like shooting targets at the carnival. No one would escape, not with all the bullets in Billy's gun. He's got enough slugs to kill them all three times over and still have one for himself.

It's the worst nightmare or the craziest thrill.

The cops, the ambulances, the TV crews can all descend on this place and Billy will blow a kiss to the sharpshooters before he puts the gun in his mouth and pulls the trigger.

"Billy, do you want me to call someone?"

There's no one to call, you stupid pig...

"No, I'm all right."

Billy uses all his strength to move his hand away from the lump under his jacket, drops a twenty from his wallet on the counter, and makes the treadmill march through the frigid air to the front door while everybody in the place watches.

"You take care, Billy."

He waves limply over his shoulder, pushes against the door, and it feels frozen solid, trapping him in this tomb. He pushes hard, uses so much strength he's about to fall on his face, and it's all done in total silence with the AC breathing down his spine and these bastards staring at him.

The last time Billy was this fucked-up at least he had Lora to keep him going.

Help me, please!

The door finally moves an inch, Billy slams his body against hard against the glass to get free, and staggers into the sunlight.

Scotty nails a spot behind an elm tree across from the rest stop and crouches down on one knee for a test run.

Yeah, this should do fine. Nice view of the whole spread, like old Lee Harvey down there in Dallas. And Superman himself could X-ray eyeball these woods until he got cataracts and he wouldn't so much as spot a hair on Scotty's doublewide ass.

He pops open his Atlantic City souvenir binoculars and scopes out the drop zone up close and hostile. The place sure looks right, Scotty thinks, working a chaw around his mouth. Now if only it felt right.

He puts the binoculars away, shifts his body against the tree trunk and winces as the pistol pushes hard against his gut. Careful there, brother, or they'll be picking your nuts up in Tennessee.

Moving slightly, he pulls out the .38 that his cousin swore was clean—and God help that trailer park parasite if it ain't—and puts it behind his back.

Scotty's thinking just how dumb, how bonehead Grade A stupid it was to let Billy, the fucking enemy for Christ's sake, pick the location for this thing when the cheapshit walkie talkie that he picked up in JC Penney squawks in his front pocket.

He jumps like he's been zapped by lightning. Shit, he thinks, that can't be good for the old sperm count. He pulls the damn thing out and tugs on the antenna.

"What?"

"Hey, Scotty, it's me—"

"I know it's you, dipshit." The sound of his cousin's voice makes him angry. "What do you want?"

"I got an idea—"

"No, you don't." Scotty scowls in the vicinity of where his cousin is hiding with the .30-06. "You have no idea about nothing at all. Got it?"

"Yeah, but—"

"—listen," Scotty growls. "If I want any shit from you, I'll squeeze it out of your head. Just shut your pie hole and be ready to move when I say so. And Larry, I swear, if you fuck this up—"

"—I know," his cousin says all hurt and dejected, "you'll kill my ass."

"Good boy. Over and out."

Scotty puts the walkie talkie away. Knew this was a mistake. Ask that meth monkey to get him a piece and the next thing Scotty knows he's got a partner. Nobody else in the family would give that *non compos dickus* the time of day and it's easy to see why.

Larry didn't have a pot to piss in or a window to throw it out of, but that doesn't stop him from flapping his gums about how he's going to head to Miami someday real soon, and live the high life with a hot tub full of freaky-ass bitches.

Yeah, slick, no doubt; I'm sure your welfare check will go a long way down there in South Beach.

Still you don't want to pull a gig like this without some kind of backup and while Larry may be borderline spastic, he can still shoot the pecker off a gnat from a hundred yards away. That kind of firepower could come in handy on a day like today.

Scotty takes out the .38, aims it Dirty Harry style toward the rest stop, and pictures Billy kneeling before him with his hands up begging for his life like a frightened little fag.

Die, scumbag, die, Scotty thinks, fantasy firing round after round into Billy's coal black heart. Die, you New York greaseball faggot mother fucker!

The daydream feels good for a few seconds before it melts like ice cream in a blast furnace. Stop jerking off, lard-ass. You haven't got much time.

Now when that animal shows up, Scotty is going to wait to see if everything looks kosher, string Billy along a little bit before making his appearance.

Then he's going to cross the road, real cool and casual, and say, hey, bud, what do you say? Once he gets his money, he turns and walks right back into the woods, slow and steady as you please.

And if that prick tries anything stupid, all Scotty has to do is lift his cap, the signal to Larry to blow Billy's head right off his shoulders. America ends here for you, numb nuts.

Scotty wipes a patch of sweat from the back of his neck. It sure sounds like a great plan; he just wishes he wasn't standing in the middle of it.

There's been this buzzing going on in Scotty's head ever since he got up today and he's been trying to ignore it, blaming it on last night's beers or this morning's Scotch, but he knows down deep what the real problem is: he's scared shitless.

If anything goes wrong over there, if Billy tries to get rough, if Larry misses the target for the first time in his despicable, no-account life, if his gun jams, or any other such unforeseen miscellaneous bullshit comes to pass, then Scotty will be facing that psychopath all by himself in that little patch of green.

You only get one shot with a freak like that. You miss and he'll be all over your ass like King Kong on crack.

Scotty looks up and sees a van come down 611, drive by the rest stop and disappear toward Portland.

Lucky bastard, whoever you are. You may think you've got problems, buddy, you may think your life is fucked up beyond all possible repair, but at least you're not waiting in the woods for the Antichrist with no one but the village idiot backing you up.

Don't be like this, boy. You've got to show this shithead who's running this show. Just set him straight, clean him out and leave him gagging on your dust.

Scotty starts to amp up, actually believing he might walk away from this deal with the money in his pocket and his genitals still connected to his body. But his gumption steams straight out of his ears when he catches the sound of his favorite pick-up rolling down the mountain.

He watches the truck slow down and turn into the rest stop and Scotty wishes to hell and back that he hadn't started this goddamn thing. But if wishes were horses, Scotty would be neck-deep in manure. He hits the walkie talkie button.

"All right, fuckeroo," he whispers, "it's time for shittin' and gittin'."

10

WHEN HIS HEAD clears, Billy looks up from the steering wheel and sees that he's here at the rest stop, where they killed him so many months ago.

It's impossible. Billy could swear, bet his goddamn life, that he had just passed under the railroad bridge in Mount Pocono 20 miles north of here.

He had just escaped the diner, broken free of the traffic knot and was speeding down the main drag with a voice in his head saying you killed her, you killed her like you pulled the trigger yourself.

He remembers pressing down on the gas pedal, racing to the cold dark safety beneath the bridge, where he could be shielded by ageless iron. Nothing could penetrate the solid metal spine that had borne the weight of those great old trains.

Billy came into daylight on the other side, faced 611's long drop and thought he was safe until he reached the spot where Lora's brother got killed.

Fucking kid. Been a curse from the day he was born

Sunlight raked his eyes and something big, heavy, was crossing into his lane, and Billy braced for a crash because there's no time to hit the brakes or turn away—

And now he's here in the rest stop, the entire drive deleted from his memory. He must have flown down I-80 in a waking coma and God alone knows if he sparked a string of deadly accidents, left stacks of broken bodies and burning vehicles in his wake.

Billy gets out of the truck, checks his watch, sees that Scotty's due here in 30 minutes. He starts walking. Whatever he did or didn't do, none of that shit matters now.

When he's done here, Billy's going to get back into that truck and head east. He's going to take care of those bastards back in the city, do all kinds of terrible things to them and their loved ones, so that when people talk about him, they'll cross themselves and say Billy the Kid was the baddest motherfucker who ever lived.

He walks slowly over to the embankment and stares over the edge. Damn, just imagine falling into that shit…

"Lucille," he whispers into the air.

Scotty watches through the binoculars as Billy gets out of the truck and zombie walks across the rest stop. Now playing right in your face, *Night of the Living Fucking Dead.*

Looks like he's hypnotized, stomping around like that. Scotty frees up one hand to take out the radio.

"Larry," he whispers. "Larry!"

"Yo…"

"Get ready."

"10-4."

"I'll 10-4 your ass, you pea-brained son-of-a-bitch."

Just nuke the fucker now. If Billy's got the money on him, a little blood won't make it any less green. And if he doesn't, well, we're no worse than we were before.

He zones in on Billy, who is still down there, motionless, and that buzz in Scotty's head sounds more like a 747 taking off.

God damn, he thinks, this is worse than having a job.

Billy looks down at the ground, as if his footprints might still be here, imbedded in the ground for eternity like Neil Armstrong's on the lunar surface. But it's only history for him. The rest of the world doesn't give a damn.

He hesitates before looking over the edge, afraid he might see his own rotting corpse looking back up at him.

Is he dead?

If he ain't now, he never will be.

His legs buckle and the trees rise and fall before him. His lifeless body is trying to pull him over the edge, tired of being alone down here and wants some company—

Billy staggers from the edge of the embankment, pain pushing brutally through his head. He crashes into the pick-up, snaps his head up to the dying sun, and begins to scream.

"Lucille!" His fists pound on the truck's hood. "*Lucille!*"

11

Scotty's got the binoculars pushed so hard into his eye sockets he doesn't need his hands. Cannot believe this shit. We knew the guy was crazy, but this business is whack enough to make a dozen slasher flicks.

"Holy shit," he whispers. "Holy fucking shit…"

Get a load of that bastard, eyes rolling, spit flying out his mouth, screaming at some bitch who ain't even there and look what he's doing to my poor truck.

Scotty's hands shake, sweat rolls off his face in buckets, and there's a very strong possibility that he just pissed his pants.

"This thing is fucked," he says softly, afraid Billy might hear him. "Totally fucked."

What the flaming flipping hell were you thinking, tangling with this lunatic? Never mind the goddamn money; just get out of here alive.

Scotty drops the binoculars, takes out the .38 and aims at Billy with two rubbery arms. Goddamn it, he watches the gun barrel twitch all over the back of Billy's windbreaker, just relax and squeeze, you fat hump.

Billy goes into high gear just then, wailing like a dying gorilla and hammering away on the pick-up. Scotty lowers the weapon and yanks out the radio.

"Shoot him, Larry!" He croaks. "Shoot that mother fucker!"

And gunfire rips through the air.

For a second, Billy sees himself going all crazy on the truck, a sane part of his mind has broken free and watches this spectacle from the opposite side of the pick-up.

That's it, big guy, tear it up. Go crazy. Have a fucking tempter tantrum, That'll do Lucille a lot of good, won't it? You left that woman to die back there and you can't do nothing about it now. You were so stupid the night you came to this spot, let that gutless loser get right on top of you—

Billy pulls out the gun, Matty's gun, presses it under his chin, preparing to stop this awful pain, but he hears them sneaking up behind him, Sal all mealy-mouthed with I'm sorry, I'm sorry.

It's happening again, Billy's getting a second chance, only this time he's ready, and he whips around in the shooter's stance and fires four wicked shots right into those fucks, and there's no way he could possibly miss.

When the pain subsides and his vision clears, Billy sees that he's alone, the gun in his hands smoking and pointing at nothing at all. He's by himself here, shooting at phantoms.

"Jesus fucking Christ…"

Scotty throws himself to the ground, out of his mind with fear and rage, and it's all he can do to keep from demolishing his BVDs. That fucking prick almost parted my goddamn hair.

"Larry," he snarls into the radio, "will you shoot this bastard already, you stupid fucking idiot?"

Goddamn cunnerman reject, I bring him in on this thing, I do all the planning, and all I ask him to do is sit there on his ass with a rifle and—

Scotty's brain goes into vapor lock. A deep river freeze sinks into his head and drops right down to his sphincter. He brings the radio to his lips and speaks in a shaky whisper.

"Larry…?"

Billy stares at the gun vibrating in his hands like it's trying to break free from his grip. The echo refuses to die and there's a cloud of smoke around him that seems determined to follow Billy for the rest of his natural life.

There was somebody there, in the woods, Billy was sure of it. But he sees now the he just had a shootout with the trees, so lost in his fantasy battle that he dragged it out into the real world.

He could have killed some poor bastard driving by or dropped a hiker who picked the wrong time to stop and take a leak. The next one to come down this road could be a cop.

Billy puts the gun away, gets into the cab and throws the truck into a screeching reverse. Fuck Scotty and his food stamp shakedowns; Billy will take care of him later. Right now he has to get out of here; he has to run away from this place and leave the dead behind.

Billy jumps on to 611 South and roars down the road like he just committed murder.

12

Scotty stares down at the pulpy mess that used to be Larry's head and lets out a long low whistle.

"And people always said you was brainless." He spits into the tall grass. "They should see you now."

He looks over at the rest stop and back at Larry's corpse. Goddamn, being a lunatic sure hasn't hurt Billy's aim any. Screaming, crying and foaming at the mouth like a Bellevue lifer and he still manages to put one right between Larry's tweaky little eyes.

Scotty shakes his head. Shit, have I got the worst luck with partners or what?

First that asswipe brother-in-law dies on me and now the gimp-brained cousin gets in on the act. Try to help these shitheels and they can't even stay alive. This is starting to piss Scotty off.

"Jackass!" He kicks Larry's carcass in the ribs. "Can't you do nothing right?"

He looks south, the direction that his truck and that satanic son-of-a-bitch are headed. All this planning, aggravation and misery and all Scotty's got to show for it is a dead moron. Christ Almighty, Scotty hates Billy so fucking much he can hardly breathe.

Now what? You can call the cops on him, but there's no profit in putting that prick in jail. Them bastards in blue got such a hard-on for you they'll probably lock your ass up just to hear you squeal.

Could clobber the ex, sure, but the way Billy lit out of here it's pretty obvious he don't give a shit about her or anybody else.

One thing's certain, though: this shit ain't over. Scotty has no idea how, what or when he's going to do it, but he's going to hammer Billy in the worst possible way imaginable, I swear on Larry's bullet-riddled cadaver, I will hang that scumbag's balls from the tallest tree in creation.

"We ain't done yet, fucker," he says, "not by any stretch."

Scotty reaches down, removes Larry's wallet from his pockct with two fingers, and inspects the contents: Crumpled twenty dollar bill, an old lottery ticket, and an expired driver's license with a photo of Larry's former face. Quite a haul you got there, Dillinger.

He puts his mind in hyperdrive. Scoop up Larry's remains, make them disappear along with his car.

Can't see anybody in the family actually giving anything resembling a fuck over this turdasaurus, but if someone asks, we'll tell them that Larry finally made good on his Miami masturbation and won't be coming back.

Scotty takes one last look down the road.

Lucille, he thinks, I don't know what your story is, honey, but you're better off without him.

Lora sleepwalks out to the back of the house and dumps the mess she cleaned up from the kitchen floor into the trash.

She only put in a few hours at work today before telling her supervisor she felt sick and needed to leave early. And it was something like the truth, too. Lora felt godawful and it got even worse when she came home and saw the pick-up was gone.

He's never coming back. She doesn't need a letter to spell that out for her. Billy's gone. That look on his face when he was talking on the phone told her everything she needed to know.

He wanted her to stay; she could see him pleading with her through his eyes to remain in the room with him. But he couldn't hang up the phone, couldn't do that one simple thing for her. When he turned away, Lora knew she'd lost him.

She tries to think that it's better this way, really forces her mind to accept this idea over some very heavy resistance.

C'mon, there'll be no more late night mystery rides, no more suspicious odor of smoke stinking up the house, no more unanswered questions, no more lies, goddammit, no more lies. You're finally free of that grief, praise the Lord.

But none of that stuff is working. Lora hadn't been able to reach him. She'd walked out when she should have stayed to help pull him through whatever nightmare was dragging him down. She failed him and it hurts so much that Lora just wants to disappear from this place and never be heard from again.

A car seems to be slowing down in front of the house, but Lora is in no mood for company. She closes her eyes and wonders if everyone in the world could please just leave her the hell alone for a little while.

13

THERE SHE IS, outside the house, and George can't believe his luck.

He always drives by here when he's on patrol and hopes he'll actually see her and have an excuse to stop. George has spotted Lora exactly twice in the last two years using this method, but he's goddamned if he'll park the cruiser and knock on the door like a normal human being.

No, he prefers the luck of the draw rather than risk of being greeted by Billy on the front door step.

All he wants to do is talk with her, that's all, just shoot the breeze about old high school buddies, the weather, stock market, it doesn't matter just as long as George gets a chance to talk with her like they used to before Billy showed up. It's all perfectly harmless, even though George can't help but wonder if he's nothing more than a stalker with a badge.

He tries to refute his self-made allegation because it's not like he's showing up at her job or trailing her down Main Street, or going through her trash or any other sort of demented crap.

George has locked guys up for that kind of stuff and he knows that he is nowhere near that brand of crazy. He's just trying to be a good friend.

He's such a good friend that he hasn't told anybody about seeing Lora's truck the night that gangster's house went up—not the fire marshal, not the guys in the department, not even his fat-assed shadow that seems to be getting bigger every day..

He knows he could make things very difficult for Billy, the guy who saved his life, but Lora could get hurt in the process and wind up hating George forever, so he's not saying anything until he has a chance to talk to her. A chance like now.

She's standing by the trashcan and George has a legitimate reason to stop, stop the damn car, turn around and go talk to her before she goes back inside.

He cuts a fiendish U-turn, like he's responding to a terrorist attack, pulls up in front of her house, and does his very best to ignore that voice that keeps muttering stalker, stalker, stalker….

The house seems to be drifting away from her, leaving her in the middle of nothing, and it feels all right, really, like she's going into a trance and maybe she'll see her way clear of all this heartache. Yeah, it could happen…

"Hey, there."

Lora looks up and sees George, yes, it would be George, walking toward her, his patrol car hugging the curb behind him. She tries to smile.

"Hey, yourself. What are you up to?"

"Oh, you know." George nods back toward his cruiser. "Fighting crime, protecting the innocent. The usual."

Lora searches for something to say that'll make him feel welcome, but she would be very happy right now if George climbed back into his cruiser and drove on out of here.

"No work today?"

"Ah, I came home early. Feeling a little rundown."

"Nothing serious, I hope?"

"No, no, nothing serious at all."

"How's Billy doing?"

"He's okay." She lies with such ease now. "He's still getting those head-aches, you know? But I try and get him to see the doctor…"

George nods in fraudulent sympathy; he's trying to be nice and supportive, while some dark corner of his heart is strenuously praying for Billy to drop dead.

It's cold out here, colder than it has any right to be and Lora knows she really ought to send George on his way, but the thought of going back into that house by herself makes her shudder.

"You want to come in for some coffee?"

All right, cowboy, take it easy; it's just a cup of coffee. It's not like she's asking you to move in with her.

"Well…" George tries so hard to sound casual. "Yeah, why not?"

He radios in to let them know he's 10-7, and follows her into the kitchen.

His eyes sweep around the room, notes that the floor is shiny from just being mopped and the stinging smell of whatever cleaner she's using still hangs in the air.

She pours two cups of coffee, hands him one, and George nods his thanks. He spots the paper on the kitchen table.

"That was some business from last night, huh?" George sips at his coffee. "Poor old guy."

"What…?" A dark wave crosses her face and vanishes. "Oh, yeah, that was terrible."

"And we got all these arsons going on, and more people keep moving in. God, Lora, this place has changed so much since we were kids."

"Yeah." Lora looks down to her coffee. "Some days I don't know where I am."

He hears the despair in her voice and he knows, just knows, that it's because of Billy, that no good son-of-a-bitch, *knew he was trouble the moment I laid eyes on him.* George wants so badly to holler through all this polite talk, tell Lora what he knows and demand to know what's going on here.

But he has to go slow with her, real slow, or she'll think he's just trying to take Billy's place and he'll spend the rest of his life driving by her house in a police car.

"You know," he says so gently, "you can always come to me if you've got a problem. You and me go back a long way—long before I was ever a cop. So if anything's ever bothering you, just let me know, okay?"

"Good old George." Lora sips on her coffee. "Always there when I need you."

"You got that right."

And she starts crying. Nothing loud or out of control, just a slow line of tears rolling down her face like rain on a windshield.

"Lora…?"

It's awful to see her in such pain and he takes one arm and pulls her so gently, almost no power at all, and she comes to him, her face resting on his chest right by his badge, and George can't believe this is happening, that he's actually holding her in his arms.

"Ah, Lora, what is it?" He whispers. "What's wrong?"

"I-I don't know…"

"C'mon, Lora, it's me."

"Everything is just…wrong." Her voice sounds so distant, as if she's lost in the woods. "I-I don't understand it. It's all gotten away from me, my whole life, and I don't know what to do."

He slides his arm around her waist and, Christ, he hasn't held her close since they danced in high school.

"It's okay, it's okay," he says softly. "What happened—you two have a fight?"

She's trembling and George knows she's going to tell him the whole story, and he's going to make it better, she'll get over this and George will come around here more often, and not just drive-bys, but real visits; and maybe one day she will ask him to move in, yeah, even though she went for Scotty and then Billy without giving George a second look, he knows he can get it right this time.

All he has to do is keep his big mouth shut for once in his life and it'll all fall into place—

"What did he do to you, Lora? Tell me. What did Billy do to you?"

George feels her warm soft body abruptly turn to a slab of ice, knows instantly that he's lost her, and when she lifts her face she's giving him the hardest stare, looking at him like he's a stalker, a stalker with a goddamn badge.

You can't throw words into reverse, buddy. Make all the excuses you want, I'm sorry, I didn't mean it, let me explain, but once something stupid slips out of your yap, you're done.

He sees right into her mind, like opening a window in a thunderstorm, hears her angry thoughts—Goddammit, Officer Puppy Love is trying to interrogate me—and feels her firmly pushing him away from her.

"I think you'd better leave, George."

"Lora, I just—"

"—please, George."

She won't even look at him now, turns her eyes away and waits for him to waddle his ass out of her house. George stands there looking for something to say, but it's way too late for that. He nods stupidly, a big old sheepdog blundering around the living room.

"Yeah…okay…you take care…I'll see you around."

George retreats from the house, flinches at the sound of the door slamming, then locking behind him. He walks away with his head down and as he opens the door, he sees himself from Lora's point of view, a chubby, pathetic man running for the safety of his car.

14

Tommy cuts a ragged spiral around the block and sneaks up on the dark house from behind.

He staggers through the Manfredi's garden loud enough to get their stupid mutt going, drunkenly tumbles over the backyard fence and lands so hard on his ass it's a miracle the can of lighter fluid in his back pocket doesn't explode and blast him clear across the heartless sky.

Mockey-eyed, he thinks, his brain in freefall. That's what his father would have said. The stupid bastard's mockey-eyed. What a fucking pussy. Sorry, pops, let you down again.

The barking finally subsides while Tommy stretches out in the dirt and searches the black nothing for any sign of the moon and stars.

"Where are you?" He slurs up to heaven. "Where did you all go?"

His old man used to talk about how beautiful the sky was in Pennsylvania, how you could see the stars so clearly, track the satellites whizzing overhead, not like the city, where you couldn't see anything—yeah, yeah, always with the goddamn stars that prick. Maybe he was an alien.

"Fuck you," he sneers toward the craven Big Dipper. "Fuck every last one of you."

It's too bad a frenzied comet hadn't come sizzling out of the stars many moons ago and cremated Billy the Boy Astronomer right where he stood.

Tommy never would've been born, of course, but that doesn't bother him a whole hell of a lot. Billy's little bundle of joy isn't exactly setting the world on fire. He realizes the joke a few seconds later and can't help smirking. Well, at least not yet.

He opens his eyes, grabs the trunk of the cherry tree his father planted 20 years ago, and pulls himself to his feet. His stomach reels as he lurches up the deck to the kitchen door and that moo shu pork he scarfed down this afternoon is begging for a return engagement.

Tommy stops on the deck, reaches for the keys in his pockets, before realizing what the fuck, and kicks the goddamn door wide open. The glass panes crack to bits and scatter across the kitchen floor as Tommy steps through the doorway.

Drained from the effort, he slides to the floor with a heavy, leaden sound that rolls through the deserted house. Yeah, he thinks, his face resting on bits of broken glass, it's good to be home.

He'd spent the day in that empty house in Flatbush, last building on a dead end street, right up against the subway tracks so it sounded like the train was going to plow through the wall. Eddie's uncle owns the place, but he's never there, so they buried themselves alive in the basement, smoking, drinking and staring at the widescreen.

When the phone rang, they ignored it; when the doorbell chimed, they refused to move. And when some stupid motherfucker made the mistake of pounding on the basement door, Tommy grabbed up his gun and swore he'd drill the son-of-a-bitch if he knocked one more time.

Whoever it was walked off, never knowing how close he'd come to being a corpse.

Tommy finally booted Eddie out for a Chinese food run sometime in the afternoon when the hunger had overtaken him. His timing was good because the news was just coming on as Eddie was leaving so Tommy was alone when his mother's face filled the screen.

She looked so happy, as if nothing had ever troubled her. Tommy was looking at a stranger, so unlike the miserable ragdoll who had crawled around the house half-drunk and wailing all the time.

He struggled to his feet, stumbled to the screen, stroked his mother's image as if it were a lost puppy. Tears were in his eyes and he wanted so badly to slide his hand through the screen and touch her for real—

Tommy snaps awake on the kitchen floor, his mind cruelly recreating her last moments, as she stood there terrified, just stood there, unable to move, while some scumbag aims a gun right at her —

"Bitch!" He sobs like a little girl, hammering his fist down on the glass particles spread out around him. "Stupid fucking bitch…"

Billy stands wrapped in shadows, and looks across the street at the two-story mausoleum that used to be his home.

It's stupid to come here; the cops could be watching the place hoping the shooter might be reckless enough to return to this house. But Billy has to see the place where Lucille died. He has to do his penance.

The cops must've gotten whatever they needed, and knowing how Matty operates, they didn't get much.

Billy wonders if that really was Jake he saw walking into the house on the news. It's nice to think so, comforting to believe that she wasn't surrounded by strangers during those last moments.

He looks at the other homes on the block, most of them dark now, but a few with flickering TV screens in the windows, signs of normal people living their lives.

A cat wails in a nearby alley, warns him of a car coming down the street. Billy presses himself against the wall of the house and thinks, hey, this is where that nosy old bag lives, the one who spies on everything that goes on around here.

Billy's tempted to walk up the steps, ring the doorbell, and say, hi, neighbor, what's new? It'd be fun to watch the withered old skank have a coronary. But it'll have to wait.

He turns around and walks quickly around the block, slips through the alleys, until he spots the cherry tree in the backyard.

Billy climbs over the fence to a dog's barking outrage, lands softly on the grass, and moves over to the tree where he stops and stares at the house.

"What the fuck…?"

The backdoor, it's busted open. Billy's guilt morphs into rage at the idea that some scumbag has violated this sacred place. Stealing from the dead— are we in the fucking Congo or something?

He hears faint sounds coming from inside as someone moves around the house, Billy's house. He smiles, happy the intruder hasn't left yet, and wraps his fingers around the .45. Make yourself at home, big guy. I'll be there in a minute.

15

Tommy squints his way around the living room. He ignores the blood trickling down the side of his face, doesn't give a damn if he drops two pints all over the place. He has to see this house one last time.

He had told Eddie he was going out, none of his fucking business where he's headed or when he's coming back.

Eddie whined about how you can't go out now, son, the cops are looking for you and you're fucked up now, and made it necessary for Tommy to slap him around until Eddie shut his mouth and gave up the car keys.

Tommy halts when he sees the dark blotch on the carpet. Jesus Christ, look at that. So much blood, Tommy can't imagine it all coming from her. Like someone slaughtered a calf on this spot, conducted some kind of demonic ritual and summoned evil spirits from every corner of hell.

Tommy can't take his eyes off that stain, his mother's life spread out at his feet. It seems to be moving in the feeble light, growing larger, and his own blood drips down from his face and joins the mark on the floor.

Get off me, you fucking animal!

His eyes remain on the ugly mark while he takes out the lighter fluid and snaps it open. We're going to do this thing right, so old pops down there on the Ninth Circle will be real proud of his only misbegotten son.

There won't be any trace of this house when he's done, not one thing you could ever identify, just the front walkway leading to a patch of scorched earth

And when he's finished here, Tommy is going to visit Uncle Matty, tie the old bastard to his wheelchair and talk about the good times they had when Tommy was a kid. And then he's going to soak Matty in the good stuff from head to withered toe, and drop a match on him.

Tommy grins coldly. Dad would have wanted it that way.

He tilts the can and pours, pours, lifting up and down with a flourish, bullwhipping the stream of gas through the air. C'mon down, drinks are on the house.

Tommy empties the can, tosses it into the gloom over his shoulder, and reaches into his pocket for the lighter. He's snapping out sparks when he hears the kitchen door gently swing open and he knows it ain't no breeze.

Motherfucker, he mashes the lighter in his hand; some spic, nigger or whatever is looking to do some late night shopping. Not that Tommy is mad or anything, oh, no, not at all. It's nice to have company drop by, especially during your time of need. Too bad this fuck won't live to use his food stamps.

Tommy takes out his nine and presses himself against the wall.

"Come on in," he whispers in the dark.

Billy moves through the kitchen gently, hands wrapped around the .45, barrel down, and does his best to step around the bits of glass on the floor. The house is so quiet each crushed fragment sounds like boulders falling off the roof.

The bastard's in the living room, trying to be quiet. All right, we'll let the little wonderboy think he's in control.

It feels like he's been gone for decades. Billy wants to focus on what's going on now, but he keeps looking around, struggles to recall the good times they had as a family in this house.

There's got to be something in his scrambled brain, a birthday, a Christmas morning, a barbecue in the backyard, one event that can make him smile. But it's just a blank.

He remembers sneaking in through this kitchen door here late one night after banging some tramp, the light coming on and Lucille standing there in her robe screaming and cursing at him. He backhanded her across the face, nearly slammed her onto the floor before he left and stayed away for two days. He remembers that night just fine, but—

Billy stops when the smell reaches him—lighter fluid. Son-of-a-bitch, he's planning to torch my house? Oh, man, are you fucking serious? Billy is the master firebug in this part of the world and now he's going to make this asshole lap up every drop of that shit and drop a match down his throat.

He steps out into the middle of the room, senses his victim is just over his right shoulder, pressed against the wall like a bug. Billy makes himself a target, plays like he doesn't know anyone's there.

Okay, faggot, make your move…

He's all ready for the attack when he looks at the space over the couch and sees something's different, something's changed since he's last been in this room all those ages ago.

It's dark but he can still see that there's a painting on the wall and he peers at the image until he can make it out, and, shit, it's that fucking atrocity with the clowns, the one that sparked their last big fight.

Billy hated that thing so much he told her to get rid of it, get it out of his house, but Lucille had different plans. He wasn't coming back, so he didn't have shit to say about what went on here, and this was her little way of telling Billy to rot in hell—

"Cocksucker!"

The guy bum-rushes him and Billy just has time to drop low, turn, and clout his attacker across the face with the .45.

A gun falls to the floor and Billy headbutts the bastard under the chin as he doubles over, fires three sharp punches to the shadowy face, savors the pain in his knuckles and the sound of dead weight hitting the floor.

"You want to shoot me, big guy?" Billy kicks the bastard in the gut. "In my own house? Shame on you…"

Billy drops to one knee, clamps his fingers around the exposed throat and squeezes; yes, nothing gets their attention like impending death.

He dodges the flailing legs, turns from the mauling fingers desperately trying to blind him. Billy's been doing this a while, so he knows what to expect.

"That's it, buddy boy," he whispers. "Go down fighting."

But Billy feels something seeping through his bones, something he sensed the moment he started pounding this guy. He knows goddamn good and well who this is, who's dying in his grip. And that makes Billy squeeze even harder.

The kid's bigger, stronger than Billy remembers, but he's just as stupid as ever.

"How's it going down there, slick?"

His son gags and chokes and it feels good having the power to slowly grind someone's life down to nothing.

Just a few hours ago Billy was whimpering all over that rest stop in PA, shouting at mirages and firing at ghosts, and now here he is, back in the city and fucking up every loser he sees.

Billy never had the chance to do this with his old man, tangle mano-a mother-fucking-mano. Lucky you, he thinks, you always wanted to dance with me, so here we are. Now you can show me what a man you are.

The air grows thinner, his vision goes cloudy, and the harder Billy squeezes, the worse it gets. The walls are moving, his eyes fix on that painting, and he's slipping away from this place, this time.

I will sail to the Sea of Japan—

The pain gets worse and if Billy keeps squeezing he knows they're both going to die, which seems only right in a rather fucked-up way.

Charley, it's me, Billy. Don't you remember me? You were my best friend in the whole world.

The room sways and rolls, the pain in his skull pounds away relentlessly and finally he can't hold on any longer. His fingers go slack and he feels his body crashing to the floor, right on top of the ugly red stain on the rug.

16

THE LIGHTER FLUID brings him back, the sharp, murderous smell pushes into his nostrils, up into his brain, and he's on all fours, not quite dead, and groaning in tandem with his son. One of them is rapidly wheezing out fucking bastard, fucking bastard, but Billy can't tell who it is.

He inhales again, rises on wobbling knees, and reaches for the back of the sofa to keep from falling. The swearing fades and Billy sees Tommy stretched out on the floor, one hand weakly massaging his throat. Billy kicks his son's leg.

"Hey…get up."

Tommy groans and sputters, but stays on his back. Billy kicks him again, harder.

"Get up, asshole."

Tommy opens his eyes, slowly turns his head and the men stare at each other in the bloodless light. They don't move, they don't speak; they just look at each in mutual disbelief.

Billy never thought he'd see his son again. He planned to live as long as he could without ever having contact with his only child and it really wouldn't have bothered him all that much.

He stares hard, tries to give off a deadly vibe, but he's exhausted, and if Tommy decides to continue this little wrestling match, Billy won't be able to stop him. A passing car breaks the silence and Tommy slowly sits up.

"I thought…" His voice is a rough whisper. "I thought you were dead."

"Thinking was never your strong suit."

Tommy touches the side of his head, gently rubs his neck and Billy can just make out the angry splotch on the kid's throat.

"What happened? Where were—?"

"—none of your goddamn business."

Tommy keeps staring at him and it's making him angry, like the kid expects Billy to sprout horns and float over the coffee table.

"I should have known they couldn't kill you."

"Yeah, you should have known."

The lighter fluid stench fills the room. It's going to be daylight soon and Billy doesn't want to be anywhere near this house when the sun comes up.

"They killed her, didn't they? They killed Mom?"

Mom sounds so strange coming from this kid's mouth. Billy nods.

"Yeah..."

"You're going after them, right? You're going to kill them?"

"Take a guess."

Tommy stands up a little quickly and Billy almost flinches.

"I'm coming with you."

Billy shakes his head.

"Forget it—"

"—I'm coming with you. I'm going to be in on this and there's nothing you can do to stop me."

Billy looks hard into Tommy's eyes.

"I stopped you once already, asshole."

Anger flashes across Tommy's face and Billy glares at him until the kid looks away.

"We're done, you and me. I've got business to take care of and it's got nothing to do with you."

"But—"

Billy leans in, cocks his head, and points to the scar.

"You see this, scumbag? You see this fucking thing?"

"Yeah, but—"

"I got this because I was stupid. I turned my back on people I thought I could trust and they tried to kill me. So I work alone. Now and forever."

"You gotta let me come with you."

"I don't gotta do shit."

"She was my mother!"

Tommy screams in his face and Billy almost grabs his throat again to finish him off for raising his voice, for being here tonight, for being born in the first place, for forcing Billy to become a father. He turns away from Tommy and he's back looking at that goddamn painting again.

"You can't leave me behind," Tommy whines over his shoulder. "This is my business, too."

He can't argue, can't listen to any more of this crap. It was supposed to be simple, in and out, start things up and watch the place burn. Now he's got this horseshit hanging over him.

"I'm not letting you do this alone—"

Billy reaches up, rips the clown painting off the wall, smashes it over his knee. His son stops talking.

The noise is like a cannon blast in this crypt and after he drops the two halves to the floor, Billy turns back and sees Tommy's mouth is hanging open.

"You got a match?"

They wait in Billy's truck at a corner one block away until they can see the orange glow lighting up the sky, hear the sirens getting closer. The house is fully involved, so beautifully involved, and Billy wishes he had torched a few more of the dumps on that block just to crank up the mayhem.

"All right…" Tommy shakes his head and smiles. "Look at that thing burn."

Billy remembers driving Lucille out here the first time 20 years ago, a beautiful spring day, and she busted out crying when she saw the place she loved it so much. Matty had spotted him the money, and they moved right in.

He became a father, a homeowner who tended the garden, chatted with neighbors over the backyard fence, and worried about leaks in the basement. He knew it wouldn't last forever with the life he had chosen, but he never thought it would end like this.

"Follow me," Billy says.

He drives away from the noise, keeps going until the end of the island, near the Outerbridge Crossing. Tommy tails him in his own car and they go to a deserted underpass where Billy stops and climbs out of the truck.

He stands there for a long time just looking at the pick-up, instead of doing what he knew he had to do.

Lora was driving this truck the night they met. She was behind the wheel of this thing when she stopped to help him, a total stranger; there's probably traces of Billy's blood in that cab. And she half-carried him to this truck when his head caved in at the diner and Billy could hardly walk.

What is it, baby? Please tell me, what's wrong?

Billy pours lighter fluid on the front seat and takes out Tommy's matches. He feels like he should say a prayer and he might have done that very thing if he were alone.

"I want you to listen to me," he tells Tommy. "You come with me, you do what I say. You don't question me, you don't mouth off, and the second I say 'jump' both of your feet better be off the ground. You give me any kind of shit whatsoever, I'll kill you on the spot. I don't give a fuck if we're outside St. Patrick's Cathedral on Christmas morning, you're dead. You got that?"

"Loud and clear, big guy."

That's almost worth a bitch slap right there, but Billy turns back to the truck, lights a match and tosses it onto the front seat.

The roaring heat climbs up his back, but he doesn't want to look at his handiwork, not this time. He climbs into the dead man's seat and slams the door.

"Let's go," he says.

17

It's late, way too late, and all Rex wants to do is bounce these last two hard-ons and go the hell home.

He's leaning against the register, evil eyeing this pair of douche bags who can't seem to get the hints that Rex has been dropping like blockbusters for the last half-hour.

Franco, sawed-off little shitheel, sits just on the other side of the taps and fumes into a glass of melting ice cubes, furious about something, as always.

Down at the end of the bar, Teddy Farina got his freaking cell phone stuck to his cheek like a push-button tumor. He's gotta be talking to his asshole amigo, Carmine, the only person he ever calls, and they gotta be arguing about something stupid.

"Ah, man," Teddy groans into his palm. "You're so full of shit it's embarrassing. I mean, you're not even here and I'm embarrassed *for* you."

And I'm embarrassed for the both of yous. Rex is tired tonight, right down to his ankles. This place, these stiffs, all this other bullshit, it's sucking the life right out of him.

There was a time when Rex thought he had the best gig in the neighborhood, boy, working for Matty and the crew. People looked at you different when they heard your story. They got out of your way, didn't give you no lip. It was all right.

But things have changed around here and Rex feels like he's going nowhere fast enough to break the sound barrier. The neighborhood is filling up with all kinds of foreigners, the old timers are getting senile, and the young ones are so stupid it makes you wonder if somebody changed the laws on inbreeding.

It's like he's invisible behind this goddamn bar and that stained white-tiled ceiling over his head is moving down on him an inch at a time. One night it's going to grind him right into the floor.

The Cigar has been talking since forever about moving Rex up in the world, but talking is about the only thing that gets done around here and with all the grief that's been going on lately, it's suicide to even think about asking Matty again.

It all makes Rex so angry that he wants to take that baseball bat he's got below the register and start swinging at everything he sees.

Maybe it's time to pack it in, he thinks, scare up some cash and open his own place in Jersey or wherever. The only trouble with that is Matty tends to get upset when people leave the fold and he's been known to give them an oil drum farewell.

But Rex has got to do something now, before the old man dies because the moment the Cigar kicks off it's going to look like downtown Bogota around here.

Everyone knows that Sal is the biggest pussy on five continents, so the young bangers are going to make their play, along with the Russians, the Albanians, the Israelis, the Eskimos, the Watusis and every other schmuck in this town who's got a gun and something to prove.

"Yo, Rex, you sleeping over there or what?"

He looks up and there's Franco's waving his glass around with a snotty look on his face that practically begs you to palm heel the little dink into the next zip code.

"What's your problem, Franco?"

"My problem is that I'm calling you like a dozen times over here and you're just standing there like a wax dummy."

"So?"

"So?" Franco is stunned by the question. "So whose cock I gotta suck to get a drink in this shithole?"

Rex looks at this insect, this waterbug, who struggles to fill that atrocious maroon jacket hanging off him like a stolen bed sheet. Franco is somebody's cousin or nephew and he likes to throw his weight around whenever Matty's not here.

"No, goddammit," Teddy scolds his phone. "You're wrong on this—dead wrong!"

Rex usually puts up with Franco's bullshit because it's not worth getting into it with a runty little fag like this. Only tonight Rex isn't feeling very usual.

"I think you've sucked enough cock for one night, Franco."

The small man's eyes bulge halfway out of his head.

"What? What did you say to me?"

"It's time for you to go home."

Franco glares at him.

"Go home? I want a fucking drink, dipshit. Now stop jerking off and make it happen and maybe you'll keep your job."

Rex stands up and folds his arms across his chest.

"Go home, Franco."

"What the fuck?" Franco slams his glass on the bar and sends up a midget geyser of stale water. "You prick, do you know who you're talking to?"

"Yeah..." Rex smiles tightly. "The little cocksucker."

All right, he shouldn't have said that and he knows he's going to be in seriously deep shit with Matty tomorrow.

But right now it's worth whatever abuse he'll have to take later just to see Franco's face screw up like somebody threw him a surprise enema. He slams his hand down on the bar hard enough to turn Teddy's head around.

"You fuck!" Franco starts to take off that hideous jacket. "Come over here and say that to—!"

But Rex is already on the way, so happy to oblige his favorite customer. He comes around the bar, snags the back of Franco's neck before the runty little prick has a chance to get his coat off. Rex squeezes hard, makes Franco wince up on to his toes and takes him to the door, tip-toeing this screechy munchkin like a ballerina while Franco swears and flaps his arms.

"What the fuck are you doing?" Franco screams. "Let go of me, you mother—"

"C'mon, Franco, it's time to say goodnight."

"—you scumbag—"

Teddy grins, shakes his head at the commotion that's going on right in front of him and gives his little phone the play-by-play.

"You won't believe this shit," he says, "Rex is throwing Franco out of the goddamn bar. I swear to God, he's got him by the neck and he's hauling him out like a sack of laundry. Huh? I'm standing right here watching it, you asshole!"

Rex pushes by Teddy and his goddamn phone friend, hip checks the door open, and drags Franco out to the deserted avenue, while the sawed-off little hump spews out curse words like a mynah bird in a microwave.

Yeah, he thinks, I'm gonna be in trouble over this one.

18

THEY'RE ACROSS THE street from Matty's club, foxholed in the dark of an empty storefront, Billy in the lead, Tommy over his shoulder. They came here straight from the burning van, over the bridge with the smoke from two fires still hanging off them.

He feels Tommy vibrating behind him, high on the thought of hurting someone. The kid says he wants to avenge his mother, but Billy knows that he just wants to destroy something. Okay, badass, he thinks, the show starts now.

Sal's house is in the wrong direction, back on Staten Island, too close to the roaring fire that used to be Billy's home. And Matty's place is a fortress with cameras, alarms, and floodlights.

This place is different, just guys hanging out. The club was where it all began for Billy and it's where he wants it all to end. He feels the life he had in Pennsylvania fading away like a mirage. This is where he belongs, in the city, with the mutts, ready to raise hell

"You fucking prick!"

The club's door explodes back on its hinges, Billy squints and, hey, look, it's Rex the Wonder Dog, Matty's chosen bitch, coming out of the bar half-dragging, half-carrying that hostile little pygmy Franco.

Can't think of the last name, but Billy used to have fun teasing the screechy jerk by calling him Franco-American and watching the smoke come out of his ears.

"What's going on?" Tommy whispers.

"Irate customer."

They watch Rex shove Franco down to the sidewalk, dust off his hands, and swagger back toward the doorway that glows like an open furnace. Franco struggles to his feet and screams as the door closes in his face in slow mocking motion.

"I'll be back, motherfucker!" Franco's squeal bounces off the bar's shaded window. "I'll be back and I'll burn this fucking place to the ground, you see if I don't, you fat bitch!"

Billy shakes his head. Get in line, peewee, get in line.

Franco lingers in front of the bar as if the whole building will come tumbling down under the weight of his terrible threat and Billy wonders if Rex will come back for a curtain call and smash Franco's head into the pavement.

Franco-American abruptly spins around and lurches down the block muttering "fucking bum, fucking bum," until he disappears around the corner. Billy turns to Tommy.

"Wait here until I call you."

Tommy nods and Billy heads out across the street, toward Matty's holy place.

Rex comes back inside from bum-rushing Franco feeling rather proud of himself. One asshole down; one to go. Teddy the clueless is still on the batphone, naturally, still running his mouth.

"Oh, man, you should've seen it," Teddy narrates into his talking canker. "Serves him right, too, that obnoxious hump. He thinks he's hot shit, but he's just cold diarrhea."

"Hey, Teddy…"

Teddy puts his traffic cop hand up and Rex clenches his teeth.

"What—you're still with that? Oh, c'mon, how come you gotta be so stupid?" He turns to Rex. "Hey, big guy, help me out with something."

"I don't think so, Teddy, it's getting late."

"C'mon, it won't take a second." He points to the cell. "I got Carmine here—"

"—hey, how come you guys do everything over the phone? You live two blocks away from each other for Christ's sake."

Teddy plugs his open ear with an index finger and shakes his head in a vigorous negative.

"Bullshit, Carmine! You don't know nothing." He looks to Rex. "You know that show *The Twilight Zone*, right?"

"The what…?"

"*The Twilight Zone*." Teddy rolls his eyes. "It's a classical TV show. They do the marathon on one of the stations every New Years, all day long. C'mon, Rex, you gotta know this show. It's got the music."

Teddy peppers Rex's brain with this stupid do-do-do-do noise like he's never going to stop.

"Teddy, I don't know it—"

"-sure you do. There was a show about this bum who puts on a dead gangster's shoes and he, like, turns into the guy? Then he goes to the gangster's bar and orders this drink, this special drink, that only the dead guy has."

Rex can barely shrug at Teddy's words.

"Yeah…?"

"So what's the name of the drink?"

Rex stares at Teddy, who nods rapidly, trying to coax the answer out of him, and he's got the phone away from his head so Carmine can hear the response in real time.

Finally, Rex raises his arm and points toward the door.

"Get the fuck out of here!"

"Hey, Rex, c'mon, I got five hundred bucks on this!"

"I don't give a shit if you got your first born on it, get out!"

"But you're a bartender," Teddy protests. "You should know stuff like this."

Rex is so happy that the baseball bat is out of his reach because if he so as much touches that black-taped handle, Teddy's head, phone attached, will go sailing out onto the avenue like a soccer ball. And Teddy will probably still be talking on the goddamn thing.

"Hit the bricks, Teddy."

"C'mon, Rex, don't be a hard-on."

Rex stands tall and uses his bulk to corral Teddy toward the door.

"Say goodnight to your girlfriend in the Twilight Zone and fuck off."

"Can you believe this bastard?" Teddy pleads to his wireless sidekick. "Now he's throwing *me* out of the place!"

He holds the phone up for a second so Rex can hear the outraged squealing.

"Fucking guy thinks he's top dog around here." Teddy angrily moves in reverse. "You just wait, you wait till I tell Matty about this bullshit. You'll be out of here so fast your head will spin!"

Teddy backs out of the club yakking his fury into his hand. Rex closes the door, and the place is suddenly quiet, so peaceful, like God hit the almighty mute button. Rex draws the bolt and exhales loudly. Being alone never felt so good.

He shakes his head on his walk to the bar, appalled at how the whole operation is falling apart. I should know this stuff because I'm a bartender? What the fuck?

He pops open the register, looks at that money and the bills look back at him. Rex wonders how all that cash would feel in his hip pocket. It wouldn't be stealing, really, more like combat pay for the crap he puts up with around this place.

Rex hears a noise coming from the back room, which is funny because he knows the back door's got the keypad lock and he, Sal and Matty are supposed to be the only ones who know the code.

He grabs the baseball bat, maybe Franco's come back to start some more trouble and give Rex an excuse to crush his skull.

He takes one step when the door to Matty's office flies open and there's this guy, this fucking guy who is supposed to be dead sliding out of the room grinning crazy and holding a .45.

And now Rex hears that *Twilight Zone* theme loud and awful in his head, wonders how he could ever have forgotten that singular piece of music, and watches the jubilant corpse approach him with the gun aimed straight at Rex's heart.

"Tequila," Billy says, "with a lump of sugar."

19

BILLY FEELS LIKE he can hold on to this moment for as long as he wants, as if he can command time to take a break and start up whenever he says so.

There's Rex, his jaw dropping toward the basement, eyeballs swelling with shock, like a swimmer who's been suddenly yanked five miles out to sea.

And here's Billy holding Matty's gun, feeding on the terror in the big man's face and nodding at the perfect timing of the deafening ghetto blast of a thumping car stereo passing by at this very instant that is loud enough to swallow the sound of a gunshot whole.

He thought the club would look different in some way; paint job, new chairs, maybe replace that old Flash Gordon TV. He figured they would mark his departure in some way. But no, a taxidermist couldn't have done a better job of preserving the place just the way he remembers it.

Billy restarts the action, pulls the trigger, and the recoil is wicked, but the gunshot is barely audible beneath the boom box camouflage. Rex slams back against the bar, looks down at the gushing hole like it's a food stain spreading on his chest.

The only thing keeping him up is the thunderous noise and when the music fades away, Rex tumbles down behind the bar.

Billy takes his time, walks slowly toward Rex so he can sweep his eyes around the room and take the tour of his own life. He listens to his even, deliberate footsteps, looks over at the chairs and tables, the fading pictures on the wall, the pool table and juke box.

He follows the circle all the way around until you reach the back room where Billy had just come from, where he swore his loyalty to Matty a generation ago.

I hear good things about you.

Over there in the corner, that's where Billy stood over the old man and cursed him all to hell. It was a pretty short walk, wasn't it?

Rex gags up the little bit of life he has left and Billy comes around the end of the bar until he's looking down at the dying man's inverted face, at the failing eyes rolling in a terrified orbit within their sockets.

"Hey, big guy, how's it going?" Billy lifts the nearest bottle from the shelf. "You mind…?"

He tilts the bottle in a mock toast, cranks his head back, and pours it straight down his throat.

He can tell it's Scotch, by the burn of it, and after he wipes his mouth with the back of his hand, Billy hurls the bottle clear across the room. It smashes against the wall and showers down in glass and whiskey all over the table where he stood before Matty and roared out his suicide solo.

"So, Rex, did you miss me?"

Liquor drips down the wall as if the building itself is bleeding and Billy reaches for another bottle. A fiery hit of something and then the glass bursts against the wall.

"I hope so because I sure missed you."

He reaches for his third bottle, his third drink, he's not even tasting this stuff now, and lobs another missile across the room. The stain deepens, spreads across the wall, while the shards of glass pile up on the empty table.

"Yeah, there I was, down there in Hell, just burning away with all the other damned souls; pitchfork up my ass, little devils gnawing on my balls, when I suddenly remembered I forgot to tip you the last time I was here."

Rex is barely breathing he's so close to death, but Billy is still thirsty, and he chugs another drink, another fastball right down the middle. He stops when he sees the baseball bat on the floor near Rex's head.

"Now how could I possibly stay there and fry for all eternity knowing that I had screwed such a decent, hard-working man out of his tip?"

Billy picks up the baseball bat, holds it in his two hands, loving the flawless feel of the thing, and he turns to the bottles lined up on the shelf. Look at them bastards, sitting there, defying him, with the pourers capping each one like hooded falcons.

He goes to work, swinging the bat and smashing everything on the shelves, all the birds of prey blow up, spill their guts, and the air reeks of spilled alcohol.

Billy whips the bat madly, like he's taking on Satan himself, nearly falls over from swinging so hard, and stops only when he sees the mangled face of an aging madman holding a Louisville slugger staring at him.

The wicked are estranged from the womb...

He winds up, because he knows that the wicked go astray as soon as they be born, speaking lies, and he destroys the mirror into flying bits of bad luck, knocks over the cash register which cracks open when it hits the floor and pukes out reams of panicked dollars.

Finally, he looks down at Rex, who still manages to be living. Billy is, too, though he's breathing hoarsely, his head inches away from breaking apart.

He raises the bat, stretches his shoulder and back muscles to their limit, and the pent-up energy surging through his veins makes his entire body quiver.

"So here you go, big guy," Billy says, "here's your fucking tip!"

At some point he becomes aware of hands reaching for him, pulling him back; he doesn't know who or why and he doesn't care. Someone is talking, but it's drowned out by the horrible wheezing noises coming out of his chest.

He shakes the hands away, goes back to swinging the bat again, again, that's all Billy can do, keep hitting over and over.

The hands grab him again and Billy whirls around, raises his club, and roars in pure Neanderthal.

"Get the fuck—!"

"Hey!"

He stops, the bat vibrating over his head, and the world comes back into focus. Someone is standing in front of him, Tommy, his hands up, ready to block, ready to attack.

"Relax, son, it's just me."

Billy tightens the grip on the bat for a second before loosening up. He lowers the bat slowly, sees the gore spread all around him, the blood smeared on his leg, the demolished body at his feet. He grabs the lapel of Tommy's jacket.

"Don't you...ever touch me again, you fuck!"

Tommy grins, places his hand over Billy's and slowly and pulls his father's fingers away.

"I'll try to remember that."

The two men stare at him other before Billy drops the bat beside what's left of Rex.

"What are you doing here?" he says. "I told you to wait until I called you."

"You were taking so long I wanted to see if something happened to you."

Billy wipes the perspiration from his face. The kid's right and that makes him even angrier.

"You got the stuff?"

Tommy holds up a knapsack.

"Right here."

"Then get to work."

Tommy takes out two cans of lighter fluid from the knapsack. He turns his head to look at the body on the floor, gives off a sick smile and a low whistle.

"Goddamn," he says. "You fucked his ass up. He owe you money or something?"

Billy ignores his son, picks up the lighter fluid and douses the corpse, then the bar and shelves. Tommy gets the hint and spreads the stuff around the pool table and furniture.

It's too bad Sal and Matty weren't here, so Billy could end this thing. But they got one less place to hide now.

Drunk last night and drunk the night before, gonna get drunk tonight like we never got drunk before...

When they're finished, Billy turns to Tommy.

"Go wait for me outside."

"Can't I watch?"

Billy gives Tommy a hard stare to let him know some things must be done in private. Tommy shrugs and leaves through the backroom.

Billy lights a match. He feels like he should say something before letting it go; maybe pray, cry, or howl like a coyote, something to acknowledge what's about to happen here.

"I'm sorry," he whispers and drops the match.

20

THEY GET TO Matty's place shortly before three in the morning, just as the firefighters are lugging the swollen body bag through the entry wound that used to be the front door.

"Hey, Jake." Stan grins and points toward the mayhem. "Somebody stole your idea."

Jake can't say a word. He feels bad enough being out of the house at this ungodly hour, the time when Billy's spirit usually shows up in his bedroom. What will that lost soul think when he finds Jake isn't there to greet him? Maybe I should've left a note, he thinks.

And now this. Much as he hates the place and wishes all kinds of horrors upon the clientele, Jake always believed that nothing short of the hand of God could destroy Matty's rat's nest. Looks like the Lord was working overtime tonight

Floodlights torch up the street to a movie set's brightness, so all the world can see the heart of Matty's ruined fortress, the blackened walls, shattered windows and smoldering furniture.

Fire engines are strewn all over the street, streaks of revolving red lightning slashing the surrounding storefronts. Waves of smoke rise from the rubble and stretch out over the cops, firefighters, EMTs, TV news crews, and a small knot of locals who stand around the barricades, many in robes and pajamas, murmuring toward the wreckage like mourners at a bishop's funeral.

The younger ones don't understand, Jake thinks. They don't know the importance of this smoke. All they see is the charred remains of a broken down saloon that's been in the neighborhood since the Redcoats moved out; where a bunch of old guys with big cars, clunky jewelry and loudly outdated clothes like to hang out. They'll forget all about this dive before the debris is hauled away.

The older people, though, the ladies with the white hair, the men with the canes and the hearing aids; they know what's going on. They remember how Matty ruled the streets from this place, how people who wanted to stay in one piece never went in there, unless it was to pay off a debt or show their respect. They know the smoke means the end of an era.

Think of all the crimes, all the sins, venial and mortal, that have been planned, celebrated, denied and committed within those crumbling walls.

No wonder the place went up so quickly, Jake thinks as they get out of the car.

"Hoo-wee, I smell barbecue!" Stan slaps his hands together. "Let's break out the weenies!"

A couple of uniforms laugh, but Jake doesn't join in. He recalls his visits to this place, where he'd walk through the front door and be greeted by a rolling wave of amnesia, an acrid fogbank of I don't know, I wasn't there, I didn't see nothing before he even asked a question.

Billy was different. Sure, he'd lie his ass off like the rest of the them, but at least he was cordial. He'd be reading the paper or collecting money from some jerk-off who'd been stupid enough to challenge him to a game of pool, see Jake and give off the biggest smile.

"Hey, big guy, have a beer."

"Can't drink on duty, Kid."

"Ah, c'mon, Jake, live a little. Nobody here's gonna rat you out."

That much was certainly true. Secrets were about the only things that were safe in Matty's place.

He remembers going in there after Billy disappeared. Matty sat in the corner, big stogie grafted to his fingers, Sal and Vince perched on either side of him like matching bobble heads, nodding at every lie that dripped out of the old bastard's mouth.

Oh, I don't know where he could be, Jake. He's been acting funny lately, you know? Not his old self. And he's been having trouble with the wife. I think he said something

Lying old crocodile, couldn't tell the truth if you put a gun to his grandson's head. Driving back that day, with the cigar smoke still clinging to his lungs, Jake finally exploded.

"Son of a bitch," he snarled, pounding on the steering wheel. "I'd like to burn that place right down to the ground."

And, of course, Stan made a note of it.

Keller, a detective from the six-two, gave them the basics. Fire broke out at around 1:30 AM, suspicious in nature, but appears to be arson, big fucking surprise, as evidenced by the rapid spread of the flames.

One male victim found inside, believed to be one Rex Carbone, 27 years old—and he won't be getting no older. Said victim may have a gunshot wound to the chest and severe head trauma, though that's a little hard to call right now seeing as how the flames roasted the living shit out of this loser and gave him the kind of suntan that never goes away.

"Maybe we should pick up Colonel Sanders," Stan says. "We got a bucket of Extra Crispy here."

The blaze also damaged two upstairs apartments and a neighboring deli, but no decent human beings were harmed in the making of this disaster, thank God for small favors.

Keller tells them about the leads they're working on and as he finishes Jake sees Sal standing shell-shocked near one of the barricades.

He can't believe how bad the guy is looking, hollow cheeks, two-day stubble, Sal is little more than an upright slab of flesh.

"Christ, will you look at that hapless fuck?" Stan asks. "If a funeral home did a corpse that way, the family would sue."

Jake and Stan walk up behind their man and Sal is so out of it, no idea that he's got company. He just stares at the fiery wreckage like he's ready to hurl himself on top of it. Stan leans over and gets right next to his ear.

"Boo!"

"What the fuck—?" Sal whips around, furious and terrified.

"Easy, Sal," Jake puts up his hand. "We're the good guys."

Sal steps back and glares at Stan.

"Yeah, I keep forgetting."

"So what happened here tonight, Sal?" Stan asks. "Matty switch to exploding cigars?"

Sal shakes his head wearily.

"Is there something I can do for you guys or what?"

"We want to know about the fire," Jake says.

"So do I, Jake."

"Well, why don't you tell us everything you know?"

Sal scowls and falls into the routine.

"I don't know nothing about this. Rex was here by himself and he was supposed to close up, like he does every night. Next thing I know, the Fire Department is calling me to get down here."

"Alas, poor Rex." Stan puts a sarcastic hand over his heart. "The world has lost a great man."

"Hey, a young guy is dead here—"

"—and not a minute too soon."

"You shouldn't be making jokes like this." Sal tries to put an edge to his voice. "I gotta call his mother tonight and tell her what happened to her only son."

"Rex had a mother?" Stan raises an eyebrow. "I thought he crawled out of the sewer like the rest of you rats."

"Hey, I don't gotta put up with this bullshit!" Sal throws up his hands. "You guys are unbelievable..."

"Take it easy, Sal," Jake says. "You know Stan likes to break people's balls."

"Yeah, well, his timing ain't so good, Jake."

"Okay, settle down." Jake nods to Stan to back off. "But I think even you'd have to admit you guys been having a serious run of bad luck lately."

"I guess so, Jake."

"Well, let's take a look." Jake counts off on his fingers. "You got Billy missing and presumed dead. Your cousin gives his own brother a standing cremation. The cops in PA tell us Matty's summer house got torched—the place he's had for years. And then Lucille, that poor woman, gets shot dead in her own home."

"Look, I—"

"—we were there, Sal; me and Stan. We saw her body and I have to say that only the lowest piece of shit in the world would do something like that.

Don't you agree?"

Sal looks at him with bloodless contempt. Jake is giving him the business and he can't do much about it.

"Whatever you say, Jake."

"And now the bar gets cooked." Jake says. "From where I'm sitting, it looks someone's got it in for you guys. And yet you got no idea what's going on?"

"No, Jake, I don't. Some crazy bastard murders my bartender, burns down my place and I'm supposed to have all the answers? The world is full of freaks."

"Say, speaking of freaks," Stan says, "what do you hear from Vince, the chef of the future?"

"Christ Almighty, give that shit a rest, huh?" Sal rolls his eyes at the new line of questioning. "I ain't seen my cousin in God knows how long and the last time I did, he had one foot in the grave. He's probably dead by now."

"He's got a lot of company."

"I ain't seen Vince. Period."

Jake nods, accepting the answer for the moment.

"Okay, you ain't seen your cousin. What about a guy named Franco? You seen him lately?"

"You mean Franco Bova?"

"Yeah, asshole, that's who we mean," Stan snaps. "Franco Bova, they call him Franco-American, that's the guy we're talking about."

"So?"

"We hear he got into it with Rex tonight and the thing ended up with Franco getting tossed out on his ass, yelling in the middle of the street that he was going to burn the place down. Doesn't sound very cordial, now does it?"

Sal waves the suggestion aside.

"C'mon, Franco was a loudmouth, but it was all talk. He'd never do nothing like this."

"And where is Franco now?"

"Gee, I don't know, Jake. Maybe you guys could like, ah, try his house?"

Stan steps into Sal's face zone and stands a little taller, a little wider.

"We already did, jerk off. A couple of detectives went over there a little while ago and guess what? No Franco."

"He wasn't there?"

Jake studies Sal's face. He's trying real hard to play stupid, but it's not working.

"No, Sal, he wasn't. His wife said he got a call, went out the door, and hasn't came back. That happens to a lot of your friends, doesn't it, Sal?"

"Look, I don't know where Franco is."

"Which means you're gonna kill him."

Stan steps in a few more inches. Sal looks to Jake like a battered club fighter, appealing to his corner with blood-drenched eyes. Jake doesn't move.

"C'mon, Sal." Stan keeps pushing. "We all know what happened here…"

"Maybe you know…"

"Matty is having Franco tortured, isn't he? Can't let something like this go unpunished, right? Burning down his club? Oh, hell, no, the Cigar's got to make an example out of this miserable prick. He's got to show everybody that he's still got it."

"…I don't know nothing—"

"Probably slice off some of his fingers, huh? The ears, hell, maybe one of you ghouls will go for the schwantz, sick bastards that you are. Is that what you're doing to poor little Franco? Are you cutting his dick off?"

Sal is a melting candle and when he tries so hard to stand straight and look Stan in the eye, it's pitiful.

"I ain't seen Franco in ages. I hardly know the guy, for Christ's sake. If he's in any kind of trouble, it got ain't shit to do with me."

Jake inhales a streak of burnt air and coughs into his arm. He's very tired all of a sudden, exhausted by the lies, all this dancing around. He spits on the ground.

"We want to talk to Franco, Sal—real bad," he says. "If something did happen to him, we're going to be very upset. And you're going to be the first one to know about it."

"Thanks for the warning, Jake."

"It's not a warning, it's a promise."

Stan snaps his fingers and his face brightens up like he's just figured out all the answers.

"Hey, I got it. Maybe Billy did this. He liked fires so much, maybe he came back from the dead to zap all you scumbags one by one."

"Yeah, Stan, very funny…"

Sal turns to leave and Stan starts walking after him in a stiff-legged Frankenstein march. He puts his arms out and lowers his voice to a drive-in movie baritone.

"*Saaal!*" He groans. "I'm coming for youuu!"

"Grow up for Christ's sake." Sal keeps walking. "You look like an idiot."

But Stan keeps the show going, follows after Sal. A few people nearby start to laugh.

"Sal, I'm coming for you. I'm going to fuck you up the ass and make you wash the dishes. Saal…!"

It's the kind of stupid stuff that Stan is famous for and anyone who knows him just ignores it. Jake sees it's hitting Sal hard, but the really strange thing is that the routine is getting on Jake's nerves, too.

It feels like all the people here are really laughing at Jake, the stupid cop who talks to ghosts and mourns murdered gangsters as if they were fallen soldiers.

What a loser, that's what they're all thinking, *no wonder his wife left him.*

Jake wants to tell Stan to stop, please, knock it off, shut up, you stupid Polack bastard; it's not funny anymore. But Sal breaks before he does, just as he reaches the barricades, inches from the real world, he spins around and glares at Stan.

"Fuck you, you cocksucker! Fuck all you fucking cops!"

Everyone on the block hears it, even the old guys who forgot to switch on their hearing aids. Two EMTs poke their heads out of the ambulance to see what's going on and all the locals fall silent to stare at Sal. Stan is shocked, but only for a second.

"You hear this, Jake?" His voice rumbles with a locomotive's bulk. "You hear how this prick talks to me?"

"Stan…"

"No, Jake, this is some crazy shit. All these years of sucking Matty's cock, I always figured him to be a fag. Now he suddenly grows a pair of balls. It's a miracle."

"Look…" Sal seems like he wants to disappear. "This is harassment."

Stan goes in for the Eskimo rub, just as Jake steps into the empty space between the two men.

"We don't want to do this, Stan."

"Sure we do, Jake." Stan pushes against Jake in a low-key show of strength. "Me and Stainless Sal here, we can do this right now."

Standing between them, Jake sees a TV news reporter and cameraman threading through the crowd like sharks moving toward their prey.

"Stan, enough already…"

"C'mon, you little scumbag." Stan glares at Sal, deaf to Jake's words. "Make your move. We'll keep it just between us, swear to God, no badge, no nothing. C'mon, you little cunt, give me an excuse to tear you apart."

Sal stands there and suffers. People, ordinary, working chumps are witnessing this, watching Sal choke in front of the cops. The old timers must be shocked at what they're seeing.

"I'm leaving," he says finally. "You got anything else to say to me, call my lawyer."

Jake nods and Stan steps back. Sal walks through the crowd, which parts before him and closes in his wake.

The camera crew, smelling the blood, goes off in Sal's direction, their lights flare up seconds later and they hear Sal bellow "get the fuck away from me!" before his car roars off down the block.

"Fucking pussy," Stan says, his chest heaving. "I fixed his ass, didn't I, Jake?"

Jake listens to the car engine fade down the block and knows that he's not the only one dodging ghosts tonight.

"You sure did, big guy."

21

BILLY STRETCHES OUT on a busted lounge chair, his arms folded across his chest, eyes closed, while his mind carves a tight circle around the room like a Doberman on a one-foot leash.

He's not awake, not asleep; not really in the room. A jet passes overhead and it feels like the rumbling engines are crushing right into his brain.

"What the fuck is this?"

The last time Billy looked, Tommy was squatting in front of the TV as if it were a satanic idol and thumb-jabbing the remote through every channel on the dial. Judging by the noise, he's still there.

"Shit…" Click-click-click. "There's nothing on this fucking thing."

Voices stab at Billy in a fragmented recital of weather reports, nature documentaries, sports scores, Spanish soap operas, classic movie lines, and talk show screamers.

It's like sticking your head into a blender and switching it up to puree, but at least it's better than talking to that lunatic.

"This fucking sucks…"

"Indeed it does," Billy says, his eyes still closed.

They came to this empty house in Flatbush a few hours ago after getting clear of the burning bar and Rex's mangled corpse.

Billy had stopped to linger at the back door, as if someone had called out to him, and he had to watch the flames climb up the walls and crawl across the room right toward him.

Wood cracked in the heat and clouds of smoke poured out of the building and even though he was choking on the foul air, almost melting in the fire, Billy felt the urge, a craving, to walk into the burning room as if the flames weren't there.

He was taking the first step when Tommy's sharp whistle pulled him away.

"C'mon! We gotta get outta here!"

He followed Tommy down the street, tried to keep up with the younger man, who all of a sudden was able to run so goddamn fast. They should've been here, Billy thought as he struggled to catch up with his son, them two bastards should've been here tonight.

Sal and Matty should've been sitting at a table, looking at the TV, patiently waiting for Billy to gun them down while he took a chest full of bullets.

They should've been here tonight so Billy could finish this thing instead of bashing some lowlife to pieces and being forced to walk away alive.

The pain collared him just as he reached the car, cruel and vicious, and Billy dropped to his knees and howled like he was going to die right there on the spot. He could sense Tommy hovering overhead, looking down at him.

"What is it? What the fuck is wrong with you?"

Billy looked up and through the agony he saw a shape, a body silhouetted by a street light, and he tried to talk, but nothing came out of his mouth.

Help me—please!

He felt Tommy grabbing, putting his hands on him, the little son-of-a-bitch, but there was nothing Billy could do about it.

"Give me the keys," Tommy was saying, "give me the fucking keys!"

Air was filling Billy's lungs, pushing the pain out of his body, and as he got to his feet, he found enough strength to shove his son away.

"Get your fucking hands off of me!"

Billy staggered to the driver's side, got behind the wheel and they were flying down the street, no idea where he was going, just had to get away from that place before it dragged him back into the fire.

He was swerving all over the road, pinball bashing into parked cars. A hand gripped the steering wheel, steadied the car, a voice whispered take it easy, you got it.

Billy powered down the window to get more air; his vision cleared and by the time they reached Eddie's house, the pain had vanished.

Billy sits up on the lounge chair and looks at Tommy.

"You ditch the car?"

"Drove it out to Coney Island just like you said."

"Anybody see you?"

The kid won't take his face away from the TV.

"I changed car services twice."

Billy waits for his son to make some remark about his seizure, about nearly getting them killed or caught, but Tommy doesn't say a word.

"So where's this friend of yours?"

"He'll be here." Click click. "He had to take his old man to the doctor. Just chill."

Chill. Shit, I could've sworn this kid was white when we brought him home from the hospital.

"I want somebody reliable, not some jerk-off with an alkie father."

"Eddie's a good man. He's my dog."

"Really? Your dog housebroken or is he gonna shit on the rug?"

"C'mon, you remember Eddie."

"I remember him being an asshole."

"He's matured."

"Let's hope so."

Billy watches Tommy linger on ESPN for a few seconds before changing the channel yet again. It kills him that this kid, this punk, was one of the last people in the world to see Lucille alive.

There's so much Billy wants to know about her life after he had disappeared, how she had taken it, what she had said about him. But he's not about to reveal himself to this stranger with the matching DNA.

"Holy shit! We're on TV."

Tommy points to the image on the screen, but Billy eases back on the lounge chair. He doesn't want to see his handiwork.

"Look at that," Tommy calls over his shoulder. "That shit is history."

Billy listens to the reporter's voice; place is a total loss, one victim, name hasn't been released pending notification of the family. Witnesses saw two men running from the building, one of them may have been injured in the fire.

Detectives are also investigating a possible connection to a house fire on Staten Island that once belonged to missing mob enforcer William

"Billy the Kid"—

"They're carrying that fat bastard out now," Tommy says. "Shit,those guys probably got a hernia lugging that big tub of shit. You want to see?"

"No thanks."

"They'll be scraping that guy's brains off the Statue of Liberty, the way you pounded him."

"Uh-huh…"

"You really went to town on that fuck."

"Hey," Billy says sharply. "I was there, remember?"

Well, yes and no. There are parts of the evening that are as unrecognizable as Rex's face.

"Why were you busting on the guy like that?"

"He asked too many questions."

Another plane rolls overhead, shoves him another notch closer to hell. Where the fuck is everybody going?

"Goddamn!"

"What?"

"It was Sal." Tommy points at the screen. "Just now on the news."

Billy looks at the screen but all he sees is some Minnesota blond from one of the local stations flapping her mouth at the camera, the remains of the bar smoldering silently behind her.

"You sure?"

"Fuck yeah." Tommy nods. "It was him, alright. But he looks so old, boy."

Billy looks at the screen hoping he might get a look at Sal, but the reporter signs off and the anchorman comes back.

All right, so Sal was at the bar. So what? His name is on the deed; of course he'd be there. If he had gotten there a little earlier, he'd have been riding out in a body bag, too.

Billy goes back to the lounge chair, closes his eyes. Going non-stop for nearly 24 hours, he's earned the right to sleep. Only it's not happening; he's so twisted, so agitated that he finally gets up and goes into the bathroom.

The closed door mutes the TV's noise and Billy stares at his reflection in the mirror, remembers the snarling maniac who looked back at him while he was working on Rex. And now he sees the bloodshot eyes, gray stubble, the exhaustion coming off of him like gusts of steam. Damn, boy, you look old.

Billy kills the light, walks over to Tommy and launches a sham stretch.

"You ready for this, big guy?"

"Fuck, yeah." Tommy keeps his eyes on the screen. "I'm mad ready."

"You're pretty sure of yourself."

"It's no big thing."

Billy fights the urge to give Tommy a sharp slap on the back of his head.

"You know what Sal and Matty are like," he says. "They're not just going to roll over for us."

"So? They can die just like anyone else."

"You're a real tough guy, huh?" Billy stands over his son. "How do I know you won't piss your pants and run away like a little bitch?"

"You'll find out soon enough."

Billy fingers grind into fists. He doesn't want to hear this fag's badass bullshit. He's run into enough of these assholes in his life, seen them fall apart and start crying when the shit gets critical. He's seen them betray their best friends.

"You ever kill anybody?"

Tommy turns around deliberately and looks up at Billy as if he'd just sprung up from out of the carpet.

"Excuse me?"

"You heard what I said."

"Well, I don't know if I—"

"Answer me!"

You never ask a question like that. It's the kind of lethal information that can put somebody on death row or at the bottom of river. You ask a question like that you better have something to give up in return. Billy knows it's wrong, the worst thing you ever could do, but he can't help it.

Tommy turns back to the shimmering screen and raises his shoulders an inch or two.

"Anything's possible."

Billy stares angrily at his son, so many questions racing through his brain. He wants to know everything, every goddamn detail, who was it, where did it happen, and why, why in Christ's name did you have to kill him?

You got no business asking this kid anything. Tommy's a big boy, so if he dropped one guy or a thousand, it doesn't have shit to do with you. Except that it has everything to do with you.

"Yeah, sure," Billy says. "You're a real animal. Too bad you weren't around when your mother was being killed."

"Look who's talking."

The TV voices blast through Billy's head at full volume. The room tilts to one side, he lets out this subhuman roar as he grabs Tommy's collar and tries to haul this little prick to his feet.

"You scumbag—!"

Tommy spins quickly, knocks Billy's hand away, and gets to his feet, up and ready.

"Take it easy, big guy." He bares his teeth in a deadly smile. "We ain't at home."

"You fucking cocksucker…"

Billy wheezes, his heart beat climbing, and a low frequency voice whispers you're letting this kid tie you in knots. You're supposed to be the brains here. Drop this shit now before it's too late.

But Billy's not listening.

"You talk about my wife that way, you fuck?"

The look on Tommy's face says everything. You, playing the outraged husband? After all the grief you put her through now you want to defend her honor?

"You sure you want to do this?" Tommy asks.

There's no emotion in his voice, no anger, no fear. He can either fight to the death or go back to watching TV. He just wants to know which one it's going to be.

Billy stares at Tommy, haloed by the TV's glow. He sees the gun butt sticking out of Tommy's waistband and feels the weight of Matty's .45 hanging off his shoulder. He aims his index finger at Tommy.

"If you ever say anything like that again—"

"—I know, I'll curse my mother for giving birth to me." Tommy winks at him. "Shit, I've been cursing you both for years."

A jet flies overhead, low enough to take off a chunk of Billy's scalp. A talk show audience applauds while the two men stare at each other.

"I'm going for a walk," Billy says finally.

"Don't talk to no strangers."

21

HE CLIMBS UP the basement steps, his mind sputtering like a faulty light bulb, stumbles out the front door and walks aimlessly beneath a rusted gray sky.

His hands tremble so badly he's glad no one is walking toward him because he'd have to beat the luckless bastard into a pile of jelly.

Fucking punk, little fucking bastard…

He let Tommy get to him, let that kid run rings around him. Christ, his son came off as the smart one.

It's just short of dawn and he's thinking of Lora. She'll be getting up soon, walking around the kitchen in that atrocious plaid robe that Billy kept threatening to burn. She'll make breakfast, get dressed, go to work, she'll do everything she normally does, and she'll do it all without Billy. She'll push him out of her life because she has no choice.

Maybe she's not even there. Now that Billy's gone, that fat butterball George can finally stop tugging himself and make his move. I should've let that bastard burn.

He looks up and sees he's gone three blocks. The sky is becoming lighter, the neighborhood is slowly coming to life, and Billy doesn't want to attract any attention. He turns back toward the house.

There's a black SUV in the driveway and when Billy enters the house he can hear voices coming up from the basement. He tries to make out the words, but its only streaks of gibberish broken up by Tommy's monkey laughter.

He's about to go downstairs when he spots the wall phone in the kitchen. If he could just hear her voice, just a few seconds, then he'd hang right up without saying a thing.

But maybe he could stay on long enough to say how sorry he was, beg her to please, please jump in the car, meet him at JFK and they could get on one of these goddamn airplanes that won't stop crisscrossing the sky.

Billy picks up the receiver, flinches at the sudden eruption of the dial tone.

His fingers tremble as he stabs out the number and the shaking travels the length of his body as the phone rings once, twice, three times before he hears her voice, her lovely, sweet voice, asking him to leave a message.

Billy goes mute, unable to make a sound as the answering machine records his choked silence. The receiver grows colder and heavier in his hand until he slams it back on the hook and goes down to the basement.

The voices and laughter are louder as Billy takes the cellar steps lightly, like Kwai Chang walking on the rice paper, until he gets down to where he can see Tommy sitting on the lounge chair and this pale, pudgy kid in a blue sweatshirt.

"Police—nobody move!"

Billy comes down the rest of stairs and the kid almost throws himself through the wall.

"Take it easy, bitch," Tommy says. "That's our new partner. Have a nice walk, Billy?"

Billy approaches his son, residual anger still rumbling through him.

"I could've killed you two assholes just now. I hope you know that."

"Thanks for the tip, chief." Tommy looks to Eddie. "Don't worry, son. He likes to fuck with your head."

Eddie is sweating and shivering all over the room and he seems to be seconds away from puking up his breakfast.

"Y-yeah, I know…"

"Shit, you turning queer on me?" Tommy laughs at his friend. "Most days I can't get you to shut your hole and now all of a sudden you won't talk."

Billy looks at this frightened kid, this oversized baby, standing in front of him.

"Eddie, huh?"

This kid doesn't have it, not even close. He doesn't have the madness you need to be leading this kind of life. He's too fearful, too desperate to live to ever accept murder and death as part of the daily routine.

Get out of here, kid, Billy thinks. Go get a lousy job, marry a heavy girl with thick ankles and have a bunch of ugly screaming kids. Fight every night in front of the TV and struggle to pay your bills. Do anything but get hooked up with me.

Tommy, he's hopeless, there's only one life for him and it's going to be brutal, violent and brief. You, you're different. You still got a chance.

I had to get him out of there.

Billy wants to drag this kid upstairs, point him toward home and give him a swift kick in the ass. Go back to your family and let Tommy and Billy grab their weapons and finished what they started.

The kid stares at him, waiting for some kind of word. Planes move through the morning sky, more people getting away, escaping. Billy should say something to this guy to set him straight, but he's on autopilot now and can't help but go ahead with the ritual.

He grabs hold of Eddie's outstretched hand and crushes the kid's fingers.

"I hear good things about you."

THE SCREAMING STARTS just as Sal enters the basement of the old mansion and the only thing that keeps him from running back to his car is the heavy crash of the door closing behind him.

"Keep screaming, you little fuck, it ain't gonna help you!"

Sal forces himself to step closer toward the single light that burns in a corner near the furnace. He sees Train, swollen muscles straining against a blood-splattered sleeveless t-shirt, the face of Christ emblazoned on his arm, a box cutter in his hand.

He's standing over Franco, that poor, pathetic son-of-a-bitch, who is tied to a chair, stripped to the waist and bleeding from a dozen awful wounds.

Train looks up and gives Sal a smile that burns like acid.

"Glad you could make it," he says.

This night is so bad that Sal wonders if the sun will ever rise. Matty's place up in flames, Rex murdered, and Franco about to join him any minute.

He can't believe he blew up at Stan like that and then made it even worse by backing down to the fat Polack bastard.

Everybody saw it, the whole neighborhood witnessed Sal cave in to the cop. They watched him tuck in his nuts and slink back to his car like a faggot. They all saw that he was afraid.

The old timers will be talking about this one, that's for sure. Matty would never have cowered like that, they'll say, he would've stood up to that cop even if they beat the shit out of him and threw him in jail with a dozen man-eating niggers. Matty Cigar ain't ascared of God.

And just when he thought it couldn't get no worse, that goddamn TV crew had to light up Sal like he's an escaped convict and record his screaming breakdown for the folks at home. Fucking beautiful…

God, Sal wanted so badly to just go home and pull the blankets over his head and die. But even as he was driving toward the bridge, he knew he'd never make it home; he knew the cell would ring and it would be Matty telling him to get the fuck over to the place on Arthur Kill and deal with Franco.

"You need to be there," the old man says, "you gotta take charge of this thing."

They both knew that wasn't true. Sal's second in command, in line to be skipper if Matty ever stops breathing. Guys of his rank should have nothing to do with this kind of business. Train clearly enjoys his work; there's no reason for Sal to supervise this atrocity.

But Matty wanted to show Sal who still gives the orders around here, who's the real skipper. This was punishment.

Sal kept driving out to the big old mansion that sits up on a hill like that house in *Psycho*. The place is huge, built by some rich German bastard over 100 years ago who wound up blowing his brains out in the basement. Wait for me, Adolph…

The caretaker got into a jam with Matty so he lets the crew use the place for special occasions and word is that old furnace can burn anything in this world once you get it going.

"They say this place is haunted." Train says. "Do you believe in ghosts, Franco?"

"I didn't do it! I didn't fucking do it!"

"Sure you didn't, Franco; Matty's bar just burned down all by itself, right?"

Sal stands behind Train and Franco eyes swell with desperate hope.

"Sal! Sal, please…" Franco strains against the ropes binding him to the chair. "Sal, tell him, tell his guy I didn't set no fire!"

Sal can't speak, can't say anything in this foul place at this ungodly hour. He's only a spectator tonight, just like he was one night with Billy so many lifetimes ago. Only Sal's got no place to hide now.

"Sal!" Franco wails. "Sal, please, tell them I didn't do this. Tell him, Sal, please! C'mon, you know me! You know me, for Christ's sake!"

No, Sal doesn't know anybody, not on this night. He's got no friends, no family, no acquaintances, because none of that means shit when Matty Cigar is mad at you.

"Sal!"

Train slashes across Franco's chest with the box cutter, another terrible scream, and Sal looks away. He's taunting him, this animal, taking his time with Franco just to let Sal know that he wasn't in charge of fuck-all tonight.

"He keeps lying to me, this little prick—"

Franco wasn't lying; Sal knew that the second Matty accused him. Franco didn't begin to have the kind of rocks to pull something like this.

The old man likes to wrap things up quickly, though, and if he gets an idea into his head that fits his view of the world, it becomes gospel. So when Franco ran his mouth earlier tonight with Rex, he talked his way right into the best seat in the house at Matty's private torture chamber.

And Train doesn't care about the truth as long as he gets to peel somebody's skin back and show poppa how loyal he is.

"All right, you little cocksucker," Train reaches for a black gym bag resting at his feet. "I'm done fucking around here."

He pulls a long blue canister out of the gym bag and Sal stares at this thing, refusing to believe what he's seeing, even though he knows it's a blowtorch and he knows goddamn good and well what Train plans on doing with it.

You'd do the same thing. You'd do the same if you was in my place!

Franco sees it and starts screaming, no words, nothing resembling a language, raw terror pours out of his mouth. The echo bounces off the walls and fills the cavernous basement.

"What is this?" Sal shouts over the noise. "What the hell are you doing?"

Train looks Sal up and down, outraged by the interruption.

"Hey, pal, this is what Matty wants."

"I'm not your pal, asshole, and I want you to put that thing away right now."

Train spits on the floor, almost hitting Sal's shoe. He looks at Sal with poison blue eyes and very slowly pulls an igniter out of his pocket.

"Look...*pal*..." He snaps sparks in front of the hissing blowtorch. "You don't have the stomach for this—leave. But Matty told me to burn this mother fucker—his exact words—and that's what's going to happen."

The blow torch erupts, hacks out a line of intense blue flame, just as Train finishes speaking and Sal jumps back.

"Y-you know who you're talking to?"

Train smirks, the controlled blaze illuminates the lower half of his face. Yeah, he knows; he knows exactly who he's talking to and he knows he's got absolutely nothing to worry about. It's the second time tonight Sal's backed down.

"Sal!"

Do something, Sal tells himself. You can't save this poor bastard, at least put him out of his misery, like Billy did. You got a second chance here. Take it.

"—please, tell them to stop—!"

Sal puts his hand under his jacket, wraps his fingers around the butt of his .38 and squeezes. Kill him, shoot this poor guy through the heart before this freak gets hold of him. When Train turns around, shoot him square in the face, I don't give a shit who his father is.

Sal looks at the furnace glowing and heaving. And then kill yourself.

"Lamb of God who takes away the sins of the world have mercy on us…" Franco speaks in a terrified blur. "Lamb of God who takes away the sins—"

Train advances toward Franco grinning savagely as he levels the blowtorch. Franco squeezes his eyes shut, tries to turn away, but he's not going anywhere.

"Sal, please!"

Hotheaded little prick, had to run your mouth, didn't you? Had to make that stupid threat, force Sal to come all the way out of here to helplessly watch this demented changeling jizz his Jockeys by burning your skin—

"Sal!"

—and then he's running faster than he's ever run before, toward the door, away from this outrage, Franco's hideous shrieks chasing after him.

He crashes against the metal door, staggers up the stairs and out to the desolate street. The screams are coming from a distant place, but Sal still hears them.

His knees buckle, he drops to the ground, and while the haunted house leers over his shoulder, ready to fall down upon him, Sal empties his stomach all over the lawn.

"I'm sorry…" He whispers in the dark. "I'm sorry…"

23

BILLY GETS OUT of the car on Eighth Avenue by McKinley Park and walks down the block with his head low and his cap pulled down over his eyes.

He feels drained, almost weightless, as if a good gust of wind might lift him right off the ground and carry him out to the Narrows.

His right hand is stuck deep in his pocket gripping this cell phone that Tommy gave him so they can stay in touch. Tommy said it was easy to work, a fucking moron could do it; Billy just nodded and thought, it'd better be, buddy, for your sake.

This is Billy's first taste of sunlight after nearly two days of being locked up in that basement with Tommy, Eddie, and the remote. Eddie went out to a Chinese restaurant down the street and they barely said a word to each other until it was time to eat.

He watched the TV in silence; went for walks late at night and stayed away from the telephone.

Last night he sat down with Tommy and Eddie and told them how it was going to happen, no mistakes, no slip-ups, no excuses.

"And don't try to blow me in the car," Tommy told Eddie, "or I'll tell my daddy on you."

Billy let the wisecrack slide, fucking asshole just wants attention. Eddie was sitting between them with the color draining from his face.

"What are we going to do after…y'know…it's over?"

"What do you care, numb nuts?" Tommy laughed. "You're gonna be dead anyway."

Billy eyeballed his son while poor little Eddie tried to hold down his chicken lo mein.

"You just do what I tell you," he said, "and you'll be okay."

Billy walks by the black iron fence surrounding McKinley, toward Angelo's, Matty's favorite restaurant, where he and the rest of the crew go anytime they bury one of their own.

Tommy wanted to take them out at the cemetery, but Billy said no. Rex was being buried at St. Joseph's in Staten Island, where Billy's mother was put to rest so many years ago, alongside that shitheel husband of hers, while Billy stood with a half-dozen wheezing relatives and family friends and watched her casket being lowered into the ground.

There were only a few flowers and the biggest bouquet was a beautiful standing spray of red and white roses from Matty with a banner reading *In Loving Memory.*

Billy, his knuckles bruised and a wad of Matty's cash swelling his pocket, stood apart from the others, a streak of night in his shades and immaculate black suit.

He didn't want to be near the friends and relatives, with their stupid prayers and pathetic sobbing. Billy wasn't going to cry, not for his mother, or for that loser he left bleeding back in the Poconos; he wasn't going to cry for nobody ever again.

Billy wasn't just burying his mother; he was putting his old life into the ground as well. No more parasites, no more drunks hanging onto him, weighing him down. He was going to take whatever he wanted from this world and fuck any motherless loser who got in his way.

He caught a few of the mourners sneaking glances at him while the priest spewed gibberish over his mother's coffin, but they quickly averted their eyes when he looked back.

Yeah, some of them bastards were mad at him, wanted to know where Billy was the night his mother died, why he wasn't home at that ungodly hour to help her, to call for an ambulance, so she wouldn't have died all by herself on the living room floor.

That's what they were thinking, no doubt, but none of them would ever say it to his face. No, they seemed to be a little afraid of him, concerned maybe that Billy might hurt them if they talked out of turn. And they were right.

Some of the faces were familiar. They were little old ladies now, but Billy recognized the women who came over to his house after the old man nearly killed his mother. The morning he left for Pennsylvania with Charley.

He wondered how he must look to them, so far from the terrified child they watched walking out of his room that day.

Poor little guy. Gotta see his mother beaten like a putana.

The sister, what was her name—Frieda? She wasn't there. Maybe she was up in PA, taking care of her brother. That guy was going to need a lot of help now after the pounding he got.

But he was asking for it, the stupid bastard, stiffing Matty like that, just a matter of time before someone chucked a horrendous beating on him. Shit, other guys would've had him killed, no warning, no mercy, no nothing. You got nobody to blame for this misery but yourself, big guy.

Sal crosses the street over here and comes back down on this side. I follow this bastard up the block and Vince is behind us...

It almost happened, Billy nearly cracked when they were lowering the coffin into the ground, so his mother could spend eternity with the old man, and he finally understood that she was really gone forever.

The earth heaved beneath his feet and Billy's black steel armor wavered when he thought of that poor woman, who suffered all her life, who only wanted her son to say just once that he loved her, and who died so terribly alone while her only child was miles away savagely betraying one of the few people who had ever cared about him.

In that moment Billy wanted to scream, tear off the Ray-Bans, throw himself on the casket and pound on the polish wood, beg forgiveness and tell her that he loved her over and over.

The wicked are estranged from the womb; they go astray as soon as they be born, speaking lies.

He glared at the priest, convinced the son-of-a-bitch was taunting him, like he thought that stupid white collar would somehow protect him from Billy's rage, when in fact it would just guarantee that the Kid would fuck his ass up even more. But the guy wasn't saying a word.

No, Billy can't do this. He breaks down here and word will get back to

Matty, sure as shit, he'll find out about it. And the old man will wonder if he was wrong about this new guy; maybe the kid doesn't have what it takes, maybe he's not man enough to work for Matty Cigar if he's gonna break down and cry like a little girl over deadbeats and alkies.

Billy held it in, used all his strength to stand silently over his mother's grave, shoulders back, eyes dry and looking straight ahead. A ferocious battle was raging within his heart. And Billy won.

He pulled back from the hole in the ground, thought of his family's house, how he hated the place, from the basement where he staged his flaming disasters when he was a kid to the attic he hadn't seen in so long he wasn't even sure it existed.

The old man croaked owing so much money on that dump that the bank was going to foreclose on the place, so even if Billy wanted to live there he was shit out of luck.

Billy started making his plans, right there in the cemetery, figured what he'd do when he was done with this stupid ritual, finished with these assholes.

He wasn't going to weep or seek absolution. After they were done here, after the lunch, and all the bullshit sympathy and worthless promises to stay in touch, Billy was going back to that house one last time.

As the priest approached him, Billy slipped his hand into his pocket and smiled when he found what he was looking for.

A book of matches...

24

THE PAIN TAKES hold of him. Billy stumbles over to the wrought iron fence and holds on tight. He's hurting so bad he's afraid he'll look up and see his own head stuck up on a spike, gushing blood out of the stump and wearing a shit-eating grin three blocks wide.

All right, he takes in a few breaths so he can get grounded; listens to the kids playing in the park; watches the people walking by; an old man tapping his cane on the ground; a woman pushing a baby carriage.

Billy closes his eyes, this empty husk holding on to the cold iron bars, and tries to get his heart beating again.

C'mon, big guy, it's just a short walk down the block and then it's over. All you have to do is take those first few steps; you'll be fine once the shooting starts.

He pulls in more air, feels stronger, and he senses someone coming up alongside of him, someone he knows couldn't possibly be there, but who is still just as real as this iron fence he's clutching; someone who's come such a long way to lean over and tell him that the wicked are estranged from the womb, they go astray as soon as they be born, speaking lies.

Billy stands up, pats Matty's gun, and smiles.

It's time.

The wicked are estranged from the womb. They go astray as soon as they be born, speaking lies…

The words enter Sal's head while he's driving over the Goethal's Bridge. He just switched off the stupid goddamn cell phone and tossed it over his shoulder onto the back seat, thinking what a nice word "incommunicado" was, and those lines just slid across his brain.

That's it, he thinks, that's what Billy said to the old man the night he came into the bar.

Sal could never remember the exact phrase, even though all the guys grilled him about it afterwards. Like he was taking notes or something.

But now here he is in the middle of the sky, all by himself, and it comes to him so easily. Maybe it's the lack of sleep, the memory of Franco's screams, or this business he's doing today; whatever it is, Sal's got it down like it's his home address.

He checks his watch. The funeral should be over now. They'll go to the cemetery and then to Angelo's for lunch like they always do. They'll all be there, all the guys, except Sal, who's been feeling pretty estranged himself lately.

Everybody's will ask how come Sal isn't there, why isn't he attending such an important event. All his friends, his buddies will be so shocked and appalled that Sal didn't make it to Rex's funeral.

They'll dog pile all over him, badmouth his name all over the map, just so they can get in good with the Cigar. That's what Sal would do if he were there talking about somebody else. The absent are always fucked.

At least he went to the wake last night, arriving at the funeral parlor just in time to see Matty offer his condolences to Rex's mother.

It was a rite Sal had witnessed many times. They wait until the place is full and then they wheel the old man up to the front of the room where he hugs the grieving woman, pats her shoulder, and speaks soothingly into her ear.

Everyone in the room falls silent and watches, so touched that Matty is making this beautiful gesture. The guy in the box is all but forgotten as Matty looks into the mother's eyes and tells her with such heartfelt sincerity how sorry he is and that if there's anything, anything he can do at all, just call him anytime day or night.

It's the same thing he told Lucille and so many other widows and mothers. Sounds great, but you don't ever take Matty up on his offer. The promise is for show, not for real.

Sal watched Matty kiss Rex's mother on both cheeks before one of the young guys wheeled him away, and Train, bulked up in a fine silk suit now, stepped forward and discretely placed an envelope into the sobbing woman's hands.

That used to be Sal's job, the money guy, and he was good at it. He really felt for these poor ladies; he was genuinely sensitive and caring. Sal took the time to talk and listen, and more than a few of these women wound up crying on his shoulder. The guys used to razz him about it, hey, Sal, you should've been an undertaker, but Sal took pride in what he was doing.

As he went to speak with Matty, Sal noticed that none of the guys would look him in the eye, pretty clear evidence that Train had given everyone a full report about what had happened the other night on Arthur Kill.

"That lying little bastard," Matty said as they sat in the lounge. "Couldn't die like a man, could he?"

Yeah, Sal thought, them blowtorches can really take the fun out of everything.

"You're right, Matty."

Neither man wants to be around the other, not after all the misery that's happened lately. And even though they're sitting a few feet from each other, Sal feels a gap opening up between them and it keeps getting wider.

"All right, Sal," Matty says, "why don't you go home and get some rest? Train will take me home. I'll see you here tomorrow for the funeral."

"Yeah, Matty, that's the thing…"

He said it real quick so he wouldn't lose his nerve, Sal was speaking lies, while Train was just a few feet pretending not to listen. He spewed some bullshit about having to get up to his country place because a water pipe busted and the plumber needed him up there.

He hated, really hated, to miss Rex's funeral, felt terrible about it, but this thing just came up. Christ, is sounded so pathetic Sal half-expected a lightning bolt to slice through the roof and strike him dead.

Matty didn't complain, didn't challenge him or say how bad this looks for someone in Sal's position to miss a funeral and then to make it even worse by telling him at the very fucking last minute with the corpse stretched out in the next goddamn room.

The old man didn't do anything like that, but the long scalding silence told Sal just how angry he was.

"All right, Sal," Matty said after an eternal pause. "Go take care of your business."

No, Matty didn't actually call Sal a no-good lying sack of shit, at least not directly. But you didn't need a secret decoder ring to know what the old man was really thinking behind those words.

The message came in clearly as Sal was leaving and looked across the canyon in the middle of the room and caught Train grinning at him: the next funeral might be yours, big guy.

The wicked are estranged from the womb...

Billy's words come back to him again, a tune he can't shake out of his head. Sal gets off the bridge, heads for the turnpike. He'll be up there in an hour or so and hopefully put this all to rest.

Let the crew talk all they want. It won't matter much longer.

25

MATTY SITS IN the back of the Buick, looks out the window onto Seventh Avenue, and wonders what the hell happened.

Train's behind the wheel, massive, silent, ready to attack. Teddy's next to him in the front passenger seat, and Louie and Paolo are in the back next to Matty, and everybody's dressed in black.

Another funeral, another one in the ground. The bar, the country home, both gone, and now they're saying on the news that Billy's old house burned down last night.

Christ, Matty's never seen it this bad, not since he took the bullet that crippled him for life. It's feels like God is casting a plague down upon them.

It hurts, hurts like hell this fucking misery, but all this suffering only proves what Matty's been saying for years; you've got to be tough to survive in this goddamn world.

Matty puts a hand on his wasted leg, recalls Jake, that ugly Irish son-of-a-bitch, hanging all over him in the ER trying to get Matty, Matty fucking Cigar, to turn rat. But Matty just took all that terrible pain and laughed in that stupid cop's face.

He looks at Train, admires at how the kid keeps his mouth shut and listens. Matty smiles. The kid takes after his old man, don't he? That's the way it should be with the young ones, listen, learn, and don't get stupid. This one's going to go a long way with the crew. Matty knows it.

Of course he's said that about others who will go unnamed, the ones who got too goddam smart and had to be taken down a few notches.

"I thought it went good today," Matty says. "It was a nice ceremony."

"Oh, definitely, Matty; it was beautiful."

"The only thing was that priest. I could hardly understand him."

"Yeah, they must've brought him up from Ecuador or someplace. Should've had them subtitles, like the movies, you know?"

"Rex's mother was very touched by all you did for her," Teddy says. "You could tell just by looking at her."

"That poor woman's suffered enough already. It was the least we could do."

"Oh, yeah, it was terrible what happened there. I mean, what gets into people? What makes them do these sick things?"

"Who the hell knows?" Matty waves his hand. "People are just crazy. But at least this thing was taken care of fast, no bullshit, no jerking around. His mother can rest easy knowing that much."

"Oh, yeah, Matty. Done deal."

The heads around him all nod in agreement the way they've been taught. You have to make them respect you or they start thinking you're soft. Matty's too old, he's in a wheelchair, we don't gotta worry about him no more. Yeah, well, why don't you ask Franco how soft Matty is?

"The flowers looked good," he says. "Real nice arrangement."

"Oh, yeah, weren't they nice? I told the florist to do something really special for us."

"That's good, Carmine. Make sure we take care of him."

"You got it, Matty."

They pull up to a red light at 83rd Street and watch a heavyset woman pull a cart full of groceries across the street.

"What happened with Sal today?"

Matty shakes his head.

"He told me he had to go up to his house in Pennsylvania. The pipes are broken or something like that."

"He had to go all the way up there for some pipes?"

"That's what he said."

"Jesus, all you gotta do is call a plumber and let him take care of it. You don't gotta drop everything and go running out of town."

"Sure," Paolo says. "Hire one of them locals to look after it. Them bastards got nothing to do anyway."

The other men click their tongues and wonder what's wrong with that guy, how could he do something like this? It's disrespectful, that's what it is, just plain disrespectful.

"Sal never really got along with Rex," Teddy says.

"That's got nothing to do with it." Matty snaps. "When someone dies, you go to the goddamn funeral; that's all. You like him, you don't like him, I don't give a shit. You go to the service. What are we, animals, for Christ's sake?"

"You're right, Matty. No two ways about it. You're right."

The light changes and Train steps gently on the gas.

"That business with his cousin—it's got Sal's mind all messed up," Louie says.

"We all got problems." Matty returns to the window. "Nobody's special."

You see that man there? You see him, fuckhead? He don't like you very much…

Billy wraps his fingers around the cell phone in his pocket, ready to call Tommy, one ring, no talk, the signal that says the enemy is coming.

His back turned, he senses the big car approaching the light at the corner before taking a quick look.

Thar she blows. Look at that big son-of-a-bitch rolling to a stop there; like the old bastard's going to invade a country. Remember all the times you rode in earlier versions of that car, back when you were the favorite son, sitting right next to the old man?

Remember looking out the window at the losers in the neighborhood who'd pimp their own mothers just to trade places with you for five minutes?

They all wanted to be Billy back then and it felt so good knowing how everyone envied him. Now, here he is on the sidewalk, the big car lumbering by him like he's just another lowlife.

Except Billy knows he's much lower than any life form known to man. He takes out the phone and hits the button.

Eddie hunches over the steering wheel like they're riding through sniper fire and brings the SUV back onto Seventh Avenue. Tommy's in the dead man's seat and drums a wicked tattoo on the dashboard.

"We're gonna die," he chants, "we're gonna die…"

He grins as Eddie turns an even sicker shade of green. Look at that little fairy, for two cents Eddie would dive out of the moving car and run crying for his mother, if he knew who the stupid bitch was shacking up with.

They just dropped Billy off by the park and now they're waiting on the other side of the highway for the phone call.

Tommy's pissed, he wanted to do this shit at the graveyard, when they had all these old mummies lined up out in the open and ready to go. Next to torching them on the crapper, there was no better time to nail these phony bastards than when they're pretending to mourn some hump they never liked in the first place.

Shit, most of these geezers were half-dead anyway; killing them at the bone farm would save a lot of time.

But Billy wouldn't go for that, put his foot down and said no, it wasn't happening. Maybe he was worried the dead would rise from their graves and start gnawing on newborn babies if they started a gun battle on God's holy turf. What a dick.

Billy wants to do it at this restaurant where these old timers come to stuff their sagging faces. Talk about hallowed ground; this place looks like a mortuary with valet parking.

Tommy's wearing a dark blue running suit so he looks like one of those assholes jogging his way to an early heart attack. The pants are a little tight, but the jacket is just bulky enough to cover the nine he's got tucked in his waistband.

"So you ready for this, big guy?" He pokes Eddie's ribs with an index finger. "Huh? You ready for your big debut?"

"Of course I'm ready."

"Yeah, ready to start crying."

Eddie glowers at him.

"I'm not fucking cry—"

"—oh, please. You're scared shitless for Christ's sake."

"Fuck you, faggot. I'm not scared of nothing."

He ain't ascared of God. That's what they used to say about Matty— unlike Eddie who's ascared of his own trembling shadow.

Just look at this pathetic bitch; hard to believe this is the same guy who was talking shit all over town when Tommy was going to cap that Polack bastard.

"Hey, it's not like you're actually doing anything, y'know. You're just driving, nigga. That's all you ever do. No reason to be scared—"

"I'm not scared!" Eddie pounds the steering wheel. "You watch me today, mother fucker. You just watch me."

"Watch you shit in your pants? I don't think so."

"Drop dead, asshole!"

Eddie pulls into a spot near the footbridge and angrily shifts the SUV into park. Touchy little fag, isn't he? Probably shouldn't break his balls so much, especially today. But it's just so much fun.

"You know what you're supposed to do, right?"

"Yeah." Eddie's all surly and pissed off. "I know what I'm supposed to do."

"So let's hear it."

"Give me a fucking break, will ya? I'm not some retard—"

Tommy cracks a backhand across Eddie's face without looking and the sound is wicked in these closed quarters.

"—what the fuck—?"

Tommy shifts in his seat so he can stare fiercely into Eddie's eyes.

"I told Billy you were ready for this," he says, soft and satanic. "I told him you could handle yourself. Was I wrong?"

"No, no, but—"

"—because if you fuck this up, if you make me look bad in front of my old man, I swear to God, I'll chop your little pinky dick off with a broken bottle."

"I-I'm not gonna let you down—"

Tommy turns away from him.

"Good girl. Now tell me what you're supposed to do."

Eddie looks down at the steering wheel and speaks in a shaky voice.

"When you get out, I drive up the overpass, make the turn, and pull up by the park…"

"Right…"

"I pop the hood and make like I'm checking the engine…"

"And then?"

Eddie rolls his eyes.

"When the shit goes down, I get in the car, tear-ass down the block, pick you guys up, and we blast the fuck out on of there."

"Very nice, son. Your moms would be so proud of you."

There's no more talk of afterwards. Even if they all survive this little hoedown, Billy and Tommy are going to resume their drama from the other night and put all the bullshit to rest.

And once he kills his father, Tommy will be goddamned if he'll have Eddie, with everything he knows, trailing after him like a lovesick poodle. All good things must come to an end. And it really hasn't been that good anyway.

"So, Tommy, I was wondering…can you hook me up?"

Shit, I knew this was coming. Why can't this little dildo just sit in the background and stay quiet?

"You're just driving, remember?"

"I know, I know," Eddie says quickly. "But something could go wrong. There may be more guys in the restaurant and you and Billy will need back-up."

"I think we can manage without your help, killer."

"But I feel naked out here, man."

"Now there's a fucking thought…"

Tommy doesn't want this dipshit carrying any artillery, not with all that spastic trembling he's doing. Give Eddie a gun and he might actually be dangerous for the first time in his life.

But Tommy can't stand all the goddam whining, so reaches down for the .38 he's got strapped to his ankle and butt-firsts it over to Eddie.

"All right," he says. "Here you go, wild man."

Eddie takes hold of the gun with both hands. He stares at the thing, tilts it from side-to-side as if it might start talking to him.

"It's just a gun, slick, not a vibrator. Try not to shoot a load."

"Yeah, yeah…"

"Now put it under your shirt. Don't do nothing unless I give you the sign. Billy and me are going to be pretty busy out there and we don't need no amateurs getting in our way."

"Yeah, yeah, Tommy. I got it."

The little dweeb is so excited Tommy hasn't got the heart to tell him the gun ain't loaded. But that's okay. Let him think he's an animal. God knows the poor boy doesn't have much else going for him.

Tommy's cell goes off, one ring, and the two of them stop breathing for a second.

It's the signal from Billy, one ring telling them that Matty and his crew are heading this way. One ring means no more talking, no more beating off.

We're gonna die, we're gonna die…

Tommy puts the phone away, pats the gun under his jacket, and flicks Eddie's nose with his index finger.

"Later, bitch," he says, and slides out of the car.

26

STAN TOOLS DOWN 75th Street chewing on a mystery dog when he catches sight of Matty's wop-mobile going by on Fort Hamilton Parkway.

"Well, I'll be dipped in shit," he says around a mouthful of possible beef. "Look what we got here."

Them scumbags must have finished tucking Rex McNuggets in for his dirt nap and now they're off to Angelo's to tie on the feedbag.

He's been running into these fuckwads a lot lately and Stan is really tempted to run into them right now, broadside these stiffs at top speed like a pirate ship and send them all down to Davy Jones' locker or wherever the hell guinea scumbags go when they finally die. But there might be a few laws against that kind of thing.

And after that grief outside of the bar with Sal, it's probably best to tone it down a little bit with these shitheels. As much as Stan hates to admit it, Father Jake might be right this time.

Jake was busy this morning making the pilgrimage out to Billy's house— or what was left of it. Being Jake, of course, he's got all sorts of eerie feelings and strange vibrations about the recent run of death and destruction. That guy should be reading palms down at Coney Island.

Stan will readily admit that some extraordinarily strange shit has been going on around here lately. This stuff with Matty's bar and Billy's house going up on the same night—that is most definitely fucked up.

But that doesn't mean Stan has joined the league of the living dead and started believing that rightfully deceased assholes are coming back from the great beyond to do some four-alarm renovations. There's a rational explanation for this stuff and all we have to do is find it.

The big vehicle moves out of Stan's line of sight and though he probably has more pressing things to do right now, he wonders if maybe he should tag along after these no-necks and make sure they get to Angelo's without incident.

Protect and serve, Stan thinks, that's what we do.

"Look at that scumbag," Matty nods at the guy in baseball cap leaning against the fence. "Bastard's drunk or high, some goddamn thing. Middle of the day and he can hardly stand up."

"What a jerk-off."

"Fucking bum."

"I'll tell you something," Matty says. "He's lucky I'm not a few years younger. Not too long ago, I'd see a guy like that stumbling around near the park with the kids and their mothers—I'd bust his fucking head for him."

"You want me to take care of him, Matty? Train, pull over, I'll fix his ass."

"No, no, don't worry about it." He puts his hand on Paolo's shoulder. "We got other things to worry about now. But shit like this, it's no good. It makes the neighborhood look bad."

Louie powers down the window.

"Hey, asshole," he shouts, "get a job!"

Hey, asshole, get a job!

Billy keeps his head down and chuckles ugly into the sidewalk as Matty's car rolls by like a four-wheel thundercloud.

He recognizes Louie cursing at him, so desperate to please that rotting old cadaver, just like the rest of those rejects.

Billy wouldn't mind taking out the .45 now and jumpstarting this massacre, but he has to put the rage on hold for a little bit longer. Let them park the car; let them start unloading Matty from the backseat like an old circus bear. Then he'll go over and say hello.

He hears the Buick slowing down; they're just outside Angelo's. They'll get out of the car slowly; one of the boys will go inside first, scout around, make sure everything's okay before coming back and getting Matty out of the car.

Billy starts walking again, watches his feet take one step after another, while his hand grips each successive picket. *Curb Your Dog,* a sign blares down at him. *It's the Law.*

Walking is such a miraculous thing when you think about it, all those muscles, bones, tendons and whatever working together for the sole purpose getting of your ass from here to there. Poor old Matty is missing out on all that; maybe that's why he's such a prick.

He quickens his pace, the spikes roll by faster and faster and it's funny that he never noticed that there was such a steep decline here. It's like he's running downhill.

Car doors click open and Billy allows himself a fast look, and sees Train, blond hair, biceps bulging beneath a fine black suit, get out on the driver's side and go into the restaurant. His buddy Louie gets out next, looks over to the jogger doing stretches by the footbridge, and pauses like he recognizes the guy in the running outfit.

Keep your head down, Billy thinks toward his son, they know what you look like, you stupid bastard.

Tommy looks away at that second, smoothly, no panic, just twists his upper body in the opposite direction.

Louie turns back to the car. Billy tries to do a headcount through the darkened back window, even though that's pretty much impossible, and he braces himself for the moment Sal steps out of the car.

He wants to see that son-of-a-bitch, eyeball him one last time before he kills him, come on, you fucking fag, get out of the car and let me have a look at you.

Should've called dibs on Sal and the old man. Should've told Tommy to take out the others and leave these two for Billy.

The aching starts again with his next step and it's going to get worse, insanely so, unless he calms down, and so he prays, please God, not now, of all times, not fucking now, and that just makes the agony come on faster, stronger.

His breath grows short and the sidewalk rolls and pitches like a rope bridge stretched over a mile-wide chasm.

The pain pushes against Billy's skull, inflates his head like a Jiffy Pop pan, and he's ready to fall down to the ground and scream for Lora, dear Lora, to please come and take him away from here.

Shit, he can't die, not when he's 20 yards from the fucking goal line. He's suffered so badly, given up too much, lost a fine, decent woman so he can pull off this suicide mission. After all this misery, Billy can't go to into the body bag without firing a shot.

He focuses on a fire alarm box on the corner of 72nd Street, forces himself, orders himself to walk toward that goddamn thing, come on, get over there, put one foot in front of the other. It's the law.

He reels, stumbles, like his old man staggering home from a shitfaced night at Gallagher's. His numb hands wrap around the alarm and he tries to keep from falling.

His mind slides back to when they were all kids hanging out in the basement of Sal's house. They had a small bar set up down there and right at the end there was this cheap little statuette of a smiling drunk hanging onto a lamppost. The guy was wearing a bow tie and a top hat and he looked so joyfully mockey-eyed.

Billy is enjoying this memory, certain the worst is over, when his guts explode and he's losing his insides all over the street. He holds on tight and the words come out of his mouth right behind the puke.

"Lamb of God, who takes away the sins of the world…"

Tommy does one of those fruity warm-up routines he's seen runners do, where you step forward and drop down into long, low stretch.

Christ, this ain't too fucking gay, is it? Let's hope nobody comes up from behind and rams him up the ass.

He's at the triangle where the street splits and he hears the car slowing down nearby. He looks to the memorial in front of him, a monument to the douche bags who were too stupid to keep their heads down in the middle of a war.

How do you assholes feel now? They named a patch of cement in Brooklyn in your honor and there's a flagpole with the American and POW flags flapping overhead. Does that make you any less dead?

Tommy twists to take a look at the monstrous car coming to a stop a few yards away. Jesus, look at that goddamn ocean liner. You could fit a whole family of Dominicans into that thing.

He cranks his head a little, sees the big muscle freak getting out of the car, walking into the restaurant and then one of the old bastards climbs out and looks in Tommy's direction.

Tommy turns slowly away, makes it look natural, nothing to worry about here. Gives it a few seconds and he turns to see the loser is walking around the car; beyond that, there's Billy coming down the street with his baseball cap tugged down over his face.

Damn, is he walking funny or is it just the angle?

A little farther up the block, Tommy spots Eddie pulling into a spot, pumping on the brake so it looks like the engine is choking on him. Atta boy, you didn't drive off and leave us flat like I thought you would.

Now play around with the car and don't look at Billy who's right behind you, grabbing onto the fence like he's inspecting the goddamn thing.

Tommy sees the fossils wobbling out of the car and into the daylight like Count Dracula's extended family. Why even bother ambushing these old grannies when most of them will probably croak next week?

He turns back to the monument, pictures the battle will take place here in a few seconds, wonders if he'll die here today, wonders if anyone will put up a statue in his honor for people to ignore and pigeons to shit on.

On this spot, a young man from Staten Island gave his life shooting the living fuck out of a bunch of old—

Billy's wobbling now, no question about it. The guy's staggering around like he's on a sheet of ice and, fuck, Tommy knew they should have greased these bastards back at the graveyard.

His mind tumbles end over end. What the hell is he supposed to do now? Billy's cooked, Eddie's useless; so that means Tommy's on his own. Another minute and those pricks will be safely in the restaurant, they'll have to scrub this thing, and the craving Tommy feels now will only get worse.

He didn't plan for no one way trip today but he got up this morning ready for war and aching to kill, and if he has to take on these cocksuckers all by his lonesome, so fucking be it.

Tommy pulls out his phone and speed-rattles Billy in a Hail Mary bid to save this thing. The phone rings and rings and Tommy watches completely helpless as Billy staggers over to the fire alarm on the corner and starts puking.

"Oh, shit…"

27

BILLY HUGS THE firebox like it's his best friend and his first love and waits for his stomach to return to his body.

There's not much inside him since he skipped breakfast and he's being ravaged by the dry heaves; it's like someone is reaching down his throat elbow deep to rip out his intestines.

His body temperature erupts like a flash fire. His head is buzzing and Billy thinks he must be having a stroke until he realizes that it's this stupid fucking phone ringing in his pocket as Tommy tries to pull off a long-range rescue.

The thing keeps whining at him, sends his blood pressure even higher, and Billy wants to reach through the goddamn phone and strangle that schmuck on the other end.

"Ah, that's fucking disgusting…"

Can't argue with you there, buddy; this shit's grossing me out, too.

Somebody's approaching him, a real human being, live and in color, and Billy can't do much except empty his gut and hope that he'll be able to stand up before this guy gets any closer.

C'mon, bitch, act like a man, keep breathing, inhale, exhale, make this happen, show them all how the wicked are estranged from birth.

The pain lifts as the footsteps get closer and that goddamn phone won't stop ringing.

"Hey, scumbag…" The voice drops down on him. "What the hell is wrong with you?"

That's Louie hanging over Billy now, itching for any excuse to use his fists so he can impress Matty.

"C'mon, asshole, stand up straight so I can punch your fucking brains out."

Louie wants you to take the pain. He's wheezing just from the walk over here, but he's such a badass he can beat the shit out of some puking bum.

Billy slides his hand into his pocket, takes hold of the cell phone, tosses it in the air, a perfect pitch, right to Louie, who catches the thing as Billy raises his head and the two of them look into each other's eyes.

Louie doesn't know what to do with this ringing phone and the guy who's supposed to be dead standing in front of him, and while he's trying to make sense of this Billy takes out the .45 and jams it right under Louie's chinny-chin-chin.

"It's for you," he says and pulls the trigger.

Tommy presses the phone against his ear, his hand reaches for the gun, ready to nail that fat load of shit waddling over to Billy, who hangs off the fire alarm box like a wet beach towel.

All right, he thinks, new plan. Shoot the warthog in the back, run to the car and kill Matty and anybody else in the vicinity.

If Tommy's still alive by then and Eddie's done shitting in his pants, they can get out of here and let Billy take care of himself. It's a shame they won't have their little grudge match, but it wouldn't have been a fair fight anyhow given how Billy's so fucked up—

But then Tommy sees Billy toss something to the fat guy and he knows what's coming next even before he hears the shots.

"What it is!"

Billy shoots Louie again even though he knows the first shot did the business; hell, right in the face like that, it's over, I don't care if you're the Incredible Hulk. But he's feeling generous today, so he puts another bullet though Louie's heart and sends him to the street over and out.

And then he's running. Yes, he should have waited until they were getting Matty into the wheelchair, but he's leaving that idea in the street with Louie. You can't change your mind once you jump out of the plane.

Tommy runs in from the opposite direction, gun out, shooting the car's windshield to pieces and with the hood on, he looks like death in a track-suit. While he's running toward the car, Billy's eyes get stuck on the words

carved into the war memorial honoring those who made the supreme sac-
rifice for their country.

He reads that line again even when he sees one of the guys, Paolo, burst
of the car and fall to the ground aiming a gun straight at him. Billy really
ought to be doing something instead of just standing here, but he recalls
this one night a few years ago when he and Paolo were hanging out together.

It was just a couple of days before Christmas and neither one of them
were in any hurry to go home to their wives. They wound up in some place
on 18th Avenue and drank for most of the evening.

Paulo got lit and told jokes all night long like he was doing stand-up.
They bought rounds for the whole bar, everybody had a great time, and they
wound up closing the place.

Billy's still thinking of that night when he shoots Paulo right through
the chest.

"What the fuck?"

Stan almost crashes into a parked car when he hears the gunfire going
off behind him. Everything was so quiet a few seconds ago when he drove
by Matty's car.

He had thought about pounding the horn just to shake these douche
bags up a little, but it seemed so undignified.

And he was all set to bounce on out of here when what sounds like
the Tet Offensive breaks out half-a-block behind him and Stan thinks, shit,
they're trying to take the old bastard out—whoever the fuck "they" may be.

He cranks out a ferocious U-turn while he's shouting into the radio. "Shots
fired! Shots fired!"

Everything's moving again.

Billy runs toward the car and Train charges out of the restaurant, faster
than you'd think for someone with all those bloated muscles.

It was supposed to be different between these two. Billy was going to
guide the young hitter, channel his savagery and turn Matty's brutal spawn
into a fearsome piece of work. They were going to be a team.

Now they are the worst kind of enemies and Billy feels something
strange looking at this young guy, an instant loathing he can't explain, a force

way beyond self-preservation, like the Holy Spirit flew down from Heaven, fluttered by Billy's ear and whispered, shoot him, shoot this mother fucker right between them sick gray eyes.

He takes careful aim, like he's out on a target range with nothing but time and no place to go, waits until he's ready to pull the trigger and when he does, the blond head snaps back and the hyper-pumped body tumbles over a potted plant. The next generation ends right here.

Billy moves quickly; he feels protected, certain that no harm will come to him today and that all these bullets ripping through the air will never touch him.

Somewhere a woman starts screaming and Billy runs even faster. He sees Teddy's half out of the driver's seat and Tommy laughing insanely while he pumps bullets through the car window. Teddy sags to the ground, propped up against the half-open door, but that's not enough for Tommy.

"Bitch!" Tommy screams as he fires round after round into Teddy's jerking body. "Bitch! Bitch!"

Eddie tears up to the scene, even though nobody gave him the signal, stupid fucking punk, nobody told him to move; while another car screeches down Seventh Avenue in the wrong direction.

Cops, Billy thinks, *fucking cops*—

This one's huge, a real big bastard, who gets out from behind the wheel with his gun out, just as Eddie stumbles into the kill zone, a .38 wrapped in his rattling hands.

The scene skips like an old silent movie and Billy wonders what Eddie's doing here, how he got a gun, and why the kid is aiming at the cop, taking the shooter's pose and pulling the trigger again and again.

Only nothing happens. No flash, no explosion, no bloodshed, just click-click-click, coming out of that useless weapon and the only thing missing is a red "Bang!" flag popping out of the barrel.

Eddie's face drops and his eyes expand in shock while the cop turns, sees the gun, and shoots him through the heart. The kid goes down screaming and the cop turns around to Billy, both aiming their weapons at each other and Stan stops and mouths the one-word question.

"Billy?"

28

THE HAND-CRANKED PEEP show halts in mid-turn and the two men gawk at each other in mutual disbelief.

That's Stan, Jake's partner, staring at Billy with that dumb shit look on his face. Billy wants to stop the scene, call a timeout like a football referee, or put up his hand and shriek *"Hoooooooooold everything!"* like the old Dick Tracy cartoons.

These guys shouldn't be shooting at each; they should be able to stop, put down their weapons, and back away from each other slowly, hands held out and spread wide. They should be able to talk to one another.

But this is not a cartoon and Tommy has no idea of the history between these two, so while Billy and Stan are still trying to make some sense out of this insanity, Tommy comes up behind Stan and before Billy can say a word, fires a stream of bullets into the cop's back.

"Die, mother fucker, die!" Tommy is shooting and screeching like a jackal as Stan crumples to the ground.

The big man falls to his knees, then on all fours, and he looks into Billy's eyes, like Billy is the one who did this to him. He slides forward and Billy gets down, grabs hold of his arm and squeezes.

"Take it easy," Billy whispers because there's nothing else he can say now. "Just take it easy."

The Polack bastard fights hard to stay alive even though they both know there's no way he can win.

Stan looks up at Billy for an answer and Billy knows that by all rights Stan should be alive and he should be the one bleeding all over the street. He's one of the good guys, while everyone knows Billy's been a curse since the day he was born.

Billy wants to apologize, sorry my son murdered you, sorry you're dying here among all these mutts. But it doesn't matter what Billy wants as Stan's eyes roll up into his head and he departs this sinful place.

Billy glares at Tommy who smirks back, like, what—that guy was going to kill you. Fuck was I supposed to do?

There's nothing Billy would like more right now than to blow his son's head off, but he still needs him; he's still shackled to this maniac.

He looks at Eddie twitching and gagging on the ground and he really wants to help the kid, at least comfort him until he dies, but Billy's got something to take care of right now, so Eddie's on his own for these last few moments.

Taking a deep breath, Billy pulls open the rear door of Matty's car and dives in.

The outside world disappears. Pure static crackles out of the car radio, the air is thin and musty, and Billy feels like he's broken into an ancient crypt.

The wheezing old man desperately pulls himself to the other side of the car, his withered legs dangle uselessly off of the seat, and Billy thinks he must be in the wrong car, that this shrunken cripple trying to scuttle away from him looks nothing like the heartless killer he remembers.

Matty Cigar is an animal. He had so many guys killed they should name a graveyard after him. He ain't ascared of God.

The static from the speakers clears his vision, though, and assures Billy that, yes, he's got the right man.

He had wondered what he'd say when this moment came, when he finally stood over Matty with a gun in his hand. Curse him out, do the old "at last we meet again" line; taunt him, break the old man down until he cries and whimpers for his life.

But now that he's here and it's happening in real time, Billy feels detached, a bystander in this little revenge story.

Matty claws at the rear door, unable to speak, he's reduced to making monkey noises of desperation, looking in all directions as if there's escape hatch, some secret door that will lead him to safety.

Billy leans over the old man very slowly, presses Matty's own .45 flush against the Cigar's forehead. Matty screams, tries to grab the gun, claws at the Jesus tattoo, and Billy decides to keep things simple.

"Do you still love me?" he asks. And pulls the trigger.

29

Billy tumbles backwards out of the car, half-blind, nearly deaf, stained by Matty's blood. He falls through the sky, miles above the earth, with nothing but a whirlwind of haunted voices ripping by his ears.

He's a curse, this fucking kid—

—I will sail to the Sea of Japan—

You're gonna love it up there, big guy—

—Charley, do you know me?—

Billy hits the ground hard, opens his eyes to see the sky, blue and clear, except for a single dark cloud floating right over him. He wants to touch it, find the man-shaped hole he made on his way down to earth, levitate his way right back up there and escape this bloody street.

"Get up, get up out of there!"

He hears a car horn shouting at him, sees Tommy behind the wheel of the SUV, waving at him to get the fuck up and get out of here.

"C'mon!"

Billy climbs to his feet, scans the battleground in search and destroy mode. Where is he? Where the fuck is he?

"Let's go!"

He mentally tags each corpse and there's no sign of the bastard, impossible, he has to be here; he has to. If Sal's not here, this thing will never end and Billy will take the pain for all eternity. A ringing comes off one of the bodies and Billy figures that Teddy just got his last phone call.

Something moves out of the corner of his eye, and he sees Paolo is somehow still alive, spitting up blood as he crawls in the gutter like a dying dog. Billy runs to him, flips the poor chump over on his back and kneels down on the massive chest wound.

"Jesus Christ!" Paolo tries to push Billy's weight off of him.

"Where is he, Paolo?" Billy leans down harder, erases all memory of that special Christmas Eve. "Where's Sal?"

Poor old Paolo made the unforgivable mistake of dying too slowly, couldn't croak fast like the rest of this bunch; no, he had to hold on to whatever flicker of life he had left, blood tracing out of his mouth, his eyes roll in agony and shock. He's just a few inches from the edge, but Billy won't let him go.

"Tell me where he is, Paolo."

"Please…"

Tommy shouts the cops are coming, and yes indeed they are, Billy can hear the sirens and he pushes on Paolo's ragged chest like he's heading for China.

He clamps his hand around Paulo's throat, feels the fading pulse, warm blood dripping through his fingertips. Paolo grabs weakly at Billy's arm to get free and die.

"Tell me." Billy pushes the gun against Paolo's head. "Tell me where Sal is or so help me God when I'm done with you, I'll go over to your house and start on your wife and kids."

Tears roll down Paolo's face as he tries to pull Billy's fingers away. Billy shoves the feeble hand aside with the gun barrel and presses it against Paolo's head.

"Don't make me do this, Paolo, don't make me hurt your family…"

Paolo's face softens as the life leaves his body and Billy shakes him.

"Don't die like this, Paolo. Think of your wife and kids. God will never forgive you if you let this happen to them."

The sirens grow louder, mix with Tommy's screams and the SUV's horn; Billy's going to start screaming himself in another two seconds; he can't keep this bastard alive much longer.

"C'mon, Paolo, die like a man."

Paolo's eyelids flutter; his hand slips away, and his lips quiver as he calls up his last bit of life to speak.

"Penn—"

Billy pulls the trigger on the first syllable and Paolo's brains explode out the side of his head, a dreadful, meaty sound. Happy holidays, big guy.

"Billy!"

Tommy's howl cuts through the air and Billy rises, sprints toward the SUV. His feet hit the ground like cannon blasts, the sirens screech at him to freeze, don't move, but fuck that, Billy runs toward the SUV like Frank trying to escape to Switzerland.

Eddie blocks his path, stretched out before him with two holes in his chest, his eyes blank and staring. Eddie, who wanted to be a tough guy, who looked up to Billy like he was the Pope, is dead on the ground with a look on his face that says don't leave me here, almost daring Billy to keep coming. And Billy jumps.

You just do what I tell you and you'll be okay.

He's in mid-air and it feels like Eddie is going snap upright, grab Billy by the ankles, and pull him down to the ground. You did this to me, the corpse is telling him, it's your fault I'm dead. Yeah, Eddie, you and so many others.

Billy hits the ground, his knees buckle and he almost goes down. Recovering his balance, he dives into the passenger side of the SUV, the dead man's seat, his legs hanging out the door while Tommy stomps on the gas.

They fly down Seventh Avenue with the wind tearing at him; Billy's grip weakens, his fingers slide against the leather seat and his feet come closer to the moving ground. He's going to fall, drop back down there with the other corpses.

He looks into Tommy's eyes and it's like his son is pausing, thinking over what he wants to do next. Billy almost smiles at the situation because he knows never should have trusted this psychopath. You should have seen this coming, big guy, Tommy, the sole survivor.

Tommy cuts a wild turn on to 68th Street, cars spin out of control to avoid a wreck, and Billy feels a hand on his wrist, his son grabbing him, pulling him into the SUV.

The force of the turn slams the door shut and they're speeding away, cutting off other cars and blowing through every traffic light in their path.

Tommy holds onto the steering wheel with one hand, a huge grin on his face, and his earsplitting laughter nearly cracks the windshield, sounding so crazy that Billy wishes he had fallen out of the car.

"That was fucking glorious!"

Part Eight: What Can the Matter Be?

1

Hours after his birthday party, Billy comes down off the bridge in a curving predator's decent and searches for a nightmare in a blue sweatshirt.

We're going for a little ride tonight…

It's late, incredibly late, a time when all decent people should be in bed, but here's Billy rolling down the blacktop at this ungodly hour with the radio squelching harshly and the AC encasing his heart in ice..

Billy sees Manhattan's scorching lights in the distance, so far off it's like a drawing in a kid's storybook. He stares harshly at the slumbering houses and apartment buildings along Shore Road and wishes unrelenting agony upon anyone who can sleep well tonight.

He bails at 65th Street, drives through Bliss Park, and comes back on Colonial Road. The restaurant is closed and dark now, like every other business in the neighborhood. No lights, no people, not even a stray cat. The world is empty, except for Billy.

He cranks out a U-turn, skitters like a roach beneath the Gigantor legs holding the highway in the sky and swings back onto the Belt.

Aiming the car at the Verrazano, Billy swears to God Almighty and all the angels in Heaven that if he doesn't see anything between here and the entrance ramp he's going to forget this bullshit and go home. Fuck the ghosts and the ghouls and all the other children of the night. Billy needs sleep.

Now tonight we're gonna take care of some business…

As he passes a huge freighter plowing through the Narrows, Billy tries to put the splintered pieces of this night together.

A few hours ago he was celebrating his birthday with Lucille, Matty, all the boys and the wives, everybody was drinking to his health and breaking his balls.

"You're getting old, big guy," Sal shouted over his third margarita. "Your next party is going to be in the nursing home."

"And you'll be sitting right next to me, dickhead!"

They were all laughing, enjoying themselves. All the worries hanging over their heads were put off for another day. Somewhere well into the evening, Billy drifted over to the bar and watched his party like he was a stranger who just walked in off the street.

Billy remembered the first night he entered Matty's place, how frightened he was, how he tried to act like a tough guy so they wouldn't see how desperate he was to be part of the crew.

And now Matty wants Billy to show Train how things are done, but don't give him no special treatment. No, he's got to earn his keep just like everybody else and the old man knows the kid will do just fine. Matty's heard good things about Train.

You don't know what that man done to me, what he done to my family!

"Having fun?"

Matty was looking up at him from his wheelchair.

"Yeah, Matty, I am."

"You mean you're actually happy for once in your goddamn life?"

"Looks that way."

"Shit," the old man smiled at him. "Somebody should call Eyewitness News; we got the scoop of the fucking century here."

"I don't give no interviews."

Matty laughed and threw his arms open wide.

"C'mere, you prick."

Billy leaned over, the two men embraced and held on to each other for a long time. All these years, Billy thought, all this time, gone by so fast. He felt Matty's hand slip an envelope into his pocket as the old man whispered, "God bless you, Kid."

"You, too, Matty."

"All right," Matty gently pushed free. "People are going think we're a couple of faggots."

"Hey, the evening is still young."

The Cigar laughed, gave Billy the cross-armed salute and went around saying his good nights. The thing was breaking up and the boys helped the old man out to his car.

"Sal, take me back to the club for a nightcap," Matty said.

"Jesus, Matty, don't you ever sleep?"

"C'mon, don't be an old lady."

Billy was tempted to join them, but he decided to go home with Lucille, convinced there was nothing that could make this night any better.

And that should have been it. Everybody gets into their cars, have a good night, see you tomorrow.

But it didn't happen that way. No, this old bum, this drunk in a navy blue sweatshirt, hood pulled up over his head, came walking out of nowhere like an extra in the wrong movie.

The memory breaks as this point, crumbles like a distant radio signal. Billy felt a burning spike sink into his soul, he was staring down the block and everybody else was staring at him. And then he was dragging Lucille back to the car, telling her to shut the hell up.

They fought all the way home and he came so close to bashing her face in while they were going over the bridge. When they got to the house, she stomped upstairs, shouted "fucking lunatic!" over her shoulder and slammed the bedroom door.

Billy didn't care, didn't even hear what she said. He was too busy pacing around the living room, muttering "it can't be him," and praying for the Lamb of God to grant him some fucking peace.

But there's no peace to be found on this night and Billy drives down this lifeless stretch of highway cursing his mother for giving birth to him.

...if you don't pay your debts, you gotta take the pain...

This is so fucked up, so crazy, crawling around like this in the middle of the night searching for some busted old gin rat who could be halfway to Canada by now and isn't even the fucking guy you think he is anyway.

It's just some loser who happens to look like somebody Billy knew when he was a kid. He had the hood up; Billy couldn't get a good look at his face. This is all in Billy's head and in a little a while, when the sun rises all of this nonsense will disappear.

Billy thinks he'll have to get something nice for Lucille to make up for the way he acted tonight. Tickets to a show, some expensive jewelry, something that will calm her down and shut her up. Maybe run her up to the Poconos and show her the place he wants to buy.

He was just getting ready to switch to the exit lane when he sees something on the bike path. In that second the car hits a pothole, goes wild, and Billy has to put a chokehold on the steering wheel to keep the bastard from flipping over.

Static screeches into his face and Billy rapidly pumps the brake until he regains control and eases the car into the rest stop right below the bridge.

He looks out the window and prays the figure is gone, begs God to please make it an illusion, a mirage, or a bad dream. But he sees someone sitting on a bench, someone who has no right to be there.

A man in a navy blue sweatshirt...

2

Billy kills the headlights, switches off the engine and watches the guy on the park bench. He's still got his hood up, his hands are in his pockets, his chin pointed down to his chest.

The guy is like a puppet sitting there, a dusty Halloween decoration that someone forgot to put back in the attic.

Billy gets out of the car and eases the door shut. He's angry, feels stupid for spying on some old alkie when he should be home in bed. It's his birthday, for Christ's sake; he deserves to enjoy it and not get all twisted over stupid shit like this.

He walks slowly, very slowly, toward the figure on the bench, careful not to step on a branch or broken glass. It can't be him—not after all this time, not after all the drinking, the hard living. Not after a savage beating he took from three punk scumbags in a dark alley one night so many years ago.

He hears a line of chatter coming from the figure on the bench, sees the covered head nodding toward the water. It sounds like gibberish at first, but words slowly emerge from the noise and take shape until Billy understands them perfectly.

"…who takes away the sins of the world…"

Billy stops dead, his right heel up and ready to take the next step. A screaming devil chorus is telling him to stop, that he's made a terrible mistake by coming here tonight.

He doesn't want to know the truth or dig up the past or solve any mysteries. He should jump back in the car, put about a hundred miles between him and this pious bundle of rags.

The tide pulls him toward the bench, though, makes him walk around until he's standing over the shrouded figure that reeks of bad booze and worse luck, who gives off an aura as deadly as plutonium. And still Billy has to know.

"Hey," Billy says, his voice little more than a rasp. "I want to talk to you."

The guy doesn't react, makes like Billy's not even there. He thinks he can ignore Billy the Kid when most people jump three feet in the air if Billy so much as clears his throat. He kicks the guy's foot.

"Hey, asshole, you deaf? Look at me when I'm talking to you."

The covered head rises slowly, so deliberately, like this bastard is trying to be funny, and Billy is ready to grab him by the throat, yank that hood back, and fry this loser's face under the streetlight's beam.

But he waits, holds his temper. If this prick wants to be cute, fine. Let him play his little game.

The neck cranks back, the chin rises, like some ancient piece of machinery coming to life after years of rusting neglect and Billy feels wind rushing by him, gets the same sick feeling he had when he was running down Main Street in Stroudsburg.

—it can't be him, it can't be him—

He looks into a pair of feeble, bloodshot eyes and Billy's chest begins to vibrate, wonders if this is what it's like to have heart attack because it feels as if the goddamn thing is going to bust clean out of his body and sail over six lanes of blacktop.

"Big guy," he croaks, "you're a mess."

3

CHARLEY'S HAIR IS mostly gone and what's left has turned white. His face bears the wounds of time and drink; there's a purple bruise fading from his cheek and a fresh cut on his forehead.

His hands hold a trembling grip around a bottle in a paper bag, he twitches as if he's being stung by bolts of electricity. His eyes strain to focus on Billy.

"What…?" The voice is cracked and raw. "What do you want?"

Jesus Christ, look at him, look at Charley, who used to carry you around on his shoulders and make you laugh so hard; look what you did to him.

"Charley…" Billy fights the urge to throw his arms around him. "Charley, it's me, Billy."

The old man scowls and tenses up, ready for an attack.

"Wh-what do you want?"

"Take it easy." Billy holds up both palms to show he means no harm. "Don't you know me?"

Don't talk to me, motherfucker. You don't know you me! You don't say shit to me!

"Know you?" Charley looks away, shaking his head. "No, I ain't never seen you before."

God, it hurts so much to hear Charley deny his good buddy. Billy drops to one knee, looks into the old man's face. There's so much he wants to say.

Look at me, Charley; I'm a man now. I got a kid of my own. You should see him, you should see my boy.

"C'mon, Charley, it's me, Billy—Billy the Kid." His voice cracks like he's five years old. "You used to work for my father. Y-you were my best friend in the world."

"I don't know you." Charley intones like he's saying a prayer. "I don't know you."

"But—"

"—I come here to be by myself. I ain't bothering nobody. Why don't you leave me alone?"

He bundles up and turns away, his eyes aimed toward the Narrows. Billy just wants to help the guy, make things right. Take him home, get him cleaned up, give him a decent meal. Find some kind of rehab place and get him off the booze. There's got to be somebody that can help him.

You see that man there? You see him, fuckhead? He don't like you very much.

There's got to be someone who can undo the damage Billy's done.

"Charley, please—"

He touches the old man's shoulder and Charley pulls back, his eyes bulging.

"What are you doing?"

"It's all right." Billy speaks softly. "I just—"

"—I'm not looking for no trouble, I just want to be left alone here—"

Billy gets down on both knees, kneels before this old drunk, grips his shoulders and he starts crying, crying like a girl.

Somebody get him a skirt.

"Charley," he says, "I-I'm sorry, I'm sorry about what...I-I was young, I didn't know no better. I wanted—I wanted to be part of Matty's crew so bad. I-I didn't have nothing else in my life..."

Billy squeezes the old man's shoulders until it feels like the bones beneath these rags are going to snap. Charley stares at him and Billy sees the recognition in his eyes. He knows who Billy is.

"Let go of me—"

"Please, Charley, you gotta forgive me."

"I don't know you—"

"Stop it," Billy yells. "You know who I am."

Charley struggles to break free of Billy's hands, twists his body, fights to stand up.

"Charley, just take it easy—"

"—let go!"

"—please, Charley, let me help you."

There's raw panic in Charley's eyes and he fights to get free. Billy won't let him go, even when he sees Charley rear back and swing the bottle like a club.

"—let go of me—"

Billy blocks the attack, knocks the bottle out of Charley's hand and hears it crash to the pavement.

"Stop it!"

The old man keeps fighting, spitting, tries to bite Billy's wrist, cursing the whole time while Billy shakes him and tells him to calm down, please, Charley, calm down.

"Let go of me, you fuck!"

Billy's got all these memories, of his friend taking him to the movies, driving him to Pennsylvania, riding so fast on the Horn that he flies out of his seat. But he can't find Charley anywhere inside this drunk, this deadbeat, this fucking parasite, the more you give them, the more they fucking take—

I had to get him out of there.

He stands up, tears rolling down his face, and wraps his fingers around Charley's throat.

There's no one around. A few cars flash by on the Belt. The air is thick and stale, the Narrows is dead calm.

"Billy?"

Billy turns his head and looks at the water while his hands do their business. He sees the big freighter lumbering toward them, massive, silent, the brilliant lights casting a perfect reflection in the water, so it rides atop its mirror image.

He'd give anything to be standing on her decks right now, on his way to the Horn of Africa, the Tuamotus, and the Sea of Japan.

"Billy!"

His grip tightens and he refuses to hear the gasping breaths, ignores the weak punches, the fingers reaching for his eyes, tearing at the face of Jesus tattooed on his arm, Billy just keeps looking at the freighter.

I will sail to the Sea of Japan...

The freighter passes by them, water crashes against the huge bow and Billy feels like he could step right on board, it's so close. Charley fights savagely and Billy sobs as he squeezes harder and harder.

He wonders if anyone on board can see what's happening here, someone who might raise an alarm, radio to the shore for help, or fire off a flare to ignite the black heavens.

But nothing happens. The huge vessel rolls by, blind to the distant figures on land. The water becomes calm again and the life between Billy's fingers goes still.

24

HE CAN'T CLOSE the eyes, no matter how many times he drags his hand over the bloodless face, Charley's still staring at him.

Billy doesn't want to move from this spot by the water even though he knows that he's got to get away from here. But Charley won't let him go.

He imagines sitting on this bench until the sun comes up and shines down upon the two of them, so that everybody will see what Billy's done. Only then does he get up and stumble to the car.

Billy drives aimlessly, no thought of where he's going, because there's no place on God's green earth for someone like him.

He finally pulls into a gas station on 92nd Street and 7th Avenue, across from the bridge entrance, convincing himself he's low even though the needle is a sliver short of full. Billy's always been good at lying.

There are only few other cars in the place, clubbers heading home, late shifters going to work, people who have nothing to do with Billy's life. One car's hood is up while the attendant, Indian, Pakistani, whatever, checks the oil.

Billy stares at the Verrazano looming ahead of him. He draws an imaginary line down from the red lights on top of the bridge way down to the place where he left Charley. He wants so badly to push away the night, back things up to that morning when he and Charley escaped the city on that deserted bridge, and left this world behind.

You're gonna love it up there—

Billy gets out of the car, walks slowly back to the pump and picks up the hose honestly believing that he's just going to top off and go home.

But he can't get the nozzle into the damn gas tank, keeps missing, shit, the thing moves on him every time he gets close, c'mon, you bastard, enough already.

Billy stops, his hand falls to his side. He's wondering what the hell to do next when he sees his arm slowly cobra rising, lifting the hose higher, higher, until the nozzle is right over his head.

You burn that son-of-a-bitch!

He squeezes the handle with that killer grip of his and the reeking fuel pours over his head and down his back.

Billy does a thorough job, brings the hose around, puts his head back, covers his chest, arms and legs, while the runoff forms a puddle around his feet and the whispers float around him.

"What the fuck—?"

"Look at that guy; look what he's doing!"

The stink is unbelievable, almost knocks him over, but Billy keeps on pouring until the pump clicks dead in his hand.

The Pakistani drops the dipstick and charges toward Billy waving his arms and screeching in some kind of English.

"Hey, hey, what you doing, what you doing?"

People get out of their cars to stare at Billy as he digs into his pocket, takes out his lighter and holds it up high like Lady Liberty.

They all stop dead, the Pakistani guy wails no, no, no, while Billy snaps the lighter once, twice, three times, and gets nothing but sparks for his trouble.

"—call the cops—!"

The faces, stupid, ugly faces, encircle him, and Billy cracks the lighter again, c'mon, just this one last time and I'll never bother you again.

And the thing must've heard him because a flame, a beautiful little blue flicker, abruptly sprouts in Billy's hand.

The ring of bodies widens, the intruders jump back yelling and waving their arms, and Billy feels so powerful, because he's in control here, everyone is this grease bucket is shit scared of him.

He crushes the lighter in his hand, ripped between the driving will to survive and the chronic need to atone for his sins.

C'mon, big guy, you gotta take the pain.

Billy brings his right arm to eye level, calculates where that suffering face of Jesus is located beneath his dripping sleeve and closes his eyes.

That's it, son. Just bring that flame up a little bit higher. Touch the fabric, that's all, touch that nice coat of yours and all your troubles will be over. That's what you want, right? That's what you've always wanted.

His body vibrates with rage and fear, but Billy knows he can do this, and, it's happening, it really is, he's bringing the lighter right up to where it's got to be, he's about to burst into flames, when some son-of-a-bitch roars out "no!", breaks from the group, and crashes into Billy's gut.

He's strong, this guy, Billy thinks as they slam to the concrete and roll into a filthy puddle, a weightlifter or some goddamn thing, who easily straddles Billy, pins his left arms, and shouts like he's scolding a little boy.

"Take it easy…take it easy!"

The kid's got the buzz cut, the neck tattoo, the goddamn headphones, all that shit that Billy hates, and he's young, so powerful, the bastard, with a crushing hold that can't be broken, and Billy hates that most of all.

"Get off me! Get the fuck off me—!"

"Just calm down—"

"—fucking cocksucker—!"

The others get a little braver, step forward to look down at this crazy old man, who is so weak that a teen-ager can knock him flat and it looks like they're all going to gang up on Billy and beat him until he can barely walk.

You see that man there? You see him, fuckhead? He don't like you very much…

No, this is bullshit, he's no parasite, he's no loser, he's Billy the mother-fucking Kid, and nobody ever puts their hands on him.

"It's gonna be okay," the bastard says, "it's gonna be all right…"

No, you scumbag, it'll never be okay, not after what Billy's done on this night and so many nights before, and while the muscle head is trying to calm things down, Billy gets crazier and crazier, so savagely deranged that he pulls the .38 out from under his belt, clubs the son-of-a-bitch across the face, over and over, until the iron fingers let go and Billy shoves this gorilla away.

Billy's up and aiming the gun at his foul savior, who looks at him in terrified confusion, blood dripping down his face.

"You some kind of fucking hero?" Billy screams. "Huh? You a fucking hero?"

"I-I—"

Billy's never had such hatred for anyone as he has for this kid, this meddling fuck, who tries to say something in his defense, the worst thing he could possibly do because Billy doesn't want to hear any bullshit tonight.

"Shut the fuck up!"

Billy shoots the kid in the thigh, the punk screams like a little girl, somebody get him a skirt, grabs his bleeding leg, and so naturally Billy has to shoot the scumbag in the other leg so he'll learn how to take the pain.

The only Good Samaritan is a dead Samaritan.

The guy wails even louder, curls up into a ball, and shrinks into the ground as Billy clips him with the 38.

"I said 'shut the fuck up!'"

The bystanders all jump back, horrified at how this thing has turned, and Billy staggers toward them waving the gun and dripping gasoline with every step.

"We got any more goddamn heroes? Anybody else want to save my life?" Billy sweeps the gun in a loathsome arc and settles on the Pakistani guy. "How about you, Mohammed? You wanna see Allah tonight, you low-life camel jockey scumbag?"

The attendant's eyes swell and he looks ready to faint dead onto the concrete. God-damn, will you look at me? I'm terrorizing these mother fuckers.

Billy feels omnipotent and helpless at the same time; and he's angry, so unbelievably furious at being alive that he whirls and takes deadeye aim at the gas pumps.

"Hey, check this out!" He shouts. "How about it, huh? How about I blow us all to hell, you fucking pricks?"

Of course Billy will be the only one going to hell and he's so primed and determined to obliterate all evidence of this night that if has to take out a whole city block in the process, so be it.

"You think I won't do it?" Billy glares at his tormentors. "Huh? You think I give a shit about any of you scumbags?"

They all suck in their breath, knowing that Billy is as serious as nightfall and there's no way of outrunning this disaster if he pulls the trigger.

"You're all a bunch of fucking parasites!"

Go ahead, big guy, make it happen. Somewhere in the freezing dark sky a passing satellite will record a bright orange flash and move on, never helping, never intervening, doing nothing while five freshly-minted souls streak towards paradise and Billy tumbles into the fiery pit.

They got nothing to say, these faggots, and it gets so quiet that Billy can hear the blood pouring out of the kid's wounds. Only the gas pumps defy him, they stand sentry tall, refusing to cower before him.

You know who I am, mother fucker? You know who I work for?

Billy's finger trembles against the trigger as he tries to loose the fateful lightning, but the suicide drive is receding, he can feel it deserting him when he needs it the most, as the animal mind turns to escape.

He scoops the lighter up off the ground and hurls it at the bridge, throws it as hard as he can hoping to blow the goddamn thing to pieces and send it crashing into the Narrows like a Philistine temple.

Billy crouches beside the kid leaking all over the ground, presses the .38's barrel against his cheek.

"You keep your mouth shut!" He glares at the others. "All of you shut up or so help me God you'll curse your mothers for giving birth to you!"

He's runs back to the car, crushes the gas pedal, flies back onto the street, far away from all those stupid faces.

His skin burns, as if he's actually touched the lighter to his coat, and Billy wonders how long he's got before the cops get him, if they'll try arresting him or just open fire the second they see his car.

Matty should be happy, he thinks, that old bastard should come in his pants when he hears there's one less deadbeat in the world tonight.

Somebody really ought to tell the Cigar, Billy decides as the gas fumes fill the car. This is big news, an old debt finally settled. He needs to know.

And then Billy smiles so coldly he almost frosts up the windshield. Yes, he thinks, the old man should know as soon as possible.

Billy plots the course, reduces his speed, and makes sure to stop for red lights and obey all the traffic laws. He doesn't want to risk being pulled over by the cops, not now.

He wants to talk to Matty.

Part Nine: Fully Involved

1

They brought Stan here to Lutheran after the massacre on Eighth Avenue where the bodies were wildly strewn about as if they had been hurled from the Chrysler Building.

The hospital is a madhouse of TV cameras, gawkers, every cop in creation from the commissioner on down storming into the place.

When he walked in here, guys that Jake didn't even know came up to him, gripped his shoulder and asked, "Jake, are you all right?"

I can't do this, Jake thinks as he rides in the packed elevator. He can't face Kathy, Stan's wife, now his widow. He's completely incapable of looking into that poor woman's eyes because he knows he'll only make things worse.

Goddammit, Jake went through this once already when Connor got killed—isn't that enough for one lifetime? Just pry open these massive doors and let Jake swan dive down the elevator shaft.

Dumb Polack bastard walks right into a firefight. Christ Al-fucking-mighty how stupid do you have to be?

Jake is supposed to comfort Kathy, tell her what a fine man her husband was, offer her any kind of support she needs. But right now he's so angry he's afraid to open his mouth.

Stan was always too loud, always had to have the last word, and he was always right even when he was completely wrong.

That fiasco with Sal outside the club was a perfect example. I mean, what the hell? We all know Sal's a gutless shitheel, but that doesn't mean you go out of your way to break the guy's balls, especially when there's a TV news crew crawling around. Jake is starting to wonder if he even liked the guy.

His breath halts dead in his lungs. Oh, you're going to hell for that one, big guy. No doubts there. You just bought yourself a first class ticket to the Lake of Fire.

Father, will you hear my confession?

They'll want him to see a shrink, get some counseling, to help deal with the grief of losing his partner.

But Jake knows that once he starts talking, he won't be able to stop at Stan's death. He'll keep yammering about all the other stuff that's been tormenting him and pretty soon the whole world will know about Billy's nightly visitations.

Maybe he should flag down a surgeon and ask for a walking lobotomy.

I can't do this…

Jake was in Staten Island when it happened, when his partner was being murdered, after making the journey to the remains of Billy's house.

Looking at the rubble, Jake thought he should know more by now; he should have corralled all these random pieces of information and come up with some kind of answer. But all he had was a pile of smoke-stained debris and a heart full of doubts.

The place had burned down on the same night Matty's bar got torched and Jake knew there had to be a pattern here, but what the hell did it mean?

Maybe Tommy burned down his own home then hauled ass over to Brooklyn so he could scramble Rex's skull and torch Matty's rathole. But if he did, he sure as hell didn't do it alone.

It's funny how this thing keeps coming back to Billy, a guy who is missing and most likely dead in a ditch someplace with a bullet in his head. He didn't cause this much trouble when he was alive.

And it felt so strange being here just days after he and Stan were inside the place, looking down on Lucille's body. It felt wrong, a violation of some kind, and Jake wanted to get the hell out of there.

"Shots fired! Shots fired!"

Stan's voice coming over the radio and Jake ran to the car, raced down Hyland Boulevard, siren going, smashing down on the horn, cursing every other driver in the world, and flew over the Verrazano like it wasn't even there.

But even as he drove, Jake knew he'd be too late, that Stan would be dead, and that radio transmission would be the last time he ever heard his partner's voice.

"It's a bloodbath, Jake," DiPalma, a detective from the six-eight, said, trying to prepare him. "A fucking bloodbath."

There they were, the top men in Matty's crew all on the ground, all shot to shit. This was unheard of, old time gangster stuff that went out with straw hats and Al Capone.

"Listen, Jake, I gotta tell you—"

"—where is he?"

DiPalma led the way, but Jake recognized Stan's hulking frame even with the sheet covering his body. And those God-ugly shoes, like they were mass-produced in Romania.

It was dreadful pulling back that flimsy cover, looking down on Stan, while cops and EMTs raced around, ambulances streaked up the avenue, and helicopters ripped through the sky.

One of Stan's eyes was open, his hand reaching for the gun just a few inches away, and his back ripped apart by what seemed like an endless stream of bullets.

Jake looked down at Stan and felt he should do something crazy; thrust his fist into the sky, vow bloody revenge, swear before the Michael the Archangel and everyone else to track down the rat-fuck maggots that killed his partner. But he couldn't do much more than shake his head and mutter, "God damn it..."

He felt a hand on his shoulder.

"Jake, are you all right?"

There were three shooters, DiPalma said, an older guy with a scar over his eye and two younger ones. It looked like Stan dropped one of them before the bastards got him.

The dead kid, who had showed up for this shindig with an empty gun, was stretched out in the middle of the street, eyes bulging in terror, forever watching Stan drawing down on him.

"I know this one," Jake said softy. "His name is Eddie...Eddie Scala. He's Tommy's buddy."

"Tommy—as in Billy the Kid's son?"

"Yeah. This one spent so much time up Tommy's ass he could be a proctologist. If he's part of this, then Tommy was one of the shooters."

"And what about the other one?"

Jake let the question blow by him like a high pitch.

"Where's Matty?"

His legs trembled slightly as he walked to the car. One of Matty's goons was half out of the driver's seat, face down on the street with blood pooling around him.

And Jake thought if Stan had just come along a little sooner, avoided this carnage, they'd all be celebrating right now—Stan the loudest. All these scumbags killed in one day? That's like Christmas and St. Pat's back to back.

Jake kept walking, around the back end of the car, to the rear door, and looked inside. Matty was bunched up in the backseat like a terrified monkey, blood and brains sprayed all over the back window.

Whoever killed him didn't waste bullets in a madman's staccato like the guy who shot Stan. This one put the gun right up to the old bastard's forehead before pulling the trigger. Even Matty couldn't beat that.

"The guy was close enough to give Matty a blowjob," DiPalma said over his shoulder. "He wasn't taking any chances."

Jake stared at the corpse, still not believing his eyes. This guy had terrified people for a generation, survived a shooting that took his legs away, and beat a score of prosecutions. You figure he'd just die gagging on his oatmeal one morning and young people on both sides of the law would ask "Matty who?"

Jake didn't think there was anyone left in this world who hated the Cigar enough to pull a stunt like this.

Sal was the only holdout, the one guy in the crew who didn't have the decency to die along with the rest of them. By skipping out on Rex's funeral he'd avoid his own. At least for the moment.

He wasn't home and they tried calling his house in Pennsylvania. But a brutal storm had knocked out the power to most of the county and the troopers up there had their hands full.

Jake looked down at the old man's body. Hey, gramps, how's it going? How'd it feel having that gun pressed against your skull?

Jake wanted to spit in what's left of Matty's face, stomp the shattered head into jelly. He wanted so badly to douse the rancid carcass with gasoline, set it on fire and dangle it over the Gowanus with piano wire.

Here you go, big guy, this is for all the grief you caused, for the people you had killed, beaten, and terrorized, all the lives you've ruined. Here's a little something to send you off to hell where you'll be taking the pain for all eternity, you piece of shit.

Jake was rearing up his leg to kick the Cigar's corpse when he decided that it might be a good idea to walk away.

2

THE BELL RINGS, the elevator stops, and Jake prays the doors don't open, and they all go back to the ground floor.

But the huge metal doors slide back, he steps out into the hallway, where there are even more cops, some of the top people, and they all look his way when Jake steps out onto the floor. A deputy chief steps up to him and grabs hold of his hand.

"Jake, are you all right?"

"I'm okay, I'm okay." Jake says, fooling no one. "I-I need to see Kathy."

"Sure, Jake, sure. You go ahead."

The crowd parts as his legs carry him forward, down the hallway, to a small waiting room where he sees the department chaplain and a priest. There are two young girls standing in the room, Stan's daughters; one is trying to be strong, while the other sobs hysterically, like she may never stop.

They're all gathered around Kathy, who turns as Jake gets closer and looks right at him, her eyes burnt crimson.

She stands up, throws her arms around and wails right into Jake's battered heart. He holds onto her, keeps her from sliding to the ground. This is where you belong, helping her, sharing her pain. This is what you deserve.

Tell me, Paolo, tell me!

Billy opens his eyes in the dead man's seat, his fingers clawed in strangle mode. They're somewhere in Jersey, plowing through the belly of a murderous thunderstorm.

Tommy is hunchbacked over the steering wheel and squinting through the slapping windshield wipers as the rain picks up. He looks toward Billy and grunts.

"Shit, I thought you croaked on me."

"Sorry to disappoint you."

Billy shakes the death from his hands, stretches the fingers until he feels they're back under his control.

He avoids looking down at his pants where the smear of Paolo's blood on his knee seems to grow larger with every passing mile. His sleeves are rolled down so he doesn't have to see the bleeding face of Christ, ripped raw by Matty's fingernails.

He's heading back up there again, getting closer to Lora; so close to her that it hurts.

What is she doing now in this dreadful storm? Is she safe in the house or is she out on the road someplace with this wind raging all around her? And why the hell isn't Billy with her?

"Look at them fucking clouds up there," Tommy mumbles behind the wheel. "It's like they're clearing the way for us."

Such a beautiful day when they left the city; just a single dark cloud framed in brilliant blue over the Verrazano. Now they're the only car on the road and the sky is a lethal shade of black that threatens to explode at any second.

It's our fault, he thinks; we caused all this destruction when we killed Matty and unleashed his putrid soul. All that hatred, rage, and evil wrapped up in that twisted body, it had to go somewhere after he died.

"That was some shit back there at the restaurant, huh?"

"Yeah, you could say that."

"Did you hear Eddie screaming?" Tommy's pops a half-grin. "Did he you hear that little bitch? He sounded like a fucking faggot."

"He was your friend, for Christ's sake." Billy feels like he's speaking inside a metal drum. "Doesn't that mean anything to you?"

"Eddie was a loser. All he had to do was sit there, drive the goddamn car, but, no, he's gotta come running into the middle of everything and gets his ass killed instead. Who needs a fucking idiot like that around?"

"Where'd he get that gun? I thought we agreed he wouldn't be packing."

"Who the fuck knows? Guess he wanted to show you what a badass he was. Too bad the little pussy choked."

"Didn't look that way to me," Billy says. "It looked like that gun was empty—"

"—he choked." Tommy swerves the car around a large pool of water. "Fuck him. He knew what he was getting into."

"You think so?"

Tommy completes his smile.

"If he didn't, it's a little late now."

Billy looks at the clouds roiling in front of them, tries to blot out the memory of Eddie shrieking as Stan shot him.

"So that guy who nailed Eddie back there—he was a cop?"

"Yeah, he was."

Tommy nods with cold satisfaction.

"And you knew that guy?"

"We ran into each other a few times."

"For real?"

"Yes, dick." Billy scowls. "For real."

"Hey, sorry, I didn't know you guys were so close."

Billy glares at his son, recalls that depraved look of joy on Tommy's face as he fired into Stan's body over and over.

"You know what you did back there, right?"

"Saved your ass?"

Billy shakes his head.

"You made us cop killers. So now every cop in creation is going to be searching for us from now until doomsday. And they're not going to worry about taking us in alive."

"What was I supposed to do—let that prick fill you full of holes?"

"You should've let me handle it. I had it under control. I didn't need no help from you."

Every word is a lie; Billy had been completely powerless, but it didn't matter because Stan wasn't going to shoot him, not if Billy stood there all day; you could see it in Stan's eyes. He was too stunned to do anything. They both were.

"Whatever, pal," Tommy says. "You think they'll do a show about us on one of them cable programs?"

"Yeah, right after we get our heads blown off."

Billy knows Jake will blame himself for Stan's death and hate himself even more than he does already, if that's possible. Fucking Irish.

But Jake's mind will be working the whole time, clicking with a calculator's detached precision. They must've ID'd Eddie, made the connection to Tommy, and tagged him as one of the shooters.

Jake will know that Sal is the next one to die and get word to him and the state troopers so that when Billy and Tommy show up at Sal's house they'll be a small army waiting for them.

It'll be suicide going up there, but that doesn't bother Billy all that much.

He tries to imagine what he could possibly say to Jake if they ever do meet in this life. *Sorry my son murdered your partner, big guy, but Stan knew what he was getting into. You gotta take the pain.*

"Who was that guy you nailed—the one you were yelling at?"

Think of your wife and kids.

"Paolo. He was one of the originals."

"Paolo?"

"Yeah, why?"

"Nothing," Tommy says. "It's just that I thought you called him 'Charley' a couple of times."

Heat builds up around the bloodstain on Billy's leg. He keeps his eyes on the storm clouds before him.

"I don't think so."

"I'm serious. You were saying 'tell me, Charley.' I was like, what the fuck?"

Billy tries to believe that it's impossible, that he could never have said the wrong name, especially that name.

"Getting old, I guess."

God will never forgive you if you let this happen to them.

"Well, that bastard was pretty confused when he died."

The drying blood becomes hotter and Billy thinks this is a good time to change the subject.

"This isn't going to be easy, you know."

"You mean with Sal?"

"He's going to know we're coming. And the cops are going to be waiting for us."

"You mean them assholes with the Smokey the Bear hats? I'd love to nail a few of them pricks."

"I'm sure you would."

They come around a curve and see a van on its side in the eastbound lane, one headlight gouged out with the wires hanging loose, the other shining uselessly into the rain. The windshield's cracked up into a white inkblot and debris litters the road. A black Toyota sits nearby on the shoulder wheezing steam from its mangled hood.

No cops or fire trucks yet, the accident is only a few minutes old. A small cluster of walking wounded move around the vehicles and squint in the relentless wind.

A woman in a yellow rain slicker breaks from the pack, runs across the divide waving her arms at them frantically. As she gets closer they see a gash on her forehead. Billy wants no part of her or her troubles, but he feels the car slowing down.

"What's going on?"

The woman is just a few feet from the car door when Tommy slams his middle finger against the window and floors the pedal.

"Later, bitch!"

The look on the woman's face shifts from relief to rage and Tommy's laughter mixes with the roar of the engine as they pick up speed. Billy raps him on the arm.

"What the hell's wrong with you?"

"Just having a little fun."

"We're all over the TV, schmuck. We can't afford to get any more attention."

"Shit, you worry too much."

Billy shakes his head. Just enough brain power for eating, fucking and killing. He pictures Lora getting into a wreck, some jeering scumbag driving right by her, and his fingers start to curl.

Billy switches on the radio and gets sprayed with squelches and feedback. Garbled voices fade in and out and Billy slowly puts the story together.

Massive storm moving through New Jersey and PA. High winds, hail, reports of a small tornado touching down in Monroe County. Phone service down, sporadic blackouts, a house set on fire by a lightning bolt. Scores of traffic accidents, including one involving a state trooper.

"It's the end of the world," Tommy says in a faggy whine, "we're all gonna die!"

All this mayhem, all this destruction, cops getting wracked up, emergency services stretched thin; so frayed, from the sound of it, that maybe protecting some greaseball hood from New York is way down on their to-do list.

But Billy feels so weak now; whatever time he's got on this earth he wants to spend it with Lora. Too bad all these cops are looking for him.

They get off at Portland and when they reach the toll booth, Billy pulls his cap down, turns toward the window and pretends to sleep.

He feels the car crossing the bridge, high over the Delaware and he imagines how violent and angry the waters must be, churning up black and furious.

"Can you believe this weather?"

The toll booth attendant feels like talking.

"Yeah, it's something."

"You drove up from New York? Must've been a hell of a ride."

"It was tough."

Get your change and go, asshole.

Billy hears the loneliness in the toll booth guy's voice, the need to talk to another human being. He hears it and he doesn't give a shit. He just wants to get out of here.

"The roads are pretty messed up around here. There are tree limbs and power lines down. Where you headed?"

"Up to Stroudsburg to visit some friends."

Billy feels the guy looking him over, like maybe he's heard about two Caucasian males from New York who might be driving up this way.

"Well, you take care now."

"Yeah, you, too."

They get off the bridge and Billy keeps his eyes closed as they drive into town. He doesn't open his eyes as they drive up 611, enjoying his chosen blindness. The miles roll by and he's almost convinced that he'll get by safely, but seconds later every bone in his body goes cold.

Billy knows without looking that they're passing the rest stop, the place where he should have died, the place where he met Lora; the spot where he fired wildly into the woods when he tried to ambush Scotty. Maybe he should just get out here.

"You okay? You seem a little jumpy."

"I'm fine."

They pull into Delaware Water Gap and Billy wants to tell Tommy to drive up to Mount Pocono and leave him off at Lora's house.

Let Tommy go ahead and finish this thing by himself, he likes killing so goddamn much. Say hello to Sal for me and hopefully the troopers will blow your ass all over these mountains.

"Which way?"

Tell him Mount Pocono. Forget your stupid revenge fantasy. Go to her.

"Head toward Marshalls Creek," Billy says. "That's where we have to go."

3

THE LIGHTS COME back on just as the scream tears out of the upstairs bedroom and Sal prays to God, please, let this be the end of it.

"Sal…?" The voice sinks down from the second floor with frail urgency. "Sal…?"

He gets up from the couch where he'd been sitting in the dark since he arrived hours ago to find Vince walking naked around the backyard in the pouring rain, crying, drooling, and raving about Billy, always fucking Billy.

He looked like a concentration camp victim, his body was so wasted. Sal grabbed hold of his cousin, threw a blanket around him, and got him upstairs. It had been pretty quiet around here—until now.

The death smell hits him three feet from the bedroom door. Sal stops for a second to steady himself, and goes inside.

Vince is curled up under a damp sheet and in this feeble light it looks like he's aged 20 years in the last two hours. Sensing his cousin's presence, Vince looks up and reaches out to Sal with glass fingers.

"Sal…"

"Easy, Vince, easy." Sal takes hold of the withered hand. "Try not to upset yourself."

"Sal…my daughter…I want to see my daughter. Please, I want to see the baby one last time…"

"Vince, you're too sick to travel. You gotta rest. I'll try and have one of the boys bring her up here—"

He hopes the lie will settle Vince down until the life drains out of him, but his cousin is shaking his head.

"We gotta…" Vince struggles for breath. "We gotta get out of here. We gotta get away."

"It's all right, buddy. We're safe here."

Vince clamps down on Sal's wrist with a shocking burst of strength.

"Billy, he's coming here—"

"Vince…"

"He's coming for us, Sal. He's coming to punish us for what we did—"

"Vince, don't do this to yourself. Just try and rest."

"But he's coming—"

"No, he's not!" Sal hears his voice rise. "Billy is dead, all right? He is fucking dead."

Thunder cracks right outside the window and Sal nearly throws himself into the closet.

"Please, Sal…"

He eases his hand free of Vince's grip.

"Just rest, okay?"

Sal walks to the door. Vince tries to speak, but a coughing fit cuts off his words. He finally recovers, closes his eyes and appears to sleep, thank God.

Sal is closing the door when words leak out of Vince's body.

"The wicked are estranged from the womb. They go astray as soon as they be born, speaking lies."

Sal grips the doorknob. He listens, listens hard, for the alien voice to speak again through his cousin, but all he hears is Vince's tormented breathing.

He closes the door and goes downstairs.

4

"GODDAMN—!" SCOTTY IS wrestling with the Chevy's frenzied steering wheel when lighting slices overhead and the car jumps clear off the road like a raped baboon.

Holy shit on a shillelagh, Scotty thinks as he bounces down the embankment, one dead cunnerman coming up.

The Chevy tears up bushes and low-hanging branches before slamming into a log and scrunching to a halt. Scotty's body snaps forward, his mug just a pussy hair away from the windshield, and slams back into the driver's seat.

"Motherfuck—!"

Scotty does a quick inventory to see that all the body parts are still attached, his bowels haven't misbehaved, and the gun is still tucked under his belt.

The car is another story, though, and Scotty has to struggle to get the door open a few inches so he can get the hell out. He finally squeezes into the clear, surveys the battered car with the busted grill and the smoke pouring out from under the hood, and decides, all right, well, fuck it then, I'll walk the rest of the way.

He staggers up the muddy hill with rain pounding on him, thinks about all this aggravation, all this bullshit he's going through, Scotty goddamn well better be the richest monkey on the mountain when this thing is over.

The rain tapers down to a drizzle by the time he reaches the road and ascertains that no one else is stupid enough to be out on day like this.

It's only about a half-mile, give or take, and it'll be worth the effort of dragging his fat rear end to that house if he can hammer Billy and get rich to boot.

All he has to do is tell these ginzos where to find Billy and hold out his hand. If Scotty's got this thing right, these wops will pay big time to get their claws on that scumbag.

Too bad he won't be there to see old Billy getting the business, but the money will more than make up for it. And once that shitheel is sleeping with the fishes or wearing a cement overcoat or whatever the fuck those animals do to him, Scotty plans on swinging over to the ex-wife's place and loosening a few of her teeth just for old time's sake.

He's picturing how he's going to spend his first thousand when he comes around a cluster of trees and there it is, that big ass house, sitting right in front of him.

The place looked normal the last time he was here, but now Scotty feels like he's facing Frankenstein's summer hideout. And the sun's going down.

Scotty's thinking that he may be a little out of his league on this one. Maybe he should reconsider. Maybe he should turn around and run back to the trailer park and hide behind the refrigerator for next six months. But he can't flake now, not after coming this far; not after getting his cousin killed. He's got to go through with this thing. Especially since he's got nothing to go home to.

Scotty steps up onto the porch and stands there dripping in front of the door.

He imagines a gang of guinea hoodlums waiting for him, cooking up mounds of spaghetti, with tommy guns slung over their shoulders, 12-inch daggers clasped between their teeth. Scotty swallows hard. C'mon, son, grow a pair of balls and make this shit happen.

He watches his index finger float toward the doorbell.

They're talking to him, all the voices. They're all calling out to Vince, now at the hour of his death.

Well, well, well, look who's here. It's the big time hoodlum himself.

He's curled up in the huge bed, eyes welded shut as he tries to block the profane choir. Leave me alone, you cold-hearted bastards, he thinks, I got a right to die in peace.

But the voices won't stop. The harder he tries to silence them, the louder they speak. The living, the dead, and whatever's in between, want to have their say.

So how's it going, tough guy?

The words push through the floorboards, bleed down the walls and drip from the ceiling. They will be heard.

Is he dead?

No, not yet, you sons of bitches; Vince still has a little bit of the life force still in him. He thinks about all the guys in the crew who kept saying that Vince was a pussy, didn't have no guts, and always hid behind his cousin.

They should see him now, those fucks, they should see Vince fighting to stay alive while his body is crumbling to pieces. Them bastards would've croaked a long time ago if they had to go through anything like this.

You're a disgrace to our family.

He's been thinking more and more about Willy, poor guy, he was the best one of the bunch. And look what you did to him.

For a while it had been easier for Vince to deflect memories of his brother's death. He was able to shake it off as a tragic accident, one of those things that could have happened to anybody. Just a few inches back from that pool table and Willy would still be alive.

And it was all Rocco's fault anyway. If that prick hadn't been beating on Vince the whole goddamn thing never would've happened.

But he's too sick to fight off the truth now and the facts overrun his mind like an invading army. He sees Willy engulfed in flames, hears him screaming, and there's no denying that Vince murdered his own brother.

You're gonna burn for this, mother fucker!

There's no penance for what Vince has done. He's going to hell the second his heart stops beating and he'll burn there for all eternity. Those nuns were right about him. He really is evil.

Vince, you gotta get ahold of yourself. Forget about Billy, for Christ's sake. We got a lot more important things going on around here.

He tried, God knows he tried to warn his cousin about Billy. They've got to get out of this unholy place before Billy gets here and burns it right down to the ground.

The storm paved the way for Billy, gave him a clear path to come back from the dead. But Sal won't listen, doesn't want to hear it. He's just sitting on his ass downstairs waiting for Vince to die.

Vince is never going to see his little girl again. She's going to grow up without him, never knowing who her father was. If he could just do something, one good thing, before he dies to prove that he's a decent man, worthy of such a beautiful child, then he could pass quietly from this life.

You'll get your Iron Cross now, Col. Von Ryan!

Vince opens his eyes, raises his head off the pillow. That's no voice from beyond the grave. It's coming from the TV downstairs, a war movie, that Frank Sinatra picture that Billy liked so much.

Vince has to get out of here, away from this doomed house. He wipes the sweat from his face and looks at the window, just a few feet away.

All right, he takes three deep breaths, swings his feet to the floor, and stands up.

"Jesus—"

The building tumbles forward, and Vince, blind from the pain, falls to one knee, and pukes up the little he's got left in his stomach.

Get up, you gotta get up, and he reaches out, groping for the window frame, and with one pull he's up on his feet and looking out at the sudden night on the other side of the glass.

Vince coughs, barely fogging up the pane with his feeble breath. It's so dark out there, like the sun has gone and will never come back. He wipes the window clear and squints into the gloom.

This is where he was standing that day when he saw Billy, saw him alive and walking around outside when the guy was supposed to be dead. He called Sal, when he was driving Matty around, and told him that he was looking right at Billy. But Sal said Vince was imagining things.

He's struggling into a windbreaker when he sees something move outside the house, a flash sliding through the trees. He squints, looks closer, harder, and sees nothing. But he knows what that means.

It's too late, he thinks, he's here.

Vince steps into his sneakers, zips up the windbreaker, and heads for the stairs.

He's floating down the stairs, no effort, no sense of movement. He can see his feet touching each step, but he doesn't feel anything.

Maybe he's dead already; maybe his heart gave out in that effort to stand up and now he's a ghost haunting this place.

He hears gunshots coming from the living room, the sound of a beer can popping open. Peering through the stairway's wooden bars, Vince sees Sal bathed in the light of the TV, staring blindly as he lifts the beer to his lips.

He looks at the front door, impossibly distant, even though he knows it's only a few yards away. Vince's knees buckle and he grabs at the railing to keep from tumbling down the stairs.

He regains his balance, inhales, exhales, c'mon, goddammit, it ain't that far, and he resumes walking down the stairs, taking the banister with a mountain climber's hand over hand grip, until he reaches the bottom and wraps his fingers around the front door knob.

Vince waits a few seconds before pulling the door open and stepping into the soaking night. Sal's voice follows him out the door.

"Get him! Get that bastard!"

5

FRANK SINATRA IS running down the railroad tracks, just like he always does at the end of *Von Ryan's Express*. Bullets are zipping all around him, but Frank keeps on going.

Sal probably should've been shocked when he hit the remote and saw that Billy's favorite movie was on. But he's numb to just about everything now.

The phone has been ringing over and over, apparently the lines are back up, but fuck it, Sal's not talking to that old bastard until Vince is gone. Whatever bug Matty's got up his disabled ass, it'll keep.

Shit, he's getting away.

You're supposed to root for the hero, but nothing seems right with the world tonight and if Sal can't escape from his nightmare then neither can anybody else.

The Nazi officer snatches the submachine gun away from one of the dimwitted soldiers and draws a bead on Frank's back. Sal tenses up as the kraut takes the longest goddamn time to aim; it's a machine gun, you asshole, you don't got to be no Annie Oakley. Just pull the fucking trigger.

"Get him," Sal snarls at the TV. "Get that bastard…"

And then *brrrp*! Frank's back arches, his head snaps back in exquisite anguish, and he tumbles slowly to the tracks. The train pulls away and Old Blue Eyes shrinks into infinity.

"Good," Sal sits back in his chair. "Shoot him again."

The rolling credits tell him that he's out of excuses, that he should go upstairs and be with his cousin now, comforting him, trying to ease his pain, even praying with the guy if that's what he wants.

The commercials start and Sal tells himself it's best for a man to be alone at a time like this. Let him reflect on his life and make his peace with God. It would be wrong to trespass at this most sacred moment.

Ah, shit, who's he kidding? Sal doesn't want to go up there and watch Vince choke out his last few breaths. There's nothing more anyone can do for him; holding his hand won't make him live no longer.

The best thing to do for Vince would be to go up there and shove a pillow over his face, but Sal's already murdered his best friend. He's not going to kill his own blood. Just wait a little longer and it'll all be over.

Sal picks up the remote, hits the mute button, and sits in the silent living room. There is that nagging little question about what to do with Vince. He thought about driving out to a lake someplace or burying his cousin in some distant, lonely part of the woods, but neither one feels right to him.

Sal looks around this house that he never wanted. He hates this place, this dead man's home that Matty made him buy. He pauses to take a long look at his thoughts. And Sal sees how he can take care of two problems at once.

6

THE WOODS CLOSE around him quickly as if they've been waiting for him, and when he looks over his shoulder, the house is gone.

Vince stumbles blindly through the brush, covered in sweat and rain.

The voices are all around him now. They're pretending to be crickets, but Vince knows it's the dead talking to him. They want revenge; they want justice, but Vince keeps walking.

"Lamb of God who takes away the sins of the world have mercy on us…"

The ground shifts beneath his feet and Vince falls, rolls through the grass and rocks as if the earth has opened up around him. He stops somewhere in the blackness, bleeding, burning with fever. The wet grass soaks his clothes and Vince starts to cry.

Let it happen now, let him die here and melt into the ground, so he'll never feel pain or fear again.

"Renee," he whispers. "Renee, I'm so sorry…"

Something is standing over him and he wonders is this how it happens—the skeleton in the black robe holding a scythe appears from nowhere and takes you away?

Vince exhales and the fear drains out of him. His mortal life is finally over and if he has to suffer for all time, so be it. He's ready for his punishment. He's ready to take the pain.

Vince hears laughter, harsh and familiar, and he sees someone standing before a sky full of churning black clouds. He struggles to regain his breath as he locks eyes with the demon.

"Hey, big guy," Billy says from up above. "Fancy meeting you here."

Tommy runs through the trees with the gas can in his hand and his heart pounding double time against his chest.

He dodges imaginary machine gun fire, sidesteps phantom land mines, and leaps over invisible tripwire. Every move is sharp, quick, and true; no hesitation, no stumbling, like he was born in these here woods. He's a kung fu ninja master mother fucker, psyched, amped, and ready for war.

Tommy slows it up when he sees the house through the trees and slithers down to his belly so he can get a closer look without spooking the enemy.

He crawls up to the ridge and there it is, the big bastard standing tall and radiating pure light in all directions. The old man's wet dream house—until it got hijacked by Uncle Sal.

He still can't believe how Billy gaped at the place when they first got here, like he was going to shoot a load and burst a blood vessel at the same time. Please, Pops, don't zone out on me now.

But even though he never took his eyes off the house, Billy still kept one foot in reality as he told Tommy to spread gasoline all round the place.

"Wait for my signal before you do anything," Billy said.

Tommy nodded and took off, satisfied that this was the last time this scumwad would ever give him an order.

Up and running, Tommy goes to the back of the house and starts pouring gasoline. He listens to the deep gurgle and smiles; shit, it's going to be fun smoking this dump. After that Pops and me will have our little chat.

He hears someone walking up on the front porch, hits the ground, like, what the fuck? Tommy didn't see no car drive up here, so where did this loser come from?

He moves through the bushes until he reaches a place where he can eyeball the front door and spots this fat load of pig shit ringing the bell. Oh, man, will you look at this crotch-scratching fuckwit? He makes that "Dueling Banjos" kid look like Robert Redford.

Tommy looks closer and sees the outline of a gun straining against the peckerwood's shirt and he smiles.

Chubbykins, I don't know who you are, but if you're looking for a fight, you've come to the right place.

And then he's running again.

7

SAL WALKS BACKWARDS up the stairs spreading lighter fluid as he makes his way to the bedroom door.

He's already soaked the couch and curtains in the living room and he's trying to gauge the remaining fluid in the can so he'll have enough to cover the bed and Vince's body.

He wishes he had some more of this stuff, but there should be enough here to get things rolling.

Sal had stocked up on the barbecue crap in anticipation of all the great cookouts that never happened. Nobody ever came to visit this place and nobody ever will. Only the dead belong here.

You can see why Billy loved setting fires so much. Nothing else comes close. All Sal has to do now is drop a match, skip out the front door, and let nature do the rest.

What happens after that, when Matty finds out that Sal lied about killing Vince, torched the house the old man so desperately wanted him to keep, well, Sal will probably wish he had stayed in here with his cousin.

It'd be nice if they sent one of the old time guys, somebody he knows, to do it nice and quick. But there's little chance that Matty will let that happen.

The Cigar is going to be so angry he'll want Sal to suffer unbearable pain and humiliation, just like Jerry and Franco. He'll want to send a message to everybody else in the crew. He'll send Train.

The desire to call his son in Michigan comes over him so quickly, so powerfully, Sal wants to throw the can over his shoulder, run down to the phone and dial the number.

This is what Vince must be going through, a chronic longing to be with your flesh and blood as your life slips away. Sal's had so little to do with his son they're almost strangers. And now that his time is so short there's nothing he can do about it.

He wants his son to stay out there in Ann Arbor. Get an honest job, raise a nice Midwestern family, always tell the truth and don't ever wind up like his old man.

Sal doesn't move, though, as he looks over the disaster he made of his life and he knows the best thing he can do for his son is leave him the hell alone.

He looks at the bedroom door. Vince has been so quiet lately; no screams, no moaning or crying. Maybe it's finally over. Maybe that awful disease is finished with his cousin. But a second goes by and Sal feels something darker come over him, drops the can of lighter fluid, and walks up to the door.

He waits a few seconds, hoping he'll hear a noise, no matter how faint, coming from the room. Finally he reaches out, pushes the door back with two fingers. The hinge lets out a long sorrowful lament as it swings back to allow the hallway light to fall over Sal's shoulder and reveal an empty bed.

He stares down at the disrupted sheets and blankets, the sweat-stained pillow bearing an image like the Shroud of Turin.

Sal can't believe his cousin had enough life left in him to stand up, let alone walk out the door. He does a slow 360 as if he'll find Vince stuck to the ceiling or hanging over the door like a hex sign. But the room is empty now, except for that terrible smell.

He wonders how Vince could've gotten by him like that, how a dying man was able to walk right out of the house. But Sal was so mesmerized by the image of Frank Sinatra trying to escape he never thought Vince might do the same thing.

For a few seconds Sal feels a strange kind of relief. Vince is gone, melted into the dark like a sugar cube in steaming coffee; Sal is free.

This is what you wanted, to be rid of that sickly dying bastard. You didn't see him sneaking out of the house because you didn't want to. So fine, let the woods have him and be done with this torture.

He stands still in this impossibly barren space and knows he can't let that happen. Sal had gone too far, given up too much to let Vince limp off to some dark place like a sick dog.

He runs down the stairs, grabs a jacket, and tears through all the drawers in the kitchen until he finds a flashlight. Vince couldn't have gotten far and he won't put up much of a struggle when Sal finds him.

He's fumbling with the flashlight to see if the goddamn thing works when some son-of-a-bitch starts ringing the doorbell.

8

Who the fuck is that?

Sal glares at the front door. He's not expecting anyone, hardly knows the neighbors, and he doubts Vince has decided to come back from his walk.

He was hoping Matty would wait a few days before doing the business. Hell, they just buried Rex today. They ought to show a little respect. But then Matty's never been the most patient guy in the world, has he?

The buzzer goes off again and Sal puts down the flashlight, walks to over the gun rack in the living room and takes down the double-barreled shotgun Matty gave him when he first got the place.

It's a beauty, this thing; single trigger ejector, splinter forearm, English grip. And it's never been fired.

Sal keeps his eyes on the door the whole time he breaks the gun, takes a box of shells out of the bureau, and slips a cartridge into each barrel.

He pauses for a moment, seriously thinks about blasting right through the door and killing whoever's on the other side. Just for the hell of it. All they could do is put him in jail.

The buzzer sounds a third time. Sal snaps the shotgun closed and it sounds like a bone cracking.

"Be right there," he says softly.

Walking to the door, Sal looks through the peephole and sees some fat yahoo bulging out of a cheap windbreaker, baseball cap stuck on his head.

Maybe his car broke down; maybe he's found Jesus and he's looking for converts. Whatever it is, Sal don't know this schmuck from a can of paint and he plans on keeping it that way. He opens the door a crack.

"What do you want?"

"Oh, uh, hi—" The guy nearly jumps out of his drawers. "I was hoping to speak to the owner of the house."

"Who are you?"

"My name is Scotty. Scotty Fuller."

"Never heard of you."

"Yeah," Scotty says, "but I sure heard of you."

Sal pulls the door open a little wider, keeping the shotgun hidden, and glowers at Scotty.

"Really? What have you heard about me, asshole?"

"Easy, easy." Scotty shows his palms. "I didn't mean nothing by it. I just thought we might be able to help each other out."

"And just how exactly could a fat tub of shit like you ever do anything to help me?"

"Well, there's this guy named Billy—"

Sal yanks the door open wide, puts the shotgun's barrels right up against the stubble on Scotty's chin, and cranks the guy's head back as far as it will go.

"Come on in…"

Sal guides Scotty into the foyer, backs him up against the wall, and kicks the door shut without looking. Scotty's got his hands straight up in the air like a referee signaling a touchdown and his bulging eyes suggest that he's exerting some serious sphincter control.

"L-let's not get excited here, buddy—"

Sal nudges Scotty with the gun barrel, puts out his hand, and Scotty pulls out the .38 with two fingers. He hands it over to Sal.

"I'm not looking for no trouble, mister. I just—"

"Shut up." Sal keeps his eyes on Scotty while he puts the gun on a shelf. "So you think you can just walk up to my house and talk to me like I'm one of your asshole drinking buddies?"

"No, no, it's not like that at all. I swear to God—"

"It's not?" Sal jabs Scotty with the shotgun. "What's it like then, fat boy? Huh? Tell me what it's like."

Scotty's about to say something, but he pauses as his nostrils flare, reacting to the smell of all that lighter fluid. Sal gives him another poke.

"Go on."

"I was just trying to tell you about this guy Billy."

"So tell me."

"He lives in Mount Pocono with my ex-wife and he's crazier than a fuck-ing loon."

"What's he look like?"

"About six foot," Scotty says. "Black hair going gray. Got a wicked scar over his forehead and it must've scrambled his brains something fierce."

Sal lowers the gun slowly. He's doing everything he possibly can to keep from screaming. No, he's not going to show this stupid hick any sign of what's going on inside him right now.

Is he dead?

"And what is this guy to you?"

"What is it to me?" Scotty's working his way up to a fury. "That lowlife son-a-bitch killed my cousin."

"What for?"

"Who the hell knows? The bastard's crazy, screeching and shooting up the whole countryside. That kid never had a chance. And there was that poor old guy over in—"

"—so you were spying on him?"

"Goddamn right I was. That fucker was putting the arm on me. Jumped me right outside my favorite bar and almost split my head open. I started tailing his ass and he led me right up to this place."

"What else do you know about him?"

Scotty smiles with a set of yellow teeth.

"I don't think he likes you too much."

The shotgun is a steel girder in Sal's hands. Remember when Vince called you that day you were up here with Matty? Remember how frightened he was, convinced that Billy was outside the house? Do you believe in ghosts now, big guy?

"So why did you come here—like I couldn't guess?"

"Look," Scotty says. "I just figured we could help each other out here. This fucker is gunning for both of us, you know."

"And. . . ?"

"And I know where he lives; hell, I used to live there myself. All you gotta do is just go over there, grab that skank ex-wife of mine and wait for Billy to come riding to the rescue."

"That's your plan?"

"Easy as scratching your ass, bud." Scotty tries to grin. "That guy is crazy about that stupid bitch. He'll come for her, all right. You can crack open the piggy bank on that. And when he does, you and your boys can nail his ass."

You wanna be sure? Here, take the fucking gun and go back there yourself.

"So what's in it for you, pal?"

"Oh, now, I'm sure we can work out something." Scotty says. "I'm not greedy or nothing and I can keep my mouth shut, believe you me. All I need is a little traveling money and you'll never see me again."

Sal barely hears the words coming at him. He's thinking about Billy, still alive, still walking this earth, and living in some small town just a few miles away from here.

And this woman he's with, Sal wonders what she's like, what she did to make Billy care for her so much. Billy always got the nicest girls, that lucky son-of-a-bitch.

Sal is still thinking about the woman as he leans over and spits in Scotty's face.

9

Billy hauls Vince up off the ground and props him hard up against a tree. The guy is so light you could hurl him up into the sky and hang him off the Big Dipper.

"Hey, Vince, you been taking your vitamins? You're looking a little sickly."

Vince looks deeply in Billy's eyes, long and steady, with no intention of turning away. He should be terrified, begging for his life now that's facing Billy, the walking dead man. But Vince isn't frightened at all.

"I'm dying, Billy," he says finally. "Just like you."

Billy smiles and tries to suppress the shudder that passes through his body.

"So you're a doctor now, Vince?"

"I know what death looks like, Billy."

"That's good because you're about to see a whole shitload in the next two minutes."

Vince looks down at the ground and shakes his head.

"I knew you weren't dead. Somehow I just knew you didn't die that night."

"No thanks to you and that scumbag cousin of yours."

Vince lifts his head and stares toward the heavens like he's appealing to the divine.

"Don't do this, Billy. Please—"

"Don't do what, Vince? All I want to do is visit my buddy Sal. What's the harm in that?"

"Sal didn't want to do it, Billy. It was Matty, he made him do it."

Billy scowls as the words slice into him.

"Oh, yeah, Vince. Poor guy. I'm sure Matty really had to twist his arm. Kind of like this."

He spins Vince around, slaps him up against the tree, and cranks his arm up behind his back. Vince bites down on the pain, refuses to make a sound.

"Is that what Matty did, big guy?"

"Billy—"

"And what about my wife? You heard what happened to her, Vince?"

"Sal had nothing to do with that. You know he'd never hurt Lucille."

"I didn't think he'd ever hurt me and look at how that turned out."

He slowly eases his grip. Vince will never cry out, not if Billy snapped his arm clean off. Billy turns the stick figure around to face him.

"If you want to blame someone, Billy," Vince says, "blame me. I was jealous of you guys and I always hated you. I pushed Sal to do it that night."

It angers Billy to see Vince being so brave, so noble. Vince was always the rat, the backstabber. This is Billy's time to claim his scared revenge and now he's being left behind.

"That's mighty decent of you, Vince, but I'm not leaving without taking care of Sal."

"Billy, please," Vince speaks urgently. "You don't have much time left on this earth. Don't get any more blood on your hands."

Billy clamps his hand around Vince's throat and starts squeezing. Vince looks at him, no sign of fear in his eyes. C'mon, let's hear your whimper, beg me to let you go…

Vince isn't cooperating, though, his legs buckle, his eyelids begin to flutter, but he doesn't struggle or fight for his life. He just keeps looking at Billy.

"Yo, you guys busy?"

Tommy emerges from the woods as Vince starts to sag to the ground. Billy lets go of Vince, who staggers back, his face a terminal shade of red.

"You do like I told you?" Billy asks.

"Yeah. And listen—we got company. Some fat douche bag showed up at the front door just now and went inside."

"Who is he?"

Tommy snorts.

"How the fuck should I know?"

Billy kicks it around his head. He doesn't like surprises, but there's no stopping this thing. Whoever this guy is, he's shit out of luck.

He pulls out the .45, grabs hold of Vince and shoves him toward the house.

"C'mon, big guy, let's go see your cousin."

10

Scotty stands there in the hallway with Sal's spit all over his face. Shocked, he raises his hand to wipe himself, but Sal lifts the shotgun.

"Leave it there!" Sal puts the barrels under Scotty's chin. "You touch one single drop of that shit and I'll spread your brains all over the wall."

"What the fuck—?"

Sal clubs Scotty with the butt of the shotgun and knocks him bleeding to the floor. Scotty raises his hand to his bloodied scalp and looks up at Sal.

"Are you fucking crazy? I'm trying to help you, you stupid greaseball!"

Sal kicks Scotty in the groin and the guy howls into a fetal position. It's been so long since Sal's actually chucked a really good beating on somebody, anybody, instead of ordering someone else to do it. He hasn't felt this powerful in years. And he doesn't want to stop

"I'm sorry," Sal says as the smile on his face grows wider with each blow. "I'm sorry, I'm sorry…"

Scotty covers up as best he can, but Sal is relentless, kicking his ribs, pounding his back with the gun butt. He should be thinking about his cousin wandering in the woods, about Matty planning to kill him, and Billy, oh, Christ, alive and coming after him. But right now he just wants to enjoy this madness.

"Fucking rat!"

Sal kicks the fat bastard again as he tries to crawl away. He flips Scotty over on his back, straddles the bloated beer gut, and aims the shotgun straight at the bastard's face.

"No! Jesus Christ!" Scotty puts both hands up. "Don't, please!"

"That's it, fat boy," Sal says, "let's hear you whine, let's hear you cry like a little bitch."

Sal clicks back the hammers on the shotgun. He's going to give Scotty both barrels. No doubts, no puking, no losing his nerve. Sal is going to commit bloody murder tonight.

"Fuck you, you guinea bastard!"

And just as he's about to pull the trigger, an image on the TV catches his eye.

"Matty…?"

He sees an old arrest photo, followed by video footage of Matty, Vince and himself coming out of the courthouse. He keeps watching and there's Angelo's blocked off with yellow tape and surrounded by gawkers.

The man on the floor no longer exists as Sal is pulled toward the glowing screen. He sees Matty's car, front wheels up on a curb, driver's side door gaping open. He looks for the remote, the goddamn remote, grabs it off the coffee table and aims it at the screen.

"—killed in a gangland slaying—"

The fat hillbilly moans and curses somewhere in another part of the world, while the TV tells Sal that his whole way of life has just been erased.

Matty's dead. Sal is trying to understand this, wondering if it's even possible for Matty to die and how the earth could keep on turning without the Cigar overseeing things.

All the boys, an entire generation of guys that Sal grew old with, all wiped out as if by the hand of God.

"Hey, big guy!" The voice cuts through the walls. "Come out and say hello!"

11

BILLY PUSHES VINCE out onto the lawn with Matty's .45 pressed against his head. He feels helpless out here, away from the dark woods, nothing for protection except this twitching little straw man.

That's it; that's my new home.

His eyes look over the house for any signs of movement, but the place seems devoid of any natural life.

"Please, Billy, this is wrong…"

"Shut up, Vince."

"Billy, listen to me. You got to save yourself. Before it's too late—"

He drives his knee into Vince's tailbone.

"Don't worry about me, Vince. You got enough problems of your own."

They walk out to the middle of the lawn with the pain working its way up Billy's neck until he has to stop.

"What's wrong, Sal?" His voice is hoarse, tattered. "Aren't you happy to see me?"

The echo of his own voice rolls back over him and Billy is so weak it almost knocks him over.

He shoves Vince forward, closer to this house, his house that hangs over him with such menace, like it's going to come crashing down on top of him..

"Vince is happy to see me, aren't you, Vince?" Another twist of the arm. "Aren't you, Vince?"

"Sal, don't come out of the—!"

Billy cracks Vince behind the ear with the .45; Vince's legs crumble, and it takes every bit of strength Billy has to keep his hostage up.

He's so tired he could drop the gun and Vince, fall into that freshly cut grass and never get up. But not just yet. He pushes Vince toward the house.

"Matty was real happy to see me. You heard what happened to Matty, Sal? Him and the rest of the boys?"

The house maintains its silence and the air grows heavy on his shoulders.

"They're all dead, Sal!" Billy roars. "Every last one of them, big guy. Can you hear me in there, Sal?"

Sal turns from the TV, walks toward the sound of the dead man's voice. He pulls the curtain back just enough to see him, finally see Billy, alive and standing on the front lawn, corkscrewing Vince's arm up behind his back.

Look at him, look at Billy out there, using that withered body as a shield; he looks almost as bad as Vince. His skin is so pale, his legs wobbling; Billy looks like he just climbed out of his own casket.

He could end this thing right now if he wants to. Pull the trigger, put Vince out of his misery and take care of Billy at the same time. Neither one of them is going to last the night anyway.

"You stupid mother fucker…"

Sal looks up and sees Scotty's up on all fours. Blood pours from his nose and fresh bruises sprout all over his face. One eye is nearly shut, the other glowing with hatred and trained on Sal like a sniper's scope.

"I tried to warn you, you brain-dead son-of-a-bitch. I was all set to hand him over to you on a silver fucking platter."

"Looks like you were a little late, big guy."

Scotty spits a mouthful of blood onto the floor.

"Well, you better get your boys out there and take care of that fucker because he sure means to kill your ass dead."

Sal turns back to the window.

"There ain't no boys."

"What the hell…?" Scotty tries to get up, but the pain in his ribs holds him back. "Are you fucking serious? That guy is out of his mind. You gotta call somebody, buddy—"

"—there's nobody to call."

Scotty sags to the ground, sucking air in through his teeth. Sal can hear the gears in his head working on the problem, looking for a way out.

"Look, brother, this ain't my fight—"

"It is now, killer." Sal looks at Scotty. "You wanted a piece of the action, well, you got it."

Sal hefts the shotgun in a way that tells Scotty if he tries to leave this house he'll be doing it without his head.

"Goddamn New York scumbags." Scotty snarls, spit running down his chin. "I can't believe it. Why does this shit always happen to me?"

Sal is about to tell Scotty to shut his hole when a bullet smashes through the window inches from his face and destroys the TV in an eruption of crackling sparks.

He drops to a crouch clutching the shotgun, broken glass all around him. Scotty's dropped back onto his belly, covering his head like he's in an air raid, frantically whispering, *oh, shit, oh shit.*

Sal looks out the window and sees Billy grinning like a teenager and aiming the .45 right at him.

"Hey, Sal, you still love me?"

Billy's ears ring from the gun blast, goddamn this baby's got a nice kick. He hadn't actually planned to shoot; the thing just kind of went off in his hand. Vince ducks down, his arms covering his head. Billy yanks him into the upright position.

"You all right there, big guy?" He whispers into Vince's ear. "Didn't mean to spook you."

Vince coughs and starts slumping to the ground, but Billy holds onto his arm. The house is so quiet, like Sal thinks Billy will get tired and go home. But this is his home. A low inhaled whistle reaches his ears, Tommy telling him that he's ready.

"Looks like we have a real problem here, Sal." Billy is almost shouting. "I think maybe you should come out and talk to me before anybody else gets hurt."

Vince starts nodding his head, whispering as if he's deep in conversation and Billy feels the wasted body vibrating, barely able to make out the words.

"Lamb of God, who takes away the sins of the world…"

"Vince…"

Oh, no, Billy's not going to tolerate this, he's not going to stand by and let this hump get religion at the bottom on the ninth and skip through the pearly gates. He presses the barrel of the .45 against Vince's head.

"…have mercy on us…"

Nobody ever had any mercy on Billy, not his family, not these so-called friends of his. The one good thing he had was yanked away from him when he was a kid. Where was the hell was that Lamb of God when Billy needed him? Billy looks at his right hand gripping the gun, the hand that choked the life out of Jerry LaRocca, shot that old guy, half-strangled Lucille, and Charley, poor old Charley, what Billy did to him.

"Lamb of God who takes away the sins of the world, have mercy on us…"

The voice is stronger, sounds nothing like a dying man. It's like some saintly spirit has commandeered Vince's body.

"Vince…please…"

Billy feels so weak and frightened that he's tempted to join in, to ask that Lamb of God to peace grant him some fucking peace.

"Lamb of God who takes away…"

He feels the throbbing in his head increasing as the prayer goes on, killing him a piece at a time.

"…stop it…"

"…the sins of the world…"

He wants to be with Lora now, drop the gun, leave his hostage, his house, his son and his treacherous best friend, walk away from all of it and go to her for whatever time he has left.

But this prayer, these words that he has no right to hear, it's tearing him apart. Billy doesn't deserve mercy, he doesn't deserve forgiveness, he doesn't deserve—

"…grant us—"

"Shut the fuck up!"

He screams into Vince's ear, infuriated by this holy roller bullshit, and the sounds sets off a chain reaction in his body, a domino effect of nerves and synapses that ignites a sneaky burst of psychotic energy which breaks free of his brain, streaks up his Jesus arm, into his hand and tugs back on his index finger.

12

THE NOISE IS massive, a blasphemous upheaval that inhales every ounce of sound, snaps Vince's head forward, and sends a spray of blood and tissue up to the sky.

The discharge steamrolls over the surrounding hills and whips back like an arctic wind.

Nothing happens for a moment as if everybody is waiting for God's permission to continue. Vince, the back of his head blown off, stands there dead in Billy's grip while Billy stares at the traitorous fingers clutching the gun.

Then gravity goes to work. The stream of gore showers back to earth and Vince drops through the heavy night air, arms at his side, head turned to the left and his eyes staring into eternity.

Billy stands still, vaguely aware that Vince has slipped out of his fingers, that he's got no shield, no protection. He's all by himself out here on the front lawn.

A scream erupts from the house and jolts Billy back to his senses. It's a long sickening wail coming straight from a human heart that shudders through the trees and slices through bone.

Sal is howling, insane with grief after watching his cousin die and Billy drops to the ground a second before a shotgun blast rips through the air.

He lands next to Vince, rolls over the bleeding corpse while another shot tears up chunks of earth and grass.

Billy's alone out here, naked as a hound and his mind shrieks, *Tommy, where the fuck is Tommy?* when gunfire tear through the woods behind.

"Mother fuckers!"

Tommy screams, laughs, and fires all in one twisted symphony. Billy aims the .45 at the house, fires one round after one, shattering the windows, there, bitch, try that on for size.

He sees his son throw a flaming bottle across the lawn, into the hedges, where it explodes and conjures up a line of flame that wails a warpath around the house. Billy rises to one knee as Tommy lights up another bottle and cranks back his arm.

Sal staggers away from the window as bullets shatter the windows and rip into the walls, still in shock after seeing Billy execute Vince right before his eyes.

He's gagging on the smoke, his shoulder aches from the shotgun's pounding recoil, and his face bleeds from a dozen glass cuts.

Sal was supposed to protect his cousin, see that Vince left this world peacefully. The man had suffered enough in these last few months, at least let him go out easy. And Billy destroyed all that.

Fucking maniac, Sal aims at Billy and tries to nail him with a ton of ferocious buckshot. But Billy's got a sixth sense or a stainless steel contract with the devil himself because he rolls clear every time Sal pulls the trigger.

"Fuck—!"

Sal sees some other guy, Billy's back-up, run out of the darkness and toss a burning bottle at the house.

Flames encircle the place. Cinders will blow in through the shattered windows any second now, make contact with all this lighter fluid and the whole goddamn thing will go up.

"Hey, scumbag…"

Sal turns and sees Scotty limping toward him, the .38 in his hand.

"Take it easy—

"We're way passed that stage, Baba Looey. Bashing my mug with a shotgun butt was kind of pushing things, don't you think?"

Sal nods toward the window.

"This ain't no time to argue."

"I'm not arguing with you, scumwad." Scotty laughs harshly. "I'm just going to take care of you and the fruitcake bastard outside."

"C'mon, we'll settle our business later—"

"Fuck that." Scotty raises the gun. "We'll settle up right now…"

Sal looks at the box of shells on the coffee table. Reach over there, grab a shell, slam it into the shotgun—not even close. Shit, you'd have a better chance just throwing this goddamn blunderbuss at him.

"Look, you came here looking for money—"

"—shove your money up your ass, pal."

Sal watches Scotty take aim, but he's fresh out of ideas, can't believe this small town loser is going to kill him, after all he's been through over the years, when a firebomb sails through the shattered window, explodes at Scotty's feet and engulfs him in a cloak of fire.

Billy sees the living room transform to a furnace, watches a piece of the blaze break away and rush towards him shrieking like a newborn demon.

He takes aim at the burning figure intent on putting him out of his misery, but the shotgun roars again and he sees Sal retreating from the window.

Billy looks at the flames tearing through the house and he knows there's something wrong, that this fire could never spread so quickly on the strength of that one firebomb, no fucking way. This thing had help from the inside.

Tommy runs by him laughing insanely and heads into the house. Billy tries to grab him, shouts for his son to stop. The place could cave in any second; it's not worth going after Sal. Let him die there. But Tommy smells the blood and nothing can turn him away.

Billy watches his son disappear through the front door of the burning building. He pauses to look down into Vince's eyes that look so peaceful now, free of pain and fear. "Lucky bastard," he whispers, and follows Tommy into the fire.

The heat embraces him from 20 feet away and Billy keeps running until he crosses the threshold. The flames sweep around him to feast on the furniture, carpets, and walls. Sweat rolls off his face as if he's been running for miles. He sees his son heading for the stairway.

"Tommy!"

He shouts over the roaring blaze. His son stops, turns and looks at Billy with a smile that says Fuck you, pops; I'm running this show now.

Billy looks past his son, though, to the shadow that he can see falling from the second floor. He waves his arms frantically and points, but Tommy sneers and turns to go up the stairs.

The explosion lifts Tommy into the air and sends him crashing down to the landing. Billy runs to his son, sees the blood pouring out of him, while Tommy kicks his legs in agony, and begs Billy with swelling eyes to do something, please, make it stop.

But Billy can't do anything to help his son. He cradles Tommy in the middle of the burning house, holds him tight, and slips back to the first day he ever held this life that he helped create.

He came straight from the hotel in Coney Island with Sal, right to the hospital to cradle this beautiful crying baby. Look at that little monkey, listen to him wail, drowning out the sounds of death. What a set of lungs on that kid, huh? Billy's going to call him Tommy, he thinks, slipping his hand around Tommy's throat to feel the pulse thumping weaker, weaker. That's what I'm going to call my boy. I'll teach him how to fight. I'll teach him not to take no shit from nobody.

Billy looks into his son's eyes and sees the squawking infant who used to look up to him like he was God Almighty in those early days.

I'll call him Tommy, Billy thinks as the legs finally stop kicking. *That's what I'll call my boy.*

He kisses his son's forehead and walks up the stairs.

13

SAL STUMBLES DOWN the smoke-filled hallway and locks himself in the bedroom. He puts his ear to the doorway and listens for any sounds above the roar of the fire.

There's nothing at first and Sal wonders if he's alone in this inferno. And then he hears the footsteps, heavy, methodical, getting closer.

He just killed Billy's son. All he saw through the smoke and the flames was a guy running toward him with a gun in his hand, Sal had to shoot. He didn't know he was killing Billy's only child, the baby that he and Billy went to see in the hospital, after Sal had puked all over himself in that hotel room.

He was Uncle Sal back then, when he held the kid in his arms, carried him on his back, and read bedtime stories to him. The baptism, first birthday, first Christmas, Sal was there for all those sacred moments of the kid's life.

But that's the law of the jungle, right? Eye for an eye, blood for blood. Matty would be so proud.

He sits down on the bed, still damp with Vince's sweat, and puts two shells into the shotgun.

The light overhead flickers, and goes out, so the only light comes in rolling crimson waves from the burning trees around the house.

Somebody must have seen the smoke, heard the shots. Somebody must have called the cops and the firefighters by now. But it doesn't matter. This will be settled by the time any of them get here.

The footsteps grow louder, like a scene from an old radio play. A harsh voice fills the hallway, enters the bedroom wrapped in smoke.

"Glorious, glorious, one keg of beer for the four of us…"

Sal aims the shotgun at the door.

Billy's legs give out on him as he climbs the stairs. He grabs the banister and leaves a palm print in Tommy's blood.

He stops, waits for the weakness to subside, and starts walking down the hallway. He's nearly blind from the smoke and the sweat rolling down his face and the roar of the flames is all he can hear.

The fire stands aside for him when he reaches the landing, points the way toward the master bedroom, and Billy thinks it's so glorious, glorious, glory be to God there ain't no more of us.

He coughs, wipes the perspiration from his face. The bedroom door is right in front of him. Billy raises his fist, heavy as a cannonball, and pounds on the carved wood.

"C'mon, Sal, open up," he says, "It's just us now. Everyone else is dead."

He turns away just as a load of buckshot blows a hole in the door where his head was and sprays the opposing wall. Goddamn, the boy's still got some fight in him.

Billy fires through the door three times, carves away pieces of wood, until the .45 clicks empty in his hand. He throws the gun aside, kicks the damn door, throws his shoulder against the crumbling panels until it flies open, crashes into the bedroom and falls to the floor.

Looking up, he sees Sal in the corner like a naughty schoolboy, aiming the shotgun at him.

They stare at each other, the first time they've been together since the night at the rest stop.

Billy's got no weapon, no chance of getting away, and no strength left to run, even if he wanted to. He gets to his feet slowly and Sal tracks him with the shotgun. Sal's got one barrel left and he can't possibly miss.

"What's the problem, big guy?" Billy asks. "Finish what you started."

The fire builds all around them, smoke fills the room, and Sal still doesn't pull the trigger. Billy takes a step toward him.

"C'mon, Sal," he whispers. "Do it right this time."

Sal doesn't move, doesn't do anything, even as Billy steps closer, closer, until he plants his chest up against the shotgun barrels.

"You gotta take the pain."

Sal closes his eyes and starts crying, his entire body shakes as if he's standing in a freezer instead of a four-alarm fire. Billy pushes up against the shotgun.

"Just fucking shoot!"

Sal opens his eyes and looks at Billy. The lines in his face go smooth and he stands up straight. He looks younger, as if the fire is burning the years off his life.

"I'm sorry," he whispers.

Billy waits with the cold metal pressed to his heart, braces for the explosion that will set him free.

Sal nods, smiles, and it's like they're kids again, getting into all kinds of trouble and laughing the whole time. And the fucking fool keeps smiling as he shoves Billy away, steps back and puts the shotgun under his own goddamn chin.

"No—!"

There's this roar, like a crate of dynamite going off and Billy staggers back covered in blood. He sees Sal's body spin through the air, crash onto a night table and tumble facedown to the floor.

Billy stares down at Sal, watches the blood leaking from what remains of his face. He wants to lay hands upon him, heal the dreadful wounds, and go back to when it was just Sal and Billy ruling the world.

"Son-of-a-bitch." Billy shouts over Sal's body. "You stupid son-of-a-bitch…"

The floor shifts beneath him and Billy limps out of the bedroom as the world tilts like he's on a sinking ship. His legs buckle at the top of the stairs and he falls, over and over, he falls, like these stairs will never end, until he reaches the ground floor.

Billy is stretched out on his belly, still alive, nothing broken. He raises his head, looks through the smoke, sees the front door, and the night beyond it.

The air is fresh and clear out there and too bad Billy is never going to reach it, just like Frank never reached that train heading to Switzerland.

He wonders what this burning building must look like from a satellite high over the earth; a tiny orange spark in the darkness that flares for a few seconds before it disappears. From up there, it looks like nothing.

It's a shame, really. Billy's done all kinds of evil, but there was this brief moment when he had a pretty decent life. He was happy; had a good woman who took care of him, worried about him. He almost got it right.

Lora, dear, Lora, please pray for me.

Billy closes his eyes, puts his face on the carpet and waits for the lady on the white horse. A hand reaches down from the stars, tears through the suffocating smoke, and grabs him by the collar, pulling Billy back to this world.

He's up, standing on his two feet, someone is shaking him so roughly, and Billy is thinking, leave me alone, bitch, let me die. But this prick won't let go and when Billy's vision returns, he sees Georgie Porgie, local flatfoot, standing in front of him.

"We're even now, big guy," George says.

14

Georgegets under Billy's shoulder and half-drags him through the burning hallway to the front door. Billy tries to push him off because he knows there's no way they're going to get out of here together.

He wants to tell George to get out of here, you asshole; get out while you still can. But he can't form the words and this thick-headed bastard wouldn't listen to him anyway.

A portion of the roof crashes to the floor and blocks their path. Billy points behind them and they head toward the kitchen with debris falling all around them. They reach the back porch, George kicks the door open, and hauls Billy out to the backyard.

The fresh air cascades over them like an ocean wave, so clear and cool and it closes around them, shields them from the heat and smoke.

Billy feels some energy returning to his body; he's able to walk on his own and they get to a tree where he leans against the trunk, and tries to exhale all the black filth from his lungs. He glares at George.

"If you don't mind my asking…what the fuck are you doing here?"

"Scotty's a suspect in a bunch of break-ins around the county," George says. "I was hoping I'd catch him in the act. Followed that fat tub of shit through the storm, right up to this place. And then everything went to hell."

Billy looks at the fire consuming every inch of the building. It really is a dream house now, a place that only exists in his mind. He hears sirens in the distance and looks at George.

"And what happens now?"

The question lingers between them. George turns toward the fire and shakes his head slowly.

"Well..." He stretches the word out long and wide. "Maybe I could tell the staties there was nobody around when I got here. Maybe you could just sort of...disappear."

Billy listens to the flames snapping and growling. It's not like he can hug the guy or shake his hand, not with all the business between them. It's best to take the offer and fade.

"All right, then..."

He turns to leave, while the house collapses behind them, and thinks about Lora again, knows that he has to be with her now, and he wonders if she'll hear him out when he shows up tonight or slam the door in his face the second she sees him.

He hears a loud click, it comes in over the fire and the approaching sirens, something he's heard so many times in his life, and Billy whirls toward the noise because there's only one sound in the world like it.

Scotty is standing behind them, his face blackened, one good eye pushing out of his head; half his clothes burned away, blistered hands wrapped around a gun.

"You fuck—!

He starts shooting, bullets that are meant for Billy, and God knows he's earned them and more. But it's George who takes them all in the back.

George throws his arms in the air, tumbles onto Billy, who prays to Almighty God as they're falling that George is packing an off-duty weapon, his fingers wrap around a .38 sticking in George's waistband, and as the two of them hit the ground, Billy squeezes off three shots into Scotty's gut.

Scotty falls shrieking and grabbing at his ripped belly while Billy stumbles to his feet and stands over him.

"You scumbag!" Scotty screams, holding out two blood-soaked hands. "Look what you did to me!"

Billy puts a bullet through Scotty's throat, here, big guy, this'll take your mind off it. Scotty gags, claws at his Adam's apple, and Billy watches him until his body goes limp. He turns and drops to one knee beside George.

"C'mon, George, don't let go," he says gently. "I saved your life once, you prick, you can't die on me now. George, please..."

But George isn't hearing him. His eyes are glassy, looking off to nowhere, and his breath is shallow and failing.

Billy should be praying for George now because there's nothing else anybody can do for him. But he's not going to give in; he won't give God the satisfaction.

And then it's over. George stops breathing and his eyes lose all signs of life and now someone else has died because of Billy. The only Good Samaritan is a dead Samaritan…

He tries to stand, but loses his balance, pitches forward, caught in the wake of George's rapidly departing soul.

Mayday! Mayday!

Billy fights back, forces himself to pull back and fight the undertow. He's not going to die here, not on this heathen land. He steadies himself, stands up straight and starts walking.

He stops once on his way back to the car, to look at the inferno that seems to threaten Heaven itself.

Fire trucks are pulling up to the house, but nothing can save that place and nothing should. Let it burn, pave over the ground with concrete, and let no one come within 100 miles of the place.

He turns his back on the fire and digs out his car keys. It's time to go home.

He can barely control the car, he's so frail, and he tries to negotiate with the unruly steering wheel as his life drains out of him with every passing mile.

"Just a little further," he whispers. "Stay with me a little longer."

The road is slipping away from him, the radio squelches out an alarm, and Billy's ready to just let the wheel go and be done with it when Johnny Rivers eases out of the speakers and starts singing "Poor Side of Town."

Jake sits in a patrol car with one of the local guys and watches the house on the corner. It's such a nice little town, like something you see under a Christmas tree encircled by a model train set. You could almost talk yourself into believing that nothing bad ever happens here.

He thought about getting a house here at some point in his life, a long time ago, before his son's death, before his wife left. Or maybe he's just fabricating memories to fill the gaps in his life. It's been so hard to tell lately.

The troopers are finally getting out to Sal's house and they're hearing reports of a huge fire at the same location, but Jake is barely listening. He knows this is where he should be.

He's thinking about who could be in the house on the corner, why the guys who killed Stan, who killed Matty, the ones who were staying at Eddie's place, why they would call this particular house. And why would they make such a bonehead rookie mistake of calling from the house where they were hiding?

"I know the woman who lives here," Ryan, one of the cops, tells him. "She's a nice lady. She had some guy living with him, though I haven't seen him lately. His name is Billy…Billy something, I can't think of the last name."

Jake doesn't react. Of course his name is Billy and now Jake wants to go home, say he's made a mistake, and get back on the highway.

No pleasing you, is there, big guy? You couldn't accept Billy being dead and now you can't believe he's alive.

A car drives up the hill, no lights on, swerving all over the road, comes close to hitting a parked car as the driver pulls in the driveway.

Ryan radios the backup units and everybody gets ready to move.

"Hold it…"

"What?"

"Let me get a look at him first," Jake says.

Ryan taps his finger on the steering wheel. He clearly doesn't like outsiders, especially New Yorkers, telling how to do his job and Jake doesn't blame him. But tonight is different.

"I'm coming with you."

"All right." Jake is already half out of the car. "Let's go."

There are cops all over the place, Billy knows, sitting in their unmarked cars. Like they're actually fooling anybody. If he weren't so weak, he'd have some fun fucking with their heads. Buy them all coffee, kick the bumpers of their Crown Victorias, or press ham against the windows. Peek-a-boo…

But he doesn't care anymore. He just wants to get inside, see her one last time.

Stopping at the side door, he looks up at the sky and thinks of the satellites circling the planet right now. Eventually their orbits will deteriorate, they'll tumble back toward the Earth and burn up when they re-enter the atmosphere.

As Billy raises his hand to knock on the door, he thinks that there are worse ways to die.

Lora watches the live news broadcast about the big fire and she feels the emptiness of the house closing in around her. Last one out of my life please turn off the lights.

Fuck it, she thinks, I'll sell this goddamn place and move to my cousin's place in Wisconsin. She'll set me up with a job and all these nosy bastards around here will have to find something else to talk about.

She doesn't realize she's crying until she hears the faint tapping on the side door. What the hell, she turns, senses the wetness in her eyes. She wipes the tears on her old ESU sweatshirt as she walks to the door.

And there's Billy, half-walking, half-falling into her arms. His face glistens with sweat, his clothes reek of smoke, and a trickle of blood runs from his nose.

"Am I late for supper?"

Jake and Ryan peer into the house through a back window. Ryan points to Billy, raises an eyebrow and Jake nods, yes, that's him. That's the kid I smacked all over Fort Hamilton Parkway in a distant time. That's Billy the Kid, the hands down craziest mother fucker that ever drew a breath, being eased to the couch now by that kind, gentle woman.

Billy is speaking and at first Jake thinks he's talking to Lora, but he's looking up to the ceiling while she wipes the perspiration from his face. Jake watches the lips moving, deciphers the words, and whispers in tandem.

"Lamb of God who takes away the sins of the world…"

Ryan calls for an ambulance. Jake nods to the side door swinging open and Ryan goes in first, his hand on his weapon.

Lora senses their presence and she turns to glare at them. She stands in front of Billy and scowls.

"What are you doing here?"

"Now, Lora, take it easy." Ryan holds up a hand. "Listen to me…"

How does he do it, Jake thinks. How does he get them to love him so fiercely?

"Please," Jake says, "I want to help him."

"We don't want your help. Leave us alone!"

Billy smiles and gently touches Lora's wrist. He looks at Jake, like it's been years since they've seen each other, and waves him in closer.

Jake stands over the Kid, who looks like an 80-year-old man now, sitting there, covered in four-alarm smoke. He's little more than smoke himself, a hazy image in the shape of a man. And this all feels so familiar to Jake.

"Big guy," he says, "you're a mess."

Billy nods and gives him a sad smile, as if to say, look who's talking, Jake. Still a fucking smartass.

He looks to Lora once more and smiles. Then he waves Jake over, c'mere, I want to educate you a little, and Jake leans over, strains like a bastard to hear every word Billy is whispering into his ear because he wants to know why all this is happening.

When he's done, Billy sits back and closes his eyes, the smile still warm on his face.

Jake stands up, still looking at Billy. Lora comes alongside him, tears rolling down her face.

"What did he say?" Her voice trembles. "Please tell me. What did he say?"

Jake turns to the window, toward the lights of an approaching ambulance that he knows will never get here in time. He takes Lora's hand, braces his fractured heart for yet another assault that is only seconds away, and looks into her eyes.

"He said 'God is good all the time.' "

Fomite

A fomite is a medium capable of transmitting infectious organisms from one individual to another.

"The activity of art is based on the capacity of people to be infected by the feelings of others." Tolstoy, What Is Art?

Writing a review on Amazon, Good Reads, Shelfari, Library Thing or other social media sites for readers will help the progress of independent publishing. To submit a review, go to the book page on any of the sites and follow the links for reviews. Books from independent presses rely on reader to reader communications.

For more information or to order any of our books, visit
http://www.fomitepress.com/FOMITE/Our_Books.html

Nothing Beside Remains
Jaysinh Birjépatil

*The Way None
of This Happened*
Mike Breiner

*Summer on the
Cold War Planet*
Paula Closson Buck

*Foreign Tales of
Exemplum and Woe*
J. C. Ellefson

Free Fall/Caída libre
Tina Escaja

Speckled Vanities
Marc Estrin

Fomite

Off to the Next Wherever
John Michael Flynn

Derail This Train Wreck
Daniel Forbes

Semitones
Derek Furr

Where There Are Two or More
Elizabeth Genovise

*Snake in the Spine,
Wolf in the Heart*
Barry Goldensohn

*The Three Lives
of Jonathan Force*
Richard Hawley

Father Figure
Lamar Herrin

The Fall of Athens
Gail Holst-Warhaft

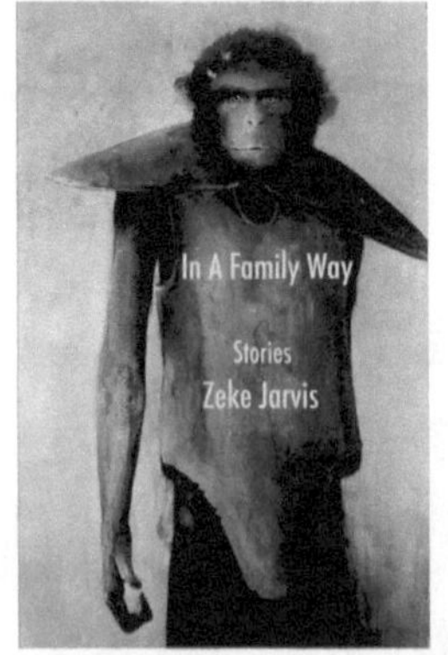

In A Family Way
Zeke Jarvis

Fomite

*A Rising Tide of People
Swept Away*
Scott Archer Jones

A Free, Unsullied Land
Maggie Kast

*Shadowboxing With
Bukowski*
Darrell Kastin

Feminist on Fire
Coleen Kearon

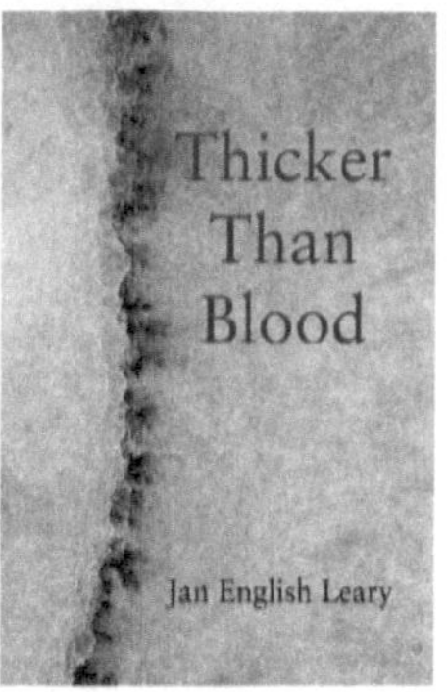

Thicker Than Blood
Jan English Leary

*A Guide
to the Western Slopes*
Roger Lebovitz

Confessions of a Carnivore
Diane Lefer

Born Speaking Lies
Rob Lenihan

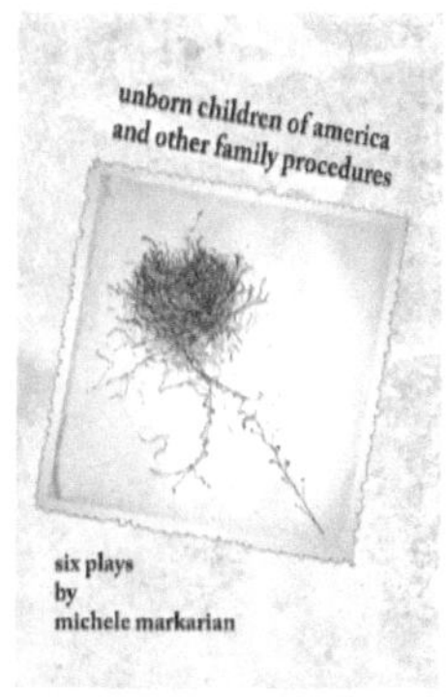

*Unborn Children of
America*
Michele Markarian

Fomite

Interrogations
Martin Ott

*Connecting the Dots
to Shangrila*
Joseph D. Reich

Shirtwaist
Delia Bell Robinson

Isles of the Blind
Robert Rosenberg

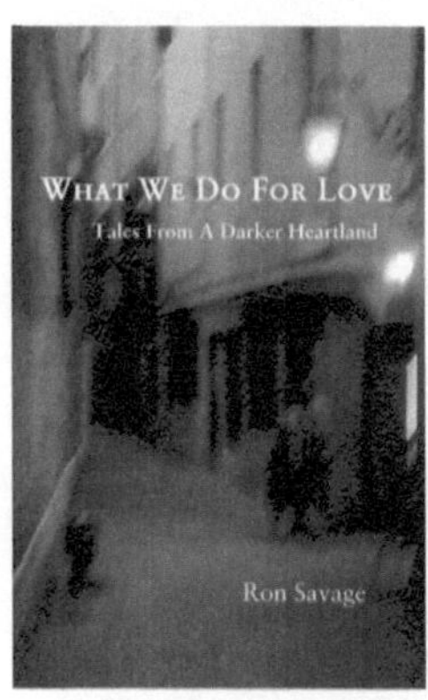

What We Do For Love
Ron Savage

Bread & Sentences
Peter Schumann

Faust 3
Peter Schumann

Principles of Navigation
Lynn Sloan

A Great Fullness
Bob Sommer

Fomite

To Join the Lost
Seth Steinzor

Among the Lost
Seth Steinzor

Industrial Oz
Scott T. Starbuck

Among Angelic Orders
Susan Thomas

A Day in the Life
Tom Walker

*The Inconveniece
of the Wings*
Silas Dent Zobal

Fomite

More Titles from Fomite...

Joshua Amses — *Raven or Crow*

Joshua Amses — *The Moment Before an Injury*

Jaysinh Birjepatel — *The Good Muslim of Jackson Heights*

Antonello Borra — *Alfabestiario*

Antonello Borra — *AlphaBetaBestiaro*

Jay Boyer — *Flight*

David Brizer — *Victor Rand*

David Cavanagh — *Cycling in Plato's Cave*

Dan Chodorkoff — *Loisada*

Michael Cocchiarale — *Still Time*

James Connolly — *Picking Up the Bodies*

Greg Delanty — *Loosestrife*

Catherine Zobal Dent — *Unfinished Stories of Girls*

Mason Drukman — *Drawing on Life*

Zdravka Evtimova — *Carts and Other Stories*

Zdravka Evtimova — *Sinfonia Bulgarica*

Anna Faktorovich — *Improvisational Arguments*

Derek Furr — *Suite for Three Voices*

Stephen Goldberg — *Screwed and Other Plays*

Barry Goldensohn — *The Hundred Yard Dash Man*

Barry Goldensohn — *The Listener Aspires to the Condition of Music*

R. L. Green When — *You Remember Deir Yassin*

Greg Guma — *Dons of Time*

Andrei Guriuanu — *Body of Work*

Ron Jacobs — *All the Sinners Saints*

Ron Jacobs — *Short Order Frame Up*

Ron Jacobs — *The Co-conspirator's Tale*

Kate MaGill — *Roadworthy Creature, Roadworthy Craft*

Fomite

Tony Magistrale — *Entanglements*

Gary Miller — *Museum of the Americas*

Ilan Mochari — *Zinsky the Obscure*

Jennifer Anne Moses — *Visiting Hours*

Sherry Olson — *Four-Way Stop*

Andy Potok — *My Father's Keeper*

Janice Miller Potter — *Meanwell*

Jack Pulaski — *Love's Labours*

Charles Rafferty — *Saturday Night at Magellan's*

Joseph D. Reich — *The Hole That Runs Through Utopia*

Joseph D. Reich — *The Housing Market*

Joseph D. Reich — *The Derivation of Cowboys and Indians*

Kathryn Roberts — *Companion Plants*

David Schein — *My Murder and Other Local News*

Peter Schumann — *Planet Kasper, Volumes One and Two*

Fred Skolnik — *Rafi's World*

Lynn Sloan — *Principles of Navigation*

L.E. Smith — *The Consequence of Gesture*

L.E. Smith — *Views Cost Extra*

L.E. Smith — *Travers' Inferno*

Susan Thomas — *The Empty Notebook Interrogates Itself*

Tom Walker — *Signed Confessions*

Sharon Webster — *Everyone Lives Here*

Susan V. Weiss —*My God, What Have We Done?*

Tony Whedon — *The Tres Riches Heures*

Tony Whedon — *The Falkland Quartet*

Peter M. Wheelwright — *As It Is On Earth*

Suzie Wizowaty —*The Return of Jason Green*